A HALLOW OF STORM AND RUIN

THE WINTER COURT SERIES

A CROWNS OF MAGIC UNIVERSE SERIES

ASHLEY MCLEO

MERAKI PRESS

Editing by Owl Eye Edits

Cover art by Sanja Gombar

Interior art by Joey Kao

Chapter art by Anna Spies of Altra Luna Art

Map by Cartographybird Maps

Ebook ISBN: 978-1-947245-94-5

Paperback ISBN: 978-1-966080-03-9

MAJOR SETTLEMENTS ◎
MINOR SETTLEMENTS ◉
NOTABLE LOCATIONS ◇

VIRTORIS
ISLAND

MORIAL
HOUSE
ARMENIL

NORTH LANDS

LEIRE
HOUSE
VIRTORIS

FARVERG

THE

SHIVERING

SEA

AVALDENN

KETHOR

AALBORG
HOUSE AABERG'S
ANCESTRAL SEAT

BITRA
HOUSE RIIS

EASTERNLANDS

VANTALIA

STORMY
BAY

SOUTHLANDS

GRINDAVIK
HOUSE
ITHAMAI

ICE TOOTH
MOUNTAIN RANGE

FOREWORD

Dear reader,

At the back of the book there are two reference pages.

One details the nine kingdoms of Isila.

The other dives into the greater noble houses of Winter's Realm. If, while you're reading, you want to know more about the Sacred Eight families, that's where you will find the information.

There is also a map at the front of the book.

Welcome back to Winter's Realm,

Ashley

CHAPTER 1
VALE

S now crunched underfoot as an icy gust of wind whipped my stinging cheeks. I shivered and wished our ragtag group of fae and humans were closer to our destination.

Of those humans Roar had enslaved in his mines or endeavored to sell to the Vampire Kingdom, not a single person remained at Gersemi Mine. None wanted to go to the grave not having fought for a better life.

I respected their fight and will to live, but traveling with them was eye-opening.

I'd vastly underestimated how slow humans traveled when compared to fae. Their fragile natures too. In two weeks of travel we'd lost thirty humans to the cold, bringing their number down to one hundred and sixty eight. Before we reached the hiding place I sought—an ancient and now deserted dwarven stronghold in the far southwest of Winter's Realm—we'd probably lose at least a dozen more lives. Likely those people who were bent at the spine and weak at the knees. As much as I hated to acknowledge that we couldn't save them all, I had to be realistic. So much was on the line. My wife's life, most importantly.

We'd left Avaldenn by an untraceable gateway and had hidden in Riis Tower for days, but was there still some way the Red Assassins could have followed Neve? The Vampire Queen Narcissa *had* placed a high bounty on Neve's head. The assassins would surely do all they could to find my wife and earn their coin.

Fates, I hated feeling so powerless in protecting those I loved.

But out here, skirting the Red Mist Mountain Range, in the remote reaches of the kingdom, I was a fae of few means. Particularly against highly skilled vampire assassins. Skies, even a medium-sized horde of the most dimwitted orcs would be too much for me and my best friend, Sir Caelo, to take on. So while I understood that Neve cared for the humans, I remained largely focused on her. I would not put their lives—or *any* lives—above hers.

This female I'd only known for but a moon cycle was my end and my beginning.

"We'll need to eat and rest soon." Caelo came up next to me. "Buy more food for the horses too."

The five horses we'd taken from the now deceased Lord Roar's stables in Guldtown were still with us, and thank the stars for them because the weakest humans often alternated riding. But as with any creature, our horses required food to continue, and we hadn't packed enough for such a long, unforeseen journey. Thus, Caelo would ride the horses, one by one, into passing towns to feed them as the group kept walking. We traveled so slowly, it was easy for Caelo to feed each horse, give it a rest, and catch up later the same day or the next morning.

"More food for us too. Our meal tonight will be meager," I replied.

Gersemi Mine had held more sustenance than I would have thought, largely thanks to the earth fae guards Lord Roar employed. Alas, those guards were no longer walking the face of this realm, and Neve, Caelo, and I did not possess earth magic to grow so much as a potato. We were quickly running through provisions.

"I believe we'll be in the next town by tomorrow morning." Caelo raised an eyebrow. "For such a large haul, you, me, *and* Neve will have to venture into the town. I can't go alone and carry so much back."

"Of course," I agreed, even while weighing the concerns of leaving the humans defenseless against us all starving to death.

After we showed them to the Kingdom of Dergia and got the humans settled in, we'd leave. From that point forward, they'd have to make it on their own since the place was abandoned, which made it both perfect for the humans and dangerous if they did not have the skills to survive. Humans were not made for this world, but fate, or whatever they worshiped in their world, had brought them here and as they'd already eaten the food of the fae, they could never go home.

I suppose leaving for a few hours will be a testing period before we reach Dergia.

"When we make camp tonight, we should see if any

from the mines can hunt properly," I added. "They can do that while we go into town the next day. Knowing someone can use a bow will ease my mind over leaving them."

Caelo nodded. "Some say they supplemented the food brought in or grown by Roar's men with wild game and fish."

I'd noticed a few carried the weapons, though I figured them knowing how to use the weapons as likely as the humans simply bringing bows and arrows to make themselves feel better. They had not aimed well at all when we'd been their targets.

Caelo twisted as a pair of men began grappling about something. "I'm going to break that up. No use in wasting energy on petty squabbles."

He left, and I took in the humans again. One young man limped, though determination shone in his face. He was one of the few with a bow on his back, a quiver full of rustic arrows too. I placed him on the top of my list of humans to test and moved on and on and on, assessing each person. As a result of work in the mines, many of the younger humans appeared strong, if a touch malnourished. That left me with a list of about twenty candidates who appeared to have the strength, dexterity, and enough determination to hunt in the barren lands of Winter's Realm.

"What's going on in that big brain of yours?" From behind me came a voice that made my heart skip a beat. I twisted to find Neve tromping through the deep snow, closing the distance between us. Red roses colored her cheeks, and though she had to be as cold as the rest of us, Neve beamed at me.

"Rhistel would laugh to hear you say such a thing about my brain."

It was a common enough belief that I was, in fact, the stupidest Aaberg. Not that I was a true Aaberg at all, but a bastard male of the Riis line, though precious few knew that fact. Nor was I *stupid* by any means. King Magnus, the male I'd always believed to be my father, gave preferential treatment to his own blood, but he would not allow an idiot relative to command his armies. Still, when compared to my intelligent family members, all well-versed in other languages and academic fields, I often felt left behind.

"Your brother is a cruel arse." Neve looped her arm through mine. The soft curves of her body pressed into me, and that familiar hunger for her came roaring back.

During our travels, we'd lacked privacy for intimacy, and it only made me more ravenous for my wife.

"What were you thinking about?" she asked again. "I caught you sizing people up."

"Caelo and I were talking about teaching the humans to hunt. We're hoping that some already know, but if they don't, we'll do our best. I plan to start at the next camp."

"Which is where?"

Out of all the parts of the kingdom, I'd spent the least amount of time in the west. However, I had studied the maps. With the names of the villages, towns, and cities Caelo brought back after feeding the horses, I'd worked things out. We had passed far west of Vitvik earlier that day. The city was too far east to detour to for supplies, though we could have found all that we required there.

"In three to five hours, we should reach a small lake

nestled up against the Red Mist Range. We'll camp there. Then tomorrow, you, Caelo, and I will go into the small town down the road and purchase food for horses, humans, and fae alike."

"A good plan." As she spoke, white puffs of air bloomed from her lips. Unable to help myself, I lowered my head to kiss those lovely, soft lips.

On her tongue, I tasted a sweet hunger for me. When her hand traveled to my chest, pushed through the folds of my cloak and stroked upward, I groaned. More than anything, I wished to throw her over my shoulder, take her deeper into the woods, and feast on another part of her. One I still remembered the sweet taste of as though it were yesterday.

But before I had a chance to act on such pleasurable thoughts, Neve pulled away and took my hand in hers.

"The sooner we reach the lake, the sooner we might find a quiet place?" She looked up at me with those eyes of violet. Eyes that came from her mother, Queen Revna, a healer queen, whereas Neve's silvery-white hair came from the Cruel King himself, Harald Falk.

Once, that information would have terrified me. The Cruel King was nothing short of a monster, and to fall in love with his daughter would have seemed too risky.

No longer. Neve—born Princess Isolde Falk—was nothing like her cruel father.

"A quiet place sounds perfect." I grinned back at my wife. "It will have to be quite far away from the group for the things I have planned for you."

She arched an eyebrow. "*Hmm*, naughty things?"

"As naughty as you'll allow."

"Promise?"

A deep laugh left me, and I winked. "You know not what you're hoping for, little beast."

"Maybe *you* know not what I dream about." She wagged her eyebrows as her hand drifted past my fur cloak again, brushing my hard cock.

Stars alive, this female will be the end of me.

I stood at the forest's edge, watching the humans practice archery.

Out of the twenty humans I'd tested with a bow and arrow, eight showed reasonable skill. Anna was one of them, which came as no surprise.

While most humans had been quiet and prone to resting when we stopped to make camp, my wife's best friend was different. Ten days ago, Anna asked Caelo to tutor her in the ways of the bow, and she had continued to practice diligently each night. No other human had been so forward to ask for help, though they'd complied when I'd requested to see their skills.

More promising than Anna, however, was a trio of people. They were novice hunters and all three had brought down birds and hares during their time at Gersemi Mine. While I remained with the other five, giving them tips to hone their skill, Caelo had taken the three best hunters deeper into the woods to look for small game. Secretly, I hope for a boar too, which Caelo possessed the skill to bring down. Unfortunately, during our travels, not a single one had crossed our path. I'd wondered if, as winter deepened, the game would start moving south to the Autumn Court.

It had been far too long since the land was bare of snow. That limited what grew without the aid of an earth fae or the magic of a holy Drassil tree in the area.

"Very nice, Samantha," I said to a young woman when she struck the dead center of her target, the ultimate goal of the exercise. "Try to hit that same place three more times."

Samantha beamed at me, her cheekbones protruding so much that it looked painful. She looked to be around my squire Filip's age. In the stage of life where she was growing a lot. The lack of food always hits the youngest ones the hardest.

I smiled back and tilted my head toward the makeshift target. The young woman turned back around and nocked another arrow. It flew, hit near her other arrow, and warmth stirred inside me.

There was hope for these people yet. A small bit, but it was there. And hope, no matter how little, was never mere.

If these humans could hunt, and if the stronghold in the mountain was enchanted with the ability to grow food as it was said to have been way back when the area was bustling with dwarves, the humans could make a home there. We only needed to make it to Dergia without incident or additional deaths.

Crack!

I turned to see Neve, still hard at work. Beneath her power, the lake ice buckled and broke. My shoulders loosened as I watched her, hands shaking as she pressed her magic into the thick ice covering the lake and shifted the loose slab up and over the rest of the ice.

Since we'd arrived at the lake, she'd divided her attention between building compacted snow and ice domes for the humans to take shelter in during the night and cracking the lake ice that repeatedly froze. Fifty domes were already up, and though they were misshapen and often used trees for support on one side, each had enough space to house three to four humans.

That much effort, over many hours, would have drained most fae, but not my wife. Since we'd been on the move, I'd helped Neve practice her magic daily. As a result, her already prodigious power had only grown.

She possessed the rawest winter magic I'd ever seen. What Neve lacked, however, was in her finesse, as evident by the clunky shapes of the shelters she created. Not that anyone cared when the domes protected them each night.

Give her time. She's only had full rein of her winter magic for a little over two weeks.

For their part, the rest of the humans fished, gathered water and wood, or remained on the lookout for fae—whether they be malicious like orcs or ogres or simply passing by. To us, both posed a threat.

Until darkness fell, there would be no rest for our weary group.

Footsteps crunched through the snow within the woods. Ever on alert, I twisted to find the humans I'd sent hunting with Caelo had returned.

Ronaldo, a man of about twenty turns, beamed. He had

three white hares gripped in his scarred hands. "Look at what we got!"

One was of decent size, sure to have some meat on its bones. Of the other two, one was average size, while the last was small, so small, I suspected they'd killed a mother and a baby that had not yet left her side.

"Nice work," I said, aware that in our situation, we could not afford to be picky. Out here, a small meal might be the difference between life and death. "See anything else out there?"

"Foxes. We didn't get any of those, though," Ronaldo shrugged. The young man had been unwillingly working in Roar Lisika's mines for most of his life, and yet, he still managed a positive attitude. "Sir Caelo said he thought he heard something larger too. He's still looking."

Maybe my hope for a boar was not too far-fetched after all? If Caelo caught one, it would go a long way in feeding these people.

"I heard it too," the huntress of the trio piped up.

"Sure you did." Ronaldo rolled his eyes. "Your hearing is worse than mine."

"Because I'm older?" She scowled.

Age did not dull fae senses, not until we were many centuries old, which this woman was nowhere near.

"Things go at forty," Ronaldo teased.

The huntress's scowl only deepened. "*Anyway*, someone was playing a fiddle. Is there a home nearby?"

We'd spent the first two hours scouting around the lake and found no structure in sight, and on a fast horse we were four hours from the nearest town. Perhaps she'd heard a wanderer or bard going down the road we'd been avoiding. I prayed to the stars that it was not a violent fae or creatures who might want to hunt us.

Like the orc tribes I'd often battled. They weren't known to play music; however, a minority of them might. Perhaps those who did not seek out food or land for their tribes.

"We'll see what Caelo finds," I replied, not about to strike fear in their hearts when I had no bleeding idea what might be out there. "For now, let's skin the hares and prepare them to roast."

CHAPTER 2
NEVE

The hares were gone, and we were down to less than two days' worth of small, portioned meals.

As a blood slave, I'd been fed regular meals and while I'd never starved, I'd also never received as much food as I wanted. Often, I'd go to bed hungry, but this hunger was different. A stronger beast gnawing at my belly. And yet, I didn't dare complain.

What would be the point? The hunters shot three hares and then went back and found two more. The meat hadn't gone far, but it was something, and they were trying their best.

In our situation, every little bit counted.

"Take this." Vale held out a cooked bit of hare.

"That's yours."

"Between cracking the ice repeatedly and building shelters, you've been using a lot of magic. You need it more than me." He extended the still steaming chunk of meat again. The savory, charred scent made my mouth water, but I made no move to take it.

Vale sighed. "Neve, *please*. I want you to have it."

Something in his voice broke my resolve, and, swallowing, I took the meat. It was little more than a bite, but Fates alive, it was delicious.

"Thank you," I whispered after I'd swallowed it down. "I don't deserve someone as good as you."

"You deserve more than me." Shadows crawled over his dark brown eyes.

Not this again.

Since learning that he was a Riis by blood, Vale had fallen into periods of moodiness. When we'd been busy with finding Roar, Vale had been able to accept that we were together. But with too much time to think during our journey, he dwelled on the fact that he was a bastard-born fae, and I was a trueborn princess. An inappropriate match, or so he said.

He seemed to have forgotten that he'd been willing to marry me—a former blood slave—to save my life. More than that, I could tell he wanted me. Vale might be falling in love with me, and I was falling for him too. We hadn't said as much, but I sensed the changes between us. That our marriage of safety, of honor on his part, had taken a turn.

Is it time to find a quiet place and talk?

I looked up at Vale. "Night is upon us. Would you like to make good on your earlier promise?"

His lips twitched and that sadness in his eyes vanished. "I'll tell Caelo to keep watch."

My stomach fluttered as he walked away. The journey so

far had been long, exhausting, and offered no privacy. Vale and I had stolen kisses, but a hotter desire hung like a weight over us at all hours. I hungered for every part of him, as well as a chance to tell him how I felt. Hoping we might be gone and lost in one another for some time, I scanned the area around the lake.

The sun had set, and our horses were bedded down, sleeping together by the fire and covered with what wool blankets we could spare. Most of the humans had already disappeared into their ice shelters to sleep too. A few remained outside, mostly the younger ones.

I spied Ronaldo, one of the best hunters in the group, talking to Stephanie and Lei. Both young women were listening, wide-eyed, and though they were far away, I caught a few words. Ronaldo was boasting to the girls about his hunting experience. No doubt he wanted to impress Lei, a raven-haired beauty about his age. I thought that, if she liked him back, they would be a good match. Other humans trusted Lei, and she was interested in healing, a valuable skill in any realm. Ronaldo was a handsome man and turning into a provider for their group. Give him a couple more turns, and I could see him being a leader one day too.

Not that this was any time to play matchmaker. I needed to focus on getting all three of them to safety.

"Caelo is on watch. Anna too," Vale said, alerting me to his presence once again.

I took his hand in mine, and as we left the lake behind, I exhaled, a quiet peace settling between us deep within the trees.

"There's a certain weight to leading," he said.

"Yes," I agreed. "One of the heaviest is never getting you to myself."

He smiled, drawing me in closer and under his large fur cloak as we walked. Snow and frost clung to every tree limb, glittering prettily in the moonlight and weighing the branches down until the lowest ones grazed the earth. Above, a star-filled sky churned and blinked, making me feel so small in such a big world.

When I was a slave, I hadn't thought about the dead gods living among the stars—or maybe *the gods were them*, according to some sources. During our journey south, I'd decided that if we lived through this, and if we returned to a shelter where there was a library, I'd do well to research the dead gods.

After all, if I was to go through with the desire burning in my heart, I might very well need the help of those same dead gods.

"What are you thinking?" Vale murmured, his voice warming me from within in a way no one else had ever managed.

"About the stars. The gods."

"Oh, is that all? By the look on your face, I thought it was something important."

I swatted his barrel chest. "It was more me thinking of all that I don't know. I'd like to learn more."

He didn't reply, and I had a hint as to why. We hadn't discussed what we'd do after we saw the humans to safety. What few options would be open to us? Few knew my true identity and fewer still knew Vale's secret parentage.

Vale was waiting for me to make my choice first. To speak it out loud and claim my blood right.

And then there was the matter of the Ice Scepter, a lost Hallow of Winter's Realm. One that could have the power to change so much, if only I could find it.

From reading Brogan Lisika's note to Roar, I learned that their parents had seized the Ice Scepter during the chaos of King Magnus's Rebellion about two decades ago. The Lisikas had then taken the Hallow on a journey with them south and then west—in the direction of Myrr, where House Balik reigned. A journey that had ended in the deaths of Lord and Lady Lisika and their young heir. The Ice Scepter's disappearance too.

But if I found the Hallow, I might use my magic to heal this land. In doing so, I'd be primed to claim the Crown of Winter's Realm, and no matter how I looked at that choice, it was terrifying.

"Did Caelo find the fiddler?" I asked, wishing to stray from the seriousness of what lay before me. Tonight was supposed to be about pleasure. For getting lost in one another. *For us.* As soon as we were far enough away from camp, I didn't want to talk at all.

"No."

"Did he go all the way to the road?"

"He did. There was no one there, but there were footprints and sleigh marks." Vale shrugged. "If a fiddler traveled the road, they're long gone."

The air turned white and misty with my breath. The explanation made as much sense as any. We hadn't checked on the roads often, but each time we had dared to do so, there was not much sign of life. According to Vale and Caelo, people didn't move about as freely in this part of the kingdom. If they did, it was to go toward Guldtown or east, not closer to where the Red Mist Mountains and the Ice Tooth Range collided.

Few fae lived and lurked in these mountains, which made them both dangerous and the best place to hide the humans. We only hoped no monsters had taken over Dergia. Vale seemed to think it was unlikely. That we weren't leading these people into more danger—that the one place where they might find peace in this world wasn't closed off to them too.

"That tree looks cozy." He pointed to an enormous pine, so large that at one point, an earth fae, or many, had to have helped it grow. The lowest branches were up high, so high that they cleared Vale's head. Perhaps once upon a time someone had used this tree for shelter and shaped it in the process.

"Should we get a closer look?"

The heat in his eyes told me we were on the same page, and we trudged through the snow, closer to the tree. When we reached the outer branches, the snow began to thin and slope downward. I gripped Vale's hand, our gloves a barrier between us, but hopefully not for long.

At the base, I leaned against the cold bark, felt snow flutter into my hair, which was a rat's nest after days of travel. I preferred not to think of that, though, especially not when I had my handsome husband in front of me.

"Finally, alone." I wove my hands around his neck.

Vale responded, coming closer so that his thick cloak

covered me as well as him. No matter how much space we'd put between us and the group, Vale was a possessive fae male. He wouldn't want anyone straying upon us and seeing the female he was with.

"Couldn't have said it better myself." He dipped his head so that our lips met.

The cold brushing over my lips thawed at Vale's touch. One hand splayed at my back, he drew me closer, and my breasts ached for his touch. There was far too much material between us for my liking, so my hands slithered up the muscled plains of his torso, sliding his tunic up with them.

"Up," Vale whispered, and before I could process, his hands dipped to my arse.

I laughed, breaking our kiss as he lifted me. My legs wrapped around his waist, seeking closeness.

Secure around him, he eased me back into the tree and his wings wrapped around me to make a sort of seat. My eyelids fluttered. Vale, besides being one of the best males I knew, was kind and strong and miraculously made. Possibly in the image of some dashing dead god. Feeling up his chest, I rolled my hips into him, wanting to be closer. Together, in every sense.

Vale groaned, the rod in his pants now pushing into me, making me wet. Loving the sound of his want, I ground against him again. The ache between my legs grew, and I peppered kisses along his strong jaw as I sought a rhythm with my hips.

"Stars Neve," Vale murmured, his face nestling into my hair. "You're going to be the death of me."

"Death isn't the plan, Vale. Though I may want it to

seem like that." My lips found his again, and I gave him a searing kiss. "Right up until the moment we both find ecstasy."

He laughed, low and rumbling. "We should have found a cave."

"Hmm?" I kissed his jaw again.

"Warmer. I want you spread out before me. Want to feast on you, and I'd like for you not to freeze as I delight."

I shuddered at the image, and though what he wanted sounded delightful, there was no way we were stopping now. "Next time. Tonight, we can make our own heat." I rubbed against him once more. The way his face softened, and his eyes glazed over when I did that made me feel so powerful. So sexy. "I—"

A female scream cut through the night shrouded land, then two, then three. Different pitches. I froze, my legs still wrapped around Vale's middle. He grew rigid, and his hands, which had wandered beneath my shirt, stilled.

"The camp," I said upon breaking a kiss, that sumptuous ache between my thighs fizzling in an instant.

He set me down, and I whirled to run, but Vale gripped my shoulder.

"Fly. The snow will slow us."

He was right, of course, and it took me less than a minute to tease my wings through the slits in my thick fur cloak. The frigid air brushed across the sensitive membranes, which was slightly painful, but I pushed past it and beat them to rise.

Walking deep into the woods had taken a fair bit of time, but with our wings spread and catching air, we soared above the trees, spotting the camp fires right away. Fires still burned and, thanks to Vale's air shields, they hadn't dimmed. The horses were fine then. I squinted. From what I could see, a few people poked their heads out of the ice tents, looking for the source of the screams too.

"The lake," Vale yelled into the wind. "Screaming stars, it's a nøkken!"

"A what?" My attention veered into the center of the lake and found a white horse standing on the ice. I hadn't noticed it before, for most of the camp was dark and the horse blended in so well with the surrounding snow. "That horse, you mean?"

"A nøkken is a freshwater creature. It lures people, mostly females and younglings, into the water and drowns them. It can shapeshift into a horse or—*fates!*—a fiddler." Vale let out a stream of curses.

My heart rate sped up. As we got closer to the lake, I could see better. Not so far from the horse was a hole in the ice, and a young woman thrashed.

"I think that's Lei!" I wished that we'd brought weapons. Especially when five more women drifted toward the ice as though sleep walking. Men tried to hold them back, but a supernatural power controlled the women, giving them the strength to move forward. What if they couldn't stop them?

My stomach dipped as a more dire thought slammed into me. What if Lei wasn't the first? We'd heard three screams.

Ahead, Ronaldo and Caelo sprinted for the lake, both armed with bows and arrows. They reached the edge of the ice, positioned so they would not hit the humans, aimed, and let their arrows fly.

The nøkken stepped out of the way of both arrows, unbothered as it glanced down at the hole in the ice. The screaming had stopped, and Lei's body remained in the hole, still as death.

"Neve, I don't want you landing," Vale said as we soared over the first ice hut—seconds from the lake at this pace. "You might be susceptible."

"Vale, I—"

"Please Neve!"

The desire to respect his wishes fought against that of helping defeat the creature, and compromising, I soared for the stars, hoping that if I went high enough, I'd stay out of the creature's sphere of influence.

Appeased, Vale scooped up a bow and arrow, leaning against an ice hut and soared for the monster. High above, I followed, heart hammering. Before my husband got there, another arrow flew, and the nøkken didn't see this one coming.

It struck the creature in the side, blood blooming over white hair. The monster shrieked. The chilling sound was nothing like a horse would make, but rather human-like. Another arrow, Ronaldo's, came at the nøkken, then Caelo's joined. Both hit their marks, and finally, the creature fell.

When it hit the ice, the creature shifted into a dark black beast with the face of a human and a wispy body cloaked in sodden, filthy rags. Yellow eyes blazed in the nøkken's face for a second before that fire dimmed.

I plummeted, hoping to get to Lei in time.

Seeing as he was already so close, Vale reached the hole first. He plunged his hand into the ice and gripped Lei's arm, still clinging to the ledge.

I joined him, feet hitting the ice, jarring me. Hard. Her arm looked so hard and cold.

My stomach churned as he pulled Lei from the hole. A small amount of relief flooded me as I watched her suck in air, but it was dashed a moment later and my entire being filled with dread. Lei hadn't been the only one in the frigid water.

Samantha had grabbed onto Lei's ankle, and her hand remained stuck in that position, allowing Samantha's body to bob below the surface until Vale broke her grip by pulling Lei from the water. Her eyes still wide with the terror she'd felt when she died, Samantha sank.

I dropped to the ice to help, plunging down to my waist. Reaching. Reaching. Reaching.

My skin tightened. Stars, it was freezing! Far colder than the river I'd thrown myself into to escape the vampires who hunted me. That river bordered the vampire and winter fae kingdoms, but this lake lived in the heart of Winter's Realm and filled with water from the mountains. Far more frigid.

"Vale! Neve!" Caelo's garbled voice hit my ear through the water.

Someone grabbed my feet as my fingers wrapped around Samantha's hand. I pulled back and the person who had a hold of me helped. When my head broke the surface, I gulped down the cold air.

"Neve! What were you thinking?!" Vale growled.

"I couldn't leave her!"

He said nothing, but the set of his jaw told me that Vale didn't agree. I ignored his ire, and he helped me pull the girl's body to the ice, next to Lei, who was breathing shallowly.

"Get Lei to the fire," I instructed. "Wrap her in blankets and put her between horses. As warm as she can get."

Ronaldo picked up the young woman and ran for the fire.

I stood and wavered. Vale caught me, though he, too, shivered.

"We need the fire too." He swept me off my feet and tucked me against his chest, which was wet with lake water.

"I'm fine right now," I protested. "What about Samantha?" I cast a glance at Caelo, saw the sorrow in his blue eyes and knew my suspicions had been right.

"Too late for her," he said. "She's gone."

I swallowed.

"The monster is too." Anger brimmed in Anna's tone.

I jolted. I hadn't known Anna was here, and belatedly, relief cut through my sorrow and swept through me. What if she'd been caught in the nøkken's thrall? I hadn't considered such a thing.

"Are there more?" my best friend asked.

"They're solitary. One to a body of water," Caelo replied. "That was sharp shooting. Good work."

"You made the first shot!?" I met Anna's upturned eyes, brimming with pride.

"I did," she said. "I was relieving myself, but something told me to go into the woods armed. When I heard the screams, I came back and saw the horse. It didn't look right, and I had to get closer to make the shot, but I managed."

"You certainly did!" I breathed, in awe of my friend.

"I'm glad you did not get too close, though" Vale said.

"Being a slower walker has some benefits then."

I snorted a laugh. Anna was always one to look on the bright side.

"Does anyone know if there are others it has already lured?" Vale asked. "Usually, nøkken's victims go silently to their deaths. We're lucky that Lei survived."

"We'll gather everyone," Caelo said. "Do a headcount."

"Anna, you do that. We'll be right behind." At Vale's command, Anna left. "Caelo, dispose of the nøkken's body, and bring Samantha back with you?"

"Of course."

With that, me still in his arms, Vale strode for the fire where Lei sat. Ronaldo had followed through, covering her and placing her between two horses. Her eyes were already open, and they were locked on me.

"You saved me." It sounded like it hurt for her to speak. Like her throat was thawing out as much as the rest of her.

"A group effort," I said, as Vale set me in front of the fire too, removing my cloak, portions of which had dipped into the lake. He took a wool blanket from the horses and wrapped me in it, then took one for himself, pressing his body to mine. We should have been changing into dry clothes first, but the fire felt so good I did not want to move.

Lei sniffled and met my gaze. "We wanted to get another horse for the group, but we didn't recognize the shapeshifter for evil. I'm sorry. God, I'm so sorry."

I offered her a small smile. "You did what you thought was best. Remember, things here are not always as they seem."

"Status on the numbers?" Vale asked as Anna approached. My husband seemed to have snapped into his military persona.

All the blood had left Anna's face, and I wondered how she'd worked so fast. Peering past her, I had my answer. From the looks of it, Ronaldo had been of the same mind. After setting Lei by the fire, he'd moved quickly and rounded up most of the people. One shouted loudly that their wife was missing, which made my throat tighten.

Anna cleared her throat. "On first count, more are missing. Ronaldo is doing another count now, but people are starting to lose it."

"How many are still missing?" Vale asked.

"Fifteen," Anna said, her voice small. "Sixteen, including Samantha."

Fifteen souls. Maybe more. I looked up at Vale. Many humans sobbed and wailed at the realization that they'd lost more on this night.

"Are you good to be left?" Vale asked.

"Yes," I breathed.

"Then stay here and warm up. I need to help Anna and Ronaldo."

"You're wet too."

"Trust me, I'm fine. You stay here and warm up."

I nodded, my stomach full of lead as he left.

"That monster got them all?" Lei asked, her voice was stronger than seconds prior, a good sign.

"We can't be sure," I said. "But I'm willing to bet it lured others before it got to you and Samantha. You shared a tent?"

"That's right. We went to bed when you and Prince Vale left, and everyone else except Ronaldo had gone to sleep. Ten minutes later, Samantha got up and walked out. I followed, saw the horse, and said we should capture it. After that, I remember little." She met my eyes.

"Back home, I always pictured the fae as smaller, but mostly, like you: beautiful and kind and spreading pixie dust or some shit." She shook her head. "How unbelievably wrong I was. There are all kinds of fae, and they're just as likely to be monsters as they are like you, aren't they?"

Lei differed greatly from the humans I'd grown up alongside. The other blood slaves knew of fae and vampires and the other creatures in this world. Countless vicious beings. But Lei and many of the humans we traveled with weren't from this world. Their lips uttered different stories of fae. They held different perceptions, some of which could get them killed. We'd taught them much along the way, but tonight drilled into me how much more they have to learn.

"Fae of my race, faeries, can be monsters too. Anyone in Isila can. You have to remember that."

She stared into my eyes before dropping her gaze to the fire. "I'll never forget."

Guilt crashed down on me. *Vale and I left for half an hour and we lost so many lives.*

Could I lead these people to safety or were their lives the price I had to pay for the night Prince Gervais had ripped out Anna's throat and I'd made a bargain with the powers that be?

Secretly, I feared that was true, but couldn't bear to think that any power above, be it the dead gods, the Fates, or the Faetia would be so cruel. They wouldn't punish so many people because I'd made a deal to save Anna . . . right?

All I knew for certain was that I'd failed to keep two hundred humans safe. If I couldn't do that, did I really have the ability to reclaim, lead, and protect Winter's Realm?

I didn't know, but it seemed to me that the odds weren't in my favor.

CHAPTER 3
VALE

E yes followed us as we rode our horses into the closest town. On my right, Neve remained quiet, just as she'd been since the number of the humans lost came to light.

At the final count, nineteen died at the hands of the nøkken. One man killed himself after others found sleep. We'd discovered his body at first light near the woods, wrists slit by a dull knife someone brought from the mines, blood staining the surrounding snow. His wife had been one of the women the nøkken pulled into the lake.

My stomach churned. Yesterday, I'd been teaching young Samantha to draw an arrow.

This morning, we'd buried her in snow along with the other fallen—everyone realizing the dead would not stay there. Once we left the area, animals would find the bodies and feast, but the humans agreed they'd rather the dead be buried.

As it stood now, under one hundred and fifty humans

remained. The number unsettled me as much as remembering the faces of the dead, for I was fae and prone to looking ahead for long lengths of time. I worried over what would happen when they got to Dergia. And after.

Their reproductive ages were more limited than my kind. It was often difficult for fae to conceive, but to balance the scales, they could have younglings for hundreds of turns. Humans rarely lived to see a century and could not have children for that long. Was the human population too small to sustain them? Protect them? And even if they survived a few turns, one day someone with no regard for their kind could find them—orcs probably.

The longer this journey stretched, the more I doubted our plan.

"Stables are over there," said Caelo. "Let's stop there first. The horses are exhausted."

For this trip into civilization, my old friend was playing the part of a wandering soldier named Týriel—Caelo's middle name. Just to be safe, I too, would go by my middle name of Trahal, and Neve had shortened Isolde to Isol. As an added precaution, Caelo had glamoured us all to be unrecognizable.

All this in case the King of Winter, or even the Red Assassins, still searched for Neve at the command of the vampire queen. For now, we wished to remain hidden.

"Once the horses are taken care of, we should visit the inn and eat before we procure supplies." I said, and the other two nodded their agreement. It had been a long ride into the village, and we not only wished to gather food, but also gossip.

Stories and tales, true or not, were feed for the masses and always being traded at taverns. Had there been any word of us in the area, we'd hear of it while others spoke over horns of ale. Additionally, we were curious as to what was happening at court.

Was the Festival still happening? How many Red Assassins remained in Avaldenn?

The horsemaster saw us coming and rushed out. After giving the price to feed, water, shelter, and groom our horses, we left the creatures in the horsemaster's hands, and he pointed us to the best inn.

"I can't wait for a mulled wine and a very hearty stew," Neve said as we walked down the street. It was one of the few times she'd spoken in the last hours.

"Agreed." Caelo sniffed the air. "And one of those cinnamon buns I'm smelling too."

"We can bring some of those back to camp." Neve smiled at that.

"Let's see how much *levae* we can carry first. Buns might take up too much space," I said, thinking about space and practicalities.

Levae bread was often used by the army, the Royal Nava, and travelers, for it was lightweight and a small amount filled one up. The bread was rather expensive, but in our case, worth it. If we could continue to hunt, a saddle bag full of *levae* could last for weeks. The hope was for the humans to stretch the supply out for a couple of moons.

Neve's face fell at my frugal comment, and Caelo shot me an annoyed look. Frustration at myself surged. My wife's first smile in hours, and I dimmed it with practicality.

"Perhaps it would be best to find cinnamon biscuits," I amended. "Smaller. More transportable."

Bakers made them from scraps of dough and sold them cheaply. Normally, gold wouldn't be an issue, but I had brought relatively little with me and needed to use much of it on the *levae*. Thankfully, my compromise seemed to lift Neve's spirits ever so slightly once more.

"There's The Golden Crossroads, up ahead." Caelo angled his head to the right.

The combination tavern and inn were obvious by the sign and the masses of people exiting, all rosy-cheeked and talkative. One faerie had stunted wings, a victim of the blight of magic in the land if I ever saw one.

The coinary stood out, just beyond the tavern. Even without the sculpted pot of gold on the building's roof, one would know it was a place of wealth as it was made of white stone while most of the buildings were crafted from logs.

This coinary was the first I'd seen since the day we'd arrived in Guldtown to confront Roar. As tempted as I was to go inside right then and there and withdraw more gold from my account, I held back. Despite being low on gold, silver, copper, and anything of value to sell that wasn't the use of my sword or the actual weapon itself, going into a coinary and dealing with the cunning leprechauns who ran the interconnected financial institutions through the kingdom meant exposing where I was in Winter's Realm.

Disguise or not, to access my coin, I'd have to give my name and my magical imprint. Though my account was my own, I was sure the king had ordered anyone with information on me and Neve to share that information.

Things of great value motivated leprechauns. What was the favor of the king if not value?

We wanted the king to know as little as possible of our whereabouts, for as long as possible.

"Golden Crossroads," Caelo murmured. "Reckon one of the Lisika mines is nearby?"

I didn't think the Lisika family had any mines this far south, but then again, I hadn't believed they'd lure humans into Isila through their mines and sell them to the Vampire Kingdom, either.

"Anything is possible with that basket of snakes. We should question the barkeep." Neve's eyes narrowed.

"*Careful* questions," I added. "If there is a mine in the area, and it's anything like Gersemi, not many fae will work there anyway. Roar would not have entrusted that information to just anyone."

The determined expression remained on Neve's face made my chest swell with pride. Her fight, the way she stood up for what she believed in, was one of the things I admired most in my wife.

Wife . . .

I'd gotten used to referring to Neve in that way. First, because I'd had to. Then I'd wished to.

Now, knowing who she was, how much better she was than me, I considered myself foolish. How long would it take for her to decide that she wished to reclaim her family throne? After that, how much longer would it be before she realized being bound to me was a terrible idea? Our attraction and growing bond meant little when faced with the fact that marriage was one way for her to secure alliances, which she'd need to beat the king. I'd been taught that all my life, and for Neve, an alliance would be valuable. Far more valuable than a single sword. Or even a male she enjoyed in her bed.

A pang cut through my chest at the thought of losing her. Of one day not being able to call her mine when she was, very much so, the one thing I wanted in this world. But before that pain could take hold, I shoved it down deep. The time I feared would come, and I'd deal with it then, like a warrior and upstanding fae would.

Though barely midday, fae of all races bustled about the lower level of the tavern, below the inn. To the side of the main room, fires roared inside multiple hearths, keeping the ever-present cold at bay.

The barkeeps, two nymphs—one male, one female— noticed us the moment we walked in. The male pointed to three seats at the bar.

"Only spots left. Not near the fire, though."

Not one of us complained as we claimed the stools, and the male nymph's gaze found Neve. He looked her over appreciatively, and annoyance rose in me as I stood behind her to relieve her of her cloak.

"Wife," I spoke the title a bit more loudly than normal, "I'll put this by the fire for you."

"Thank you." Neve sighed wearily. I doubted she noticed the nymph eyeing her, but I noticed him look away and become engrossed with the glasses on the other side of the bar.

If the nymph wasn't so handsome, I wouldn't care, but

nymphs were known to attract all sorts, and my emotions around Neve were raw. Hot-blooded, but raw.

"Hang mine up too." Caelo tossed me his cloak with a wink.

I rolled my eyes but took the furs to the fire where they would warm and dry. Along the way, I listened. Gathering news was one reason we were here, but I heard nothing of value, only normal village gossip, so I rejoined Neve and Caelo and found an ale waiting for me.

"Bottoms up," Caelo said. We toasted silently to being warm and eating a full meal for the first time in days as Neve sipped her hot, spiced wine. "We ordered bowls of stew and rolls. If you want something else, they have roasted boar."

I salivated but shook my head. Stew cost less than roasted meat. And though we needed a full meal to keep our magic strong, I saw no need to go overboard.

"Here you go." The female nymph approached, flowers growing out of her long pink hair. She set two bowls down, which I insisted Caelo and Neve take as the nymph returned to the kitchens for the last. When the barkeep arrived with my steaming bowl, I thanked her and she turned to leave, but Neve lifted a hand.

"I was wondering, is there a crier in the village with the latest news from around the kingdom? Or a pamphlet? We've been on the road for so long, and I'm curious if anything has happened."

"Like?" the barkeep arched an eyebrow.

"Well, I'm quite interested in the Courting Festival." Neve ducked her head as if embarrassed to say as much. As if she was some romantic female drooling over the idea of an event.

The nymph softened, and a smile grew on her heart-shaped face. "Aye, the balls and the betrothals. I can understand wanting to know more about that! So romantic!"

I forced myself not to scoff. As the king strong armed matches he preferred, the Courting Festival was anything but romantic, though I supposed that, to the commonfae who had never so much as visited Avaldenn or seen the inside of the castle, such an event would draw the imagination.

The nymph wiped down the bar top. "And since you're asking, I *did* hear a bit of news two days back. *Scandalous* news!"

"Is someone already wed?" Neve asked.

No doubt she was thinking about Sayyida Virtoris or Marit Armenil, both betrothed against their will for bearing witnesses at Neve and my wedding.

"Not that! Better! The Warrior Bear and his new bride are nowhere to be found!" The nymph leaned a hip against the bar, happy to indulge Neve in her gossip.

I started in on my stew. Caelo had already demolished half his bowl, and fat dribbled down his chin.

"Oh, do you hear that, Trahal and Týriel!" Neve's face relaxed as she dropped our middle names, the first false cover trail. Like me, I doubted she'd considered news of us had reached this far west. "Do you have any idea where they went?"

"No," the nymph said. "Though some are guessing they

left the city because the new princess was already with youngling. *Lord Roar's youngling!*"

The barkeep looked scandalized, and my wife proved she could have acted at the Royal Theater for she clapped a hand over her mouth.

"No!"

"Yes! Maybe they're going to the midlands to have the child and leave it somewhere. Old King Magnus wouldn't abide bastards in his castle. Ironic, wouldn't you say?"

It *was* ironic, though not for the reason the barkeep surmised. And apparently, she wasn't done, for she leaned closer to Neve. "I wish there would be a sighting of them. They—"

The tavern door banged open, startling me so much that I dropped my spoon into my bowl. "A healer! We need a healer!"

Everyone spun to find a brownie yelling at the door.

The barkeep straightened. "Yeel, what's going on?"

"Gerda had her youngling!" Yeel said. "Born with no wings and a horrible gaping hole in her chest. The healer who delivered the babe needs help. Another knowledgeable set of hands."

A patron stood. "I'll help."

They swept out the door, and the barkeep let out a long, sad sigh. "It'll be Winter's magic acting up again. The last three younglings born here weren't right either. No wings or, if they had them, they might as well not. Shredded to bits, the poor things. And a dryad was recently born with hair as black as the night. An oddity if there ever was one!"

"That's so sad," Neve said.

"That it is," the nymph agreed.

"A little help back here would be nice!" The male nymph yelled from the back.

The barkeep gave a long-suffering sigh. "Let us know if you need anything else."

Once we were alone, Neve began to eat with a far-away look in her eyes. A few bites in, she set her spoon down again.

"Eat it all," I urged. "We need your magic for the final few days."

"I constantly feel like I'm failing those we travel with. These people too." She gestured to the bar, to those who suffered from the blight. "Their issues aren't natural. It's a problem with the magic of the realm, and I might be able to fix that."

There was no denying such a thing. "But you can't blame only yourself. You've only recently been freed from slavery and have learned much since then. The king might also have the power, and he's been failing them for far too long."

She picked up her spoon, and I shared a sidelong glance with Caelo. Neve had said nothing about claiming her birthright. Seeing as she'd only had a couple of weeks to come to terms with such a monumental notion, no one had pressed, but it seemed to me that she was tiptoeing closer to claiming herself as the rightful ruler of the land.

CHAPTER 4

NEVE

The humans waved excitedly when we rode back to camp, laden down with *levae*, other dried goods, and useful supplies. Things like the weapons and tools the humans would need once they settled into their new home.

The only beings who didn't look pleased to see us were the pair of horses we hadn't been able to take to the village. From them, we received greetings of stomped hooves and harsh snorts.

"They're brimming with great irritation." Caelo nodded to the horses.

"They see how fresh and well fed their friends look after visiting a warm stable." Vale shook his head with amusement.

"Exactly." Caelo turned his full attention to the horses and clicked his tongue softly a few times. "We brought you apples and oats."

Their stances softened.

"I'll take care of them," Caelo said, eyes crinkling at the corners. He'd removed our glamours an hour out of the village, and his eyes were back to their brilliant blue color. "You two can unload without assistance?"

"We have it under control," Vale assured him, and the knight veered for the horses.

Once he was gone, I met Vale's eye. "Judging by the smiles we received, all went well in our absence."

"Agreed. It helps that the sun warmed things up today. People are in a good mood."

Two dozen people helped us unload the supplies into an ice hut. Once done, I took a bunch of *levae* in one hand and waved the other at the hut, dousing it with my magic. It was not warm enough to melt ice, but to be safe, I wished to reinforce the structure.

"One piece of this bread can last a fae Vale's size all day." I handed a woman one of the many packages of *levae* that we bought. "And as long as it stays dry, it won't go bad. So make sure to keep it stored dry."

She pressed the package to her heart, clearly grateful.

"Did the hunters go out today?" Vale asked the general group.

There had been some debate on whether that should happen. Given the nøkken attack, many humans were fearful.

"We did," Ronaldo replied. "Killed ten hares and, get this—we finally saw a boar!"

The barkeep in the village had told us boars did, occasionally, venture this far south and west, and at this further proof, gratitude welled in my chest. Maybe the boars would move further south and into the mountains. They could be regular food sources for these people.

"It ran off too fast for us to hit it, though." Anna came up behind and added to the tale. "Next time, we'll be ready."

"Excellent." Pride rolled off Vale at his students' progress. "Perhaps we should practice shooting again before we lose the light? Those who are adept can help those who are still learning."

Ronaldo grinned. "I'll gather people."

Vale kissed me before going off to help the archers. I loosed a sigh and glanced around. For the first time all day, I was at a loss at what to do and though the day had been long, I wasn't yet ready for sleep.

Anna nudged me. "Let's collect snow for water."

"Good idea." I fell in line with my friend.

Now that we knew human bodies, along with that of the dead nøkken, were in the water, no one dared to drink from the lake. We were back to scooping and melting snow like we did in the forests—a never-ending task.

"So," Anna began as, with her hands, she scooped snow into a watertight basket. "Anything interesting happen in the village?"

My mind flashed to the fae affected by the blight, then to the brownie who had called for a healer for a poor youngling.

"People are talking about Vale and me. Apparently, I'm pregnant with Roar's youngling, and we've left Avaldenn until I give birth."

"What are they saying you'll do with the child?"

"That I'd abandon it," I said. "I'd never do such a thing, but such a youngling would certainly be in danger. I'm willing to bet King Magnus would throw it in a lake. One with a nøkken."

I meant to remain lighthearted, but the image of a nøkken coming across an innocent youngling and pulling it below cracked my voice. I swallowed and tried to fight the emotion rising inside me. Emotions I'd tried hard to hold back all day.

Perhaps it was just a matter of time, but it still surprised me when I failed. Fat, hot tears sprang to my eyes.

"Neve," Anna whispered. "What's wrong?"

"I-I—we saw so much in the village, and that was after what happened last night. And . . ." I trailed off before sniffling. "After all this, I'm not sure I'm fit to lead."

Soft, cold hands landed on my shoulder and unthinkingly, I slipped them beneath my furs. Anna had gloves but needed the heat my furs provided more than me.

"There, what you did with my hand, proves you're meant to help these people, Neve. That you care more than almost all other fae."

"I care but that doesn't negate the fact that so many people have died!"

"They understood the risks when they left the mine. And it's not like you can control the cold."

A lie. Or at least, it might be. As a Falk by blood, I might control the Ice Scepter, a magical Hallow of this land that mitigated the worst of winter's storms and weather. In a handful of days, we'd reach Dergia. Once we were sure the humans were safe, then Anna, Caelo,

Vale, and I would leave them there, in peace and freedom.

When that time came, I needed to have made my choice of what I'd do next. If we should risk returning to Avaldenn, or only go to Riis Tower. Both places would likely have some information on the Scepter, but I was of the mind that Riis Tower would be the safest place to begin. Even if we only stopped there for a couple of days, it would give us time to assess what exactly was happening in Avaldenn.

Anna twisted me so that I stared her dead in the eyes. "I'm serious, Neve. Those people knew that risk, and they still came. They came for a chance at freedom. *You* gave them that. A chance when they wouldn't have had one before."

What she said was true, but somehow, my heart still found everything I was doing to be inadequate.

Can a former slave really become a queen?

At first, fueled by my mother's insistence that I come west and after seeing everything Roar had done, everything I suspected his ancestors had done too, I was on fire. I wanted change. To protect.

However, after two weeks of travel through the harsh land I'd been born to, I wasn't sure. I *was* strong, but strong enough to do what needed to be done?

"Are you thinking that you'd rather go south? Like we once planned?" Anna asked, breaking my deluge of doubt as she scooped more snow into her basket. "Do you want to make a new life where no one knows you? If you do, I'll understand. No one understands more than me. And, of course, I'll come with you."

I turned, caught her gaze, those dark eyes so full of compassion. Exhaling, I scooped more snow into the basket and patted it down.

"At first, going south was an escape. Freedom." I swallowed. "Now though, no matter where I go, I won't feel free. There's always a chance someone will learn who I am and hunt me for who I am, rather than what I've done."

Anna nodded slowly. "Then there's Vale."

Unthinkingly, my gaze shifted to the edge of the forest where the prince was instructing archers. Thanks to Vale's instruction, it was plain that many had improved.

I sighed. Vale. My husband. An unexpected rock in my life. The male I was falling for . . .

Things had been hot and cold between us, mostly because he'd had more time—*too much time*—to consider his parentage. As far as I was concerned, as a father, Lord Riis was a great improvement over King Magnus. The kingdom would be better off with the current king being dead—or at the very least, tossed in a cell that was rarely visited.

"He's perfect for me," I admitted. "But this journey has brought up feelings that we're working through."

"I understand." She sounded wistful, and I was pretty sure I knew why. I'd heard that tone before from Anna when she'd spoken of a boy she fancied.

"Do you think of Arie often?" I asked.

"Yes. He's different from other people I've met. Which I realize seems obvious, seeing as I grew up with slaves and around vampires, and he's a fae lord who had everything he ever wanted at his fingertips, but it feels deeper."

"You like him?"

"I do. And I know it's crazy to say this, but I think there could be more between us too, if this place changed."

My stomach tightened in understanding. Arie was a faerie, a male of the Sacred Eight.

Anna was a human.

It was one thing for a commoner fae to be raised so high in fae society. Far less likely for a fae slave to do the same, but not unthinkable. A partnership between a human and a noble lord, however, was as likely as the dead gods returning to Isila.

But if I spoke my truth, if I claimed my real name and fought King Magnus for the throne, I could be a catalyst for the change Anna and Arie needed to be together. I could do so much good. My chest seemed to squeeze hard as I stood.

"You would be perfect together." I hefted my basket. "Better get this to the fire to melt."

Anna said nothing as I returned to my work, my head buzzing, and my heart heavy with conflict.

INTERLUDE

KING MAGNUS AABERG, THE WHITE BEAR, PROTECTOR OF WINTER'S REALM

T he throne sat cold beneath him, as frigid as many of the gazes in the crowd—of which the king noted every single one.

Enemies of my house will be punished.

The Courting Festival, the pain in the arse it was becoming, had once seemed so brilliant. A way to not only form marriage alliances that would benefit House Aaberg for many turns to come, but to discover where the Ice Scepter might be hiding. Of the Hallows the king knew existed—all lost to him—the Scepter, with its ability to influence the magic of the realm, was the most important. The one he might actually be able to get his hands on too.

The lord or lady who stole the Hallow and kept it in their possession for all these turns would, in theory, be more powerful than the rest. And if said lord or lady were smart, they'd bring it before the Crown Drassil for a blessing.

But the king had people watching the holy tree, and no one had approached the Drassil. No one Head of House seemed far more powerful than the rest either. Well, no one save for the king himself. Fitting, really, after all his positioning and training to be the strongest in the land. He'd worked too hard, schemed and fought mercilessly, to sit upon the Throne of Winter, and he had to believe that if the Ice Scepter thief was at court, he'd find them. Then he'd take the Hallow he desired most of the three, the only one seen since the Rebellion, and use it to meet his ends.

King Magnus's fingers curled around the throne's armrest, frost creeping over the royal blue velvet. "Where *are* they?"

Behind, a Clawsguard cleared his throat. "The ship arrived an hour ago, Majesty. They should be here at any moment."

How long did it take to leave a boat? To walk through his city and bring news from the Blood Court? Magnus huffed. Skies above, Lord Sten Armenil always took his bleeding time and time was not a luxury the king felt he had much of. With Red Assassins terrorizing Avaldenn, and his son and the whore who'd caused this whole mess missing, King Magnus wanted answers *now*.

He was about to demand more information from his Clawsguard, but remembered the person behind him was not Lars, his favored guard of many turns. Now dead, but faithful to the end. No, this guard was new and not of the same caliber as Lars, and likely did not have more information to give. Since Lars died in the rebellion's massacre at the Royal Theater, the king had gone through two other Clawsguards, both not up to his standards. These failings displeased the king to no end.

"I could go check, Father." Saga leaned forward in her throne, a smaller version of his own.

She and Rhistel had answered his summons, both sitting dutifully to his left. On his right, however, Queen Inga's throne remained empty.

Magnus exhaled a long, frustrated breath. Perhaps no one had found Inga. Or more likely, someone spoke to her, and she'd whispered to them, made them believe they'd never found her. Frustrating as it was, his queen only did his bidding when *she* wished.

Or when he pressed and dangled her secret over her head, which he knew better than to do often.

"The docks might be busy?" His sweet daughter leaned forward a touch more, ready to leave, though King Magnus did not believe it was purely to help. Since yesterday, Saga's friend Sayyida had been absent from court. He suspected his youngest wished to look for the troublemaking Virtoris wench at the harbor.

"No need," King Magnus replied as an entourage wearing the light gray cloaks and wolf broaches of House Armenil entered. One carried a small chest. "They've finally shown up." He pointed to the base of the stairs leading up to the thrones, eyes scanning the guards and then behind.

Lord Sten Armenil, the red-haired, plodding Lord of the North, was not among them.

"Where is your liege lord?" King Magnus barked before the knights serving the great, noble house of the far north reached the dais.

The soldiers exchanged glances, their faces masks. However, the tightness in their shoulders told a different story. Something had happened. Had Sten Armenil stopped the ship at his castle on the peninsula and told them to continue on?

King Magnus's jaw tightened. *May Odan help Sten if he did. I will not stand for him leaving court without my permission.*

"My king." One soldier came to a stop below the king's throne. "Lord Armenil is not with us."

He glared, and did not miss when many in the crowd took a half-step back. "Return to your ship and retrieve him."

"I did not speak clearly, Your Grace." The soldier unhooked the latch on the box. He lifted the lid, and the king drew back.

Lord Armenil's head, eyes flat, stared at Magnus.

"What happened?" Magnus growled, his gaze flicking briefly to the crowd and landing on the Armenil clan. The pale family of redheads shoulder-to-shoulder with those of House Balik, all brown of skin and hair—a contrast if there ever was one. So far, none in the crowd had spotted the head in the box.

Things were about to go very wrong, and the king wished that he'd not called so many witnesses.

These were people he'd wanted to be present when Lord Armenil relayed word from the Blood Court. He'd been so sure that the king and queen of all vampires would demand Neve's head on a platter, to which he'd simply have to give in, or risk all-out war. Then he could proceed with his plan to dismiss the murderous Lord Triam from Frostveil with his soon-to-be-bride, Marit Armenil. She'd be a cautionary tale, and no one would dare go behind the king's back again.

"We reached the Vampire Court and attained an audience with Queen Narcissa." The soldier's face paled at the mere mention of the queen in the neighboring kingdom. "Lord Armenil stated the facts, as you wished for him to. He told them that their prince died at the hands of a fae. That it had been a matter of self-defense."

The soldier inhaled before continuing. "The queen was angry but allowed Lord Armenil to continue. That changed when a vampire ship captain arrived. He told her the one who killed him was a member of your house. Then she demanded immediate retribution because, well, the vampire queen's temper might have been thinner than normal."

"How so?"

"She was in mourning."

He arched an eyebrow. "For Prince Gervais?"

Prince Gervais had been of Narcissa's bloodline, but vampires did not typically mourn. Not unless their mate or maker died, and only the former was a prolonged period.

"No, Majesty. King Vladistrica was killed shortly after Prince Gervais sailed west. Many other nobles too. By vampire tradition, the queen is in mourning for six moons, but I think she was bloodthirsty, hence she accepted us. Upon hearing what he had to say, she claimed she wanted revenge, and that Lord Armenil was close enough to the throne for her—*for now*. She took his head then and there, Majesty." He gave a single nod to the box, the implication now clear for all those who could not see what was in it before.

The king caught the moment Lady Orla Armenil fell to the ground, Marit and another red-haired brat he could not be bothered to recall the name of, moved to help the Lady of the North. The king looked at his hands, as if sorry for the loss.

But he did not see Sten Armenil's death as a loss. Rather, an opportunity to further his own power, which he needed to do for this act on the part of the vampires also brought new threats.

"You said *for now*," the king said, returning his attention to the soldier. Neve was one thing, but did the queen mean his children? His queen?

"As the assassins have not done the job she required of them, she seeks Princess Neve's blood next. Personally wanted to drink from the princess.."

If only Narcissa had come here, I'd have offered the female's blood up from the vein.

"Will she call back the Red Assassins still lurking in Avaldenn and the surrounding areas?" the king asked.

The guard looked away briefly before shaking his head.

So the queen would keep her hired killers here just to terrorize the fae of Winter. To make King Magnus's life more difficult. His jaw worked from side to side. The Queen of Vampires left him no choice. He would have to increase the presence of soldiers in the city and incentivize them to find the bloodsuckers and kill them.

Everyone leaned forward to hear the king's next words, the mark of unflinching power. "I see that Lord Armenil was not effective in protecting my family. Nor my people." The words were true, even if he did not like to think of that silver-haired female as his family. "I understand that we now sit on the brink of war with the vampires due to his inaptitude."

The direwolf-loving soldier blinked. "My king, he—"

"I do not remember telling you that you may speak again." Magnus stood. "Take that box to Lady Armenil."

He stomped down the stairs. The crowd parted a bit more for him, allowing him a wide passage. The Lady of House Armenil was still wailing. His lips curled in disgust. She was a weak female who only furthered his belief that their house needed to be replaced with a stronger family.

If I had the Scepter, this would be far easier.

No one stopped the king as he left the throne room. Heavy footsteps assured him that two Clawsguards were behind him, ready to defend, to fight, should he need their swords, magic, and bodies. He would not. He needed time to think and a soft cunt to sink himself into.

"Go to the harem. Find me the nymph with pink hair and large breasts. Bring her to my chambers." King Magnus did not turn as he spoke to his guards. The sounds of footsteps dimmed. Only one guard followed him to his suite. When they arrived, the king opened his own door. "Have the nymph wait until I call her in."

"Yes, Majesty."

The king let himself into his chambers and went right to the table heavy with the finest Summer Isle wines. The best spirits from the Dragon Kingdom too. He selected one of those fiery spirits, poured himself a large glass, and drank.

"*Bleeding Armenils.*" He turned, preparing to disrobe and his heart, usually so cold it was nearly frozen, skipped a beat.

He was not alone in his chambers.

"Warden Roar," Magnus said with forced calm as he took in the high lord with a goblet of wine in his hand and a calculating glint in his eyes.

Half of Roar Lisika's face bore a hideous scar, as though someone had shoved a hundred pebbles into his cheek. It had not been like that when the Warden of the West fled Avaldenn in the dead of night.

"I've been looking for you."

Roar gave a half smile that made the king's grip tighten on the goblet. "Have you, Majesty?"

The warden possessed no weapon, not that the king was foolish enough to believe that meant he was safe. Lord Roar could shift into a great beast. And, like King Magnus, the Warden of the West controlled winter magic. Not as completely as the king, but it was still a factor to keep in mind.

The king tugged on his power, ready to attack should he need to, and the temperature in the room plummeted.

Roar chuckled and swirled the wine. "My king, I have no desire to fight."

"Then why, pray tell, are you in my rooms?"

"I have information that you'll want to know. Information I didn't want anyone else hearing, hence I thought it best I wait here for your return."

So sure, so cocky. Then again, he always had been. All Lisikas were like that.

"How did you get in?" King Magnus asked.

His Clawsguard usually followed him, but when he was gone, his door was warded to not let anyone aside from himself and select slaves inside to clean.

Roar gestured to the window, left open but a crack. "You should close that. Frostflies might get in."

The king's eyes widened. He'd known for many turns that the warden shifted into a monstrous snow leopard. He'd heard from Lord Riis that Roar had also achieved the form of great antlered hart too, though that had only been in the last two turns.

"You have a third form?"

"Born of necessity," Roar drawled. "As you know, since a young age, my wings have not been functional. However, very recently, I found myself somewhere dark and deep within the ground. No one knew I was there, so I needed to get myself out." He lifted the hem of his pants to reveal a metal leg. Then Roar turned, and the king swallowed. The warden's wings were shorter and more mangled than before.

"The fall almost took my life, but shifting boosts my healing abilities. I had enough power to shift and fly out of the dark and dank. Once safe, I shifted again and again and again, rotating between my forms and healing myself more each time—to a point, of course. Some damage, like my leg and the wounds on my face, were irreversible, but I made it home and to my healer, who minimized the rest of the damage as best she could. The process took many days, so I've only just arrived back to your wonderful city despite flying on my fastest gryphon. No longer could I wait, you see."

Magnus stared at the warden. He seemed sincere. And the story was intriguing and in line with what he knew of shifting powers. "What is it then?"

Roar went to the table and poured himself another glass

of summer wine. He sipped the goblet. Sighed. "You always received the best vintages, Majesty. I dare say you pluck them off the boats from the Summer Isles before the rest of us can even try to breathe the sweet, warm air caught in those sails."

"My patience is running thin. Give me this news or I shall send you to the dungeons like I have planned to do these past weeks."

"Ah, about that. This information will buy my freedom. It is worth it. Worth a crown, I'd say."

The king's heart froze. Nothing in Roar's face or standing indicated he meant a crown for himself. But they all knew the rebels continued to spout off about an heir. Had Roar learned who it was? How?

"If it is worth so much, I vow to not harm you, Warden Lisika."

Roar did not seem worried. Rather, his smug smile grew. "I want more."

"More than your freedom when I have called for your treasonous head?"

"Indeed. I will keep my lands and title. I will also hold an advisory position to the Crown."

The skin on the back of the king's neck tightened. Only information about the rebels—the location of where they stayed—could be so valuable to him.

"Lastly, I wish for a formal betrothal and quick wedding to your daughter—Princess Saga. Within a moon, I'd like to be wed."

Ire stirred in the king's chest. The day Saga had been born, many debated over who she'd wed. It did not matter if she turned out to be the most powerful of his younglings and hence, the heir, or not. A princess was always a valuable piece of a king's power.

House Lisika, the only surviving member of which was young Lord Roar, was a natural suggestion, but King Magnus had never cared for the great house of the west. He used them, oh yes he did. Any king worth his crown would leverage their mines and large army. But trust and admiration never struck his cold heart when he thought of House Lisika. So the White Bear had spurned Lord Roar as a husband for his only daughter, despite the Snow Leopard Heir being a reasonable choice.

"*If* it is important enough, I will entertain your requests."

The warden sipped again, unbothered by the fact that he should not be here. That the king should have already killed him. "Well, Majesty, I bring the gossip of the century. After all, it's not every day one learns that Isolde Falk is alive and well."

CHAPTER 5
VALE
DAYS LATER

My thighs ached, and snow pushed down into my boots as I plowed through the deep drifts.

It should be right around the next curve of the mountain. I craned my neck and stared up the mountainside. *Or was it the next?*

I cursed myself. Had I paid better attention in classes as a youngling, I'd remember precisely where the entrance to the old Mining Kingdom of Dergia was located. But I'd always been more preoccupied with current threats to Winter's Realm over long forgotten and dead kingdoms. Particularly long-forgotten kingdoms, which were so far away from Avaldenn, the beating heart of Winter's Realm.

However, through my many frustrations, I allowed myself to take a small measure of heart. I *had* managed to get us this far. With Caelo's help, and a bit of luck, we'd found the ancient, unmarked road cutting through the forest and leading deep into the mountains, to the place where the

Red Mist Range and the Ice Tooth Range intersected. To the guest entrance of Dergia, or so it was said.

The Doors of Eitriod have to be coming up soon . . .

Caelo approached, careful to walk close to me and within my footsteps. The pathway into the mountain range had clearly deteriorated with the passing turns. On one side, a steep cliff promised certain doom to anyone who was not vigilant with their footing.

"Animals walk the peaks above," Caelo said. "Goats, I think, though I can't be sure. They were far away."

"Good." At this small mention, relief bloomed inside. "That means there's food somewhere, and the humans can hunt."

"And water is near too." My friend angled his head back to the crowd. "Should we rest? Some are lagging. Neve and Anna are having difficulty keeping them motivated."

I twisted to take in the group. Since the nøkken attack six days back, we'd lost five more souls, all to the cold.

The humans had not been conditioned to walk across Winter's Realm. Nor had they possessed the best attire. For one hundred and forty three people to have survived the cold alone was a miracle. That gave me hope for them, that they truly could live out here alone and safe and free. Maybe, if they survived for a while on their own, I could send aid. I'd already been considering whom among the earth fae I knew would be skilled enough to make this journey and would be trustworthy enough to keep the humans a secret. The list was short—consisting only of a soldier I'd fought alongside many times, and a fae living in the Tower of the Living and the Dead.

"They can stop, but I'll keep going," I said to Caelo. "I wish to see around the next bend."

"What happened to being extra careful?"

I knew precisely what he meant. The risk of other creatures in this area was slight, but present. We worried, particularly, about the dwarves.

Some dwarves had refused to integrate into the greater Kingdom of Winter. Those small clans roamed the mountains nomadically, like orcs, trolls, and giants, though they were not a nuisance, so the Crown of Winter did not bother trying to subjugate or fight them. However, it was not out of the question that they'd reclaim old mines to use as temporary camps. Stepping into their territory would be an aggression.

"What happened to following your prince's orders?" I retorted and immediately cringed. Days of travel, periods of hunger, and constant peril had me on edge, but that was no reason to talk to my best friend, a brother of my heart, in such a manner.

A testament to our brotherly bond, Caelo didn't apologize, but arched a brow. "You can't bring up the prince card when it suits you, while also lamenting privately that you're not good enough for Neve. That you're only suited to be a part of her guard."

"I know," I whispered, which seemed good enough for him because Caelo turned around and held up a hand.

"Take a five-minute break." He spoke at normal volume, and the message was passed down the line, proving the humans were heeding my warnings about avalanches. "Vale will continue forward to scout."

I left and remained focused on the bend ahead. Focused on pushing through the snow, carving a path up the slight incline to see our destination.

What would have taken ten minutes on roads beaten down by sleighs, hooves, and feet took three times as long, but at last I reached my destination and rounded the corner.

My breath left me in a plume of white, filling the air. *We did it.*

Below, still a ways away but visible, a set of wood double-doors were nestled into a mountain. The Doors of Eitriod, an intricate set of light wooded pine doors meant to honor one of the dwarves' favored gods, had once been the visitor's entrance to Dergia. My heart rate doubled at the sight of the great hammer and axe carved into the doors, illuminated by the late morning sun. The most loved tools of the dwarven artists and soldiers. Soon enough, we'd be there, we'd break the door down and venture inside for a first glimpse at the humans' new home.

"Stand back," I instructed.

It had taken far longer than I'd expected, but we'd finally reached the Doors of Eitriod only to find the great wooden double doors locked from within.

"You're going to blast it?" Neve asked.

Since I'd announced I could see the doors, her spirits had improved drastically. I only hoped that once inside, her mood would continue to rise. But who knew what we'd find inside?

Nomadic dwarves who knew another way in? Monsters that pushed their way into the mountain and made it their own home?

Hopefully nothing.

"I can freeze the door to help," Neve added thoughtfully.

"If you have the energy."

During our journey, we'd learned to let her save her magic for the dark hours when we required shelters.

"There might be wards on the door," I added. "Force may not work."

She countered. "Why would anyone ward a deserted kingdom?"

"They would be old and stout wards, Neve. Dwarven magic, especially within the mountains, is loyal and stubborn. Like dwarves themselves are known to be."

"Stubborn, are they? Perhaps I'm part dwarf." Neve stared at the Doors of Eitriod with a gleam in her eyes.

"Just be careful. Release your magic if you feel anything off." I stood back for Neve to do as she would.

She faced the doors, and I felt when she called her power to the surface. Over the weeks, Neve had delved ever deeper into the depths of her power. Bit by bit, she harnessed the magic she'd been born to wield, and though she still had a long way to go before she claimed true mastery, I remained in a constant state of marvel.

Many times when her power filled the air, I'd wondered

what would have happened if the White Bear's Rebellion had failed. Or better yet, never happened.

If Neve had been free to grow up with her parents, her four older brothers, and her twin sister, where would her power have fallen on the spectrum of their bloodline? Would she have been the most powerful, and therefore, the heir? In our world, that was how things worked, with rare exceptions—my brother being one of them.

Or had House Falk produced fae with greater winter magic? I shuddered at the thought, though I suspected it to be true. King Harald Falk had been cruel and mad during the last turns of his life. Those stories were told most often, though tales of his magical prowess were told from time to time too because whomever the wielder, fae loved and revered power.

The temperature dropped, and Caelo urged the humans to back away. Wishing to add extra protection for all of those around her, I created an air shield and expanded it to cover the humans and Caelo. The shield was barely in place when Neve unleashed herself on the door.

The pine slabs shuddered, and frost crept from the edges as gales as strong as those from the harshest of winter storms slammed into the doors. She pushed again, and the doors shook harder, the great metal locks whining under the strain. More frost covered the wood to the point where both doors were no longer a light pine color, but pure white.

When I thought she was done, and my precautions had been a touch much, the blow back came with vengeance. Hail exploded from Neve, soaring in all directions. Ice balls struck my air shield, and screams arose from the humans.

Neve spun, exhaled as she saw that I'd protected those with us. "Good thinking on the shield."

"It's always best to take precautions."

"You're used to considering the lives of others."

I'd led scores of fae to battle. Yes, I considered their lives, and I'd been considering the lives of the humans since we'd liberated them. So had she, but I suspected the challenge the Doors of Eitriod presented made her forget the potency of her power.

"Try again, but this time consider, where's the weakest point?" I asked, changing the topic. "A place you can infiltrate with a targeted strike."

"If I hit right in the middle they'll shatter inward."

One corner of my lips curled. "You're sure?"

She smirked. "I am, but I think you should try. You have better accuracy."

"As you wish."

It took no time at all to call my air magic. Once, I'd believed my powers to be a limited form of winter magic, a concentration on air magic, and maybe it was, but after seeing Neve's powers, after realizing how little of that supposed winter magic I possessed, I preferred to focus on the elemental aspect. After all, I had no Aaberg blood flowing through me, and while House Vagle, like all the Sacred Eight, possessed the blood of Winter's Realm, I did not think I'd inherited much from my mother.

No, my powers—like my vast physical strength—were likely from House Riis. I needed to make peace with that.

I formed the air into a spike, so thin and condensed it might as well have been a true spear, and hurled the weapon at the door. The ear-splitting sound of splintering wood filled the quiet of the mountains.

Neve sucked in a breath, taking in the hole I'd made before lifting her eyes upward. "Was that loud enough for an avalanche?"

"Yes." My gaze swept up the mountainsides as the wood continued to splinter. Pieces fell to the ground, and still I looked up at the peaks.

Watching. Waiting.

Only after many long seconds had passed and I still hadn't spotted movement of the snow from above, did I release my breath. "We're safe. I'll peer inside. Make sure no one is lying in wait."

Striding closer to the door, Caelo and Neve fell into step with me. My hand tingled, ready to draw *Skelda*, my sword, at a moment's notice. Neve drew her own sword—the one she'd taken from King Harald's room when we escaped Frostveil Castle.

Not for the first time, I glanced askew at the blade. Pride made me think I should know its name, but I did not.

Neve's father, King Harald, had wielded several swords, often in concurrence with the various phases of his life: The first as a young warrior, the second as a rake who also fought for Winter's Realm, and the third he claimed after he wed his wife and mate, Queen Revna Skau. The one Neve held could be any of those blades.

The closer we got, the harder I listened, trying to detect sounds of life beyond, but there was nothing but the wind. And when we reached the hole, and I peered in, only darkness stared back.

"Nothing that I can see," I stated, wishing for a consensus. "Nor do I scent anyone or anything."

Caelo sniffed at the hole and stared inside. Only once we'd both checked and deemed it safe did I allow Neve to do so.

"Smells deserted, like we hoped," she confirmed, her violet eyes sparking with hope. "Let's go inside."

Using two of the miners' pickaxes, Caelo and I attacked the wood. Our breach seemed to have broken whatever protections were in place for we felt no magic around the area. The wood chipped away easily enough and soon the horses could walk through the center of the semi-demolished double doors.

"Careful inside," Caelo whispered to each horse. "This place has been abandoned for many centuries and the ground will be uneven."

I nodded, glad he was around to communicate with the animals. Not only would we need them when we left, but I'd always had a soft spot for horses, especially Carpus, my beloved destrier back home. I hated the idea of having to end a horse's life over a broken leg.

"Everyone ready?" Neve asked.

Lanterns, also brought from Gersemi Mine, had been lit to guide the way. I took one from Lei who clung to Ronaldo, just as she'd done since the nøkken attack. Would that we had fae lights, but none of us possessed that power, so fire would have to do.

With Caelo at my side, one hand holding the lantern, another gripping *Skelda*, we ventured forth into the mountain. Inside, a sense of relief swept through me. I'd grown used to the winds and with the lack of them, some feeling returned to my cheeks.

"Watch that dip." Caelo cautioned from a few paces ahead. Horses neighed, hinting that he'd communicated the issue to them too, as Neve, who walked directly behind us, passed the word back.

The passage was large enough for three large fae to walk side-by-side. We moved carefully, clearing fallen rocks as we progressed. Without the sun, I had no way to tell the passage of time, but I felt like we walked for at least two hours. We came across torches, the wooden handles cracked and disintegrating from age. We tried to light each one and three worked, providing more light for those in the middle and the back of the column.

More sinisterly, we passed two skeletons. Dwarven by the looks of them. Had they denied leaving their kingdom and died together beneath the mountain with only memories of their kinds' glory days behind them?

"There's a curve ahead," I spoke clearly but not loudly. "And a sound coming from there too. I can't tell what it is yet."

"Weapons in hand," Neve added for the sake of those behind her. I doubted that any one of them had let go of a weapon if they were among those lucky enough to have one.

We approached the curve, took it, and the sound I'd been hearing intensified.

"Is that water?" I looked to Caelo for his thoughts.

"A waterfall, I'd wager," my friend agreed. "I heard the dwarves rerouted creeks to flow into their kingdoms. The entrances never froze, nor the water."

"Clever."

"You'd have to be to live down here."

No argument there. While I respected dwarfkind, I could not understand why someone would live beneath a mountain. It was too constraining. Too dark. Too suffocating.

The only thing worse would be living underwater. I shuddered at the thought.

The sound of water grew closer, and the tunnel widened bit by bit. Neve shuffled up to walk with Caelo and me, her eyes squinting ahead.

"I think it's a cavern."

Another twenty paces proved her right. We stopped at the edge of a cavern, the light from our lanterns illuminating enough for us to see water falling from the ceiling into a pool at the bottom.

"That's a good sign." Neve took a step forward, holding her lantern aloft and dropping her sword as she took in the area. "They won't have to go outside to gather snow to melt."

"Could sleep in here," Caelo said.

It would not be comfortable. The cavern was nothing like the living quarters at Gersemi Mine, where some of the humans had lived for many turns. Roar had been a monster to them in many ways, but even he had taken care of the basics. The humans working his mine had been housed and fed. Of course, the humans caged to be sold as blood slaves hadn't been so lucky.

In any case, Caelo was right. This place appeared safe

and until the humans had explored more, it might be a good base.

"Break for water," I said. "Fill our skins and let the horses drink."

I stepped into the cavern, ready to do as much, when fae lights dropped from the ceiling, blinding me. The sounds of heels hitting stone and metal being drawn told me that we weren't alone.

CHAPTER 6

NEVE

I thrust my lantern at the nearest human, who took it with a squawk. No longer burdened by its weight, I gripped my sword with both hands. Ready for what may come. I sucked in a breath as my vision adjusted to the bright fae lights.

I'd thought the attackers would be orcs, but no. They were dwarves. Twelve, in number. I barely had time to process the information when they rushed us, a variety of weapons raised. An arrow snapping against the rock wall at my side made me jump and look up.

"*Stars*," I yelped at my stark miscalculation.

The twelve were not alone. Peeking out of small caverns and climbing along ledges with grace that their short stocky bodies shouldn't possess were at least fifty other dwarves. We were in serious trouble. Vale might be the Warrior Bear, Caelo a powerful knight, and I had the basics of defense and fighting down, but I doubted our ability to take on so many.

Behind, the humans began to panic, and the horses whinnied and snorted. The skin on the back of my neck tightened. "Caelo! Calm them."

The last thing we needed was the horses running back through the tunnel. They could trample the humans down the line or break a leg running through the uneven tunnels.

Caelo squinted, dividing his attention from the threat ahead to the horses' wellbeing.

Another arrow soared my way. Caelo ducked, and I followed suit as the first dozen attackers reached us. Vale pushed me behind him and went on the offense.

One dwarf fell, then another, only for more to drop from above. I gripped my sword, ready to join the fight, when another arrow soared at us, and this time, the archer struck a human woman.

She screamed and fell. Others grabbed her, tried to pull her into the tunnel where the humans were retreating, but before they did so, another arrow hit a man.

My blood ran hot. We'd spent weeks walking here, and these people had lived through it all! I'd not see them die now. My magic surged with my anger and flew from me.

Cries of fear filled the cavern, bouncing off the walls and setting my teeth on edge. However, the sounds of blades hitting blades ceased. As did the clamor of boots on stone.

"Help!" another human behind me shrieked and began jerking in place. The reason became apparent as my gaze dropped.

I'd frozen her feet to the ground, like King Magnus had done during the execution of the Royal Theater actors. My stomach dropped as I put that together with the sudden lack of sound and cast a wide glance. *Every single person* who stood on the ground was frozen in place, including Vale and Caelo.

Vale met my eyes. "More might drop."

I looked up and found that he was right. My outburst of magic had not flung itself above us and the archers and more dwarves waited to fall, though now there was hesitation in their eyes.

Knowing this might be our only chance to bargain with them, I sheathed my sword and raised both hands.

"We aren't here to harm you." I spoke clearly, levelly, but did not shout. I didn't wish to appear fearful, for many fae saw fear as a weakness. "We seek sanctuary!"

Arrows lowered a touch, and dwarves exchanged perplexed glances. For the first time, I noticed they were wearing clean uniforms.

They don't look like nomads.

Before I could question further, a fair-skinned male with a large bulbous nose, a great blond beard, and long blond hair shot through with gray jumped from above. Was he going to attack?

He landed and did not grasp his weapon, answering my unspoken question, though his eyes blazed into mine.

"Sanctuary? *Here?* When the rest of Winter's Realm believes my kingdom to be not but coal dust?"

So this is their leader.

I sized him up. Yes, the pride in his face, the uplift of his chin and the fire in his voice would indicate a high station. I sought to match such an effect and tilted my chin up.

"You heard me correctly. We seek safety, not to harm or take anything of yours."

The dwarf stopped, his hand sweeping the ground. "It appears *you've* already done harm."

"I—I didn't mean to do that." I swallowed, well aware of the whining from behind us. I waved a hand at Vale's feet. "As you can see, I disabled my best warriors."

"You cannot release your power to free them?"

"I already have," I admitted. "Ice and frost do not melt so quickly."

The leader stared at me, then he pointed up to where others waited for a command. "Would you oppose me bringing down a fire elemental? One of our best?"

Fire elemental? They had one here and hadn't unleashed fire on us right away? They could have easily done so from a distance. That indicated some reluctance to attack, I supposed, but I had to be careful here.

"Only if you promise not to hurt anyone." I placed a hand on Vale's shoulder. "Including those who fought your soldiers."

And had felled many, despite the short duration of the fight. Though none had died, which I hoped worked in our favor.

"If they try to do harm, I suspect you will be quick to retaliate, will you not, my lady?" The leader again gestured to the shackles of ice around so many ankles.

"I will strike as fast as a viper."

A smirk broke on the dwarf's face, and he snapped his fingers. "Utrick!"

Another dwarf, this one shorter and stockier than the

leader, with hair like gray ash and enormous, rounded ears, launched into the air. I marveled, wondering how they landed without harming themselves when they did not have wings. A split second later, I found my answer. Nearly hidden by an outcropping of stone, one dwarf was manipulating air to assist their landings.

Utrick approached his leader. "King?"

I tucked that information away. Not only was this dwarf a leader, but a king. Nomadic tribes did not have kings. It seemed that the kingdom of Dergia may have been reformed.

"Heat the ice shackles. Free all—in fact, do these two first." The king's chin jerked to encompass Vale and Caelo. "As a sign of our good will. We wouldn't want this powerful female thinking anything else."

Utrick's magic heated the space around Vale and Caelo and with his combined magic and their strength, Vale and Caelo were freed. They came to my sides, like the queensguard they'd offered to be in the depths of Gersemi Mine, as the fire elemental spread his magic. Sighs of relief filled the cavern.

When all were freed from my shackles, the king motioned for his soldiers to get behind him as he stepped closer. I met him, stopping when three paces separated us.

"King Tholin of the Kingdom of Dergia—the Great Rock." He inclined his head and for the first time, I caught a shimmer of gold dust on both hands crawling up the dwarf's meaty arms.

"Reformed after all these turns?" I asked, unable to help myself.

"We never truly left." The king arched an eyebrow. "And who might you be, my lady?"

He had picked me out as the leader, which was both unsettling and empowering.

Now, how to answer the question? He said they'd never left, which meant the dwarves had hidden here. Since the time of Sassa Falk four thousand turns ago when she had demanded their bent knees.

I had no idea of his loyalties, nor if this dwarf's family had a relationship, good or bad, with my birth family, for it wasn't Vale's house that demanded other leaders bend the knee many turns ago. However, the Aabergs also hadn't returned individual powers to the various fae races.

In passing at court, I'd met one such dwarf, a descendant of a royal line from the Ice Tooth Range and another descendant of the sprite royals. Neither had seemed inclined to want change, to take on the troubles of the realm for themselves.

This king was clearly different. He stood before me proudly, as did those behind him. How many more might there be?

I didn't know, but I understood one thing: They weren't fae to be trifled with. For now, I'd hide my birth name until I determined if they'd take offense to the bloodline that had tried to rob them of their kingdom.

"Neve, wife to Prince Vale." I answered, gesturing to Vale. The king's eyes narrowed, but before he could say anything, I added. "We come with humans, some fated to mine rock as slaves until they died. Others destined for the Blood Court. For collars and chains. *They* are why we're here, as we hoped this kingdom—though we believed it to be deserted—could be a home for them. A place where they might guide their own fates. Seeing you here both gives me hope, and worries me, for their sake."

The king's attention went to the tunnel, where the humans huddled. Anna stood in the front of them all and not for the first time, I marveled at my friend's bravery.

"According to your laws, they should be in noble homes and select institutions."

Your laws. This kingdom did not abide by laws outside their own. Nor, if I was reading him correctly, did Tholin seem hostile to the humans. Not as if he would wish to use them. No, King Tholin looked at them like . . .

Like I do. Like people he was used to being around.

"You're right, we're breaking the law. I cannot watch these people, lured here by a malicious lord, put into forced servitude."

Tholin's eyes widened. "Interesting."

"Might I ask why?"

He stared at me, as though I was a puzzle he was hoping to solve.

"You might, but first I wonder—why are you speaking and not your husband? He is the prince, son of King Aaberg and the Warrior Bear, is he not? Have my soldiers got him so out of breath he cannot speak when his rank demands it?"

This king wasn't just unusual, he was intelligent. He recognized an atypical dynamic between Vale and me, and it raised a flag.

"You used your magic, so you can't be under the influence of Liar's Salvation and lying to me," the king added, "but I do not see why a princess—a new one, if my spies are correct—would speak for the House Aaberg. Those of the House of the White Bear are as proud as mountains and nearly as unmovable."

Too clever indeed.

"And you seem to have powerful winter magic, though, from what I heard, you are a commoner?" The king eyed me.

We were at a stalemate. I had to give him *something*, and my stomach churned at what that might mean. But I would not do it for free.

"You've asked many questions, and I will answer you, but first, these people are under our protection, and I must be sure of their safety first."

King Tholin leaned back, studying me for seconds that stretched into turns.

"You claim that you seek sanctuary," he said, "and I will grant you the safety of the great beneath, and that same safety for everyone under your protection, *if* you promise to remain quiet about what you've seen. All that I'm about to show you. You cannot breathe a word to anyone in the kingdoms beyond."

Show us what?

The question must have shown on my face, for Tholin continued. "Promise, and you and yours will be fed and treated as guests inside my halls of stone while we get to know one another." He stuck out his hand.

I took it, my hands grasping his meaty forearm, while he did the same to my more slender one. Bonded, I inclined my head. "We'll say nothing about this place and do nothing to harm you and yours."

"Betray me, or even think about it, and you'll never leave this mountain," Tholin said as he released.

I nodded, having no intention of doing so anyway, so it was an easy promise to make.

The king swept a hand to his side, indicating I should walk with him. "Then, welcome to the Kingdom of Dergia, Princess Neve. Follow me and in time your queries will be answered."

I questioned myself many times as we followed King Tholin through tunnels beneath the mountain. Was I making a mistake? Should we have run down the tunnel and left the mountain? Were we walking into a trap?

Why is this so easy?

Through my many doubts, however, my heart beat as steady as a drum, and that was the most telling thing of all. I might know nothing about King Tholin or his kingdom, but this felt right. Safe.

Truth be told, if we left, I wasn't sure how much longer the humans could last. It wasn't as if we had other options in mind. So we strode deeper into the mountains, passing by artwork, both the carved and painted kind, on to the dark walls and illuminated by fae lights.

"Look." Vale squeezed my hand. He stared at the opposite wall, at one of the paintings.

The art depicted the two mountain ranges bordering Winter's Realm to the west and south illuminated in white paint. Five castles stood apparent, and they weren't those of the fae lords I knew. These had to be the ancient kingdoms of the dwarves. I located Dergia. Small dwarven figures seemed to be gathered around the hidden kingdom but nowhere else.

The king stopped. Though we'd only been walking for five minutes or so, I'd lost count at how many twists and turns we'd taken, and now, to my shock, the king didn't choose a direction, but rather placed his hand on the rock wall in front of him.

A door shimmered, appearing out of nowhere and opening. When we marched through the door and inside, a new world appeared. Like in the mines that the humans had once lived in, nothing was open air, though the magic above that mimicked the day time sky did not make it seem so. In the parts along the edges, where the rock ceiling was not as high, stones and gems dripped from the ceiling like large icicles and those made of gems like rubies and sapphires refracted the colors on to the side walls. Rivers of blue-green glacial water ran through the city below.

I inhaled the air, fresher in here than elsewhere in the tunnels, and tears pricked my eyes. That much green meant earth, water, and light fae lived here. There was no other way such abundant vegetation could exist in one place. And judging by the many stone and metal buildings below, many decorated with shining gems on their roofs, the city was not too small. If King Tholin allowed the humans to remain here, they'd live, safe and hopefully happy.

"I can't believe this," Vale whispered. "All of it, hidden. So many fae."

"More come every now and again," a soldier said. "They seek a haven from winter. They required a respite from the nobles and their games that do not benefit the people." The dwarf looked at Vale, then at me.

Little did he know, I could not relate more to those people. I'd once been on the run for a haven too. In a way, I'd found that safety in Vale—though now we were both searching for a way to be us *and* live in a kingdom that might not welcome us if they knew the truth of our blood.

King Tholin led us down a staircase. Along the way, I took in the city and then the largest building along the left wall. Built right into the face of the mountain and far grander than anything else, that had to be the palace. At the bottom, he stopped and looked up at the soldiers and humans still streaming behind. I twisted too, caught Anna's gaze.

She shook her head and in that I read that she, too, was in a state of awe.

"The newcomers will come with me. I need only twelve soldiers to escort and make sure no one branches off and gets lost on the way to my palace."

"That would be difficult to do, considering where we're going is obvious," Caelo muttered as dwarves surrounded us and their king.

Tholin might have heard him, for he gave a snort, and continued to lead us toward the palace built into the wall of the mountain.

CHAPTER 7

NEVE

K ing Tholin brought us to Fellstone Castle, the grandest building presiding over the city deep below the Rock. He showed the humans to the grand hall, a cavernous room with walls of gray stone and rivers of gems winding their way through the slate.

The king ordered food to be cooked for them, their injuries to be healed, and temporary bedrolls brought in. Once the humans were being cared for, he'd requested to speak with a few of them, and told a servant to show us to a guest room. King Tholin would join us soon.

My friends gathered round, and I waved for Ronaldo and Lei to follow. If the humans had leaders among them, it was these two. I wished for them to be present for whatever the king wished to say to me.

Escorts led us to a stone-walled room, decorated with weathered tapestries, crystals of blazing oranges and yellows, and threadbare chairs, one of which Anna collapsed into. Between the chairs sat a small table bearing a tray with teacups and a steaming pot of tea that smelled of pine needles and citrus. None of us touched the pot, let alone drank the tea. No matter how good it smelled, no matter how much I felt I could trust the dwarves, I didn't know them yet, and we had secrets to keep. Drinking tea that might have been altered was not smart.

With Vale, I walked the perimeter of the room, taking in the tapestries. Each one told a story, and I was desperate to learn more about Dergia. To even the scales of knowledge before the king joined us.

One caught my attention more than the others.

"Is this real?" I whispered to Vale, my hand running across the fibers depicting a green land covered in mist and gray rain clouds above. In the distance, a city rose— Avaldenn, if I wasn't mistaken. Dwarves rode toward it, cutting through the mist, two with crowns on their brows. Royals journeying to treat with other royals. "It's so *green*."

A longing, a yearning, washed through my body. If this was Winter's Realm, I wanted to see it like this. Without snow, the land was able to offer abundance, if only for a short while. Vale's face had tightened, and I got the sense the tapestry was affecting him as it affected me.

"It is. I've never seen our kingdom like this," he said.

Vale was only a few turns older than me. How long had Winter's Realm been naught but snow and ice and frost? And why did it strike me as so sad that others did not speak of those days, but the dwarves beneath their mountain remembered openly?

The door creaked open. A servant, a young ruddy-faced dwarf female, rushed into the sitting room carrying a marble tray, heavy with biscuits. She smiled as she set them down, her grin brightening most when it landed on Ronaldo.

His eyebrows knitted together, and he and Lei shared confused glances. Fae did not notice humans. Let alone smile at them as she'd done.

The servant left just as King Tholin strode in. At his side, arm in arm with the king, walked a regal female dwarf with black skin that glowed from within, amber eyes, and a tumble of dark curls down her back. Gold dust sparkled on her high cheekbones, a touch of it on her large nose too, and an elaborate gown stretched over her belly proclaiming she was heavy with child. His wife and queen, I suspected.

Bringing up the rear was a younger version of the king, though with a medium complexion, where the king was very fair. The younger dwarf was tall for his kind and bore an eyepatch over his left eye. The scar running down his face hinted the eye might be gone. If so, it didn't seem to hinder him. His blue eye was trained on us, his bearing was as strong as a bears, and a battle-axe was strapped to his back.

We stood: The females curtsied, and the males bowed. After everything that we'd been through, everything that had happened, and so many days on the road, the gestures felt foreign, but we were in a palace, under the goodwill of this dwarf king. We needed to act accordingly.

"Please, sit." King Tholin's piercing gaze landed on me. We did so, only for the king, the female I presumed to be queen, and the younger male to stop and stand before us. Establishing high ground. "After speaking with some of the people in the great hall, it is clear you've come quite a long way. Also that you're more than what you seem."

I stiffened. How much had they told him about themselves? About me?

They knew I'd been a slave and was now a princess. My true identity remained a secret, though there had been moments, softly spoken words between Vale, Caelo, Anna, and me that others might have caught.

"The other humans assure me that your story is true. That the four of you," the king gestured to Vale, Caelo, Anna, and I, "rescued them from a fate worse than death. A fate that one of you experienced firsthand."

I squirmed in my chair.

"This background came as a surprise, as my spies heard you were from a small town in the west, Princess Neve." Tholin took one chair, the female the other, and the younger dwarf took the last, clearing his throat as he did so.

"Might Mother and I introduce ourselves before you chip away at them, Father?"

The king chuckled. "Observe the niceties."

The queen's amber eyes warmed. "Queen Deseana Fellhelm. A pleasure to meet you all."

We echoed the sentiment, and when I turned my gaze upon the younger dwarf, it was to find that he was already staring at me.

He looked only a few turns older than Vale's twenty-nine. As fae aged slowly after thirty turns, this made his age difficult to pinpoint, but he surely was not over a century.

"Prince Thordur of House Fellhelm, heir to the

Kingdom of Dergia." The prince inclined his head. "It's a pleasure to meet you."

I inclined my head in kind. "We're thankful for your House's invitation to see Dergia."

"One that comes with questions," the king said. He was not one to be deterred from his interrogation.

"We would expect nothing less." Vale leaned forward, placing his elbows on his knees in a show of relaxation that I'd never manage in this scenario. How did he stay so cool under intense pressure?

"Firstly," the king crossed one thick leg over his knee, "I need to hear the princess's story of her life before meeting you, Prince Vale. From her own lips."

I swallowed. Upon learning that this kingdom was not, in fact, deserted, I'd hoped the king would see us bringing humans here as a good deed. Something Vale and I did out of the goodness of our hearts, which it was, but I could not deny that my past and hatred of Roar drove me too.

"I'm not from the west of this kingdom, but further west." I didn't second guess myself because something told me the humans had already told him this part of my past. "I grew up as a blood slave to vampires and escaped two moons past."

King Tholin nodded. "And you married a prince. Did you hide your truth from Vale?"

"For a while. He knew about my past when I married him, though, and he still vowed to protect me."

"From?"

"A royal vampire at court. I killed his brother's child."

Tholin and Thordur exchanged looks. Again, they did

not appear surprised. Their spies must have come with this information already, and I found myself both shocked and awed that a hidden kingdom could have spies.

"You have winter magic too. Great power. Even if I did not see it in the cavern, I can now feel it rolling off you in waves. If you were my race, you'd cause a great earth shake with such magic. Yet I do not think you realize you're using energy to hold back." The queen poured herself a cup of tea and sipped. "Did you know, Princess Neve, that the ancient kings and queens of this kingdom put in place an enchantment against certain bloodlines with such power?"

I stiffened before loosening again to hide such a reaction. "Why would I know that?"

"Because," King Tholin spoke, "your arrival set off our boundary wards. They allowed us to be in place when you got too close."

Seeing as the queen had helped herself, I was now sure that the tea was free of poison or an unwanted potion. I poured a cup, using the moment to think of how to answer. I was pleased my hands did not tremble as I did so.

"My arrival," I said innocently. "You must mean my husband's. He's a prince, raised under the banner of House Aaberg."

"We have warded against that family too," King Tholin turned his gaze on Vale. "That protection will need to be examined, for *it* did not trigger when you stepped through the Doors of Eitriod."

My stomach twisted. I'd thought the Doors had been too easy to break open. Also strange that there were no wards.

Well there had been. Extremely specific wards that would probably take a specialist to discern.

"Then who do you mean?" I asked, still playing dumb.

King Tholin laughed dryly. "Why, you're of House Falk, of course. You hold their power. Their blood. The runes that you walked right past do not lie. So, tell me Princess Neve, are you a discarded Falk bastard? Or are you someone for us to truly worry over?"

Heat rushed through me, but I was Winterborn and used my power to cool myself before I could flush. Saying I was a bastard was impossible, but I wasn't sure I was ready for others to learn my identity. Could I spin this, use the fae tact of diversion and omission?

Thordur chuckled. "She brought well over a hundred humans here, Father. A rare fae would worry about the fate of trapped humans, a rarer one still would free them. Outside Dergia, very few fae would lead them to safety." He gestured to me. "No matter her bloodline, I do not think we need to worry about her. And this helps Dergia greatly. We direly need new blood."

The prince's words rang through me, sounding an alarm as memories of bloodletters and vampires indulging in the streets filled my mind. "What do you mean by blood? You said they'd be safe here."

"And they *will* be safe." The prince stared at me; eyebrows pinched together. "Did you not notice the humans walking the halls of Fellstone? The stone streets of my city? Those humans who arrived with you are not the only ones in Dergia."

I blinked. I had not noticed such a thing and couldn't

imagine it being true. Not after all that I'd seen of Winter's Realm. Nor in other kingdoms. "Are you being truthful?"

"I'm as fae as you are, Princess Neve. And dwarves despise deceit more than other races of fae."

"Where did the humans who live here come from?" Anna broke her silence.

"Noble houses who mistreated them," the queen spoke softly, sadly. "Some traveled all the way from the capital, searching for a way to get to another court, one where they might have a chance."

Thordur shook his head in commiseration for the weak. "The mountains are harsh enough to those of us accustomed to living here. The humans never would have survived on their own. We found many people and brought them here. Nearly all have stayed and become part of our society."

"Bleeding stars," I muttered, barely able to believe it. "Most fae look down on humans."

"Treat us worse than vermin!" Ronaldo hissed.

"We in Dergia are what remains of the dwarves from the five other kingdoms." King Tholin sighed. "Those of our kind who wished to remain under our own rule, in a home made for us. We did not want to be like others of our kind, traveling the mountains nomadically—nor did we want to serve royals we did not love—but there are few of us living beneath this mountain. Too few, and we require new blood to ensure we do not marry too closely."

My lips parted, understanding what he meant by blood. "Wait. So you *wed* the humans?"

"They enter our society as any dwarf would. Treated with fairness and given jobs that suit their builds and skills."

Ronaldo shifted. "You know that many who arrived with us are miners, right?"

"Lucky that," Thordur said. "Though there's always work for non-miners here too. Many humans who know nothing of the art of a pickaxe will bake or clean or do other tasks that are essential to a community, to earn their keep."

I was about to ask another question, but the king held up a hand. "My question has not yet been answered," the king said. "So I ask again, who are you, Princess Neve? A bastard of House Falk? And if so, do you know your exact relation to that long dead house?"

I cleared my throat. What I'd learned of the dwarves endeared me to them, but would their opinion of me change when I told the truth?

Did it matter? The king would not let his question slide, and I could no longer lie.

"Your wards didn't fail you," I admitted. "I am, by marriage, a part of House Aaberg. By blood, I was born into House Falk as Princess Isolde."

The king's eyes went wide. By such a reaction, I suspected he really had thought of me as a bastard-born Falk, which I'd recently learned was common enough. Prince Calder Falk and my own father had sired many bastards in their youth, before my father met and wed my mother. Though, of course, those same bastards might not know the truth of their fathers. And if they did, they would be smart not to flaunt that name while King Magnus sat the throne.

"Isolde Falk, daughter to King Harald and Queen Revna?" the queen whispered.

"The same."

"A daughter of Harald and Revna was a slave?" She set her cup of tea down with trembling hands. Considering Dergia was hidden, I doubted she'd known my parents. Likely, she was considering her own children living as I had done.

"My parents sought to send me to safety, but the Fates intervened. As they did again, two moons back when I escaped the Blood Court."

A pregnant pause followed in which the royals studied me with such intensity that my skin crawled. Finally, the king shook his head.

"I should have you killed. A trueborn Falk, in my kingdom, the very line we swore to protect and hide from. The same line that tried to make my ancestors bend the knee."

"Try and you'll meet your own death," Vale growled.

"The operative word is *should*," King Tholin retorted as forcefully, "I have no desire to harm you, Princess Neve. You have shown character, bringing humans here at great personal risk. You have given me the truth, a secret, if I'm not mistaken. And you have arrived when the Kingdom of Winter as a whole needs you most. I can read the signs, and bad blood between our families be damned. I am a dwarf of honor. Of ingenuity too."

I exhaled, and a knot in my chest released. Nothing in his holding said the king had been about to be violent, but watching him speak, seeing the sincerity in his eyes told me a lot. I felt, for the first time since being found by the dwarves, that we were really, truly safe.

The king held out his arm. "Might you stay for a day or two as guests to the Crown so that we may discuss matters?"

Could this turn into an alliance?

I stared at his arm. I wasn't willing to commit to a full-on alliance yet. How could I when I had not yet committed to my own name? All that aside, I wished to have a relationship. To become friends with fae who thought like me. Those who valued humans as much as the varied races of our kind.

So I grasped his arm tightly with my own hand. "Thank you for your hospitality, King Tholin. We would be delighted to stay."

CHAPTER 8

VALE

I paused before the desk in the room Neve and I had been given, and glanced down at a book, its pages open. I read a bit and chuckled. In the ten minutes I'd taken to clean the dwarven blood and grime from our travels off me, Neve had requested multiple histories of Dergia delivered. My wife never rested, just as she never ceased to amaze me.

An illustration featured on the opposite page, one that showed dwarves bearing the historical garb and colors of other mining kingdoms arriving in Dergia, pleading for a home. The king, likely one of the current king's ancestors, welcomed them with open arms. My finger ran along the old, dry page. There was so much I did not know.

I looked away from the image, into the fire that burned in the stone hearth dominating one wall of our quarters. Set into the dark stone, fiery gems gleamed, a dwarven touch if there ever was one.

There had been, for many turns, a hidden kingdom within my own. One that treated humans as equals.

The dwarves of Dergia had been here for centuries, hiding so that fae of their race might be as free as they wished. But did they love living beneath the Great Rock all the time?

I suspected no. Or at least, not always. If I had to guess, I'd say that King Tholin was hoping to use Neve's legitimate claim to Winter's Realm to bring his people out of the shadow of his mountain. To emerge into the wider Winter's Realm but continue ruling as a separate entity.

But first they're giving us a bleeding tour. I shook my head at all that had happened in the last hours.

"Ready?" My wife emerged from the bathing chamber adjoining our quarters looking fresh as newly fallen snow and smelling of her usual smokey vanilla. She wore borrowed black pants and a crisp white tunic while her other clothes were being washed.

I suspected the new clothing had to be from a human, for Neve was curvy and also not a short female. I wished I'd gotten a change of attire but had settled for handing off my dirtiest clothing to the servants and wearing the most presentable of my traveling clothes. Never had I met a human as large as I, and as for dwarves—well, just the idea of me attempting to shove myself into their clothing was laughable.

"We don't want to keep Prince Thordur waiting." She pulled on her sword belt. Not that we thought we'd need weapons, not as guests of the Crown, but like me, my wife believed it was better to be prepared.

"I'm ready." I slung on my belt bearing *Skelda* and went to her, circling my arms around her waist and pulling her close. "Thank the dead gods that you smell like yourself again."

Neve scoffed, but her eyes twinkled, telling me that she was not upset. "That's what happens when you travel for weeks!"

"Some of us bathed." I buried my face into her hair and inhaled, a smirk overtaking my lips at her gasp.

She whacked my shoulder. "I couldn't bring myself to bathe in the rivers. Not as often as you did, anyway."

"Some Winterborn princess you are." A laugh rumbled out of me as she muttered something that sounded a lot like '*I'll show you Winterborn*'. If only we had time to linger, to indulge in one another. That appealed far more than going on a tour. "You get used to streams when they are the only option."

"Well, I suppose I'll have more opportunities to practice when we leave." Neve drew back and gently placed her fingers on my chin and directed me where she wanted me. My lips on hers. The kiss proved decadent, but far too short for my liking.

"We *must go*," Neve said as a horn sounded outside, blaring the hours much in the same way the bells of Avaldenn told them. "That's the top of the hour. The prince is waiting."

A sigh parted my lips. "Fine, but after this, no more appointments. We deserve time together."

"We're having dinner with the royal family tonight."

"After that, then," I grumbled, knowing full well that there would be no getting out of it.

Dinners were a means of forging bonds, and it was clear as glass that the King of Dergia wished to get to know Neve better. I could not stand in the way of a potential alliance that could help keep my wife alive.

She smiled. "It's a deal."

A servant stood outside our chambers to show us where the prince would be waiting. I appreciated our hosts' foresight. As we'd only been in Fellstone Castle for a few hours, most of them spent in one room speaking with the king, his queen, and his heir, we did not know our way around.

Walking through the castle with Neve's hand tucked into mine, I could finally take in the fortress carved into the interior of the mountain. Sculptures and tapestries were plentiful here, much like at Frostveil and in the castles of the other great houses. Other art, however, was rare. I spied only a handful of paintings depicting the royal family.

"Vale," Neve whispered. I caught her eye, and from beneath her cloak she lifted a single finger, guiding me to look beyond our escort.

Down the corridor, two human women laughed at something a highly decorated dwarf soldier said. One woman carried a basket filled with linens while the other's dress indicated that she was of a higher class. She bent and the soldier kissed her.

The woman appeared to be highborn—or to have married into the highborn class. A human noble in the fae's land. That was something I'd never thought I'd see.

We continued through the corridors, spotting a few

other races of fae as well as more humans. Others met our curiosity with their own. While we'd passed a faerie or two, it was clear to all that we did not belong here.

The Prince of Dergia waited at the door that we'd entered the castle through. Caelo and Anna stood with him, both looking excited to see the city beneath the mountain.

We joined the trio, and bowed at Prince Thordur, who responded in kind, bowing to me and my wife. He'd changed since meeting us. He now wore armbands made of pure gold around his forearms. On the bands, runes were etched. I knew enough runes to recognize they marked him as part of the royal house.

"I hope you've been able to rest?" the dwarf asked as the doors to the castle opened for us.

"As much as one can, having learned such earth-shattering information," I admitted.

Prince Thordur nodded as if he expected nothing less. "Well, then, let us chip down your preconceived notions further, shall we?"

Green spanned as far as the eye could see. Vegetation crawled down the long cavern, up the walls, and hung from the ceiling.

I inhaled the fresh air, impressed by the sunshafts and mirrors bringing in natural light from high above. The sunlight combined with the efforts of earth and light fae allowed the dwarfs to grow crops deep within the earth. To hear Prince Thordur tell it, dwarves once mined this very cavern for minerals and gems. Once it ran dry, they reused the space to grow food. No space went wasted beneath the mountain.

"So your water fae bring water in from the mountain streams? And is there ever an issue with the food going bad before it can get to market?" Neve gestured to a rail line with many carts waiting on it. "Or do the mine carts transport food back into the city? That would be far easier than carrying the vegetation. Faster too. It's damp down here, so I expect timing is of the essence."

Throughout the tour, she'd exhibited a thirst for knowledge regarding Dergia that charmed Prince Thordur.

He smiled approvingly down at my wife, the light from a nearby sunshaft caught the gold dust in the prince's hair and sent it shimmering. Clearly, the kingdom was rich with the precious metal, if the royals, and a few of the other wealthy dwarves we'd met, could wear gold so flagrantly.

"Mostly, you have the right of it," the dwarf said, "As for the issue of keeping food fresh, there is none. The dead gods blessed my people with strong earth magic and that helps preserve food."

"I'd always thought that dwarven earth magic was of the metal variety," Caelo admitted as he ran a hand over a bunch of green onions. "But this proves otherwise. This cavern alone is as large as one of the major greenhouses that feeds large numbers in Avaldenn."

"Many of my kind do work with metal," the prince agreed, "but plant magic isn't rare. Thank the dead gods."

"Speaking of metals," I spoke up. "I'd appreciate a view of your forges. I assume they're a wonder."

In Avaldenn, dwarves ran the best forges and my own favored smith, Master Urgi, was a dwarf at Frostveil. He was also my close friend Duran's father.

"Was wondering when you'd ask, Prince Vale." Thordur turned and waved a hand for us to follow. "The forges are in the city."

Prince Thordur led us back the way we'd come, through a tunnel that exited on the outskirts of the larger city. During our hours of walking and taking in the sights, we'd learned that most of the population lived at the foot of the castle, within the massive cavern carved out by the dwarves over centuries. Though some smaller communities took up residence in smaller caverns that spiraled off the main one. Their religious fae, scholars, and healers were all examples of communities who had sought smaller caverns for their homes and to focus on work.

"This is all so interesting," Neve said as Caelo and Anna fell into conversation with the prince. "I find the ways in which they tweaked the common infrastructures quite ingenious."

"If you live beneath great mounds of rock, you find a way to survive." I looked up, taking in the magical sky, courtesy of light fae working illusions.

The magic told me the sun outside was setting. The day was ending.

Neve came closer, snuggling into me. For the first time in weeks, we were without our long fur cloaks. I wrapped my arm around her waist, pulling her softness closer.

"Hmmm, that's nice." She nuzzled my shoulder. "I have to admit, while this tour has been fun, I've been a touch distracted—thinking about how comfortable that bed looked."

"After days of sleeping in snow, a bed will be beyond our dreams."

"I don't intend to dream too much tonight," her tone dipped. My wife was coming on to me. "I hoped for quality time."

I smirked, all too happy that she was thinking about us together, even if a small, annoyingly honorable voice inside me still whispered I did not deserve her. That by having married her and allowing this relationship to progress, I did Neve a disservice.

Her best chance at gaining support among the other great houses was marriage. When my parentage came out, as I intended it to, I'd be a bastard of House Riis. The House of the Ice Spider had much wealth but a very small army, and she'd need swords more than gold if she were to stand up to King Magnus.

I will give her my sword. My life. And free her from this marriage, if it will keep her safe. Thinking such a thing sent my heart racing with denial. I hated the idea but would do whatever was best for her.

"I need to work on my seduction. What stole your thoughts?" Neve tugged on my arm.

"Nothing as important as you." I stopped following the others and dipping my head, I took her lips in mine.

Neve twisted so that her front faced me and wound her hands through my hair, her lips and tongue dancing with mine. My blood heated. I'd kissed my fair share of females. Bedded many too. But this one seemed as though she was made for me, and me for her. Though I hadn't told her as much, inside something I couldn't describe pulled us closer —a sort of magnetism that lived in my chest and deepened by the day.

Bleeding skies, it would be so difficult to let her go.

"*Ahem!*" Anna shouted. "We thought we'd lost you two, but apparently you slowed on purpose to get it on!"

Neve laughed and broke away.

"We're here already," Anna said from where she leaned around a corner, eyebrows arched and a smirk on her face "So come see. The sooner you do, the sooner you two can *be alone.*"

I straightened. "Close to the forges? But I smell no fire, no metal."

Anna smirked. "Must be the vents. Prince Thordur was telling us about it, but you were too deep down each other's throats to hear."

"That's enough!" Neve said, though there was no anger in her tone. "We're coming."

Anna disappeared, and as much as I wanted to continue what we'd been doing, Neve took my hand and pulled me along.

Something I'd been so interested in before dulled in comparison to getting to explore her, but I followed around the corner. I sucked in a breath. These forges were the largest I'd ever seen.

"There are enchantments around the entire Circle of Steel," Thordur explained as we caught up with the others. "You cannot hear the work, just like you can't scent it, unless you are in a specific smithy's business."

The Prince of Dergia led us deep into a large market with so many forges that it resembled a maze.

"*Zuprian* steel daggers!" one apprentice yelled from the door of one of the more run-down forges. He saw me watching and winked. "Half-off, today only!"

My eyes widened, but Prince Thordur wrinkled his bulbous nose, a common feature of his fae race. "Not there. All our smiths are excellent, but you can do far better than that one. I'll take you to the best and if you wish to buy *zuprian* steel, you'll have your pick."

I shared an excited look with Caelo, drawing chuckles from Anna and Neve. Laugh they might, but my best friend and I understood the value of *zuprian* steel and how difficult it was to work. Dwarves were always the best with the material, and having a blade or other implement from the best of the dwarves would be a prize.

The market kept my attention with so many swords and weapons on display. Any soldier worth his salt would love to possess a good many of them. Would that I had the coin to buy them all, but I possessed very little on my person. I'd have to make do with merely holding and admiring such fine craftsmanship.

"Many here seem to work *zuprian* steel and make weapons." I gestured around as we made our way through the workers, metal hissing and sputtering and hammers banging all around. "Your entire army must be outfitted in the best steel."

Thordur tossed a smirk over his shoulder. "We are. And the excess, we sell."

"To who?"

"To other kingdoms. *To yours.*"

I scoffed. "Our metals and gems come from a crown-owned mine."

"Not all." The dwarf prince looked smug. "My kingdom supplies much of the *zuprian* steel in your kingdom. We have our ways to transport and sell without being discovered."

"How?" I demanded.

"Nearby villages and towns are safe to trade with. As we prosper, their lives become easier. They know as well as any how hard mountain life can be, and they also have connections to larger cities where they can trade without issue. And then there are the dwarven nomads. They know about us, and trade when they need to."

"Why wouldn't the nomads live *here*?" my wife asked. "I understand not wanting to be under King Magnus's thumb, but I imagine moving all the time is a hard life. This seems like an ideal in between."

"It is. Yet some prefer to feel more than rock beneath their feet and live to see a true sky above whenever they wish. Who are we to dictate how they wish to live?"

I had no answer for that.

"And here we are. Master Smith Kolmot is the finest smithy in all of Dergia. Dare I say, in all the Land of Winter." Prince Thordur held open a metal door to a forge, and my eyes feasted on the swooping and lovely lines of gold in the metal as we passed through. An artist and a smith both.

"A hearty claim." I arched a single eyebrow.

"We don't call him The Hammer for naught."

The interior of the forge was as magnificent as the door.

Various metals created works of art, and weapons hung from the wall, beautiful and functional. Inside the door, I could hear the pounding of metal, the hiss of water as metal plunged into buckets, and the chatter of workers. The smithy had to have at least ten people working for him.

A young female dwarf entered the foyer. She wore a dress and had not a speck of dirt or grime on her.

"Prince! We weren't expecting you today. Shall I get you tea so that you might browse the wears?"

"No thank you, Yaggarra. I'm here to show my friends the forge and speak with Master Kolmot on an order, if he has the time?"

"Of course, Prince Thordur. I'll retrieve him."

"So this visit was a touch self-serving," I asked once the dwarf left to get her master.

Thordur shrugged. "Good time management."

I smirked. I'd have claimed the same.

The Master Smith appeared minutes later, wiping his scarred, wrinkled hands on a cloth. The dwarf was rather old and smaller than many we'd passed by except in his arms, which likely rivaled mine in muscle.

He approached Prince Thordur, a smile on his lips, but when he noticed Neve, the smith stopped walking.

"I'm afraid we haven't met, miss?"

"I'm a guest of House Fellhelm."

"An outsider."

She shifted, a touch unnerved. "Yes."

"One who comes bearing a blade imbued with shadows."

I drew in a sharp breath.

"Pardon?" Lines appeared on Neve's forehead as she arched her eyebrows.

Neve's blade came from King Harald's long-hidden rooms. Hence it followed to reason that it was a royal sword. One could assume that meant it was valuable, even famous, but I hadn't been able to name it.

"Your blade, miss, it has touched the shadows," Master Kolmot said, "meaning it is old, since the time of the Unification, if not older." He held out a hand. "May I?"

"Um, sure." Neve unsheathed her blade and handed it to the smith, who hadn't bothered to learn her name, so great was his interest in the sword.

"*Zuprian* steel, made the old way," the ancient dwarf murmured, "and yes, shadows." He peered at the hilt, squinting as he did so before he brought the blade to his ear, listening to the metal. His eyes widened, and he looked up at Neve. "Sassa's Blade."

"What happened?!" she asked, her tone frantic, but seeing his expression was not one of awe or ire but rather, recognition, understanding dawned on me.

"He means," I placed a soft hand on my wife's shoulder, "that your blade is Queen Sassa's sword. You carry the sword of the queen who unified the realm. It's a powerful symbol."

Legendary was more like it. Sassa and her blade had banished the Shadow King and Queen and, it seemed, in doing so, might have taken on the magic of the Shadow Fae that this dwarf recognized.

Master Kolmot nodded. "And a powerful blade, strong in legacy and magic, I think. Perhaps it can call shadows? I do not know, though I sense the darkness of that magic— something my own teachers taught me about. However, I have no knowledge of how to test it, I'm sorry to say. Only theoretical learning." The Master Smith passed back the sword. "Use it carefully."

Neve took it, her hand shaking when she replied. "I'll keep that in mind."

CHAPTER 9
NEVE

The first thing I noticed upon arriving to sup with the entire royal family of House Fellhelm was how at ease they were with one another.

Six siblings, three of them triplets, and no one appeared to despise the other. Or compete. Or egg the others on—not meanly anyhow. The family smiled and teased and laughed. To me, they looked ideal, like something to envy, and stars, did I.

And the Fellhelms' aren't done growing a family. I glanced at the queen's round belly.

Queen Deseana caught me, and her stubby-fingered hand rubbed at the bump. "I believe it might be twins."

Twins in addition to her brood of six. I'd grown up with humans, with their predictable cycles that came every moon. But fae differed greatly from humans. Most fae had trouble building large families, largely due to highly irregular female cycles and turns in which both the males and females were simply more fertile than others. Thordur aside, who I'd learned was nearing his sixtieth nameday, most of the Fellhelm children were all in their twenties.

"May the stars bless your growing family," I said as a human woman dressed in Fellhelm slate gray and gold swept in to fill the wine goblets carved from a beautiful stone and crafted to look more like inverted mountains. Tapered candles lined the tables, providing supplemental light to the torches on the walls. No faelights here, just simple, classic ambiance.

Vale sat across from me at the fourteen-person table. King Tholin reigned at the head, Queen Deseana to his right, next to Vale. Heir Prince Thordur sat to my right and the second in the royal line, Princess Bavirra, perched to my left.

The other four Fellhelm children took spots around Caelo and Anna and were involved in a lively discussion with the pair. Elsewhere, a faint din of kitchen noises could be heard, making my stomach rumble. We'd started the day rising early and walking through the mountains with a group of humans to protect and were ending it at a table full of royals. I was exhausted and so looking forward to a proper meal.

I picked up my goblet, examined the hammer etched into the stone. I ran my finger over it, lingering on the rune in the center. The same hammer had been on the doors leading into Dergia. The Doors of Eitriod, Vale had called them. "Is this your house symbol?"

"Indeed," Prince Thordur said. "It's said that the hammer used by the dead god Eitriod looked the very same."

"I see." I reached into the far recesses of my mind, flailing for something to contribute, but, as ever, when I thought of the dead gods, no specifics came. During my turns as a slave, I'd been taught nothing about the gods. We'd been told to worship the stars, and that was enough. Now though, I was no slave. I needed to better learn the customs of my people.

"I know little of that god, but seeing as he uses a hammer, I'm guessing he's for the smiths?"

Princess Bavirra, who I'd met only briefly when she'd been helping the humans by getting them food and seeing that they were comfortable, leaned over. Her long night-dark hair fell over her shoulder and her skin, as inky as Sir Caelo's, gleamed in the many lights of the candles. She had certainly inherited the queen's beauty. "Eitriod is the patron god of smiths. He deals with metal, earth, and fire. And of course, he is a dwarf, which is why our kind loves him so."

"I could have told her as much," Thordur murmured, though there was no real ire in his tone.

"But as always, I am quicker!" The princess gave a mischievous grin. "Plus, you monopolized much of their time today. Don't frown at me for wishing to get a word in edgewise."

"*Edgewise?*" The heir scoffed. "Eitriod knows that once you start, no one else will ever speak to Prince Vale or Princess Neve again."

I felt Vale's stare and glanced across the table. A look of amusement was on his face. I wondered if he was thinking of Saga, and how he and his sister often ribbed one another. I certainly was.

"Do you have a book on Eitriod?" I asked the siblings. "I'd love to learn more about your favorite god."

"I do!" the princess said. "I'll send it to your rooms!"

"Thank you so much." I inclined my head, as the king called the table's attention with a raise of his heavy goblet made of a fiery red stone.

"Beloved wife, family, and esteemed guests, thank you for gathering together for this meal." The king looked at me. "I hear you saw much of my city today, and a small part of the kingdom beyond, so I'll open the meal by toasting to Dergia."

We echoed his toast and had barely set our goblets down when the servants swept in with the first course. Other than the bread, cheese, and hot, nourishing broth given to the humans when we'd arrived, I had not known what to expect when it came to food in a city under a mountain, but the soup set before me smelled like onion and potato. My mouth salivated as I peered down at the food, noting the bowl appeared to be made of an orangish-red crystal. The dwarven presentation for most things was hard and cold, made of stone and metal and precious gems, but all of it was beautiful too.

"Please, eat," the queen said when my friends and I hesitated to pick up our spoons. "Don't let it grow stone cold."

We did as Queen Deseana commanded, and I was not at all disappointed by the soup. Rather, I felt that I'd died and gone to the afterworld. It was so good.

"My compliments to your cooks," I said when I'd finished the bowl.

"Our head cook was once a slave to House Triam. She

escaped, and we've been treasuring the benefits ever since," the king said.

"I believe she likes it here too," the queen added. "She's about to have her second youngling with her husband—an apprentice smithy."

"Speaking of smiths," the king set down his spoon, "what did you think of our Circle of Steel?"

"I found it all impressive," I said.

"Quite," Vale agreed. "The innovation to soundproof and ventilation so deep within the mountain is ingenious. Add in the actual smith work and no one can deny dwarves are the best of the craft."

King Tholin beamed, as did the heir, who lifted an offering palm to Vale. "We will need to get you a *zuprian* steel dagger before you depart, Prince Vale."

"Have you none?" the princess asked.

"My sword is *zuprian* steel. As is my friend, Caelo's." Vale gestured down the table to where Caelo and Anna were engrossed in a different conversation with the triplets and the thirdborn Fellhelm, Prince Balindur. From the looks of it, Anna had told a joke that had sent the triplets into hysterics. "But no dagger. In truth, I'd like one for each of us, but I'm afraid those purchases may have to wait."

"Why wait when you are here now?" the princess asked.

"When we'd first set out for Guldtown and then the mines where we found the humans, we'd not prepared for such a long trip." Vale shrugged. "I carried gold, but I'm nearly out. There's not enough for one *zuprian* dagger, not even at half price, let alone four."

The prince laughed. "I told you, you don't want those half-off daggers that Smith Otrig sells."

"Especially when we have plenty we can give you," the queen added.

"We can't accept such generosity," I said. "You've already given so much—a home for those we arrived with, food and safety for a night or two. Most of all, a budding friendship."

"Of course you can accept our gift." Queen Deseana motioned for her water to be refilled. "We have many such daggers, and love supporting our smiths. It would be our honor for you to leave with daggers from our kingdom."

"Helping is what allies do, is it not?" The king pushed his soup bowl to the side, where a servant swiftly whisked it away.

I swallowed, unsure how to proceed, and looked at my husband. He stared back at me and gave the slightest of nods.

He would not answer for me. That both boosted my confidence and sank my stomach.

With every passing day, it became more apparent I had but one path: To claim my name and *everything* that went with it. Fighting Magnus. Potentially starting a full-blown war in Winter's Realm.

In some ways, such as what I was doing now, treating with the King of Dwarves at his table, I'd already begun trying to take down King Magnus. In others, I held back.

I did not flaunt the name Isolde Falk. Nor did I hunger for absolute power.

Did I wish for revenge against King Magnus for killing

my family? More than anything. I considered the matter often.

Before, I wanted him to simply die, but the more I considered it, the more I'd rather see the king stripped of what he held dear. Imprisoned in a cell like he'd done to Prince Calder. Maybe magically bound if I could do so. However, to me, dethroning King Magnus was not the only hurdle I'd have to leap.

There were invisible strings holding me back, and only today, as we walked around Dergia, had I worked out a couple of those strings.

One being the bloodshed that would surely ensue. Once I came out as my true self, blood would spill. Magnus would hunt me, along with the vampires who already did so. He might hurt anyone I was with.

The second thread related to the rebels. The rebellion had claimed that they followed the true heir. Who was that? A Falk bastard? Someone pretending to be so? I didn't know, but their potential presence made me both curious and hesitant.

And yet, I was here, with a king trying to ally with me. Of course, he did so because he wished for something too. That was how alliances went. They were a give and a take.

"You're right, King Tholin," I answered finally, careful with my words. "We'd be happy to leave here with four fine *zuprian* daggers from Dergia."

"Everyone who sees them will ask about their maker," Vale added.

"The mystery you withhold will infuriate them," the king chuckled.

"That it will." I set my spoon down, and my bowl was swept away.

"Prince Vale, you'll have to give specifications for the blades," Prince Thordur said, and the pair leapt into a conversation about sizes and hilts and whatnot.

Vale began speaking of weapons, but I was more entranced by how his face lit up. Every gleam in his eye and grin as he, the king, the queen, and the heir of Dergia spoke of daggers and steel. My heart stuttered when his dark gaze turned upon me and he winked.

My cheeks grew warm, and my chest tightened. I looked down as my plate bearing some type of roasted bird and root vegetable landed on the table.

"You two are quite a handsome couple," Princess Bavirra leaned closer, and the candlelight made the gold dust on her cheekbones glitter beautifully. I made a note to ask for a tin of the dust before we left. "I'm envious."

"Thank you," I said, pleased to have someone to focus on other than my husband, who apparently turned me into a maiden at the least expected times. "Are you courting at all?"

"Father wishes it, but Mother says to take my time, and I'm not ready to seriously court. I'm only twenty-nine turns, after all. I'd like adventure before I worry about love."

The human blood slaves I'd grown up with would have thought otherwise, but their lives were short and fraught with fear. When you had centuries to live, why rush into any relationship, let alone marriage?

That was unless you were about to lose your head for killing a vampire prince—like me.

Down the table, the triplets set to laughing again. This time, Anna did too. I looked past the princess and found Caelo beaming. He looked too proud of himself, and I was dying to hear the joke, but the princess spoke again.

"What was it like, traveling here? Especially with so many humans in your care? Did you run into trouble?"

It struck me that the princess didn't just want adventure under the mountain, or in the small territory surrounding their mountain kingdom. She wanted *out*. Wanted to see the wider Winter's Realm.

I leapt into the story of the nøkken, glazing over why Vale and I had walked away from the camp, though by the gleam in her eyes, she understood all too well.

When I finished, she looked saddened. "I'm so sorry for your losses."

"I am too. I failed them."

"You didn't," she said, "so many of them are here, in a kingdom unlike any other fae kingdom. They're safe now."

I smiled softly before taking a bite of the roasted bird and chewing. The events of the day and so much socializing was wearing on me.

The princess ate too, before leaning close once again. "Also, not to be too nosey, but I got the feeling in your story that you and your prince have had little alone time?"

"How astute of you."

She grinned, and I felt as though I was back in Avaldenn with Saga before she pulled me into a clandestine game of nuchi with other ladies of the realm. A sharp pang cut through me, unexpectedly, though it shouldn't have been. I missed the princess and Sayyida—Marit and the Balik sisters too. They were the first people in Avaldenn to show me friendship. In the case of Saga and Sayyida, they'd even accepted my past. Or what I'd known of it then. Now I knew so much more, though I expected their reactions to finding out I was a lost princess would be similar to when they discovered I'd been a blood slave.

"Well, I have a place you two might want to go." The raven-haired princess curled a finger as her voice dropped into a whisper. "It will offer you privacy and a beautiful view, but you can't tell anyone else about it. Promise?"

I shot a glance across the table at Vale, still engrossed in talks with the king and Prince Thordur. A grin spread across my face as I turned back to the princess. "Promise."

CHAPTER 10
NEVE

"We have a perfectly suitable room in which to be alone together," Vale muttered, his eyes closed at my request as I guided him.

He wouldn't be so grumpy if he knew what I intended. After all, we'd been wishing for alone time for weeks, and yes, our quarters at the castle would have done well enough.

But for our first time together, I did not want *well enough*. I wanted *magic*. The sweet Princess Bavirra had shared with me a place she claimed held just that.

"You'll come with me, and you'll like it," I told Vale in a faux stern tone, and as I'd hoped, his lips twitched into a smile.

The prince might be one of the most revered warriors in the kingdom, but I'd learned that he didn't mind a female in charge. In more ways than one.

I spied the door the princess had detailed in hushed

whispers at the dinner table. A grin spread across my face. "A few more minutes and we'll be there."

"Fine," he breathed.

Beneath the cloak I wore, a silver silk dress with two slits riding up to my hip bones slithered across my skin. The dress was one I'd never have purchased for myself, but Princess Bavirra had thought I'd needed something special for tonight. At dinner, she'd covertly sent a servant out for a dress that would bring a prince, a battle-blooded warrior, to his knees.

I'd dressed in our private bathroom, with the door shut, so he would not get a sneak peek. And while the dress wasn't exactly to my tastes, after wearing regular clothing for weeks, I delighted in the feel of luxury. In the softness. The delicacy and beauty. I couldn't wait for Vale to lay eyes on the dress. I wanted him to rip it off my body.

I dragged him down the final hall and opened the door to be met with the garden surrounding the castle. Despite being inside a mountain, the dwarves seemed to love flowers and trees as much as they did metal and gemsmithing. The royal garden overflowed, and in the center of the greenery, I spied the vibrant purple leaves of a Drassil tree.

As it was night, the sunshafts and mirrors positioned above brought no light down on the holy tree. Still, in the darkness and the stillness, it was magical. Beautiful, despite the thinning of the leaves and the slight droop to those that remained.

My heart clenched as I remembered that many of the Drassils were suffering, just as the people did. Perhaps Vale or I could offer to infuse magic into this one before we left. Help it as the dwarves had helped us.

Vale sniffed. "Are we outside?"

"As much as one can be beneath a mountain," I replied.

"The plot thickens."

"You never know what you'll get with me."

He barked a laugh as we entered the garden. "Isn't that the truth?"

Once I'd been a 'commoner' to Vale. A female he'd married for honor. Then I'd learned I was much more, and my hopes and dreams for my future shifted. To include him. He was the moon and the stars and all that I ever could have dreamed of. All that I wanted.

Tonight, I planned to tell him as much. I hoped that this night would assuage all his doubts. That we could make our marriage last a lifetime. I wanted him for that long.

Will he still think of his fated? The thought filtered through my mind, and not for the first time.

Despite the occasions when we'd been intimate, no soul-mate mark had appeared on our bodies. Would it appear tonight? Sometimes to be sure, fae needed to join in the most intimate of acts, the one that could result in creation, for the mark to appear.

"There are stairs. Follow me and go slow," I said as we reached the spot Princess Bavirra had detailed.

Pushing aside vines and bushes, Vale and I climbed the stairs—about two hundred steps, cleverly hidden from the view below. I hoped Bavirra was correct in thinking that only she and her past lovers knew of this place. To be interrupted in my plans would be frustrating.

"We're here," I said when we reached the top. I edged him into a small crevice on the mountain's side. Vines draped the side of the wall. The princess had made certain no one would find her hideaway unless she allowed it. "Won't be long now."

"Nearly tripped three bleeding times going up those stairs."

I rolled my eyes. Like most of the dwarven masonry I'd seen, the stairway had been expertly carved and smoothed. "Stop being dramatic. I had you, and you know it. I'll always have you."

Again, his lips formed a small smile. Try as he might to act grumpy about being dragged from our chambers, I knew that secretly he was intrigued by the outing I'd planned.

"Through a curtain of vines." I pulled the vines aside and led him into a tunnel. The ceiling was tall enough to allow Vale passage without ducking, and the stone floor had been worn smooth.

"Is that water?" Vale asked.

"It is. I'll let you know if we come across a fall to avoid."

Vale feared little, but he'd told me once that as a youngling, he'd nearly drowned. To this day, he despised going underwater, but Princess Bavirra had assured me there was no need to do so in her sanctuary. Not unless one wanted to.

The tunnel proved uneventful, though, and when we reached the first opening, I stifled a gasp. According to the princess, there were three chambers off the main passageway, but the first one was her favorite. In one glimpse, I understood why.

A cavern opened through the rock opening, every single wall glinting with assorted gemstones made of pure fire. Thanks to Princess Bavirra enjoying this pool often, faelights hung in the air like burning coals. Their illumination refracted the light off the stones, bathing the entire cavern in oranges, reds, and yellows.

"Have we reached your destination?" Vale asked when I'd been silent for too long.

At the bottom of the cavern, a pool large enough for six to bathe in welcomed us. A serene waterfall fed the crystalline bright blue pool, and in the water's depths, those same gemstones glinted. I could not wait to jump in.

"Open your eyes."

My husband did so, and my wonder reflected in his expression, the light within the rock gleaming in his beautiful eyes as he took in the cavern.

"How did you learn of this place?"

"Princess Bavirra told me about it! Isn't it *astounding*? She claims there are private pools like this in many places beneath the mountain, but this one is her favorite."

"She shared it with you because . . ."

"I think she'd like to be a true friend. Let's get a closer look."

I led the way down the steps, and Vale's heavier footsteps followed. When I reached the bottom, I spun, looking up again, taking it all in. Isila was a world of enchantment, and though I'd grown up wearing a collar and tied to a tiny radius in Sangrael, I'd seen more of this world now. Much of it was lovely, breathtaking, and defied imagination. Few places, though, had stolen my breath so thoroughly as this cavern.

I turned to the prince, the fae I'd fallen in love with, though I had yet to say as much. His dark eyes met mine and I couldn't fathom why no one saw Lord Leyv Riis in him. Red hair aside, Vale's eyes, his muscular frame and size —and most of all, his kindness, seemed to have been inherited from his father. Maybe from Queen Inga too, though my impressions of the queen were few and not all positive. In my eyes, the queen's saving grace was that two of her children were some of the best people I'd ever known.

"So, you lured me here, wife. What will you do with me now?" Vale asked.

In answer, my fingers went to the tie of my cloak. I loosened the knot and allowed the cloak to drift from my shoulders, down, down, down. It pooled on the floor, revealing the silver dress that left little to the imagination. Already, my nipples puckered against the silk, aching for Vale to take them in his mouth.

"Fates, Neve, you nearly stopped my heart." He took a step closer, his expression ravenous.

Before he touched me, though, my wings spread, and I took off. I flew until I was above the crystalline water and spun, a laugh spilling from my lips as Vale let out a long groan.

"Why do you tease me so?"

I faced him. "It does my heart good."

He scoffed, which made me chuckle.

"I'll ask the same of you, husband! Why haven't you disrobed and joined me yet? The pool is inviting, is it not?"

"Not as inviting as the stretch of your legs." Vale shucked off his cloak and then did one better, pulling down his britches. His long tunic remained covering his malehood. Soon enough, I'd rectify that.

The prince leapt into the air, dark wings beating as he joined me, suspended in midair above the water. Before I teased him more, Vale snatched me and pulled me close.

"Got you," he growled, his hands pinning down my wings.

"Am I your prey?" I relished the thought despite my past of being prey to every vampire in sight. If I had to be someone's quarry, I'd be his. And I'd enjoy it.

"Prey? No, you have done what the strongest of warriors could not. You've felled me so thoroughly I don't think I'll ever rise the same again." He drank me in, and in his eyes I saw an entire universe. Our universe, one we would make together. "You're my wife. My queen. And the love of my life."

"Vale." I swallowed the lump in my throat. "I love you too."

"Thank the dead gods," he murmured as his lips found mine.

In all the kisses I'd received and given, none have ever affected me like this. None were so simmering. So desirous and controlling. Not like, if he stopped, the entire world might shatter.

His hands, wrapped around me, drifted up and teased

along the tops of my wings. The membrane tingled, lighting me up inside. I arched into Vale, wanting more of him.

Stars, I wanted all of him. I wanted it now.

My plan came rushing back, and unable to help myself, I smiled against his lips.

"Hmm?" Vale asked, drifting to kiss me along my jaw. "What are you thinking about, little beast?"

In answer, I pulled back enough to release my wings from his grasp. "Come find out."

I dropped into the pool, the warmth of it surprising me, and when I bobbed back up and found Vale, still in the air, his eyes wide and stunned, I laughed.

"The water is warm, and it's shallow enough that I touched the bottom when I got in."

Assured, Vale fluttered down and joined me in the pool and gripped my waist. The male had gotten a taste of me and was not at all sated. Nor was I, for that matter.

I wrapped my legs around his middle and sighed at his hardness as it pressed against my core. I'd tasted Vale before, touched him just as he'd touched me in the most intimate of places, but we'd always stopped short of sex. Laughable in a way, seeing as we were married, and attracted to one another, but now I was glad we hadn't given in to lust. Glad that we'd waited for love to come.

I kissed him again, and he reciprocated, leaving tendrils of flames on my lips as his length pressed into me, forming a delicious ache between my thighs.

He groaned. "I want you, Neve."

"Then have me."

Vale floated us to the edge of the pool. Excitement fluttered in my core at the thought of him pressing me against the rock and taking me, so when he gripped my waist tighter and instead lifted me up and out of the pool, my eyebrows knitted together. "What are you doin—"

My words died on my lips as he pulled up the sodden silk of my dress, exposing me before removing his tunic and giving me a glorious display of his muscled chest and the many intricate tattoos swirling on his skin. The two bear claws on his chest seemed to soak up the brilliant light in the cavern, making them look freshly inked. Vale tossed the tunic to the ground carelessly as his gaze trailed from my face to my thighs, spread on the rock. He licked his lips.

Never had I been one to have anxiety over my body, not even when I lived at the Vampire Court where thin females were prized, and I did not fit that mold. Not even with the meager rations they gave me. But this . . . the way he looked at me made me both excited and anxious in a way that I could not describe. I felt too much, too *seen*.

"I've never seen something more beautiful," Vale stated as though it were a fact moments before his face was buried between my thick thighs.

Air sucked through my teeth, and my channel pulsed as the Warrior Bear licked, sucked, and kissed my core. I'd known he was skilled in the arts of the bedroom but blazing stars, I learned something more about Vale daily. This skill of his was one I would, as his loving wife, request regularly.

My back arched as his tongue dipped inside me. A low rumble left Vale's lips.

"You taste amazing." He nipped at the apex of my folds and the tension within me ratcheted up higher and higher, threatening to spin to the stars as Vale's adept tongue parted my folds, and his fingers played with my clit.

His free hand ran up my thigh, pulled at my back, and allowed him to bury his face harder against my wet flesh. I stared down at Vale, lips parted, unable to speak as heat and electricity built inside me. This beautiful male with his long dark hair splayed into the water behind him, brown eyes burning with desire and a tongue that had to be gifted from the god of love was mine. All mine. No matter what he said, I was never letting him go.

"Come for me, love." Vale did not look up, though I had no doubt he felt my eyes on him. "Come on my tongue. Give me your nectar."

And as though his words were a spell, that sweet tension that made my toes curl and my every nerve ending alight released. I moaned, my head tipping back to take in the gems shimmering and winking like stars.

"That's good, my fierce *queen*."

"Bleeding moon," I hissed as another wave of pleasure rolled through me before I went limp.

Vale expected my weakness though, for he'd already pushed himself up, out of the pool. Knees straddling my legs, he caught me and kissed me.

I blinked, still rocked by the bliss rolling through me. With ease I could not fathom, he scooted me back so that no part of either of us was in the water and lowered me to the ground.

"I want you all, Neve."

"It's time," I whispered.

If the dead gods themselves appeared in the cavern with

us, they couldn't stop me from wanting him deep inside me at this moment. I ran a hand over him, savoring his deep breathing, his heartbeat, and how it sped up for me.

Vale lowered above me, one hand planting aside my shoulder as the other gripped his cock, standing tall and gleaming with pre-cum.

"I've been waiting for this moment," he admitted as he stared into my eyes. "But I have to ask. You're sure? You're my queen, and I'll not go a step further unless you say so."

"Your queen and your wife and I *love you* Vale, so please don't make me wait longer." I reached down and guided him to my entrance. "*Please.*"

He pushed in, and I gasped at his size even as my body accommodated him. When he was inside me to the hilt, I rocked my hips, and a long moan ripped from Vale's lips.

"You'll be the end of me, little beast."

"*Promise?*"

He grinned. "Promise."

With one hand, he tilted my hips upward, deepening his angle, and together we began to move. Maybe it should have surprised me that it took no time at all for us to find a sublime rhythm, but it did not. So much about Vale and I had been easy. When I was supposed to hate him, I'd found an ease, a comfort, in his presence that I had not been able to explain.

And as our bodies moved together, another wave of delicious tension and heat and electricity rose inside me, I knew it wasn't ever supposed to be hard. Now, a thread was tightening between us, pulling at my heart and strengthening our bond. Winding us together.

"Fates, Neve. I'm close." Vale exhaled and kissed along my jawline. "You are too?"

He felt my channel tightening as well as I.

"Yes." I was shocked at how breathy I sounded; how much I shivered with delight all over. Almost as though he were inside me fully. Like we were merging as one.

Vale tilted his head to the cavern ceiling and swallowed. He was seconds away. I was too, and I wanted us to come together. I rolled my hips, and he let out a long moan as he spilled into me at the same time as I came with the force of a winter storm.

My orgasm, however, seemed mild compared to the snapping of something in my chest. I let out a sharp yelp, and my eyes squeezed shut as Vale did the same.

The pain—which was also somehow pleasurable—was short-lived, however, and the bliss of orgasm took over again, a breeze on a hot day. Something novel and lovely.

When it ended, Vale stilled, lowered, though he was careful not to give his entire weight over to me. He kissed me passionately, and I kissed him back, the floaty sensation washing through me, making me sedate and tired.

He pulled away, and I opened my eyes to find Vale staring down at me, smiling.

"Stars, you're beautiful," he murmured and brought his hand to my face and brushed aside a stray lock of hair.

I stiffened. "Vale? What's on your hand?"

"What?" Instead of looking, he pulled out of me, probably still caught in the haze of our lovemaking.

"Your hand. There's a mark."

He had tattoos on his chest and arms, but what I'd spied looked different. White and glowing and—

He raised his hand, and his eyes widened before snapping to me. "Show me yours."

Body trembling, I lifted my hands, and my heart nearly exploded when a matching mark stared back at me. Intricate snowflakes, trailing down the fourth finger of our left hands. Deep inside, a tug alerted me to the fact that the strange sensation I'd felt during sex was still there. Pulsing and hot and strong as steel.

A bond had snapped into place. A symbol had marked us. Upon our bodies, our hearts, our souls.

"Soulmates," he murmured, before gathering me to his chest. He sounded as though he barely dared to believe that what he was seeing was true.

"Soulmates!" I kissed him with a passion so hot none of the forges in the city matched it. "All along! *Soulmates!*"

Vale picked me up to soar above the water. We spun in the air, hearts leaping as we laughed.

Dizziness began to set in when Vale descended into the water. He released me so that my legs were free and took a pace back, eyes burning into me.

"You're not getting away from me." I swam closer and wrapped my legs around him again.

"Never would I try, my love. We're it for each other."

"Until death." I whispered.

"Until the stars fall from the night sky." He took my chin in his fingers and kissed me again.

INTERLUDE

LADY MARIT ARMENIL, HOUSE OF THE DIREWOLF

A sleigh awaited her, the outline of the conveyance blurry through the tears pooling in her eyes. And still, she proceeded, step by step, for this was what she'd been raised to do. To further the family line, to bring glory to the great house of the far north, and to make her ancestors proud.

"Marit, wait."

She turned to find Princess Saga rushing from the doors of Frostveil Castle, pink hair streaming behind her, grief lining her face.

Like Marit was dying and not just going to her new home.

"I'll miss you so much." Princess Saga enveloped Marit in a tight hug and only when they were that close did the seer princess whisper in her friend's ear. "I'll make Mother call you back to court so you don't have to stay in Liekos. With *him*. I'm sorry that my father—"

"You could do nothing." Marit clung to her friend as her

family and other friends who she'd already said goodbye to cried behind the princess. The wind coming in off the Shivering Sea stung her pale cheeks, likely making them as red as Marit's hair.

"Maybe the rumors aren't true," the princess said softly, but not weakly.

"I don't know about that, but I can say that Jarl Triam is insistent. Forceful."

She had already assumed that quality in the jarl before their perfunctory wedding the day prior, and now she knew it all too well. The lord had not been kind or gentle when he took Marit Armenil's maidenhead. She'd heard the rumors that he relished cruelty and, after their short time together, Marit feared the whispers were true.

Would he direct the full weight of his cruelty upon Marit once they reached Jarl Egil Triam's castle? How much worse could things get? Would she eventually become one of the wives that mysteriously died at House Triam's castle?

Why did the stars forsake me? Her throat tightened, and she tried to shove away the negative thoughts that clouded her mind all too often of late. Her father, Fates rest his soul, had always said that hope endured, no matter how slim. Marit was determined to take those words to heart.

Her best chance at survival was for Princess Saga to call her back to Avaldenn—after the honeymoon period that Jarl Triam claimed to want with his wife.

Marit only hoped when that day came, she remained breathing and not with child.

To have a youngling with him would be a fate worse than death.

She did not wish for her thread of life to weave tighter with Triam's thread.

"I promise," the princess of House Aaberg hissed. "I will get you away from him for as long as I can." She squeezed her friend again, releasing only when the driver of the sleigh proclaimed for a third time that they needed to leave now if they were to beat the storm sweeping the countryside.

Feeling more alone than ever before, Marit watched Saga walk away. The Balik sisters had come to see her off too, and now waited for the princess to join them. Sayyida was still missing from court, and Marit suspected that the storm-chasing Virtoris did not intend to be found. Let alone married. Marit's stomach twisted in annoyance that barely cut through her sadness. She wished the Nava captain had confided in Marit in her plans to leave Avaldenn. Marit could have joined Sayyida.

Do not become sour. She did her best and taught you to fight, not that you learned well, Marit chided herself. Sayyida's foresight should be applauded, and Marit should not be jealous. It was unbecoming of a lady, and through this all, she was that: a lady.

Her family, her rock, stood a few paces away too, having already said their goodbyes. Lady Orla Armenil sobbed, something she'd done since the day her husband's head arrived at court. Her mother was doing her best, but for Marit, it wasn't enough. Had Lady Armenil been in her right mind, Marit was sure she would have fought harder for her daughter to become a lady-in-waiting to the queen or princess. Anything but this.

But Orla Armenil and Sten Armenil had been more

than husband and wife. They'd been mates, and there was no greater pain in this realm than losing a mate: Not even seeing your daughter carted off to the house of an alleged murderer.

Marit prayed to the dead gods that while her mother was in this condition, her other siblings who were of age to wed continued to evade the king's notice and helped their mother through this troubling time. Marit would be more certain things would turn out if the Armenil heir, Connan, was present to help, but he remained in the far north, stricken with illness.

Rune will do his best. He must.

As if he sensed her thoughts of him, Rune, her second oldest brother, raised a hand as their mother wailed. Marit's heart clenched, and when Rune brought that same hand down and to the wolf clasp that gathered his cloak, she let the tears she'd been holding back fall.

The pack endures.

Rune assured her they had not forgotten her, had not forsaken her. He would bring her to safety, for the Armenils were direwolves, and they did not forget their own.

She was tempted to go to them again. To say goodbye one last time. Her feet nearly took her in that direction, but Marit was stopped by a soft, familiar voice.

"Marit, a word?"

Marit twisted. Sir Qildor had only recently been released from the healers' care. Or so she'd heard. Marit had not had time to visit the Clawsguard knight, an old family friend. Her brother Connan's best friend, and, though Marit had never told a soul, her first kiss.

Warmth stirred in her at the innocent, sweet memory. In light of what she'd experienced lately, it made her cherish her short time with Sir Qildor more.

"I'm happy to see you out and well," Marit said.

"They didn't wish to let me go, but I had to see you before you left." His eyes, a startling violet, shone with anguish. "I hate that you're paying for helping Vale and Neve."

He'd been whipped with an ice whip for the same transgression. His back had been torn to shreds, and his life had hung in the hands of the Fates.

"I don't regret witnessing their wedding," she replied. "The king's choice later, however, well, it was too harsh. For the both of us."

He nodded, and as his long black hair slithered around his shoulders, she caught Qildor's scent of juniper. She inhaled deeply, always having loved the scent.

"You don't deserve this. You deserve only good things. The best." Qildor looked around. "And if I can, I'll help."

She smiled weakly. Qildor was a Clawsguard, an elite knight sworn to the royal family—to King Magnus. He could do nothing. Just as she couldn't.

Still, it was sweet what he said.

He's Connan's best friend. By extension, he cares for me.

"Hug me," Qildor said.

She blinked. "What?"

It wasn't that they hadn't hugged before. They'd kissed many times, and once or twice it had gotten heated. Hugging was nothing by comparison. However, since Qildor took the Clawsguard's golden cloak, he'd barely touched her, let alone hugged her.

"I have something for you. Hug me."

She opened her arms, making it clear that she invited him in. They embraced, and Marit allowed herself to lean into the familiar feel of him. He might be stronger and leaner and more masculine, but he was still Qildor, a commonborn male she'd once thought she might love. A knight she still had a bit of a crush on, though she'd never say so out loud.

His hand shifted, and Marit's eyebrows pulled together as she felt something drop into her cloak pocket before he released her.

"There are instructions on how to use the herbs in the bag. I could get only two moons worth, but it might buy you time."

"Time?"

His cheeks darkened. "To not bear his child. I assume that's what you want?"

Oh! She gasped, unable to believe what he'd done for her. She had to be very careful with the bag in her pocket. No one could see it.

"Yes. Thank you, Qildor. I—"

"We must go, Lady Triam," the carriage driver called yet again.

Triam? Oh, no, that will not stand. I'm still an Armenil, no matter the words the king forced me to say.

"Lady Armenil, actually." She did not miss Qildor's smile at her words. "I follow the rituals of the Sacred Eight and will not be changing my last name."

She may be forced to do this, but she was who she was, and Marit was more magically powerful than her husband.

Marit waved goodbye one last time and went to the covered sleigh. Thankfully, her new husband was not traveling with her, but rather riding ahead so that he and his soldiers might collect taxes on the way. Taxes the king insisted on collecting.

Marit assumed the rush for more riches had something to do with the reappearance of Lord Roar back at court. An appearance that had caused a stir and more so when the king did not punish the Warden of the West. Rather, he'd elevated the lord, and the pair seemed to always be talking. Planning? That's what it looked like, but no one Marit had spoken to could say for certain. Not even Saga.

As Marit climbed into the sleigh, one of House Triam's servants shut her inside. She swallowed. The fine velvet of the cushions turned her stomach. This carriage, no matter how lovely, was taking her to a life she did not want. A prison of a different sort.

Marit peered out the window at her loved ones, and her heart clenched. This may well be the last time she ever laid eyes on them, but the herbs in her pocket gave her hope. Just as the determined expression on Qildor's face did.

CHAPTER 11
NEVE

Leaving our suite proved tortuous, but unfortunately, Vale and I had already promised the Fellhelm siblings we'd join them for a morning training session. We did not want to disappoint our gracious hosts, nor appear flaky in our growing friendships.

Not to mention it had been weeks since we'd trained inside, with various weapons at our disposal, and without the threat of the wrong person or persons stumbling upon us. Our bodies wanted to stay beneath the furs, exploring one another, but we knew to take advantage of the situation. Once we left Dergia the following morning, we were not out of danger. Safety wouldn't come until we reached Riis Tower and reassessed the situation. After that, how would we proceed?

Back in Avaldenn King Magnus would have questions about where we'd been and why. He already didn't trust me, and I was sure that this period away had not strengthened that trust. If we did return, I'd first have to seek the king's forgiveness and then gain allies at court under Magnus's nose—a difficult and imposing prospect. Going back to court *just might* be worth it though, if only to find a lead on the Ice Scepter's location.

The Hallow had been missing for so very long, and the king had been searching for it for some time. A part of me thought it preposterous that I could find the Hallow when no one else had. Another part believed that I'd learned many secrets regarding the Scepter and the realm and that had to be a sign. Perhaps I was fated to bring it to light once more?

I didn't know, but with Sassa's Blade hanging at my side and my mate walking with me, I figured training might clear my head. Perhaps inspire me too.

"We could still return to the bedroom and . . . stay there for hours."

The raw desire in Vale's tone made my toes curl in my boots. In the weeks after a mating bond formed, mates had a greater need for each other—physically, mentally, emotionally.

"We should train for a few hours," I said. "If I'm really going to ally with the dwarves, I need to see how they fight."

"So you're considering an official alliance?"

"I would be a fool not to." I lifted my shoulder. "Plus, think of all the *zuprian* steel weapons you can try today."

He mulled that over and nodded down to my blade, which I had not yet named. "I'm curious to see if, now that we know the blade holds shadows within, we can't draw them out."

"I have no idea what to expect from it," I replied. We'd

trained often during our journey south and had seen no hint of shadows. Or any magic from the blade at all.

"Has anyone told you that Sassa's Blade is said to be a Hallow of this land too?" Vale looked at me. "I meant to mention it once we learned the name of the blade, but we've been busy since we visited the forges."

Busy with diplomacy. Then each other.

"Roar introduced me to the idea of the Scepter as a Hallow, but that was all he mentioned."

"I'm not surprised. That is the one people saw the most. As far as I know, King Harald did not bring Sassa's Blade out for the public to view. And I've never heard it called a shadow blade. Maybe that's why he did not bring it out much, but it's just as likely that he wished to keep his treasures private. The third Hallow also rarely saw the light of day."

"What's the third one?"

"The Frør Crown."

I'd heard that King Magnus wanted the Crown. However, that was the extent of my knowledge regarding the Crown.

"What does that do?"

"Only the Falks knew, I fear." Vale took my hand, kissed it along the line of snowflakes that bonded us. "Are you sure you're ready to go public? People will see our marks."

I laughed, and not just at the sudden change of topic, the thinly veiled attempt to get me back into bed. "I expect everyone aside from Anna and Caelo already thought we were having sex all the time, Vale. The mark doesn't always appear the first time, anyway. Or so I've read." I looked at him. "Besides, they'll be happy for us."

And they were. The moment we entered the castle's training room, Prince Thordur and Princess Bavirra walked over to meet us, with a sly grin on her face. The youngest of the Fellhelms, the triplets, and Prince Balindur, were mid-sparring and did not stop to greet us.

Anna and Caelo were present too, the former learning how to wield a dagger and use her body weight to her advantage as she did so. They paused in their practice, and I waved.

Anna's eyes bulged as she shrieked. "What's on your hand?!"

I laughed. My friend was human, and between humans, there was no such thing as a soulmate mark, but I'd spoken of mates often enough for her to recognize the outward signs.

I took Vale's hand and lifted them together. "Soulmates."

The next minutes were a flurry of happy congratulations from the royals and our friends.

Anna, unable to contain her joy, gripped Vale's hand and beamed. "Now we both have matching marks with Neve." She pointed to the crescent scar on her collarbone, the one she'd carved into her skin at the age of eleven, so I would not feel so ugly and alone. The scar matched the one on my temple—the same scar that made Roar suspect who I was the moment he met me.

"Family resemblances," Vale said, which made Anna's dark eyes fill with tears.

It warmed me through to hear Vale call her family because that was what they both were to me. Vale and Anna, family of the soul and heart.

Once everyone had examined the marking, Vale and I suggested getting to training.

"Yes, you'll want to make this quick, I suppose. So you can get back to bed." Princess Bavirra winked, and my cheeks flamed.

"*Sister*," the Heir to Dergia gave a warning, and the princess rolled her eyes. Prince Thordur seemed to have expected such a reaction though, and if anything, his one eye sparked with amusement at his sister's cheek. "Prince Vale, I had hoped to engage you in sparring today."

My mate smirked at the dwarf prince, and there was no denying the hint of arrogance in his posturing. "You're sure?"

Prince Thordur chuckled, all confidence and a touch of bravado that made Vale's spine straighten. "I need a challenge for once."

"I'll give you a challenge you might not be able to handle." Vale patted *Skelda's* hilt, his smirk deepening as his competitive side rose to the surface.

"My roots were formed deep in this formidable earth, Warrior Bear. Trust, I can hold my own."

"Sword against sword, it is then." Vale rolled his neck.

"More rightly, sword against battle-axe," Prince Thordur amended, and strode to a stand upon which two dozen weapons awaited. "The true weapon of my race."

I gazed at the double-sided axe inlaid with etchings of

fire and mountains blooming above the cloud line. It was a true thing of beauty, and while I'd seen such a weapon before, even watched Luccan Riis and Sian Balik use similar axes during our training sessions at Frostveil, I had the feeling the Heir of Dergia would wield his weapon on a different level.

"This will be interesting." Princess Bavirra stood by me as the warding dwarf placed a protection over both princes' skin so that strikes did not maim, and the males faced off. Elsewhere in the training room, others continued practicing, though I suspected that soon, the prince-on-prince fighting would steal their attention too.

"Your brother has the advantage, having heard about Vale. Do the dwarves of Dergia have a specific fighting style?" I looked at the princess.

The faelights above gleamed against the dark skin of her high cheekbones as she mulled over my question. "From my studies, I believe we do, though never having left the mountain range, I can't really be sure. There's much I have not seen."

"You've really never left?"

"Thordur has ventured into the nearest villages, but none of our other siblings have been allowed to leave our territory. It's why I'm so excited to help him escort you out of our tunnels."

We were leaving soon. Tomorrow. The royals had assured us we could stay longer, but I was anxious to get back on the road. To find information on the Ice Scepter so I could begin my search.

"I won't be going anywhere near the closest village," Bavirra added, "but it will be the farthest I've ventured from home."

I let out a hum, but as the princes began their session, I didn't continue the conversation. I was too entranced in watching the warriors size one another up in real time. They circled, and I knew from his instruction to me that Vale was taking in Thordur's every move, how he held his weapon, which foot he placed more weight on.

The other sounds in the training room fell away as other sessions ended. They were watching too. Assessing. Waiting to see who won.

Prince Thordur rushed Vale; battle-axe held high. My mate blocked the blow, but the dwarf prince came at him again with shocking speed and the curve of the axe gripped *Skelda* and hurled the blade to the side of the room.

Thordur let out a whoop, and his face split into a grin. For his part, my mate seemed astonished but also oddly elated. It wasn't often that someone got the best of him one-on-one.

"Round two?" Vale asked, retrieving *Skelda* and returning to the one-eyed prince.

"If you can hack it."

Vale swung *Skelda* in a wide, impressive arch, showing off if he ever had. "We'll see, won't we?"

Hours later, sweat poured down my face as I stretched my limits in the sparring arena.

After watching Vale and Thordur face off half a dozen times, I thought I understood how the dwarves of Dergia fought with their axes, and Princess Bavirra had offered to have a round with me.

I'd accepted gladly, needing to capitalize on every moment. I might have powerful magic that most could not fend off, but my power was not limitless. Nor did I hold perfect control over it yet. So I required other options to ensure my safety and the safety of those I loved.

That's what I kept telling myself anyway, as Princess Bavirra's battle-axe swung my way, and I had to dodge for the tenth time this round. We were warded across our skin, preventing serious injury to our bodies, if not our pride.

So far, the axe-wielding princess had beaten me three times, and I'd matched her—though only by a hair on the final round. This time was not looking so good for me.

Bavirra loved the show of the battle as much as the exertion, whereas I merely wanted to win. To prove myself. I felt that, if I did, it would be another signifier that I was on the right path. That I could protect and fight for what I believed in.

Bavirra came at me yet again. Spinning, I deflected her battle-axe. The metal of the axe struck the stone ground of the castle, echoing throughout the otherwise silent chamber. Bavirra recovered masterfully, as she had every other time, and charged again.

Dwarves were powerful, especially when moving quickly over short distances. In truth, they were far quicker than I'd have imagined, and I could imagine quite a lot.

Axe raised, Bavirra struck, and this time, my blade met hers in the air, hooking on the curve and stopping the metal at my pommel. The princess shoved upward. I twisted to the side just in time to avoid the blade hitting the shield in front of my face.

I was at least a head or two taller than her, though in this scenario that meant I had to watch my lower half more than I usually did. A lesson I'd learned by losing the first two sparring matches.

"Did you stay up too late?" Bavirra teased. "Your arm is shaking."

I'd grown stronger in the weeks I'd been free, but Bavirra trained often—and had worked in the mines, as was her family's custom. So like her parents and siblings, her arm muscles were something to envy—and for me, something to conquer.

Though in this case, I was feigning weakness. I acted mortified, and Bavirra pressed harder, sensing a win close by. I allowed my arms to shake harder, preparing my wings for the right moment.

On the sidelines, the princes, Caelo, and Anna cheered for one princess or the other. Beyond them, I caught a flash of coin being passed around. Others had taken bets.

I hope they bet on the stranger. I allowed Bavirra to raise her axe again and as she brought it down, my wings snapped out of their protective position. I leapt.

Her body flew forward, her axe slammed into the ground as I flew and flipped. It was a move I'd seen Sian pull many times and tried once or twice myself—never to the effect Sian did, but today, it felt right. Like I might be nearing Sian's natural grace. I soared over the princess and extended my sword.

It struck the warder's protection at the base of her neck, the spot lighting up for all to see.

"That's my wife!" Vale shouted, pride lacing his voice.

The moment my feet hit the ground, he was there, scooping me up and pulling me into a kiss that sent flames through my body.

When we broke apart, I looked up at him and beamed. "I feel like pieces of everything I've learned are coming together. Slowly but surely."

"Excellent progress." He let out a chuckle. "In truth, I don't feel that I can call you 'little beast' any longer. There's nothing *little* about what you've done today—or for weeks. I believe that you need another name."

"How about a force of nature?" Bavirra came up behind us, her voice breathy from the effort of our fight. "Fighting her feels like one. It's almost impossible to believe that you've been training for only a couple of moons."

"When you have a lot to lose, you learn quickly," I said. "Not to mention, I've been lucky to have varied, skilled, and generous teachers too. People like you."

She grinned her thanks.

I leaned into Vale and looked up at him. "I think it's time to retire for a while, though?"

We'd been training for many hours and tomorrow we had a long journey ahead of us. Being tired would not help.

"Agreed, Force."

I cocked my head.

"Yes? No?" he asked.

The name hadn't resonated when Bavirra said it. Not until I heard it from my mate's lips. Although I didn't think I was quite worthy of it, maybe I could grow into such a powerful name.

CHAPTER 12
VALE

I packed the last of my belongings and, latching the bag shut, my gaze caught on the line of snowflakes running the length of my left fourth finger. I rubbed the line with my thumb.

We had shown many people the marks and had marveled at them ourselves for hours, and yet, I still barely dared to believe that they were real. My soulmate had been in front of me for weeks.

In dreams of turns past, or as I walked the countryside with soldiers, I'd often thought that if I was among the lucky few to find my fated mate, I'd know in an instant. Perhaps that Pórr, the dead god of storms and thunder, would reawaken and strike me down with a bolt.

Never would I have thought I'd wed a female, fall in love with her, and be willing to give up everything I was before I recognized she was mine and that I was hers. That we were two parts of one soul, our fates destined and woven together by the stars.

My gaze turned to Neve, standing at the door to our room and still speaking with a bleary-eyed Ronaldo and a smiling Lei, who stopped by to bid us farewell. My heart warmed. I should have paid more attention to my inklings about Neve, but it did not matter now. We were bound forever, even when we entered the starry halls of the afterworld. I no longer doubted I should be with Neve, and would do my best to live up to the great fate the stars had gifted to me.

"Hello there," Neve said, alerting me that someone else was stopping by.

A small voice came from the hallway. "I apologize for my interruption. I have a package for the prince and you, Princess Neve."

My mate stepped aside. "Could you give it to Vale while I finish my goodbyes? He's packing up."

A human we'd led to Dergia entered our room. She was around Filip's age and reedy, malnourished in a way that made her brown eyes appear too large in her gaunt face. Although she had put on weight in the days since I'd seen her, the girl still had a long way to go before she was healthy.

"Hello." I'd only spoken to this girl twice and didn't know what she could be bringing us.

She curtsied, bobbing erratically with the motion. "I'm working in the royal household until I come of age to have my very own cottage. I've been at the forge since dawn, and Master Kolmot just finished these for you." She held out a leather package tied up with a thick string.

"From the forge?" My throat tightened. The royal family

had mentioned that they'd gift us *zuprian* steel daggers, but after our first meal together, nothing further had been said. It seemed, though, that the Fellhelms hadn't forgotten.

"Do be careful," the girl said as I took the package. "They're sheathed but sharp, and the smith warned me that they might slip out."

"Thank you. Are the dwarves treating you well?"

"They are, Prince Vale. I sleep in a room with others who are around my age. I feel safe and so far, I enjoy what I'm doing. This world is so fantastical."

"Do you think you could be happy here?

"It's not what I'd imagined my life to be, nothing like where I come from, but I know it's better than being a blood slave. The dwarves are kind, and soon enough, I'll be able to get a job outside the palace. Until then, I get to save coin and learn how things work around here."

I knew next to nothing of the human world, and little more regarding the magical beings that lived with humans. From what I knew, though, our realms were quite different. I only hoped that this girl's desires came true, and she could make the best of this life.

"Good luck to you then." I bowed my head, and she performed another clumsy curtsey before scurrying off.

"That was sweet." Neve swept over the instant the girl was gone. Lei and Ronaldo had left too, and we were alone.

"I hope she'll be happy here. That they all are."

"Ronaldo and Lei told me that most of the humans have already found jobs, and some have their own stone cottages too. Those who were ill or injured are remaining in the castle until they're well, but positions are lined up for them.

Ronaldo and Lei plan to work in the mines for a while until they find work that suits them better."

"It truly worked out," I murmured. There had been many doubts as we traveled, but this outcome was better than expected.

"It did." She glanced at the package in my hands, and fanned herself. We were already dressed in furs for the journey. The furs, combined with the fire blazing in the hearth, made the room warmer than we liked. "I overheard the girl. So those are the daggers?"

I nodded. "Perhaps we find Anna and Caelo and open it together? They each have one too."

"Excellent idea! They'll already be preparing the horses, and I want to get out of this room. It's sweltering." She held up a finger. "But before we meet them in the yard, I have one thing I want to do."

"What's that?"

"The night I seduced you," she winked, "I saw a Drassil tree in the garden. I forgot all about it until now. Anyway, it was looking like it needed a magical infusion. I've touched them before, but I could try?"

"No."

She straightened. "Why not?"

"The Drassils are all connected, my love." I took her hand. "It's not likely, but my father could learn where we are if you infused one with your power. More importantly, he could learn of Dergia. I'm sorry to say, but their tree will have to continue to rely on magic being infused into the network elsewhere."

Her shoulders fell. "I didn't think of that."

"One day, you'll be able to help," I assured her.

"One day." She sighed.

I scooped up our small satchels, before looping her arm through mine. Together, we made our way to the main entrance of the castle.

As expected, Anna and Caelo were already there, beneath the dawn-soaked enchanted sky, preparing our horses for the journey. Judging by the full saddlebags, the royal house had provided us with much food and water, a kindness I would not forget. Just as I wouldn't forget my time in the Kingdom of Dergia.

"Prince Vale, Princess Neve." A dwarf appeared and bowed. "We were already preparing Prince Thordur's and Princess Bavirra's horses and tried to assist Sir Caelo and Lady Anna, but they would not allow it."

"Don't fret," Neve said. "It's not a reflection on your work ethic. Caelo likes to be thorough."

Among friends, Caelo knew how to let loose and have fun, but when he slipped into his Clawsguard duties, he liked to be in complete control. And now that he considered both me and Neve under his watch, he'd be extra cautious.

"Thank you, Princess Neve." The dwarf looked at her shyly, clearly relieved not to be found lacking. "I'll continue preparations."

He left, and we veered toward our friends before anyone else could appear. Caelo saw us first. He, like Anna, Neve, and myself, looked much rested and well fed after our time beneath the mountain.

"Is it odd that I'm looking forward to getting back in the

saddle?" Caelo asked. "To feel the wind on my cheeks again?"

"It's *very* strange, not that I'd expect anything different from you Winterborn lot," Anna retorted playfully. "You're all a touch crazy about the cold."

I laughed. "Strange or not, I agree."

"Honestly, though, why can't your kind stand a little warmth?" Anna pulled her own fur cloak tight around her.

"We're born of ice and frost. Some of us more so than others." I drew Neve closer, remembering the day winter had exploded from her, turning her blue.

Anna's gaze steered to her friend. "Well, I guess all good things must end. We're mostly packed, just waiting for—"

"A handsome prince?" Thordur's voice boomed from behind.

I turned to find the king, queen, Prince Thordur, and Princess Bavirra marching outside. The siblings were dressed warmly too, for they planned to see us through the maze tunnels beneath the mountains and down a pass before pointing out a town with a coinary. I exhaled, pleased at the small send off. We'd already said goodbye to many of the humans and the other Fellhelm siblings.

"And a cunning princess," Neve added with a grin.

She and Bavirra had become fast friends these past days.

"You get both for another day or so." Bavirra winked as she went to her horse and began checking the stirrups. "Longer if we run into trouble."

"Stars, I hope we don't run into those giant ice spiders." Neve shuddered.

We'd been told that the creatures, along with many

others, sometimes found their way into the mine tunnels that dwarves used to travel through the mountains.

"Tell me true," Neve continued, "what's the likelihood of that?"

"I've only heard the ice spider alarm sound twice," the queen assured Neve. "The path you're taking has soldiers stationed along the way to sound alarms and fight off the beasts, so it's very rare that they venture down those tunnels. I think you'll be fine."

Prince Thordur nodded down at my hands. "I see you got the daggers."

I lifted the leather package, bowing to the king and queen in thanks. "I have yet to open and distribute them."

"Well, go on," Caelo said, eyes gleaming. For a knight to own one weapon made of *zuprian* steel was unusual. Once he chose his dagger, my best friend would own both a sword—a recent nameday gift from me—and a dagger.

I untied the leather string and opened the flaps to reveal the sheathed daggers. Picking one up, I marveled at the sheath and the mountains drawn along the length. The craftsfae decorated the bronze and bone hilt with small hammers and snowflakes. Personalized for us—fae of the wider Winter's Realm who had seen the innermost secrets of the dwarves. The others looked much the same, though the patterns differed, so we could tell them apart.

"The same range that houses this very kingdom," Thordur stated. "The middle mountain, the tallest, of course, is the heart of Dergia."

"Astonishing craftsmanship." I unsheathed the blade.

My breath caught, taking in the wavy lines of the *zuprian* steel. The dagger was stunning in every regard.

"We hope you like them," Thordur commented.

"Like them? I bleeding *love* mine," Caelo said.

"And which is yours?" I teased and held the package out to him, offering him the first choice.

"This one." He plucked one off the wrappings, eyes alight. "Thank you, King Tholin and Queen Deseana."

The royals smiled at him, and after giving her own thanks, I offered the next choice of blade to Anna. Neve plucked up the third dagger, and I took the last, slipping it through my sword belt.

"I'll treasure this blade, always," I said to the royals as I bowed.

King Tholin stepped forward. "I have something else for Princess Neve. Might I present it in private?"

The others, save for the Queen of Dergia, left and continued preparations. I remained with my mate, which the king did not question. He raised a hand and a servant who had to have been waiting at the gate came running our way, a wrapped item in hand.

The servant presented the item, and King Tholin unwrapped it to reveal a small, silver mirror with a short handle glinted in the light of nearby torches.

"This," King Tholin passed the mirror to Neve, "is a special piece. Dwarven kings once used mirrors like these to communicate with each other, but since the four kingdoms are no longer, I have acquired two extra mirrors. I'd like to present you with this mirror."

Neve's violet eyes widened.

"You need only speak my name into it, and my mirror will activate. Unless I hear otherwise from you, I will keep it nearby."

"Thank you, King Tholin, but I'm not sure I can accept such a valuable item steeped in the history of your people."

"You can, and you should," the king replied. "For if you're in danger, you'll need a way to get in touch, will you not?"

His question shook me to my core. My mate had not yet claimed her birthright publicly. Nor had I pushed her to do so. She struggled with the idea—with the repercussions. With the loss of what could have been her first days of true freedom, a life where no one expected much of you, balanced against helping all those of the realm.

And war, for once word spread that a trueborn Falk was alive and wished to challenge the king, blood would stain the snow of the realm.

That blood would be noble and commonborn alike, though it was often the commoners who suffered most when high houses fought. As Neve was nothing if not a fae of the people, she hesitated, which I suspected only caused her more pain because she understood that her hesitation was in turn causing all of Winter's Realm to—*the lands and the people*—to suffer.

Neve cleared her throat. "I fear asking too much of you, especially after all this kindness."

The king's eyes crinkled at the corners. "I knew upon meeting you that you were different from other rulers. They would not have cared for humans as you do, as *we* do. The way you were loyal to them, is the same way we dwarves will be loyal to you, and you should never underestimate dwarven loyalty, Princess Neve. It's stronger than the bones of the earth and stretches beyond the soil and rock of this realm."

My mate sniffed. "I've not spent a lot of time with your people, but I do understand that much. Still, you are quite far from the places I may eventually be fighting."

The king took her free hand in his, softly, like a father figure, and stared my mate in the eyes. "I will employ any means necessary to help an ally."

There was that word again, straight from the king's lips. *Ally*. He'd not spoken the word since we'd supped the first night, but the king had not forgotten that he wanted more than friendship.

My mate stared at the mirror, a work of art, like so much in this kingdom. Seconds passed like turns and still no one in our quartet spoke, though I felt the king's gaze on Neve and thought the queen—unusually quiet through this all—might be watching me with equal interest. Did she believe I would intervene? To try to sway Neve one way or the other?

I'd never. This was her battle to overcome, and while I'd not make a choice for her, I'd support whatever she decided.

An exhale parted those sweet lips as Neve looked up at the King of Dergia.

"I'm honored by the gesture of friendship, King Tholin. Just as House Falk is honored to call House Fellhelm an ally."

CHAPTER 13
NEVE

"This is the final water refill location within the tunnels," Prince Thordur informed us as he stopped at a branch in the passage we'd been traveling. "If your skins need filling, do it now."

I dismounted, needing both water and to get blood moving in my legs. Traveling the dwarven tunnels through the mountain passages had been a novel experience and for the first hour, I'd been captivated by the idea of where we were and how much work went into creating the web of tunnels. But when things began to look the same, my mind wandered.

We had some semblance of a plan: Aim for Riis Tower. From there, learn what was occurring in the kingdom and seek information on the Ice Scepter. Despite knowing what we were doing, foreboding threatened me.

Soon, I'd officially announce myself as Isolde Falk to the whole kingdom. Preferably when we were safe at Riis Tower —or perhaps just after, if we found a need to return to

Avaldenn, which I was against. Either way, there would soon come a time when I'd shed the name Neve and reclaim the one I was born with. The name I'd known since the human slave, Emilia, an old friend of my mother's, had identified me in the hidden parts of Frostveil Castle. A name I had not completely believed was mine until my mother, Queen Revna, came to me in a vision. The time to come to terms with my royal name and the changes in the new trajectory of my dreams and my entire life had been necessary, if frustrating.

I smiled at that as I filled my skin, content with my choice. Also content to allow myself that secret for another day or two.

"Shall we eat here too?" Princess Bavirra asked as she petted her horse. The dwarven horses were smaller than the ones we'd arrived with. Small and stout, much like the dwarves themselves. "I'm *starving*."

"A good idea," Thordur replied. "From here on out, we'll travel the same tunnel, but it's smaller than the rest and there's no good stopping point."

"What time is it anyway?" Anna asked, looking above at the rock that encased us as if she'd be able to spy the sun.

"Midday." Prince Thordur shrugged. "I can't be certain, but you'll arrive in Eygin before the supper hour."

That was enough for me. We unwrapped the provisions we'd been carrying and took seats on large rocks that littered the sides of the tunnel.

"How far do these tunnels stretch?" Caelo asked.

We already knew the dwarves had dug beneath entire mountains. The tunnels were not only a means of keeping their existence a secret, but simply a smart idea. Cutting through the mountains, rather than going over them and fighting snow, altitude, and creatures that made the mountains their home, was far preferable. Dwarves were a rather ingenious race of fae.

"As far north as Sisival, and our western tunnels go all the way to the sea." Thordur took a large bite of his hunk of cheese. "Though many of the western tunnels are collapsed in areas thanks to so many frost giants in the Ice Tooth Range. They destroyed a lot of our tunnels. Probably without even knowing they were there."

"To *the sea*. Skies, Thordur." Vale shook his head. "Your people never cease to amaze."

"Don't forget it." The prince quipped with an easy grin.

I sipped my water and stretched out my legs in front of me. We'd stopped two other times, at official dwarven junctions, which were basically small villages lining the tunnels. At the junctions, soldiers remained on rotation in case malicious creatures had found their way into the tunnels. Beings like orcs or ogres sometimes did, and the tunnels gave them an easy means of infiltrating Dergia.

The soldiers at the junctions had been elated to see us and their royals. They'd happily offered us a place at their hearth, which had gone a long way in making the ride more comfortable.

We finished eating, refilled the skins once more, and were about to ride when the horses began whinnying.

Vale looked to Caelo. "What's happening?"

Caelo's blue eyes narrowed, and I got the sense that he

was using his magic to speak to one of the mounts. "Something's approaching. They—"

The surrounding rocks began to shake, and my heart rate soared. Was the mountain collapsing around us?

Stars, I'd considered a lot of scenarios when I'd been told we were to ride all day through underground tunnels, but collapse hadn't been one of them. I'd been too confident in dwarven craftsmanship and mining to think that possible.

"Which way should we go?" Vale asked, sounding far calmer than I felt.

Thordur did not answer right away. Instead, he reached out and touched the rock. Only a moment passed before he exhaled. "A mullrokk is coming. Be ready to move should it appear close by, but don't worry otherwise. It won't harm us if we don't startle it."

"I'll tell the horses," Caelo said.

"*A what?*" I asked just as some thirty paces away, rocks from a sidewall began to fall.

I spun to take in the direction we'd come from in time to see rocks exploding across the tunnel and an opening appear. From the depths of the mountain appeared a creature so ugly that I recoiled.

"It's hideous," Anna whispered. "Look at its teeth!"

Bavirra laughed softly. "Rock moles aren't pretty, and we don't want them near our cities beneath the mountain for they might destabilize the rock, but they're gentle creatures. Necessary for the health of the mountain too."

I'd take her word for it because I was with Anna on this one. The mole was as tall as two stacked horses and as wide as three horses walking side by side. Milky eyes hinted the creature was blind, but its large nose likely made up for having no vision. Its claws scooped up rocks the size of my head and the mole tossed them into its mouth. I gaped as, with reddish-brown teeth, the creature chewed the rocks as though they were well cooked vegetables.

"I'll take a run in with a mullrokk any day over an ice spider or an ogre," Thordur added.

"And it moves on!" Bavirra smiled as the mullrokk began digging into the opposite side of the tunnel with its large claws.

The claws had to be metal or a similarly hard substance. It seemed to take little effort for the mole to dig a hole into the wall.

"As should we," Thordur said, gesturing to the horses, now calm thanks to Caelo's silent communication with them. "Walk the horses away, just to be safe."

I gripped my horse's reins, and we took the right fork of the tunnel, toward Eygin. Before we got too far, I cast a last glance back at the mullrokk. The vast creature had already disappeared into the tunnel it was digging.

I shivered. Though I'd enjoyed my time with the dwarves, I would be glad to soon emerge from the mountain and into the sunlight.

CHAPTER 14
VALE

"Follow this road and at the next branch go right." Prince Thordur pointed down a path. "From there, you'll descend directly into Eygin. It's about a half hour ride."

Our journey had taken us north, to a remote village I'd never known existed. Likely, western fae founded it as a last stop for rest and resupplying for those crossing the Red Mist Mountains into the Kingdom of Fire. According to Thordur, the fae of Eygin were among the few in the kingdom who knew the lost Kingdom of Dergia survived.

"The coinary there is small, as you might expect," Thordur added, "but the leprechauns are fastidious, and their establishment is connected by the magic of their kind to all the other coinaries in the Kingdom of Winter. You'll have your gold to ease the rest of the journey."

"You are still set on the midlands, correct?" Bavirra asked, looking wistfully around at the snow-covered landscape. Along our journey, the princess had proclaimed that she wanted to go farther, to ride with us into the midlands. Her brother was having none of it. As it were, we'd just exited the mountain tunnel, and Thordur said they'd go no further.

"Our best base is in the midlands." Riis Tower was safe. Warm. With access to the Riis brothers and Lord Riis— Avaldenn too, on the off chance that we needed to return for information, which I felt was unwise. "Thank you for showing us through the tunnels and around the mountain paths."

"It's what friends do." The prince held out an arm, which I took, sealing a bond I had not seen coming. "May the Fates and the stars watch over you, Vale."

"And you," I replied.

Neve and Princess Bavirra embraced, and my mate pivoted to hug Prince Thordur in thanks.

Though the gesture was sweet and innocent, instinctively, I bristled. Prince Thordur was no threat to me, but the idea of another male touching Neve made my muscles go rigid and hot, and I knew exactly why. In every story I'd heard, the mate bond was always strongest in the weeks right after its formation. Perhaps this was something Neve also intuited from her own bond, but just in case, I'd have to explain that to her.

We finished our goodbyes and parted with the siblings. When I looked back next, I found only the road staring back at me.

"Disappeared into the rock. Hidden from a kingdom with their own mysteries. A culture lost to dwarves elsewhere," Neve whispered. "We're so lucky they allowed us to see it."

"Indeed." I cleared my throat and after making sure that Caelo and Anna were far enough behind not to hear, I barreled forth with my concern. "Neve, you cannot go about hugging other males like that for a while. Not even in a friendly manner."

She blinked. "Why not? We're allies. More than that, *friends*."

"Did you notice I didn't touch Princess Bavirra? And that she did not seem put off or bothered by that distance?"

"I—no . . . I didn't notice." Her brow furrowed.

That didn't surprise me. Around those she loved and trusted, Neve was open with her affections.

I, however, had been raised in the royal court. My mother had taught me to be chivalrous and kind, while my father pushed me to be strong, a leader among the warriors. I had select members of my family and my close friends who knew me well, but I did not openly show affection to just anyone and everyone. *Especially* not female fae. Now that I was mated, my deepest affections were reserved only for one female. At least until the time—stars willing—came that we had younglings.

"I made a point not to," I told Neve softly, not wanting to make her feel bad, as much as I wanted her to understand how it made me feel. "The mate bond is strong now, and that might have made you jealous to a degree that it could have been dangerous for Princess Bavirra. I felt some jealousy when you hugged Prince Thordur."

The confusion clouding her face disappeared, and her

lips parted in an expression of clarity. "Vale, I'm so sorry. I didn't think about that, but of course you're right. I do feel more possessive of you than before. Had you touched a female that way, I probably would have been upset too. I'll be more considerate."

"Thank you," I said, certain now that we were on the same page. "I don't believe you have to do without affection forever from your male friends, but for now, I'd appreciate it. I'll do the same."

"Of course." She smiled at me, and the mere sight of her genuine smile stirred my arousal. Neve had always been attractive to me, but that attraction had multiplied a thousand-fold. "I've been thinking. Should we glamour ourselves again before we reach Eygin?"

I chuckled dryly. "The leprechauns will use my magic to determine who I am. My reputation will follow."

"They don't keep that a secret?" Her eyebrows pinched together.

"Everything pertaining to the inside of my vault is secret, but my visit to a coinary? No. They have no obligation to keep that a secret. I'm willing to bet a good deal of coin that King Magnus has each vault our family owns on watch, so once I take money out, the coinary in Avaldenn will know and inform him. He'll soon learn I'm in the west and will correctly assume you are with me." I corrected my horse, who had veered too far right. The creature was trained but had a tendency to wander, something my destrier, Carpus, never did. I missed that stalwart beast.

Anna and Caelo had moved close enough to listen, and

the next question came from Anna. "What do you think the king will do when he learns where you are?"

"I'm not sure, but I don't wish to find out. Though the king does not know Neve's truth yet, we've been gone a whole moon cycle without word. The king will take that as an affront. Once he has a hint where we are, he'll send soldiers to collect us."

"Wonderful," Neve murmured.

"Don't worry. He'll not find us so soon," I assured her. In under two hours, the sun would set. "We'll leave early tomorrow. Too quickly for anyone to find us this far from a true city. There are no soldiers loyal to the king out here."

"If only I had some coin," Neve said. "You think I'd be used to not having two coins to rub together, but I still hate it."

I looked at Neve. "I'm sure you have claim to coin."

My mate side-eyed me. "If you mean I can sell the gems I took from my mother's rooms, you're not wrong, but I sort of hoped to keep them. A change of heart, which I know is perhaps not the best idea—"

"Not that," Caelo cut in before I could reassure her. "Vale means the Falk family vault. Isn't that right, brother?"

"And House Skau's," I added. "As you're the sole survivor of both lineages, you may be very wealthy indeed. Far more so than me."

Despite the thickness of her fur cloak, I could see Neve stiffen. It was a testament to how in tune with her body I was that I felt the shock rippling through her. My mate had spent hours considering what it would mean to claim her family name, but I was certain she'd never once thought about the many assets that went with the Falk bloodline. Let alone that of House Skau.

"But King Magnus is a Falk by blood," she replied, her words slow and thoughtful. "Wouldn't he have drained that vault or had the contents moved into his?"

"He's a bastard and hence his name would not be automatically applied to the family vault. You can be sure his father never placed his name on the Falk vault's account, either," I answered. "So no, you are the last."

"With the combined wealth of two houses, you might even be wealthier than Warden Roar—or, that is, his estate, Neve," Caelo said, no remorse in his tone over the dead noble. "Though the moment you claim any money will be a proclamation to the realm of your right to the throne."

"Why wouldn't the money have been, I don't know, donated or something?" Neve asked. "It's just been sitting there for two decades?"

"That's how the leprechauns work," I replied.

Neve cleared her throat. "I have much to think about."

I shared a look with my best friend, then Anna, hoping that they'd not push more upon my mate. They did not continue, and Neve fell silent as she urged her horse down the road leading into Eygin.

The rest of the ride was quiet, and soon enough, we approached through the feeble gates surrounding the village. Two fae manned the gate, but merely waved us in. Apparently, we did not appear dangerous enough to be stopped. Or they were simply too deep in their mulled wine. From many paces away warming spices perfumed the air.

Eygin nestled between three mountains, one of which

ran right up to the gates and, presumably, along the edge of the village. I nodded approvingly. The rock would provide a natural barrier to predators, should any dare to stray too far off the roads.

However, near the gate, there was a large, boarded up door that told me more about the village. One of the mountains bordering Eygin seemed to have also once been a mine. Possibly one belonging to the dwarves, but more likely, the villagers had once mined for coal to keep their fires going. I stared at the wood over the door. It was not so old, though I spotted older boards beneath.

Caelo gestured to the doors. "A mine might help explain the communities' loyalty to the dwarves of Dergia. Similar pasts."

"Or maybe there's a mullrokk in there? I wouldn't want one of those getting out and gnawing through my home," Neve said.

"Could be many things. There are many unnamed monsters of the dark," Caelo muttered.

"If something is in there, *whatever* it is, the boards must keep it in," Anna said. "And I'm glad for it. I need a rest."

"We continue on," I agreed, digging my ankles into the horse's side and urging it toward the buildings.

Though we wore no glamours as we rode through the village, we kept our hoods up as far as they would go. We earned a few welcoming smiles and curious stares, mostly from females and younglings out doing the end of day shopping, but no whispers followed. To these fae, we were travelers. Soon enough, though, the rumor mill would turn and the commonfae would learn that their prince and his wife were visiting.

"The coinary." I pointed up the street to what was likely the most regal structure in the medium-sized village.

"The other one was white stone and had a golden cauldron too—though this one is on the sign, not a statue on the roof," Neve mused, taking in the coinary. "Do they always look so similar?"

"Leprechauns are a small fae race with massive pride. I think it may stem from the fact that they're a type of goblin and they know how the kingdoms regard goblinkind. So leprechauns, having found acceptance, know they have to be the best. They take special care to be consistent. The insides always look much the same too—occasionally with local art featuring landscapes—but mostly, they're identical."

We reached the coinary and tied up the horses. Anna and Caelo leaned against the free posts, ready to wait and watch the horses. Not that their protection was necessary. No one in their right mind would think of theft so close to a coinary. That security extended to the horses and sleighs that parked outside their establishments too, for it was all a reflection of the leprechauns' business.

Rather, Caelo and Anna stayed outside because leprechauns were strict about who they allowed into their establishments. If one did not have an account, or planned to open one that very day, they were not welcome. As Neve was my wife, she was allowed inside, as was Caelo, who held an account, but that meant Anna would be alone. A human alone in this world was always in peril.

"Ready?" I held an arm out to my mate.

She took it, her chin lifted high. "As ever. See you two soon."

"If anyone passes by, ask for the best inn," I directed Caelo.

"I can already taste the ale," my friend replied with a wink.

Arm in arm, Neve and I swept through the front door of the coinary into a long, white hallway that led to a bustling antechamber. On either side, leprechauns worked at desks. Each desk looked the same, with a small golden cauldron on the right corner filled with false gold. Like other coinaries, the leprechauns wore a green tunic, black pants, and shiny black shoes. The air smelled like all coinaries: dry and like the very metal coins the leprechauns kept in vaults. An area their kind called The Below.

A leprechaun with a long red beard appeared at our side. As expected, he was small, the top of his head coming up to Neve's hip. "Are you a new client, withdrawing, in need of a loan, or entering your vault?"

"I wish to make a withdrawal," I said.

Seeing as I was not in Avaldenn, and I would not be staying long enough for leprechauns to transport any valuables through their internal networks, entering my vault would be pointless. Only the coinage, which they kept books on, was accessible to me.

"Very well," the small fae replied, his narrow-set eyes blinking. "Follow me."

We walked through the line of desks, and no one bothered to look up from whatever business they were undergoing.

"This is stunning," Neve whispered.

I followed her gaze up to the many antler chandeliers holding a dozen flaming candles each. The antlers gleamed so bone-pale they might have been taken from a white hart —the animal symbol of my mother's house. However, to kill the white hart spelled death to the hunter, so I guessed that they'd come from a regular stag and had been enchanted to look like the more majestic creature.

"This is Coinmaster Hyknas. She will help you today." Our escort stopped at the desk on the far side of the room.

"Thank you," said Hyknas, a female of her kind shorter than the rest, but with a stern face that hinted she was not one to be trifled with. "I have it from here."

The escort left, leaving us before Hyknas and with mere seconds of anonymity left.

"What may I do for you today?" Hyknas pulled at the hem of her green tunic.

"My wife and I wish to make a withdrawal," I said, clarifying our union.

"Very well. Place your hand on this cauldron."

I extended my right hand, calling up my magic as I did so. The Coinmasters used this same enchanted object in all their coinaries to identify clients. As long as the fae had opened an account with the leprechauns, the cauldron could name a fae with the smallest speck of magic. The moment I touched the cauldron, I felt an odd tug beneath the skin of my palm. The object taking an inventory of my magic. An inhale of breath told me the leprechaun had read my name, magically scrawled on the other side of the cauldron.

"Prince Vale Aaberg." Hyknas looked up from the golden pot and stood, only to fall back into a curtsey, "Apologies, I did not recognize you. Nor did I know that the Courting Festival was over, and you were traveling the southlands." Her dark eyes glinted with excitement when they skirted over Neve.

I didn't bother to correct her assumption that the Courting Festival had finished. It might have, but I doubted so. As Roar's family had once possessed the Ice Scepter, Father would find nothing about the missing Hallows from the nobles at court—though he did not know that. And until he did, or until he ran out of matches to make, the Festival would continue.

"This must be the new princess," Hyknas added. "Apologies that you were not greeted as such."

I refrained from sighing. "We're only here for the night. Now, might I withdraw from my account?"

"Of course." Hyknas sat back down and pulled up the ledger enchanted to perform accounting between all coinaries in the kingdom. My name had appeared on the parchment the moment I touched the cauldron, and it was only a matter of time before the entire coinary spoke our names, followed by the village, the westernlands, and, soon enough, King Magnus too. "How much would you like to withdraw, Prince Vale?"

❋

The Frozen Toes Inn boasted lodgings on the top floor, a tavern on the bottom, ale as cold as a mage's touch, and warmed, spiced wine so excellent it would thaw a frost giant. Already the tavern set itself apart with lively music and dancing.

From where we sat at a table large enough for six, it was all too easy to hear that *we* were the primary topic of interest. I leaned back in the wooden chair, indulging in the feel of the hearth fire at my back.

I had not bothered asking the leprechauns to stay quiet, knowing that someone, somehow, would leak the information, and it would spread like wildfire. Better that it looks like we weren't hiding, even if we were trying to escape the notice of so much.

Hiding from the Red Assassins.

From the king's anger at our disappearance.

From the truth of our identities. The moment that news got out, it would change all I'd ever known.

"The stew is good," Anna said, testing the food once it was cool enough. While Neve and I had been in the coinary, Caelo had not only found the inn, but decided it would be for the best to glamour Anna to appear fae. That way, she could put down her hood and no one would ask questions about us traveling with a human. She now bore pointed ears and a glow to her skin that humans did not possess. It was the basest of glamours, but so far, no one noticed, or if they did, they did not care. I suspected most were staring at me or Neve, wondering why their royals were here and not at court.

"It's goat, I think?" Anna added after taking another bite.

"Could be ice spider stew, and I'd still eat it," Caelo replied. "I'm happy to have another warm meal."

Despite having been lavished in Dergia, not one of us would soon forget the days and nights of travel and the dwindling food.

"Pardon me?" A high-pitched male voice came from the side.

I turned to find a faerie bard with skin as pale as the moon and eyes so dark brown they almost appeared black—an unsettling combination. In his slender hands, the bard held a stringed instrument. Thantrel would know the name, might know how to play it too, but I didn't recognize the instrument, though the gleam of the wood told me it was well taken care of. Prized even.

"Yes?" I asked.

"Welcome to our fair village, Prince Vale. Princess Neve." The bard bowed when he addressed us, revealing that he had only one wing pressed down his back. The other, a dark navy stub, remained stunted at the base.

My stomach tightened at the sight, hating the blight and all it had done to so many in this land. I hoped that, if we found the Ice Scepter and it healed the magic of Winter's Realm, the blight might also end. That they were, somehow, as many thought, linked—although the blight had endured longer than the Ice Scepter was lost, the effects had become far more dire in the last twenty turns.

As the storyteller didn't recognize Caelo or Anna, he nodded at them before turning back to Neve and me. "I'm

Itham of Eygin. I recently returned home from Vitvik with new songs in my heart. I was about to take over the stage and wondered if you might have a request?"

Truly, I did not care what he played, but Neve nudged me. Sighing, I pulled a silver stag from my pouch. "Whatever the princess wants."

The bard beamed and turned to Neve. "Your wish?"

"Do you have a song about the Unification? A happy one?"

Itham's eyebrows rose. "Aye, I do. A rare choice, Princess Neve."

"I like rare things."

Fitting as my mate was a rare thing herself. Singular, in my eyes. More than seeking novelty, however, I suspected Neve wished to know what the common folk thought of her family. It would be too hasty to request a song about House Falk or House Skau, but the Unification was thousands of turns past and during that time, Queen Sassa Falk had been instrumental in crafting the realm as it now stood. No one would blink an eye over such a ballad.

Itham took to the stage where a small band waited behind him. He waved the others to quiet, intent on taking the stage for himself. The others leaned back, and the bard wasted no time in beginning to strum. Chatter eased, and many turned to watch the showman as he sang.

In song, his high pitch rang like a bell through the tavern. Chills ran along my arms, raising the flesh there into small bumps.

I'd never heard the song he sang before, but it began with Queen Sassa demanding that the old kings and queens of Winter's Realm bend the knee. At first, the old royals of the land did not comply. For that, Queen Sassa put a lord of House Qiren to flame, and a lady of House Ithamai lost her head. Of the most powerful eight families only House Lisika knelt without argument and that was down to the king consort of the time being a Lisika himself.

But as the Shadow Fae invaded our land and ravaged Winter's Realm, one by one, the once-great scions of this kingdom saw that only the Falk and Lisika lands were being spared. Protected effectively. Some said mysteriously. One by one, those kings and queens hit their knees before the unifier Sassa Falk and prayed to the stars that the House of the White Hawk might turn the hands of fate.

And she did. Queen Sassa's forces swept into all corners of the realm and beat back the Shadow Fae. She fought with the common soldiers, with those who grew the realm's food and tended livestock and built homes and sailed ships to bring back uncommon goods. She stood alongside anyone who could wield a weapon well enough, brandishing her own to save their lives as much as hers. For all that, the commonfae loved her, flocked to her, and where the Unifier Queen fought, shadows vanished. Light prevailed again. No one knew how, but the Shadow King and Queen and their armies fell against Sassa.

The day the shadows disappeared from Isila was the first day of peace our kingdom had known in many turns. A war of utter destruction, followed by the dawn of a new peace.

The enemies were gone. Blood no longer stained the snow. And each house had kept true to their word to serve House Falk.

That was, until King Magnus's Rebellion.

Itham, however, did not go that far into the timeline. His song ended with Queen Sassa dying in her bed. At peace, her family beside her, the realm still united.

Silence rang through the tavern, so incongruent in a place that had been raucous before the tune began. The moment my wife clapped, others followed suit in a slow and gentle way. It seemed as though they weren't sure if they should be applauding at all with us present.

"That one was for the lovely Princess Neve." The bard gestured to our table, a relieved smile spreading across his face. "Now, how about a song for the working fae? Those of sweet Eygin? Something lively to get the blood pumping?"

Cheers rang up, and the bard snapped his fingers, to which the band leaned forward. Flutes and tambourines and the bard's stringed instrument filled the air a heartbeat later. It took no longer than that for the fae to stand and run to the small space in front of the stage.

Young and old alike danced, some more spryly than others. Many more than the bard bore signs that the blight of Winter had left a mark on their bodies and their lives, the most common of which were fae with deformed wings. And though remembering the blight almost always put me in a sour mood, the sight before me warmed my heart.

No doubt, many of these people lived a hard life. In much of Winter's Realm, there was little other way to live. But they seized happiness as often as they could, where they could, and their joy was infectious.

"Let's dance!" Anna tugged on Caelo's arm. "You too Neve and Vale."

I looked at my mate, who grinned.

"You'll have to teach me the common dances. Clem only informed me of the courtly ones."

"We'll be learning together," I said.

"Speak for yourself." Caelo stood and offered his arm to Anna. "I could dance this in my sleep."

"Then we'll follow your lead."

We took to the floor and Caelo, the cocky bastard, showed us and everyone else in the tavern how adept he was at the common dances. I snorted as he grabbed Anna by the waist, lifted her and spun. The human squealed, and Neve laughed before turning to me.

"Well, aren't you going to spin me?"

I lifted my mate, breathing in her intoxicating scent as we spun, and she laughed. Around us, villagers cheered and clapped, happy to see others happy. Caelo set Anna down, so I did too and soon enough we lost ourselves in the music, the dance,

I didn't care that I was likely doing it wrong. My friends were having fun, as was my mate. We had coin to fund our trip, and we were on our way to safety. The fae of the village danced with us, beaming and singing and laughing. A few looked as though they were working up the courage to ask Neve to dance.

My mating bond hummed inside, but when I caught Neve staring up at me, her eyes only for me, I relaxed. A villager might ask her to dance, and if she wished to do so, I'd allow it—with a stipulation that the dance partner keep his hands to himself—but she was *mine*. And I was hers. My bond might insist on possession, but when it came to our love, we had nothing to worry about.

Neve beamed. "No serious thoughts. Be with me, Vale. Dance with me."

I brushed aside a stray lock of her hair and looked her in the eyes, committing this moment to memory. "I'm with you. Always, with you."

CHAPTER 15

NEVE

A t dawn, we rode for Riis Tower. Our safe haven. There, I could continue to search for clues as to where the Ice Scepter might be. I had to believe that, at the very least, I knew more than King Magnus, who might not even know that Roar was dead.

I gazed past Vale and his horse. Ahead was an arch of stone that clung to the side of the mountain. From so far away, the passage appeared large enough for horses and their riders to go beneath one by one.

Somewhere on the other side of that arch, we'd exit the Red Mist Mountain Range. According to the Fellhelms and a musician Caelo spoke to the night prior, once we were out of the mountains, the road would run along a river that fed a lake so colossal that some called it a small sea. Vale claimed that body of water was the same lake where House Vagle built Staghorn castle upon.

I blew out a plume of white breath. The temperature

had dropped again overnight, making it so cold that my thick fur cloak was barely enough to keep me lukewarm.

I cast a furtive glance at Anna, riding third in line. She was not a winter fae, and if anyone would be the worst off in this weather, it would be her. For that reason, my friend wore thick clothing, a gift from the dwarves, and *two* fur cloaks. One down her back, the other cascading down her front, leaving only the smallest of slits for her to expose her arms to hold her reins. Judging by how her teeth chattered, her furs weren't doing the job either.

I swallowed as I turned back around, not wanting her to catch me staring. I coddled her, or so she claimed. But humans were so delicate and this kingdom so cold, so happy to take a life and bury it deep in snow.

But we only needed to last until tonight. In the nearest city, Vitvik, I'd been told, we'd once again have a fire and a warm bowl of stew. There, I could buy more clothing for Anna. Perhaps hire a sleigh enchanted by a fire fae to keep it warm?

I'll ask Vale. It won't slow us down that much . . .

The tunnel through the mountain was now upon us, and Vale held up a hand.

"Let me check the inside first."

Now that we were closer, it was clear that this was no short passage through. Darkness indicated the tunnel was of some considerable length and that meant many creatures could be within. They might simply be taking shelter from the winds, but they could also be hiding for more nefarious purposes.

"Neve, let Caelo take second position." Vale twisted in the saddle and waved his friend forward. "Just in case."

"I can fight." I patted my sword, Sassa's legendary blade, and felt the dagger on my other hip shift as I did so. Vale insisted we all travel armed to the teeth, and I did not disagree.

"Of course you can fight. That's why you're the rear guard," Vale replied with a grin that warmed my heart. "We very much need you to watch our backs, Force."

"Flatterer."

"Desire to compliment you burns inside me. After seeing you dance with that youngling last night, I worry about our future." He winked.

His jest pulled a laugh from me. Vale had allowed a bashful teenage faerie to dance with me as long as only our hands touched. The entire time, the gangly lad's face was so red, but he smiled broadly, telling me that though he was embarrassed, it was a night he wouldn't forget.

"He's a bit young for me, but he danced well enough."

"It's too bleeding cold for all this flirting." Caelo rode by me, though there was a twinkle in his blue eyes. He enjoyed seeing Vale happy.

From the depths of their cloaks, they pulled glass faelights about half the size of my fist. Gifts from the dwarves, the tools were wrapped in metal to protect the illuminated portion.

Upon lighting them, my mate and the knight allowed the lights to float at their shoulders as the pair drew their weapons. A second later, Vale, then Caelo, had disappeared into the tunnel.

My breath tightened in my chest as the fae lights got smaller and smaller. The light disappeared and still I heard no sounds of fighting emanating from the tunnel. After two minutes of waiting, one fae light approached again, and Vale emerged from the tunnel.

"Nothing. Caelo is waiting on the other side. Come along, ladies."

I urged my horse forward after Anna's and shuddered when the rock covered us. Even with the faelight, the tunnel was dark. Colder, too, than the outside somehow.

"How long is it?" I jumped when my voice echoed through the stone.

"Longer than I thought," Vale replied. "We rode through quickly after we realized that if someone was hiding in here, they'd have to move, or we'd run into them. It's narrow."

"Can we just get on with it?" Anna said before I asked another question. "I'm sweating."

Right. She had a fear of enclosed spaces.

"Go faster, Vale," I said, for my friend's benefit.

"Follow close. And watch your head just up here. There's an overhang." He picked up his pace.

When he reached the rock protruding from the ceiling, Vale had to hunch over not to hit his head. Anna, being the shortest among us, dipped her chin. My turn came, and I ducked, raising a hand to touch the stone for guidance.

A jolt of frigid cold, an icy zing, seemed to stop my heart and the hum of my magic. I yelped and pulled my hand back, and the sensation disappeared.

"What happened?" Vale asked as Anna simultaneously whisper-shrieked. "Neve! Are you well?!"

"Fine," I said hurriedly. "I'm fine." I didn't want to scare Anna any more. So we continued on and when we exited the tunnel to find Caelo waiting in the sunlight, a wider road stretching before us, I sighed.

Vale's eyebrows pulled together as he caught my gaze. "What was that?"

"I touched the rock, and it was so cold. It was like it froze everything inside of me. Even my power. That didn't happen to you?"

"I didn't touch it." Vale's eyes narrowed before he added, "but I have a suspicion I know what caused that."

My spine straightened, and I shifted in my saddle. Stars, my rear would be sore tomorrow. "What?"

"Many dark creatures live in the mountain ranges. Most stay away from towns and villages, but they lurk in the wilds, like here. You might have sensed the magic of a banshee's song, or maybe an ice spider is to blame."

My stomach twisted. I did not wish to meet either. "What do the banshees do? Besides sing of death?"

"In Winter's Realm, I think it's different in the Autumn Court, where they originate, some banshees can freeze their prey. Their songs can also lodge into natural materials. You said it froze you?"

"Yes, sort of. Magically, it did. Physically, I could move."

Caelo nodded. "Likely ice spiders in the area, then. The web was probably connected to the other side of the rock you touched, and you felt it freeze, or stall, your magic."

Prince Rhistel wore ice spider silk gloves. Was that how his powers always felt?

Bleeding skies, it was almost enough to make me pity the foul arse.

"Ice spiders can get quite big, can't they?" Anna asked, her voice wobbly.

"They can," Caelo replied. "They start as small as frost-flies but over the course of their lives, which can be hundreds of turns long, they can grow as large as white bears." He cleared his throat.

"Can you talk to them, Caelo?" Anna asked. "Reason with them if we find one?"

The knight gave her a sympathetic smile. "You could speak with an ice spider yourself. They're not normal animals, however, so I doubt any of us could reason with them."

"Which is why we best get moving." Vale turned his horse forward.

Our foursome continued on our way, but not before I cast another glance behind us. Though the sensation of bone deep, bitter cold leaving a void in me was gone, I couldn't help but think there was a different vibration coming off the rocks, something dark and powerful in the air.

I hoped I was wrong, and if I wasn't, I prayed that it didn't follow us.

Amidst the trees and creatures of the dense forest, somehow the coldness of the rock lingered, if only within me. Everyone else seemed to have forgotten the experience within minutes of it happening. Finally, sick to death of thinking about it, I decided to make the announcement I'd been holding close to my heart.

"So," I began, thankful for the cover of pine boughs, which somehow felt like a comforting blanket, "I've been doing some thinking and have an announcement."

The road through the trees was large enough for us all to ride side by side, so the others glanced over.

"Such an important tone! Should we roll out a golden carpet to hear it?" Anna teased, and as I'd done so often in childhood, I stuck my tongue out at her.

Vale and Caelo chuckled, and Anna grinned.

"No carpet necessary," I retorted, secretly glad her jest had loosened me up a little. "Soon I'll officially claim my name—Isolde." It still felt odd coming off my tongue, but the moniker, more regal and powerful than the one given to me by a vampire, was growing on me.

"Shall we call you that from now on?" Caelo asked.

"No!" I blurted. "Not yet. Maybe when we reach Riis Tower, I can send out a proclamation and the Riis brothers can secretly distribute it in Avaldenn? I don't want to rush it in case we need to return to Avaldenn for some unforeseen reason. I might also like to wait until I have the Scepter. Though I've been considering when the best time to do so will be for days, I'm still not sure. All I know is the timing has to be right, or we'll be in danger."

Luccan's gateways meant we'd be able to speak to the

Riis brothers more often. I looked forward to it, and to seeing Clem again.

Vale hadn't looked at all surprised at my talk of me claiming my name, and thus a crown. He'd known of the war waging within me, just like before our mate bond snapped into place, I'd been sure he'd been battling feelings of unworthiness. We'd both allowed the other space to work through their thoughts and feelings.

"I'd ask, when I make things public, that you three be my council."

Though it had been many days since I fantasized over living a simple, free life, deep inside me remained some lingering nostalgia for that dream. Once I announced to the world who I was and what I intended to do, I'd never be free in the way that I'd once dreamed. I'd be royal, a queen— that was, if I defeated King Magnus, who I was certain would not step down without a fight.

"At Gersemi Mine, I said I'd be in your queensguard," Vale spoke first. "I meant that."

"I know you did. And I appreciate that, but you're my husband, my mate, and it is only fitting that you will be my king consort. That's quite enough, don't you think?"

He laughed. "I suppose so. I'll defend you with my life, anyway. I meant it when I said until the stars fall."

A lump rose in my throat, and I reached out a gloved hand, taking his and squeezing it before letting go.

"Caelo?" I asked.

"I'm more suited to a queensguard than an advisory position."

"I'm not sure I agree," I replied. "But isn't the head of

the Clawsguard an advisor? Aren't they on the Royal Council?"

Sir Caelo could be more than a sworn knight. He *should* be more, for his many gifts were too valuable to waste and they would be shunted aside if he were to be merely a guard.

"The head Clawsguard is an advisor," Vale affirmed. "And Caelo would be perfect for such a position."

A blush crept over Caelo's dark skin. "You two honor me."

"Accepted?" I asked.

"Accepted."

I looked across Caelo to Anna. "And you, dearest friend?"

Tears shone in her narrow, upturned eyes. "I'm human."

I feigned a shocked expression. "How dare you hide it all my life!"

A strangled sob left her throat. "You're sure? Others won't like it."

"Then they won't like much of what I intend to do as queen. I'm not sure of what your title will officially be yet, should you accept, but it will come with privileges and responsibilities to help others who have been enslaved."

Under my rule, not only would human slaves be getting rights, but I'd do my best to discover a way for them to return to their home realm—if they so wished to. No one had ever discovered a means, but I did not believe they'd had a proper incentive either. There had to be some way. If it took many turns, decades, centuries even, I'd find a way.

"Then I accept," Anna said. "Stars! I better read the histories of this kingdom thoroughly! I—"

My best friend's delight turned into a scream of horror as orcs barreled through the trees, their weapons at the ready.

CHAPTER 16
NEVE

Twelve orcs loomed, double Vale's size, their eyes wild with the idea of captives, and fangs gleaming in the light of the setting sun. Acting on instinct for Anna, I used my winter magic to drive her horse back, far away from the menacing fae.

"Caelo, Neve, up!" Vale shouted, his wings teasing through his cloak slits.

I followed his orders, a shudder thundering through my body as my wings hit the cold air. With three beats of my wings, I pushed through the physical discomfort and soared upward until we were above the trees. Out of reach, I surveyed the area and exhaled a sharp breath. Anna's horse ran backwards, just as I'd intended. Even better, our horses followed hers, putting a great deal of distance between them and the horde. Still, we had to act quickly before the orcs ran after her. Anna was brave and learning to defend herself, but she remained an easy mark.

"Divide," Vale said. "Neve, stay with me. Caelo, you take the right."

On the right, five orcs lumbered down the road after my best friend, leaving seven for Vale and me. Caelo soared down and fought, placing his body between the orcs and Anna.

"Force, take the young female and male next to her. I have the rest."

"I can do more!" I shouted as I dove.

"Do as I say," Vale shot back.

I gripped my sword, annoyed, though he was probably right. What was giving me this surge of confidence?

I'd trained for weeks against some of the best warriors in the realm, but not orcs. While I had seen these creatures in Guldtown, back when I was naïve and unable to protect myself at all, these ones seemed larger. Harder too. I needed to not get overly confident. I had not proved myself yet.

Now is the time.

I directed my attention to the closer male orc, the second smallest of the bunch, and blasted him with frost. He hadn't seen my powerful magic coming, nor guessed that his feet would be unable to move. The male snarled, pulling and tugging against the frost that continued to build around his legs, creeping toward his torso. I flew down, sword arching his way, but he just batted my blade to the side with a dull sword of his own. Pivoting, I flipped over the orc, coming to hover behind him, where I ended the short-lived fight with a slice across his neck. Blood spattered the snow, though thanks to the frost, the orc's body remained standing, frozen in place.

CHAPTER 16

I barely had a moment to catch my breath when the female ran at me, her blade arching for my head.

She growled as our swords met in the air. The orc was far stronger than me, and pushed me back, closer to the trees. I understood her motivation. Get me away from Vale and Caelo so they wouldn't be able to help. She thought I was the easiest mark, which if we only counted swordplay and other weaponry, she was right.

However, against most fae, my magic was unrivaled. In an instant when her sword pulled back, I leapt closer to the trees, putting a bit more space between us as I sprayed her with icicles. Two lodged into her chest, and blood spurted across the white snow. The orc's eyes widened for a split second before she fell backwards. Dead.

I spun, taking in the others only for my heart to drop into my belly. In mere minutes, the orcs injured both Vale and Caelo. The former to an arm, the latter to his side and leg. They'd both taken down two orcs as well, but with their injuries, they were moving more slowly. I needed to help them.

My wings unfurled, but before I could catch the air, a net tumbled from the sky and covered me. I gasped as my cold powers receded, diminished to practically nothing inside me.

A low, rumbling laugh came from behind. The net pulled tight. "Caught you."

I strained at the cage of webbing around me, trying to rip it. My blade slashed, but though the material was as supple as water, it did not tear, and that's when my heart began to race.

This net wasn't normal, and though it differed from how I'd seen the material used before to cover Rhistel's hands, I knew this had to be made of ice spider silk. That was why I could not feel my magic. The web was negating my powers.

The orc, a massive male with fangs as long as my pinkie protruding from his lower jaw, lumbered out of the trees. I slipped my blade through the net, trying to pierce his chest.

He retaliated, hurling a dagger at me. The bastard had impressive aim too, for the blade slid right through a hole in the net and grazed my right cheek.

"Ahh!" My hand went to the injury and in doing so, my sword slid backwards into the net. Cursing my reaction, I fumbled for my weapon, but before I could pick it up, the orc was in front of me.

With a hand as large as a dinner plate, he grabbed me by the neck and lifted me. I kicked air, struggling for freedom.

"Neve!" Vale shouted.

Dead gods help him, he sounded breathy. Weakened.

I reached for my powers before remembering that they weren't accessible. My heart raced. The orc laughed again, the sound hideous, the stench of his breath rancid. He slapped me across the face, and my teeth sang, but as he pulled a dagger from his belt, I ignored the pain and kicked at it with all that I had.

He slammed his knee upward, ramming it into my arse. I groaned, and in that instant, he slipped the dagger through the net, slicing my thigh. I screamed and gripped the net.

How was I going to get out of this?

My answer came in the form of Vale, who dropped

behind the orc and slammed the butt of his sword into the orc's neck.

Our enemy's knees buckled, but he was too powerful to fall. He whirled and used the dagger he'd sliced me with to cut Vale across his chest.

I fell with a scream, my hands plunging into the snow after the sword. Some of my blood had mixed with the snow, wetting my hands. I fumbled with the blade, trying to grasp it properly, to help Vale to—

My blade glowed with a deep black light, like a dwarf had set it to a strange dark fire in a mysterious forge.

"By the Fates, what's happening?" I whispered, staring down at the blade.

As if in answer, whispers hissed through the woods as a plume of black smoke—no! A shadow so dark it had to have been born in the darkness that separated the stars—blossomed from the *zuprian* steel. My throat tightened as the shadow took the form of a faerie.

"Your bidding?" It spoke in an ancient voice, one that set my heart to racing.

Bidding? Sassa's Blade was one of legends. Legends I was, admittedly, largely ignorant of, but if such a thing were possible, surely Vale would have mentioned shadows emerging from a blade. Another grunt from my mate quickly ceased my wonder. I looked past the shadow.

Vale knelt all fours, now trapped beneath a net too. A second orc appeared from the woods and sneered down at my mate. The first massive orc stood over him, sword in hand, dripping with blood.

Where in all the nine kingdoms were these orcs getting

nets made of ice spider silk?! Wasn't the material expensive beyond measure?

"Why did you summon me?" the shadow spoke again, irritation riddling his tone.

"I didn't. I—wait, can you do anything I need?"

One curt nod.

"Kill the orcs. That one first." I pointed to the orc standing over Vale, sword now raised. "Go!"

"I need blood." He nodded to the pool in the snow.

I paled. The slash on my thigh had been shallow and between that and my quick healing, it had already ceased bleeding. I'd have to open a vein. "How much?"

"For this many? Much."

I took my sword and cut across my already injured thigh, using the tear in my trousers to better gain access to the flesh. Fresh blood welled, and I nearly dropped the sword from the pain, but pinned it against my leg. I'd stopped short of the inner thigh, knowing to cut there would be death, but a sickening amount of blood still poured. I swallowed, but a second later, the blood vanished. Not in the snow, but into the air? Impossible.

The blade glowed again, giving me another option. One I never would have guessed. Had my blood gone *into* the blade?

The question died, however, as the shadow soared to the orc—and flying straight through his body, left a hole the size of my head in the orc's torso. I gasped, but the grotesque killing was not the only reason for my shock. The moment the shadow killed the orc, a tug came at my leg, a familiar sensation. It felt as though a vampire was pulling to get more blood.

Oh, stars, what have I done?

As the shadow soared over to the next orc and the next, the tugging continued. With each drawing of blood, my vision dimmed, my body weakened. After the shadow's fourth kill, an orc twice the size of Caelo and equally skilled in swordsmanship, I toppled over and, try as I might to push myself up against the blood-sodden snow, I could not get back up.

"Neve!" Vale was beside me, pulling at the surrounding webbing. When had he gotten there? "What's going on?"

I tried to answer, but no words came, only the dimming of my sight until the world went black.

CHAPTER 17
NEVE

A fire crackled and sage and rosemary drifted by my nostrils as my eyelids fluttered open. Above me hung bushels of dried herbs and flowers and twigs. One bushel of dried cranberries, the skin wrinkled and slightly brown, stood out the most. I lay upon a thin mattress.

The last thing I remembered was the orc fight in the woods and the shadow being that had helped.

My heart raced as another question presented itself. *Did the shadow bring me here?*

My head spun as I shot into a sitting position.

"Neve! Stay still!" Vale's voice grounded me. At least he was here. We were together.

A moment later, he stood at my side, the scent of him reassuring, as his protective hand splayed across my back. "Breathe, love. You've been passed out for two days."

Days?!

I glanced up at my husband, only to recoil. Stars, he

looked bad. A black eye and claw marks, both on the right side of his face besides the injuries I'd seen him sustain to his chest and arm. My gaze dropped.

"I'm fine," he assured me and waved a hand to his face. "These are superficial, and my other injuries have been tended to and bound. They hurt but were nowhere near as bad as yours. Or Caelo's."

"What happened to him?" I'd lost track of the knight in the fight. "Where's Anna?"

"She and Caelo are both sleeping deeply." Vale stepped aside so I could view the pair. Caelo laid in a real bed, while Anna sat upright in a chair, a thick, red blanket pulled over her. "Caelo lost a lot of blood from a side wound—a serious one. Anna didn't sustain a single injury."

"Where are we?" I asked, quieter now that I know we were all alive and two of my friends were sleeping. "You said I was passed out for *days*?"

Vale cleared his throat. "The fight ended, and you went unconscious. Caelo too. With Anna's help, I got him on his horse and tied him down. You rode across my lap."

Now that he mentioned it, my middle ached. It had to have been awkward riding that way, I was sure I'd have bruises.

"We're in Vitvik. Anna and I found a healer on the outskirts of the city."

I looked around again. This place looked like a cottage. The front had been converted for work, so perhaps the back was a living space? "Is the healer here?"

"She is. Now that you're awake, I need to alert her." My chest tightened. I wanted to ask a hundred more questions, but Vale kissed the top of my head and went to get the healer.

When they emerged from the back, I studied the red-haired female, head tilting to the side. Now that I'd been in Winter's Realm for two moons, I'd seen many more types of fae, but she was unusual.

"How's your leg?" the healer asked when she got closer.

"Fine."

"Let's see it then." She pulled back the blanket, allowing me my first good glimpse of where I lay. The table had a small feather mat atop, probably a place where she made concoctions and potions, as this didn't seem to be a healing outfit large enough for multiple people to stay in long term. Someone changed me out of my pants and into a flowing nightgown.

"I'm Rynni Vamyre." She did not dally in lifting my gown up to expose my wound. "You came in with a deep gash. I disinfected the site, sewed you up, and bandaged it. I'm going to undo the bandage now to check on it." Really, she was already doing so. "My main concern is infection."

"Of course."

As she worked, I studied the healer. Rynni had black scales on the sides of her face. Not the whole side, just behind her ears. If she wore her hair down, no one would see them, but today her long red hair was tied back.

What sort of terrestrial fae looked like that? Some water fae had scales, but aside from the nøkken, I'd not seen any water fae. I shot a glance at Vale, who shook his head. Clearly, he'd noticed the scales too, and did not think it appropriate to talk about.

"Everything looks like it's on the mend," Rynni said, confidence in her large, dark brown eyes. "I'd like you to take two more blood regeneration potions, though."

"More? How many have I had already?"

"You had three upon arrival. You lost a lot of blood."

Not lost. I'd given it away. Though I did not understand how or why that shadow appeared from my sword, that much was true. Had others seen it? Judging by Vale's relieved expression, he was only thinking of me, not some frightening shadow that killed the orcs.

Rynni went to a side table, opened a drawer beneath and sighed. "I only have one potion left, and the knight will need more soon too. I'll have to ask another healer if she has some on hand. " She pulled the vial from the drawer. "Take this. I have to go before she retires for the evening. It's already so late, and we're not on the best of terms, but she owes me a favor."

The healer passed the vials over, and I noticed her hands, while normal with five fingers and all, ended in short claws. Not nails. I sucked in a breath, which made her blow one out in exasperation.

"Since you all seem too polite to ask, I'm half dragon. Do you doubt my abilities knowing that? Wish to see another healer instead?" Her chin lifted in defiance, as though someone had often told her otherwise.

"You've already helped us," Vale said. "None of us would speak poorly of your skill. My wife has just never seen someone like you."

Had he? Dragons generally stayed in their kingdom, or so I'd been told. But then, Rynni said she was a half dragon.

So did that mean one of her parents was fae, and this was where she settled?

"Good." She shoved the vials at me again. This time I took them. "I'll be back."

She left the cottage in a huff.

I turned to Vale. "Is that common? To have dragons live here?"

"Not at all, but she was the first healer I found, and I didn't care about her heritage."

"Me either. I was just curious."

He reached into his pocket. "There's something I should tell you before she comes back."

A piece of parchment appeared. He unfolded the page, and I snatched it from his hands, my heart thudding in my throat.

"That's a drawing of me!"

"This was on the way into the village. I expect there will be more posters the deeper we go into Vitvik."

My mouth fell open. "Vale, this poster says I'm Isolde Falk." And an enemy to the Crown. Apparently, the king will give a hefty reward to someone turning me in. "How did he find out? Lord Riis? Or one of his sons?"

Even as I asked, it felt wrong. Luccan, Arie, and Thantrel were friends. And because Lord Riis was Vale's father and Vale loved me, I did not think the Lord of Tongues would have told the king about me, either.

Vale shook his head. "They're as loyal of friends as I've ever had. The Riis brothers would not betray us."

Emilia? No, the human slave I'd happened upon in the hidden part of Frostveil had loved my mother. Had been her

227

best friend. Emilia wouldn't give me up. And the Riis family swore their servants were loyal. The only other person who knew was Clemencia. I refused to believe she'd put me in danger.

My back stiffened. But no, Clemencia hadn't been the *only* other person.

Cunning green eyes and a serpentine smile filled my mind at the memory of Roar admitting he'd known, or at least seriously suspected, I was a Falk. But he was dead.

Right?

"Roar," I whispered, as a kernel of doubt bloomed inside me with the memory of that day in Gersemi Mine. "Vale, you didn't see his body."

Vale snorted. "That shaft was *very* deep. There's no way he could have survived."

"There might be."

Roar was a shifter. What if he'd shifted into some sort of animal that could have broken his fall? Not his normal snow leopard form, but something smaller, with wings. It would not surprise me in the slightest if Roar, master of secrets and twisted truths, had shifter forms no one knew about. I said as much to Vale, and his face paled.

"It's far more likely than our friends betraying us," I added.

"Neve. I really don't think so. I—"

The door to the cottage flew open and a sharp wind gusted inside, and snowflakes dusted the stone ground. Rynni did not come in, though. Rather, she stood at the threshold, three vials of potion in one hand, a poster in the other.

"Care to explain why a wanted royal is in my cottage?"

Vale grabbed *Skelda* from a table she'd been resting upon, ready to cut the healer down if need be.

Rynni shut the door behind her. "Don't bother. I'm not going to hurt her. She's a patient, and my oath to Eirial forbids that I harm a patient." She dragged three fingers down her breastbone in a gesture common among the faithful and nodded at something behind me.

I twisted to find an eight-spoked wheel, the healer's wheel. I'd seen the same symbol on necklaces that the healers wore in the royal infirmary. The wheel was the very symbol of the Goddess of Healing and Gentle Deaths. Woven through the spokes of the wheel were dried vines and flowers. An offering.

"I can't harm *anyone* who isn't harming me," Rynni added. "However, I do require answers."

Vale kept his sword in hand but allowed Rynni to come closer and pass me a vial. The contents looked identical to the other vials and tasted the same as I drank the potion.

"Now, tell me why a Falk princess is in my cottage. One who should be dead?"

"I—I'm not—" My words faltered; the lie unable to escape my lips.

"You can't deny it," Rynni snorted. "Even if you could, I would not believe you. This looks like you, and there's a written description. Down to that scar on your temple. Seeing as I've seen a lot of your skin, I can say with surety, this is you."

Silence rang through the room, punctuated only by

Caelo's occasional snores and Anna's shifting. How in the world were they still sleeping?

"I gave them a draft for peaceful sleep. They won't wake. Now, answer me." The dragon healer's eyes narrowed. They were slitted, reptilian.

"You're right. That is me," I said. "Though my past was a mystery to me for a long time. I used to be a blood slave."

Her eyes widened. "Well, that sounds like a story. Tell it."

Unless Vale wanted to kill this healer, which seemed in very poor form, seeing as she'd saved me and Caelo and healed Vale, I had no choice. So I swallowed and began my tale.

Once done, I took a breath. I wasn't the only one who looked like they needed one. The healer was gaping and shaking her head at what I'd told her.

"So," I began again. "Will you turn me in?"

She did not answer me but looked at my mate before meeting my eyes again.

"The king would imprison his own son's mate?"

Though I'd told her about myself, I'd neglected to mention anything about Vale's blood connection to Lord Riis. That was his tale to tell when he saw fit.

"The king has a deep hatred for my family," I replied. "Although he has no clue that Vale and I are mates yet. Even if he did, I believe that yes, he'd imprison me. Or kill me."

"That's atrocious."

"King Magnus is not known for being lenient."

"That's not the only thing he's not known for," she

muttered and, after realizing what she said, her hands flew to her mouth. "No offense, Prince Vale."

My mate's lips twitched. He was holding back a laugh. "None taken."

"Many in Vitvik think your father should do more for Winter's Realm," Rynni said, emboldened by Vale's reaction. "Now that I think about it, if your mate is Isolde Falk, who do you plan to side with should things go sour?"

They were already going sour, I wanted to say, but Vale clasped a hand on my shoulder.

"My mate. She's my everything."

Rynni leaned back in her chair, considering what to do.

"We can offer you gold for your silence," Vale said. "I have some now, but I can get more. And we'll glamour Neve before we leave here so that no one will connect her to you."

"Gold is always needed," Rynni said. "But I want something more valuable than gold bears lining my pockets."

"And what's that?" I asked.

"You must have connections with the House of Wisdom in Avaldenn, Prince Vale?"

"I do."

"I want a spot there. To train in the White Tower. For that, I will be silent—more so, I will join you on your journey." The healer's gaze landed on me. "I have no personal relationship with the king, but I believe things could be better. Perhaps you, Isolde, might bring about that change?"

It was bold, what she said. Treasonous. But Rynni did not appear afraid. Maybe she could read me well enough to guess what I intended to do—and she wanted to be on my side.

"I can make that happen," Vale said. "Though not right away. My wife and I still are not sure when we'll return to Avaldenn."

Rynni held up the poster. "Of course, you can't traipse into the capital! Until then, it would be good to have a healer with you, no? As far as I can tell, I've already proven my worth."

"Why do you want to attend lessons in the White Tower?" I asked. "You seem to own a nice business."

Small, but it was clean and comfortable in the cottage. Many would have been content here. I would have.

Rynni snorted. "You're the first person to walk through my door in three weeks. I'm the second-rate healer in the city, but only because of my father's blood. Fae come to me when they have ailments they want to be sure no one would ever learn about. I have no friends here either. Never have, although I grew up in Vitvik."

My heart clenched. She hid her isolation well, but as she spoke, pain filled her eyes.

"An education from the White Tower, though, no one could call me second-rate with that. And who knows? I might stay in Avaldenn where it's more diverse."

"There are no half dragons there," Vale said. "But we are more welcoming in the capital."

She sighed and waved a hand in the air. "My mother is dead, my father . . . Well, he's likely still in the Court of Fire, where I would fit in worse than I do here. I have nothing here and want to train with the best. That's why I wish to go, and I'll take a chance on you to do so."

"You shall join us then," I said, understanding wanting a better life, and seizing it when that possibility came.

For the first time, Rynni smiled, and a new, softer faced person appeared. "We can leave tomorrow night, under the cover of darkness. That will give you plenty of time to rest."

"Excellent idea." Vale held up a finger. "And actually, I've been wondering if Lord Riis owns an establishment in this village?"

"He does. A brothel," Rynni looked at me as she answered, obviously wondering why my mate would be asking for such a thing, and right in front of me too. Offense was not on my mind in the slightest. Lord Riis owned many brothels and taverns. Those, as much as being a lord, were his coin makers.

"I need to get a message to him," Vale said, "and I know Lord Riis's ravens are trained to go between his establishments. Could you, once I write a note, send it from the brothel tonight?"

Rynni laughed dryly. "I'll go, but I'm adding this errand to your tab, Prince Vale."

INTERLUDE
LORD LUCCAN RIIS, HOUSE OF THE ICE SPIDER

L uccan stood with his brothers on the edge of the overflowing throne room, waiting, hoping that whatever the king called them here for so bleeding early in the day had nothing to do with them.

As far as the spymaster's son knew, King Magnus had asked no one other than Lord Leyv Riis questions about the disappearance of Vale and Neve. Luccan's father, an expert at twisting and omitting truths, had assured the king that his spiders were on the task. That they'd soon find Vale.

The only thing Luccan knew for sure was that his friends had gone west, and *something* had happened. Something important enough for Lord Roar to return to court with a metal leg, and his face scarred. Something important enough for the king not to execute the Warden of the West after he'd made the king look like a fool. Something important enough for Luccan's father to have been in endless meetings with King Magnus and his Royal Council.

Since they disappeared through his temporary gateway,

Luccan had returned to Riis Tower many times. Often to see Clemencia, who remained safe at his family home, but also to see if his friends had returned. They had not. Luccan knew that they'd need to travel the long way to come back to the Tower, but even with the ridiculously heavy snows, it shouldn't have taken them *this long* to ride from Guldtown to Riis Tower.

Perhaps they had to walk? It was the only thing that made sense since Luccan was certain that his gateway had worked. He'd not deposited them somewhere random.

He wished he could have forced the gateway into permanent existence. Then they could have returned to safety that same day, and he would have no questions. But Luccan was not yet that skilled in the magic of gatemaking. It had cost him much to create that one gateway in such a hurry. He'd been weakened for a fortnight after and had only recently ridden himself of the dark circles under his eyes.

"Fates, do you think the king is ever going to show?" Arie muttered. "This is a waste of time. I was in the middle of researching"

"Stars forbid you pull your head out of a book for a moment," Thantrel teased.

Arie's jaw set tight. "I've been reading histories, learning about the noble families and their traditional alliances. Might be helpful, don't you think?"

Luccan stiffened. Yes, the histories would be helpful. Especially if Neve came to court. Should she claim the throne in the name of her dead kin, the realm might divide. Then, war.

In contrast to Luccan's reaction, Thantrel shrugged as if he did not care, though he surely understood the serious ramifications of what might come to pass. The youngest Riis brother was as clever as his elder siblings. He simply hid that intelligence in favor of exuding a larger-than-life personality.

Before Luccan could inquire deeper into what Arie found, Princess Saga entered the throne room on the arm of Vidar Virtoris, finally healthy enough to walk about the castle after the attack on the Royal Theater. Vidar's side remained bandaged, and he still walked with a slight limp, but both matters would resolve in time—or so the castle healers assured his family and friends.

Luccan loosed a long breath. The healers had also released Sir Qildor. If Vale did not return in three more days, Luccan would call the cabal members together. He couldn't tell Vidar, Qildor, Duran, or Sian about Neve being a Falk princess. But he could at least suggest the brotherhood send out feelers and search for Vale. That seemed safe enough.

The queen appeared at the door to the throne room, dressed in Aaberg blue and gold. She filed down the long runner to her throne. Prince Rhistel followed a moment later. The rapacious Lord Roar, who looked far too pleased with himself, trailed them, and the king appeared last, his white fur cloak billowing behind him. Two Clawsguards flanked the White Bear, their faces set like stone.

King Magnus did not delay in taking his throne. Lord Roar tucked himself away at the edge of the crowd nearest the golden seats.

What could the Warden of the West have possibly said to get back in King Magnus's good graces? The king had been humiliated when Roar left court right after the king approved his betrothal to Neve—so humiliated that he'd put Neve in great danger and claimed to want Roar's head. And yet, now the Lord of the House of the Snow Leopard stood smugly before the king.

"Today, I have many more matches to set," King Magnus boomed without preamble. "The following subjects approach the thrones."

He rattled off names, those of members of lower houses, some of whom Luccan had spoken to but did not know well. Most did not live in Avaldenn where Luccan spent nearly all his time.

"Hadia Ithamai," King Magnus continued, and that name got Luccan's attention. Which was lucky, as his name was the very next spoken.

Luccan shared a wary glance with his brothers. Before him, fae parted, knowing who he was, allowing the flame-haired lordling to pass with ease. Swallowing, Luccan approached the throne.

Clemencia's sweet face swam through his mind. She had not been born noble, but Luccan didn't care. He hadn't been either. Raised a bastard, Luccan's legitimization came only mere weeks ago. All that mattered to Luccan was that he loved Clemencia, though he hadn't told her as much. He would, though, when the time was right.

The king called three more names, all from houses of the Sacred Eight: Eireann Balik, Baenna Balik, and Njal Virtoris. At the last, Luccan's throat tightened.

Since Sayyida Virtoris's disappearance from court, the king had been *furious* with House Virtoris. Luccan was not sure that things would go well for young Njal, only nineteen turns old and the quietest of the Virtoris clan.

Luccan joined the line up, standing between Baenna and Njal. With everyone present, the king stood.

"The first match of the day is for Lady Baenna Balik. She will wed Lord Arvis of Kethor. Her sister, Lady Eireann Balik, will soon be the lady of House Skuld of Vantalia."

Luccan's lips parted slightly before he corrected his expression into one of approval that the king would expect.

House Arvis and House Skuld were lower banner houses from the midlands and easternlands. These were not marriages that Lord Balik, Warden of the South, would have negotiated for his daughters. King Magnus knew that too. Which meant the king was fishing to see if House Balik, like Houses Armenil and Virtoris, would fight his selection.

But Lord Tadgh Balik was a wise and patient fae. He remained silent, and his daughters also wore masks, though Luccan was sure he could see Baenna's hand trembling. They weren't that close, but they ran in the same circles. And Luccan had always enjoyed the Balik sister's company. He wished he could reach out to comfort Baenna, but not now. Not here.

The king made other matches for those of lesser houses. They appeared, if not quite pleased, not upset by their matches.

"Njal Virtoris." The king turned to the second youngest in the Virtoris family and the last member of that Salt and

Serpent bloodline who was of age to become betrothed. "You will wed Lady Eyja of House Ra."

Luccan averted his eyes. Another midlands match for the Virtoris family. Another lesser noble house that was neither wealthy nor powerful.

Behind, the crowds shifted, and Luccan looked into the masses to find the Lady of Ships staring daggers at the king. Njal might not be a skilled sailor like his older siblings, but the Virtoris family bled saltwater. Lady Virtoris would see House Ra's ranking as the slight, but that they were land-locked was an additional, deeper insult. However, unlike when Sayyida received news of her match to Jarl Salizier, this time, Lady Fayeth Virtoris said nothing. She'd learned, and to that, the king gave an oily smile.

"Only two matches remain." The king turned his gaze on Luccan.

He rolled back his shoulders, knowing that no matter what King Magnus said, Luccan would not like the outcome. He would not like any name that did not belong to Clemencia of Guldtown.

"Lord Luccan Riis, you will wed none other than the stunning Lady Hadia Ithamai."

Luccan's stomach tightened. Stars, it could not have been worse.

Hadia was of the Sacred Eight, which most fae likely considered a great blessing for the House of Riis—but the Ithamai family were lawful in the extreme.

By the dead gods, Luccan had been brought up in a brothel, and his brother took *great* pleasure in illegal gambling! He himself was a bleeding gatemaker! Luccan's

240

power was illegal save for when used at the king's will, which he did not intend to do.

But most importantly, Luccan did not enjoy the company of *anyone* in House Ithamai. So while he bowed his head, he was already planning a way to get out of this.

The plan halted abruptly when the king cleared his throat. "Lord Vidar Virtoris, would you approach?"

Luccan blinked, as his friend, Sayyida's older brother and the heir to House Virtoris, stepped out of the front of the crowd and approached the throne.

"My king?" Vidar appeared as confused as Luccan.

"Considering your sister's refusal to accept her betrothal as ordered by the Crown, I can no longer accept you as a husband for my only daughter."

The crowd gasped, and Luccan's breath stilled in his chest. He cut a glance at Saga. Tears had formed in her eyes.

"King Magnus," Vidar spoke as if he could not believe what was happening. "I apologize for my sister's actions, but Saga and I—"

"*Princess* Saga is no longer any of your concern," the king interrupted. "From this day forward, my daughter is betrothed to Lord Roar Lisika."

"My king," Vidar's voice broke as he spoke. "I understand your wishes. Might I take my leave?"

The king released him, and to no one's shock at all, Lady Fayeth Virtoris stomped out of the throne room after her son and heir. No one stopped her. A smart choice. The Lady of Ships looked ready to call her formidable armada to war. Poor Njal had to remain behind, his brown cheeks red as the king took his throne again.

Luccan expected to be dismissed, but instead, the king waved away those standing before him, directing them back into the crowd.

"Now that the Courting Festival business is done for the day," King Magnus said, "Clawsguards, show in the criminals."

"Duran," he whispered as the door to the throne room opened, and knights shoved his friend inside.

The dwarf, a part of the cabal and lärling at the House of Wisdom, caught Luccan's eyes, shook his head so minutely that Luccan was sure most missed the gesture. Duran's misshapen hands were bound by manacles and shackles ringed his ankles with just enough chain between them so that he could walk.

Luccan hadn't talked to Duran since that night in the Warmsnap Tavern. The night Vale had gotten drunk because Neve had been acting indifferent towards him. Duran had seemed odd that night. But a criminal? There had to be a mistake.

Deciding not to return to the back where his brothers waited, Luccan slipped into the front of the crowd, determined to hear what was said about Duran Urgi, hoping that the dwarf's father, a Master Smith working at the castle, was not present to watch.

A soldier shoved Duran toward the base of the thrones, where the dwarf knelt, and looked up at the king. Wisely, he said nothing.

"Duran Urgi, is it?" King Magnus asked.

As if Duran had not grown up playing with Vale in the castle yard and the dwarf's father did not make the best *zuprian* steel weapons in all of Avaldenn. Of which, the king owned plenty.

"It is, my king." Duran bowed his head.

"You've been caught brewing Liar's Salvation. Do you deny it?"

"I—no, my king." The words sounded strangled coming out of Duran's throat.

"You brewed it for Princess Neve, did you not?"

Murmurs washed through the room.

"I did."

Bleeding skies. Why didn't Vale mention this?

"A clear admission. That's all I required," the king said, then with a wave of his hand, he spoke to his guards. "Take this male to the dungeons. Lock him up."

Duran cried out, but he was small and quickly carried from the room. Before the doors shut behind, King Magnus waved a hand at the guards at the door. They motioned outside, and a moment later, another unforeseen event occurred.

A vampire—chained and sedated, judging by how he moved—shuffled into the room with an escort of ten guards. The red rose choked with thorns on the vampire's chest declared him as a Red Assassin, and the crowd acted accordingly. Many pushed back.

"Do not move. He will not harm you." King Magnus stood again and, from beneath his thick cloak, the White Bear pulled out a stake and descended the steps leading to the thrones.

"This *parasitic creature*, and more like him, have haunted our city—our kingdom—long enough. But I wonder, do you all understand why the vampires are here?"

No one answered, the silence deafening, and likely exactly what the king wanted.

"The deaths of so many fae by vampire hands is Princess Neve's fault." King Magnus did not raise his voice as he closed in on the bloodsucker and yet it carried throughout the cavernous room. "They're here for her, and if I could find her, I'd give her over to save you all."

Sharp gasps arose. Neve was beloved by many, but Luccan was not sure that love would last long after today. That she'd been drinking Liar's Salvation was bad enough, but to be the reason vampires ran about the city, killing fae? No one would excuse that.

"You may think me cruel," King Magnus played to the crowd as he stopped before the vampire. He twirled the stake in his hand. The vampire was so drugged that the creature stared at the king, unseeing, unthinking, not caring that his death stood before him.

"But you do not know the real Princess Neve. Not as I do. Lord Roar has returned and told me much of the princess—you'll remember they were engaged before she ensnared my son? Well, the princess told Lord Roar who she is. Her *true* name."

Like a flash, the king raised the stake and struck. Sounds of surprise erupted from the crowd as the vampire fell to the ground, dead, soon to turn to ash.

King Magnus turned back to his people. "Princess Neve

has been hiding her true self, her past. Her lineage of cruelty, some might say *madness*."

Luccan's heart hammered in his chest. No! How did he learn the truth? How had Roar?

"Princess Neve is none other than the daughter of the Cruel and Cold King, Harald Falk. She is Isolde Falk, and, I believe, the reason the rebels continue attacking our cities, towns, and villages!" The king's voice rose and in response, panic, fear, and a million other emotions crossed the faces in the room.

Luccan caught Saga burst into fresh tears, saw Prince Rhistel smirk, saw Queen Inga remain frozen, ever an unreadable mask on her face.

"Princess Isolde Falk is the reason the vampires are in our kingdom. Why they're hunting and killing and drinking fae blood." The king repeated his previous claims as he tossed the stake to the ground. "She is a liar and a menace in *all ways*. She has stolen slaves from Lord Roar and, he believes, will try to convince the rest to fight for her! I have already sent notices to the countryside, sent flyers into towns and villages. They are being put up in cities as we speak." King Magnus huffed out a long breath and thick frost crawled over the floor from where he stood. People increased their distance, frightened, and rightfully so, by their king's magic. "So I say this to you all. If you have information on the pretender, Isolde Falk, the Slave Queen, and you bring it forth, you will be rewarded."

Without another word, he stomped out of the throne room.

The fae in the room, all noble, remained still, stunned,

but Luccan was already scanning the crowd, searching for his father.

He found him a moment later, his great height approaching the thrones. Luccan rushed to intercept him and grabbed his father by the hand.

"No mention of them here," Leyv Riis warned, low enough for others not to hear.

"I wasn't going to, but Father, can you free Duran?"

Lord Riis's eyes widened almost imperceptibly. "I'm not sure."

"Please, try. Bring him to safety, and I'll hide him. He's a friend."

Lord Riis shot a glance to the thrones where the princess bawled, Prince Rhistel still lounged as if nothing at all had happened, and Queen Inga remained still as a statue.

"I'll do my best, Luccan. Now," he ducked his head, moved his lips to Luccan's ear, "leave Frostveil. Go home and take your brothers. Say nothing to anyone who is not our blood. Do you understand?"

"Understood." Luccan bowed his head.

He left his father, and barely noticed when Queen Inga descended the throne and spoke to the Lord of Tongues. The throne room was almost empty, save for Luccan's brothers, who remained by the back wall, waiting for him.

"Thantrel, Arie, we need to leave right away."

Night fell. The moon rose. The fae of Avaldenn quieted.

And still the Riis brothers waited for word from their

father. The king's spymaster had told his sons to leave Frostveil Castle, to return to Luccan's home in Lordling Land, but Leyv Riis had not done the same.

Luccan hoped that was a good sign for Duran, though it was likely the king had kept his father in meetings all day. King Magnus must believe the Lord of Tongues and his intricate network of informants were crucial to finding Neve.

Little did the king know that Lord Riis had helped to get both Neve and Vale out of the city. He'd housed them, fed them, and allowed Neve the precious time to work through her past.

Vale too, Luccan supposed. He wondered how Vale was fairing with Neve. It was clear the Warrior Bear was in love with the female.

Luccan shook his head. Vale had been stormy when he learned the news that he and Neve were related by Falk blood, but then, somehow, they'd worked things out. Luccan didn't understand it and had asked his father if it had anything to do with the spymaster's private meeting with Vale. Lord Riis had only said that if Vale wished for Luccan to hear what they'd spoken of, he'd tell Luccan directly. That had been that.

"Any word?" Arie entered the sitting room.

"None. Are you taking a break from studying?"

"In a way." Arie cleared his throat. "I was doing a bit more research on Neve's family."

"Do I have many books on them?"

"No. I took the gateway to the castle and brought more books back."

Their family castle in Bitra, a city in the east of Winter's Realm, had once belonged to House Skau—Neve's mother's house. Luccan wondered if the texts their father had on hand were from that time too.

"What did you find?"

"Not much that I had not already read," Arie said. "Though there was one matter pertaining to—"

"Luccan! Arie! Thantrel!" Their father's voice boomed from the front of the home and the brothers leapt to their feet and ran to meet him.

When Luccan swept into the foyer, he exhaled. Duran stood there, dirty and pulling a rough spun hood down to reveal his face. The trembling dwarf's strawberry blond hair flew every which way.

"You're safe." Luccan went to his friend and laid a careful hand on his back, hoping to calm Duran. "Thank the Fates."

"Thanks to you and your father," Duran whispered, his voice raspy.

Luccan heard Thantrel enter the foyer. For once, the youngest Riis said nothing, just joined the family and studied Duran for any sign of injury.

"How did you get him out, Father?" Luccan asked.

"Best that you remain in the dark on that score."

He hated when his father said such things but had learned not to argue. When he set his mind to keeping a secret, Lord Leyv Riis did not budge.

Duran turned to the Lord of Tongues. "I wish I could give you something in thanks, but I'm afraid I have no money and little leverage at the moment. My father could make you a *zuprian* steel sword, but—"

"That's unnecessary, Duran," Lord Riis stopped him. "I ask for nothing but your silence that I was the one to free you. And that my sons will help you escape Avaldenn."

"Of course." Duran said nothing more, and Luccan suspected the studious lärling was fighting shock. Though part of the cabal, Duran contributed through scholarly means and opted out of the more adventurous activities the others relished.

"On our way here, I saw these." Lord Riis held up one of the posters the king had shown them earlier. Upon further inspection, Luccan saw that the poster also named Neve as 'the Slave Queen'. "They're all over the city."

"No posters lined the streets when we came here," Arie confirmed. "So they must have put them up this afternoon."

Lord Riis huffed out a breath. "Let us get a drink. Other, more important things have happened since you left Frostveil Castle, and we have much to discuss."

They moved back into the sitting room, but instead of sitting, Luccan went right to the bar and poured his father a small glass of Dragon Fire.

"Me too," Thantrel shouted from where he lounged, one leg thrown over the arm of the chair, close to the fire. Across from Than, Duran perched, looking anxious in Luccan's home, though Duran had been here many times.

"Get it yourself." Luccan held up the glass he had poured for Father. "My hands are full."

Air swirled, and the glass lifted from his hand on a bed

of air to travel to the Head of House Riis. Luccan hid his amusement. Though it was the weakest of Thantrel's powers, air magic was dead useful at times.

Luccan turned to pour two more glasses. Thantrel lifted those as well and distributed them to Arie and Duran. The dwarf took the elegant glass in his misshapen hands and sipped, pulling a face as he did so.

Luccan carried the last two glasses back, handed one to Thantrel and took the final for himself, settling into a seat next to Arie.

"What happened, Father?" Arie asked.

"The Courting Festival should be long over. King Magnus has dragged it out," Lord Riis said and paused to sip his drink. "There's a reason for that. One Vale told me before he left."

He explained to his sons that King Magnus was searching for a lost Hallow—the Ice Scepter. The king believed a noble house possessed it, and had thought that house would bring it to Avaldenn, if only so the Crown Drassil growing in the heart of the castle could bless the Hallow. That had not happened. It seemed that no one was in possession of the Hallow, a fact that, Lord Riis was sure, was infuriating the king.

"He thought *we* had it?" Arie asked in the middle of the story.

"He did," their father replied. "Vale, who was aware of the plan all along, did not. Hence, he told me. Smart lad, as only those with Winter's blood can wield it."

Their house, so newly raised in society, had not a drop of Winter's blood. On the back of that revelation came another. The idea of finding the Ice Scepter had to be part of the reason Vale had acted so oddly of late.

"I believe the king was setting the poor matches partly to punish those he did not agree with," Leyv Riis continued, "and partly to force the holder of the Ice Scepter's hand. After all, with Winter's magic in upheaval, he was not wrong to believe that the holder would bring the Scepter to court and ask for a blessing before the Crown Drassil."

"Wouldn't that establish them as royal?" Luccan asked, trying his best to assimilate the information his father had known for weeks.

"It is one sign of legitimacy." Lord Riis gave a nod. "However, now that Neve's truth is out, whoever holds the Ice Scepter will have another person to contend with."

"You *all* knew about her?" Duran's voice was small as he stared at the group. "She's really a Falk?"

"Are you surprised?" Thantrel asked, olive eyes shrewd. "You made the Liar's Salvation for her. Didn't you ask what it was for?"

"I tried, but they wouldn't tell me. Vale asked for a favor, and I granted it. He's a friend."

And that was that. Dwarves were loyal down to their bones.

"She is a Falk. Born Isolde Falk, as the king said." Lord Riis drank the last of his Dragon Fire and set the glass down. "Now that the king knows who she is, though, he will hunt her. Vale and Neve cannot return to Avaldenn, and I wish for you, my sons, to leave as well."

Luccan gaped, and his brothers mirrored his expression.

"Father, the king will be furious if we leave. And we cannot leave you here too," Arie countered.

"I will take care of myself," Lord Riis replied. "Besides, you will not be the only ones leaving."

"Of course we're taking Duran," Luccan said.

"Him yes." The Lord of Tongues cleared his throat. "But my spiders tell me that other houses are leaving Avaldenn as we speak. The Virtoris family sailed home after the scene in the throne room. I have heard whispers that the Armenils and Baliks plan to move tonight. The Courting Festival has gone on too long, and it has not gone their way. Many great houses are angry with the king, and more pressing, they do not wish for their families to be kept here if Neve claims the throne and Magnus declares war. That, more than anything, tells me of their loyalties, which is something we can use."

"You didn't mention their leaving to the king?" Thantrel asked.

"Not until you all are gone and safe." The spymaster arched an eyebrow. He knew full well that when they left, they'd not be using the city gates, but the king did not and the spymaster wanted his sons far from harm's way as quickly as possible. With the potential for war upon them, keeping Luccan's gateways a secret had become more important than ever. "And then there is the matter that if Neve is to claim her title, she will need allies. Some of those houses might be sympathetic to her. Specifically, the Great House of the North. Queen Revna's mother was an Armenil."

"The pack endures," Luccan spoke the house words of

the far north, a way of saying that if the Armenils stuck together, they'd prevail. In the long history of the great house, those words had always been true.

"And where the Armenils ally, the Baliks are likely to follow," Arie whispered. "They're so connected."

"Yes," Lord Riis agreed. "As for House Virtoris, I believe that Lady Fayeth would not take much convincing to side with Princess Neve. Not after the disrespect that King Magnus has shown her children. They are likely the safest from war as well—with their impressive armada to protect their island, no one will attempt to sail their way."

"A war of houses is on the horizon then," Thantrel said, his tone hollow.

"I fear so, and we have already claimed our side." Lord Riis leaned forward and placed his elbows on his knees. "We are all in agreement there, my sons?"

No one spoke, and though he believed in what his father said, Luccan's heart pounded in his chest. *War.* They'd all been too young—or in the case of Thantrel, not even born —during the White Bear's Rebellion.

And yet, there was no way Luccan would side with King Magnus over Vale.

"For Vale and Neve," he said, and his brothers echoed him, Duran's voice joining in with devotion.

"Very good." Lord Riis stood and wiped his hands on his trousers. "I wish for you to gather weapons, whatever effects are most important to you, and leave for Riis Tower now. From there, you will take Clemencia with you—she is too associated with Princess Neve to remain safe, and join Prince Vale, Neve, Sir Caelo, and Anna."

Luccan's eyebrows knitted together. "Wouldn't it be smarter to wait until they return to our Tower? Surely they will, if only to rest after their travels."

Lord Riis gave a sly smile. "I would not wish for them to come so close to Staghorn Castle. House Vagle will ally with King Magnus, so we must intercept Neve long before she arrives at the Tower and keep her safe."

"But *how?*" Luccan was a gatemaker, and given enough time, might make a gateway to anywhere. That was useless, though, if he did not know where the others were.

"This map will tell you where they are." Lord Riis pulled a piece of parchment from his pocket. "Right now, they're in Vitvik. Move quickly, using the gateways you've already established, Luccan. I will join you when I can."

Luccan ignored the utter look of shock on Duran's face when his father admitted he was a gatemaker. He took the parchment and opened it.

On the map of Winter's Realm, a dot of red that looked like blood glowed in Vitvik. Three other dots glowed in Avaldenn. Small names hovered above the dots. Vale's was in Vitvik.

"And these are *us?*" Luccan pointed to the dots in Avaldenn, clearly labeled with his name and that of his brothers'.

"Obviously," Lord Riis said. "I gave Vale a potion with his wine while he was in Riis Tower. One that would allow me to follow his progress. He disappeared for a time in the mountains of the southwest, which I cannot explain; however, he reappeared a couple of days ago."

"And you've given us the potion at some point," Arie muttered, annoyed.

"You're my sons, I have a right to know where you are. Some of you needed supervision." His lips curled slightly as he cast a side glance at Thantrel.

"I don't see twenty other dots on the map," Arie shot back. "And the Fates know you have a few daughters that should be monitored at all times."

Luccan bit back a laugh, knowing exactly the half-sisters that Arie referred to. Triplets who thrived on a touch of chaos. The sisters had been terrorizing the city of Grindavik practically since the day they'd emerged kicking and screaming from the womb.

"The mothers of my other children would not allow my monitoring," Lord Riis replied. "I can respect that, and all that matters is that you are safe, and you can find Vale."

"But how will you find us if we take this?" Luccan asked.

"I'm the spymaster for a reason, son. Trust, I *will* find you."

Luccan folded the parchment back up and stood. "Then I suppose we should get going. Duran, come with me. I'll get you a weapon and clothing. Brothers, meet me downstairs when you're ready."

The brothers Riis and Duran left the spymaster in the sitting room, standing before the fire, staring at the flames.

CHAPTER 18
VALE

Rynni handed another potion to Caelo. "Drink this."
That had to have been the fifth glass he'd downed in an hour. Was it a bad sign?

Darkness approached, and we'd been planning our exit from Vitvik all day, packing up items we'd need for the ride north. For Rynni, that meant packing the most precious items in her life. But now I was of a split mind about what to do. Should we leave so that no one discovered Neve or stay here so that Caelo could continue to rest and recover?

"Do you think we should stay another night?" I nodded to my best friend.

Neve's eyebrows shot up, but Rynni answered before my mate interrogated my line of thought.

"The wounds are sealed, but are not healed," Rynni said. "Sir Caelo went through a lot. Princess Neve too, however, I think they can both handle the journey if we go slowly."

"I feel well enough," Neve said. "You were injured too, Vale."

"Minor injuries." I'd dealt with much worse than I'd endured, but despite fighting side by side for many turns, I'd never seen Caelo so beat up. And Neve had lost an astounding amount of blood. During the ride to Vitvik, her face had been so pale, I'd worried the Fates would cut her life thread at any moment.

"If we go slow, the knight can ride," Rynni repeated. "Which I'd rather do. I ran many errands today that I'm sure garnered notice from my neighbors—not to mention last night."

She'd gone to another healer's establishment and one of Lord Riis's brothels for us.

"Those errands might draw attention to my leaving, our leaving, and I'd rather not others notice me in the company of a Falk princess."

If only Caelo could glamour us.

But that was out of the question. Caelo might be well enough to walk and ride, but he was magically depleted. It would take days of rest and eating and more healing arts from Rynni before Caelo should push himself. When we left Vitvik, it would be with thick hoods covering our faces as our only disguises.

"If you're a dragon, why can't we fly out of here and ride on your back?" Anna asked.

I cringed when Rynni stiffened. Anna likely did not know that Rynni would see the question as rude.

"I can shift and can carry you all," Rynni said, her tone sour. "But I cannot breathe fire well or have any other means of defending myself besides my teeth and claws, which I'd rather not use because that would mean close combat. I've spent my turns healing, and fighting is not a strength of mine. Considering *who* would be riding on my back, *and* the attention a dragon would draw in this kingdom, I believe this course of action to be unwise. That is, unless one of you is an illusionist and could mask me from those on the ground?"

"None of us," I replied. "Not to mention that with you flying, we would be less able to defend or fight from her back. Overall, I agree with Rynni."

"I'm still learning." Anna held up her hands.

"I'd tell you if I couldn't make it on horseback," Caelo repeated, clearly irritated. "We're not that far from Riis Tower."

Normally, I'd say we could cut close to the lake and ride the horses hard, completing such a journey in two days, but with his injuries and a new fall of snow, it was sure to be a three-or four-day ride.

"Very well," I said, content to drop the subject. "I—"

A knock came. Rynni froze, her face paling as she stared at the door. "Who could that be?"

"There's only one way to find out," Anna replied and stood. "I'll get it. My face isn't the one plastered on all the wanted posters."

"No!" Rynni rushed forward. "Why would I have *a human* in here? All of you need to hide."

I took Neve's hand and the four of us retreated behind a thick curtain, into the back room of the cottage—Rynni's private quarters.

The door to the cottage creaked open.

"Hello?" Rynni said. She sounded unsure, as if she didn't recognize the person at her door.

"Hello. We're here looking for friends."

I jolted, and met first Neve's gaze, then Caelo's.

"Luccan?" I whispered. "It can't be."

"Who are you?" Rynni asked.

"My name is Luccan Riis," the reply came like a balm to an injury. "I believe you may have been the one to send a raven from a *certain someone* to my family's home in the midlands?"

It was a relief to hear my friend's voice—the words of my blood brother, though he did not know that yet—but why in all the nine kingdoms was he here? In the letter, I'd stated we were soon to make our way north. I'd not mentioned Vitvik, but I supposed they could have guessed where the letter had been sent from by the brothel's raven. No matter the reason for them coming, Luccan being here was risky. I wasn't sure I liked it.

"What was that person's name?" Rynni snapped, not giving away that she had sent a note on my behalf.

"Are you always this inhospitable?" another voice asked.

"Thantrel!" Neve scoffed. "Anna, peek and make sure it's them."

Though I found it difficult to believe that this was an elaborate ruse, much was on the line, and these were the oddest of circumstances. My mate was right to be prudent. We pulled open the door slightly, enough for Anna to peek out. She chuckled.

"Oh, it's them!" Anna stepped into the healer's working portion of the cottage.

"What are you doing!" Rynni sputtered.

"They're friends," Anna explained. "Let them in before Thantrel attracts too much attention with all his gold eyeliner and blazing red hair and just *being him*."

"Too late," Arie's voice made me smile.

"No such thing as too much attention," Thantrel retorted as playfully as Anna had jabbed him. Rynni rolled her eyes but opened the door wider for them to shuffle inside.

We continued to wait in the back, lest someone in the street was walking by and could see into the healer's quarters, until my brothers filed in, their flaming red hair a mess from the wind. However, when Clemencia came into view, followed by Duran, my eyebrows pulled together. Clemencia made sense. Luccan adored her, and if there was danger—which I sensed there was—he would not leave her behind. But what was Duran doing here?

The door closed, and we stepped into the business portion of the cottage.

"Clem!" Neve ran to her once lady-in-waiting.

Clemencia curtseyed, but my mate pulled her up and hugged her. "I'm so glad you're safe!"

"And I you, Princess Neve. I mean . . . Neve."

Luccan's face loosened as he took the rest of us in. "Thank the dead gods you're still here." He lifted a finger and gestured to my face, still healing from the orc claws. "What happened to you?"

"We came across a violent band of orcs," I said, and

moved on to what I was more interested in. "I take it that, since you're here, there are posters in Avaldenn about Neve, and you've come to warn us?"

"Posters here too," Luccan replied. "*Everywhere* if what the king says is true." He swallowed. "King Magnus announced her as an enemy to the Crown."

"Called her the Slave Queen," Thantrel said as he leaned against the wall. "You stole Lord Roar's slaves?"

"You have no idea," my mate replied. "Roar didn't just have slaves at his castle. He was using humans in his mines as free labor. Also selling some to the Vampire Kingdom!"

"What!" Arie's eyes went wide. "I can't believe the king overlooked that in making him an advisor."

I stiffened, as did Neve.

"Did you say that the king made Roar an advisor?" Neve spoke slowly.

"When he returned to court with news of you, I expect," Arie replied. "Roar is also betrothed to Saga now, which the princess did not look happy about."

A cold fire spread through me at the idea of my sister marrying my enemy—a faerie who tried to kill my mate, Caelo, and me—but that fire doused when Neve whacked me on the shoulder.

"I had a feeling! Stars, Vale, you should have gone to the bottom of that stupid shaft!"

"I don't see *how* he survived," I murmured. "It was far too deep to survive the fall."

"That's why I'm sure that he had to have shifted into something that saved him," Neve replied.

I took her hand. I'd failed her, but really, did it matter

how Roar survived? He had and now danger came for my mate sooner than we'd hoped. "I'm sorry, my love. I failed you."

She let out a long breath and the tension that bunched up around her shoulders loosened. "No, you didn't. The king would have found out anyway—whether from me claiming my name or . . . apparently, this crazy scenario. I'd have preferred to have the timing on *my* side, and maybe get a leg up on him, but this is our reality." She looked at Luccan. "Fill us in on *everything* that's happened at court."

He pointed to the area where we'd accumulated our supplies. "I will, but were you leaving tonight?"

"As soon as we could," I answered. "We planned on returning to Riis Tower."

"Not now, you're not," Luccan said. "We've left court without permission and traveled via gateway, first to the Tower to get Clemencia, and then to the brothel Father owns in Vitvik."

Right. I'd forgotten that Luccan connected all the Riis properties via gateways. Somehow, I hadn't imagined that meant each of the many taverns and brothels, too, but it was an intelligent move. Useful too.

"I'm sure that our timing will lead the king to suspect us of siding with you, with Neve," Luccan added, "so we're not returning to Avaldenn and none of our holdings will be safe to stay in for long. Save for maybe the castle."

House Skau's old stronghold in the east. Even then, that castle was not as formidable as others belonging to the other seven great houses. If the king suspected Neve of being there, an army could easily infiltrate the city of Bitra.

"We know where we can go, though," Arie interrupted. "We weren't the only ones to leave the capital. Houses Balik, Armenil, and Virtoris left too. We plan on seeking refuge with House Balik—they're far from Avaldenn, heavily fortified, and with Neve's connection to House Armenil, they're likely to be sympathetic. I say we go there."

Yes, the castle of the southlands. It abutted the Ice Tooth Range, which was filled with all sorts of creatures, including frost giants. Due to constant threats, House Balik's home was the most secure castle in the realm. If we were to be safe anywhere, it would be there.

"House Armenil?" Neve asked. "How am I connected to them by anything other than being a friend to Marit?"

Her face fell on her friend's name. Marit Armenil had attended our wedding, and the king had punished her for her loyalty to Neve.

"Revna Skau's mother was an Armenil, so you are a cousin to that family" Arie answered. "And House Armenil and House Balik have blood ties too. They've always been loyal to one another, those great houses of north and south."

"If their entire house has left Avaldenn, Sian and Filip will be in Myrr too," I added. "Allies indeed."

Rynni cleared her throat, commanding the attention of the room. "Not that I'm not *thrilled* that four strange males and a female have arrived unannounced at my home, but with all that's transpired, I think we should get a move on. If you have horses and a place in mind to go, any additional tale can be told just as well on the road, can it not?"

"We can go when the rest of you are ready," Arie said.

"In the meantime, we can help pack. Our horses are waiting outside."

Rynni scowled.

"*In the back*," Arie added. "Thanks to a map our father gave us, we knew we'd find you in this city, but it's not so accurate that it pinpoints homes. We had to ask where the messenger who sent the note to Riis Tower lived. They pointed us in this direction. We figured that, if our friends were still here, discretion would be necessary."

"At least someone *besides me* has some sense."

The dragon-fae healer was right. We were putting her at risk, and in truth, I'd feel far more secure behind castle walls than in a small cottage. Now that the king knew the truth of my mate, I was sure he'd come for her. And when he did, he'd be merciless.

CHAPTER 19

VALE

We rode deep into the night and whiled the hours away by catching everyone up on what had happened in their absence. All secrets, save for my true parentage, had been divulged, and as we set up camp for the night, I could feel that final and most important secret climbing up my throat.

I wished to tell the Riis brothers most of all but Rynni's presence among my group of friends gave me pause.

I glanced at the healer, tending to Caelo as the rest set up our camp for the night. While I trusted the dragon-fae to follow her oath and mend me, my mate, and my best friend, this was different. This was the sort of information that one would profit from. Information that would turn the realm on its head.

It would endanger my mother. My twin, too, though I was of a split mind there.

Back at Frostveil, Rhistel had threatened my mate, tried to force himself upon her, and before all that, he'd hurt me many times. And yet, he was my twin. We'd shared a womb, been born as close as siblings could be, and when we were still young I thought we were destined to be friends for life.

Against all odds, I'd always secretly hoped we'd one day come together and be as we once were as younglings. Outing our secret, however, would destroy him. After that, would there ever be a chance of us reconciling?

In many ways, at many junctures in my life, Rhistel had been a weakness for me. After all, families were complex, and mine was no exception.

If only I could speak to Rhistel first and give him time to choose his fate as I had. That could be enough. That and I'd love to ask him a few questions . . .

I'd been shocked to hear he was not to be betrothed to a Balik lady. Before I left court, that had been King Magnus's plan. Such a change likely meant that the king had decided the great house of the south was untrustworthy. Seeing as the Riis brothers claimed the Baliks had left court, the king seemed to have been correct.

"Prince! Come here, let me look at your injuries!" Rynni shouted through the trees.

I looked at Neve. She was still creating her clever shelters of ice and snow. I'd not seen another fae make them, but those same shelters had saved many humans' lives during our travels south, and they'd keep us alive and as warm as we could be tonight. My mate must have felt me watching her, for she glanced my way and smiled.

No sweat poured down her brow, no appearance of tiring. Despite having ridden for hours, she was fine. No longer affected by our battle with the orcs.

"Don't make me wait. It's rude," Rynni added, her tone riddled with annoyance.

I huffed. The healer might be skilled in her arts, but her bedside manner could use work.

I took a seat on a fallen tree next to the healer. Her eyes, a darker brown than mine, took in my face. "Those wounds are nearly healed. Show me your side and chest."

I pulled off my cloak and began stripping off my many layered shirts. Before we left Vitvik, Rynni had purchased extra clothes for everyone. Now that we were heading to the seat of House Balik, we expected at least a week-long journey, and as Neve was the most wanted fae in the kingdom, we would not stop at inns, so we'd all rely on layering to remain warm.

The cold penetrated my skin. I shivered, thankful there was no wind today. A stroke of luck that we'd needed.

"Hmm." Rynni leaned closer, taking in the wounds that she'd cleaned and sealed. "No tears from riding. That was what I was most worried about, but my work held well on you and Caelo."

"And Neve?"

"She is better off than the both of you. The long sleep and blood regeneration potions did her much good."

"You're finished then?" I itched to pull my shirt back on.

"Apply the balm you carry before bed. I'm done with you for good, unless you hurt yourself again."

I dressed. With my cloak back on, I turned matters to my own thoughts. "Rynni, I have something I wish to talk about."

"Is this the secret you're hiding?"

269

I blinked. "How did you know I had a secret?"

"Most fae do, but yours makes your neck tighten." She chuckled and rubbed her hands together. "I've worked with many bodies, Prince Vale. I can tell when someone is holding something back. It shows in their muscles and posture. The eyes too, though you seem to hide your secret well there. Still, I'm willing to bet my future at the White Tower that you have a secret and it's as large as a frost giant."

Try as large as a kingdom.

"It is. And I wish to share it with the people here, which is why I must ask you to perform an eiðra with me before I share it."

She blinked. "Will the others?"

I'd asked Caelo to do so, but only because at that time, I'd been a complete mess. The precaution had not been necessary. I'd only been trying to soothe myself.

Luccan and Duran were trustworthy members of my cabal, and while I was not as close to Arie and Thantrel, I was sure that once they knew I was a brother, they'd take that secret to the starry halls of the afterworld. Anna and Clemencia were Neve's best friends and harming me meant harming Neve. That alone made me think Anna and Clemencia would never tell.

"I take that as a no," Rynni let out a huff. "Is this a life-or-death secret?"

"It is." I still was not sure what the king would do when he found out—for he would, eventually, find out. To strengthen Neve's claim to the throne, I'd share this secret publicly, but the timing had to be right.

"Why do you think I'd share a dangerous secret when I need you to secure me a spot in the White Tower? If you're dead, I've done all this for nothing." She gestured to the surrounding woods.

"I must insist. I do not know you as well as the others."

For a moment, she was silent, then Rynni reached out her arm. "Do it. I'll swear on the power of the dead goddess Eirial."

Seeing as this healer had no family, her goddess was likely the most precious bond to her.

I took her arm, pulled my power up, and I felt when she did the same, her warmer magic meeting my cold. Half dragon and Winterborn fae.

"On the power of the dead goddess Eirial, and your own magic by extension," I started the vow. "Swear you will say nothing of what I'm about to tell you until I tell you it's safe. You may only speak of it to those in this camp on this night, or your magical essence will be smothered to nothing."

My magic surged, and Rynni tightened as the cold flooded her, but she cleared her throat and lifted her chin as she spoke. "I swear on the dead goddess of healing's power *and* my own that I will keep your secret until you permit otherwise."

As her warmer power rushed over me, an exhale parted my lips. I released, as did she, the bind set.

"So? What is it?" she asked.

"I'll tell you with the rest of them." I wasn't about to tell Rynni before my brothers.

"Fair enough. Let's go then." She stood and stomped through the snow.

Neve leaned against a tree, taking a break from building our shelters for the night. Anna and Clemencia spoke with her, as the males blanketed the horses for the night.

"The prince has something to say," Rynni called out before I could. "Gather round!"

The others did as she said, most of them with looks of interest on their faces. Only Neve and Caelo appeared calm, both likely sensing what I was about to say.

So once everyone came together, I got on with it. "I've been keeping something from most of you. Something I hope will be well received. I ask that you tell no one about this news. Not until I'm ready for the public to find out."

As I'd guessed, the brothers, Anna, and Clemencia nodded vigorously. My heart warmed. Maybe I should have insisted on a binding promise from all of them, but deep down, I knew no one here would betray me.

"Thank you," I said, and then paused. I'd thought about this moment for so long, but not the exact words I'd say. A dozen options ran through my mind.

The simplest explanation struck me as the best. "Back at Riis Tower, Lord Riis pulled me aside and told me he and my mother had an affair in the past. He's my birth father. Rhistel's too, obviously. So, I'm Vale Riis by blood, not Vale Aaberg." My gaze strayed to Luccan. "I hope that's alright?"

Neve let out a snort of a laugh that she covered up, though I barely noticed because the way Luccan's face split

CHAPTER 19

into a smile, and Arie's eyes widened, and Thantrel's face took on a mischievous quality, made my stomach tighten.

I'd been quite certain they'd like this news. But I'd also have been lying if I said that some small part of me worried about it. To have me as a brother—*me and Rhistel*—changed dynamics.

Luccan swept me into a hug so tight it crushed my bones. "Bleeding skies, our father was a scamp, wasn't he? We might need to have a talk with him about keeping it in his trousers!"

I laughed, and Arie and Thantrel joined us. They welcomed me to the family by hugging me and punching me in the shoulder the way brothers did. I cast a glance at Anna and Clemencia, both of whom were smiling. Not a problem.

My attention dragged to the healer. She stood back, lips parted in shock. When she caught my gaze, she inclined her head.

No matter that selling such a secret could change her life for the better, I'd ensured that the price was too high. She'd stay silent.

For now, I got to spend a few hours with my brothers, my truth out among friends.

CHAPTER 20
NEVE

The next day, we traveled east, drawing ever closer to the main road that divided the midlands into the western and eastern portion. Once we hit the King's Road, we'd follow it south to Myrr, where we'd treat with High Lord and the Warden of the Southlands, Tadgh Balik.

So far, the journey had been easy. Happy even. The brothers Riis enjoyed having another sibling, especially seeing as they knew and loved Vale already. Clemencia and Anna continued to bond, which warmed my heart. The two were not so much alike, but they found commonalities and that they were trying meant the stars and the moon to me.

There was only one looming issue—and unfortunately for us, it proved a large one indeed. A storm brewed in the distance, the clouds so gray and foreboding that many times, we debated trying to disguise ourselves so that we could seek shelter in a village.

However, with Caelo's glamour magic still being limited,

and my face posted all over the kingdom, we'd decided against backtracking. Onwards it was. A choice that, with each step, I questioned more.

"Should we stop here and set up camp?" I eyed the clouds for what felt like the thousandth time as we came across a pool fed by a convergence of two small creeks. Nearby, large rocks jutted out of the snow. "Water is available for the horses, and I'll use those rocks as a wall for the shelter I build. Then we could all stay together for the night. If I only have to make one large shelter for us, I can work on walls for the horses too."

Last night, we'd slept in three small ice huts, but if the storm was as savage as I suspected it might be, we'd want everyone together to trap in as much body heat as possible. When the temperatures dropped so much, I was especially worried for Anna.

"It's not even suppertime," Luccan stated the obvious, "if we stop now, we'll lose a lot of travel time."

"Staying in one ice hut would be better," Arie countered, cutting a glance at Anna.

I suspected he wanted to stay near Anna as much as he wanted her to benefit from so much body heat. The pair flirted all day, but at night, Anna slept with Clemencia and Rynni, while the Riis brothers and Duran shared a hut. Only Vale and I slept alone.

"The clouds are moving faster than normal," Duran added. "They could be upon us sooner than we think. I, for one, don't wish to be caught riding in the middle of the storm. I say we do as Neve suggests and stop."

Luccan shrugged, and as no one else spoke a strong

opinion on the matter, we veered toward the pool and dismounted.

Glancing at the clouds again, I shivered. How *did* they move so quickly?

"Begin gathering wood," Vale said. "The storm will make seeing the smoke impossible, so tonight we'll sleep by a fire."

"Thank the fates," Thantrel said. He, more than anyone, disliked not having a fire.

When we traveled with the humans, the fires had been outside the huts, but as Vale said, it would be wise to bring it inside tonight. I'd have to make the shelter strong, with a hole in the top and wake up a couple of times during the night to reinforce the ice, but the work would be worth it.

Others chipped away the pool's ice, gathered water, and unpacked while I studied the protruding rocks abutting one side of the pool. After so many days of creating shelters made of compacted snow and ice, I'd developed a confidence in how best to make them to protect the inhabitants.

"Do you need help digging the snow, Neve?" Clemencia asked, like she always did. Though Clem had small magic, she was so helpful in other ways.

"Not at all." I pointed to the area where I wished to work and twirled my finger. Snow rose in one great scoop, hollowing out the area. I did that ten more times, expanding the base of the shelter until I was certain we'd all fit and then shifted to the right and made a larger dugout for the horses too.

The others were watering the horses and making sure

they ate. The creatures were tired, and I was glad we'd stopped earlier than usual. They deserved a break.

The preliminary work finished, I laced my fingers together and pushed my palms away from me, preparing for the most draining part. My magic began swirling in the air when movement in the forest beyond caught my notice.

Red . . . eyes?

I squinted. The flash of red was gone, but even in its absence, claws raked down my spine. The red had been small and luminous, and I knew one creature who fit that description.

Vampire eyes could turn red. Usually when the bloodsuckers were starving or enraged. But the Red Assassins that came after us in Avaldenn had not been shy to approach. And why should they be? They were highly touted as the best assassins in Isila.

"Neve?" Vale asked from where he worked with the others. "Is something wrong?"

My gaze shifted to find my mate watching me, reins in hand, as he guided a horse away from the stream.

"Someone is in the woods," I replied.

Vale blinked. "This far from civilization?"

"I guess. Their eyes were red, so they stood out."

"We need to scout." He turned, clearly understanding what I did not say. "Caelo and Luccan, Neve saw someone in the woods. Maybe a vampire. Help me look for them?"

"On it!" Luccan handed his reins to Thantrel as Caelo gave his over to Arie.

"Be careful," I warned, as the males gathered their

weapons and entered the woods. If that had been the assassins, they wouldn't aim to kill my mate or his friends, just me. But that didn't mean they would not harm someone who was in the way of them fulfilling their contract.

"We will be," Vale replied, worry plain in his eyes. "You'd better build the shelter quickly, Force. It's colder already. Thantrel and Arie will hold watch while you work."

He was right. The storm approached at an unnatural speed. So, as the cabal members disappeared into the deep woods, I built a shelter to see us through what was sure to be a long night.

"Catch." Luccan tossed a bit of dried meat at Clemencia, as he had twice already.

She opened her mouth and this time, the meat fell right in.

"That's my lady!" Luccan cheered, and Clem's cheeks turned pink with delight.

Next to me, Anna looked happy too, seated by Arie, his cloak covering both her legs and his.

Our evening meal comprised of dried meats and cheese; foods easy to travel with. Now that my belly was full and I was warmer than I'd been all day, I yawned. Last night we'd told stories for hours and hours, but I did not think that was in the nuchi cards tonight.

Outside, the winds howled, and snow fell at a remarkable rate. Everyone raised in Winter's Realm claimed they'd never seen snow fall so fast and thick. The fire we'd huddled around for hours was dimming, but I found I did not worry about the storm raging outside. Not when I was safe in my frozen shelter and around friends.

Vale, Caelo, and Luccan hadn't found a soul around our camp. Not a single footprint in the snow, which a vampire, with all their supernatural strength and speed could not help but make. So it was likely a vampire was not lurking.

My friends had put me seeing red eyes down to being tired, but I disagreed. I was sure I'd seen someone. Maybe something? I didn't know, but as no one had seen the red eyes since, I allowed myself a modicum of relaxation. Whatever it was had clearly moved on.

"I'll wake and reinforce the shelter throughout the night, but I'm exhausted, so whomever is on watch will have to wake me when they think it's needed." I nudged Vale, who had taken it in turns with Thantrel to funnel the smoke out of the shelter.

"Of course," Vale said. "We all need to rest well tonight. I hope to make good headway tomorrow, but with the snow falling, we might be slowed again."

"I'll take first watch," Arie offered.

A rotation was quickly established, and finally, I laid down on my cloak. A moment later, Vale cuddled around me and pulled his larger cloak over the pair of us.

The others laid down too, side by side. Arie sat nearest the door, a cloak and woolen blanket pulled around him as he peered outside.

"Good night everyone," Clemencia called out from where she snuggled with Luccan, her cheeks pink, though I wasn't sure it was from the chill.

A chorus responded, and I wiggled closer to Vale. I closed my eyes, and sleep came like I was falling off a cliff. Exhaustion pulled me deeper and deeper into a void, and I swore I heard whispers.

"You sleep," a voice said as the darkness of sleep closed in around me. *Now, I feast."*

CHAPTER 21
NEVE

P rince Gervais stood before me, his hands bloodied, his fangs dripping red.

"I require a nightcap, wildcat. Come to me. Listen to your master. *Beg me* to drink from you."

Unable to stop myself, I moved forward. Metal clanged nearby, and one glance down told me why. Not only was I wearing a familiar red collar, but shackles bound my ankles.

My muscles tightened. I was the prince's slave—sold to him. I'd never escaped. I'd never been free.

The cold of the vampire's palm against my shoulder made me shudder as he pulled me close, brought his lips to my neck, and then his teeth slid in—

Delicious. Something sweeter this time.

I barely had time to hear the voice—not Prince Gervais's voice, but a deeper, raspier one—when the scene changed.

"What in the stars?" I breathed, again looking down at my feet. No shackles. No collar. No vampire prince.

"Of course there wasn't," I assured myself, though my heart still raced. To be back there, captive, a slave—I could imagine nothing worse. "I killed him."

"Killed who?"

I turned and found Vale standing at the entrance to this room, *Skelda* hanging off his hip. Sweat glistened on his face as though he'd returned from training. Only then did I realize we were back at Frostveil. In his suite.

"Vale, why are we here?" I asked.

"This is our home. Your castle." He came closer. "Don't you remember?" His lips twitched with amusement.

"My castle . . ." I trailed off, searching the room again and this time seeing that it was different. Similar, but not exactly the same. Paintings of the Falks hung on the wall. A crown heavy with amethysts and diamonds sat in a case.

Mine?

Before I voiced such a question, however, Vale stepped before me, tilted my chin up, and his lips crashed into mine. I moaned, the sensation so heady, so electric.

Calloused but gentle hands roamed my backside, and only then did I notice I was wearing very little.

Vale cupped my rear, lifted, and carried me to the large bed we'd shared in his room. He set me down and pressed my hands above my head. His hardness pushed into my core, and my breath became tighter, more needy.

"Tell me what you want," Vale murmured. "Anything you want, wife, I'll give it."

Heat flushed my cheeks.

Now something with a bite.

The bed disappeared, and I found myself in the Royal Theater. All around me, fae ran and screamed. I whirled around looking for Vale, but he was in the air, sword swinging.

It was the night of the rebel attack. No sooner had I realized that than the female with ice-blue eyes and dark hair rose from below. Arrow pointed at me, her wings fluttering, she sneered.

"You thought you got away!" The arrow flew, sank into my chest.

I let out a scream, and my eyes fluttered open. Sleep still clung to me, but I was aware enough to know that I'd been dreaming. Feeling around for Vale, I grasped only cold air. I wasn't lying down anymore. Nor on the ground. My heart leapt.

Someone held me and judging by the jostling, they seemed to be running? Blazing sky, every step they took sent sharp pangs of pain through my head. Through the splitting headache, I blinked, looked up, and met a pair of ice-blue eyes.

I jerked as a faerie I feared, the same one who shot me in my dream, stared down at me. "I should have let the Dream Eater have you!"

"Wha—" the word caught in my throat as a voice hidden in my subconscious rose.

Come back to me. All of you come back! I'll eat you all. Drain your hopes, your life!

That voice was the one that haunted my sleep.

"No!" I screamed as a tug, something familiar but also savage, ripped into my mind.

"Fight it! Once he has control, you have to fight your way back!" the fae carrying me screamed, but it was no use.

But the other voice gripped me in a way that I'd never experienced. Above, the faerie loosed a string of curses, and kept running as darkness pulled me under again.

INTERLUDE

LORD LEYV RIIS, LORD OF TONGUES, HOUSE OF THE ICE SPIDER

The Crown Drassil's leaves swayed in the winds blowing in off the Shivering Sea, and Lord Leyv Riis pulled his overpriced bandicota fur cloak tighter around his shoulders.

Though leaves danced above, many littered the snow at the spymaster's feet. A bad omen for the future. One fae willfully turned away from. No one at court dared to bring up the fact that all Drassils were losing leaves at a worrying rate. They did not speak their concerns to the Grand Staret or the eldest Vishkus at the House of Wisdom either.

But the Lord of Tongues' spiders heard what those in the great houses did not say in polite company. All the Drassils planted on noble land were long in the dying. His own Drassil, in a protected grove near Eruhall, what used to be the castle of House Skau, was also in dire straits. And as Leyv was not the old blood of Winter, but an upstart house, he could not help his own tree as often as he'd like to. Rather he required bringing in a noble with the ancient blood of kings and queens flowing through them to enliven the tree.

Perhaps some of the wild holy trees were in a bad way too, though with other matters being at the forefront of his mind, the spymaster had sent no one out to check.

"Sorry I'm late."

The voice of the female he'd loved all his life flitted through the courtyard. Leyv turned and took in Inga.

"I was lost in my thoughts."

Her lips curled. It was a smile she gave only to him and her children, and he cherished every single one. "I hope you're ready to consider a bit more, for I have news."

His head tilted to the side. He'd called the queen here to discuss what was happening with Vale—and propose their next move. To, hopefully, push her into acting. But the way she spoke told him that whatever she wished to share was indeed important.

He nodded beyond her, to the entrance to the courtyard, where the queen's Clawsguards might stand. "Alone?"

"I sent them away for privacy in my prayer." She shrugged. "They obliged as easily as ever."

No surprise there. Inga Aaberg, née Vagle was the most powerful mind reader—and secret whisperer—in the kingdom. She'd overheard many times others thinking about how she unnerved them. How they felt she was hiding something.

They were all right, of course. Only Leyv's and Inga's family, and not even all of them, knew of the queen's true powers. How her magic made her a silent weapon, and one of the most powerful creatures in the realm.

Inga joined him before the tree. They allowed the briefest brushing of hands, nothing more, as anyone could walk into the courtyard at any time. Outside their private quarters, the pair had to proceed with caution.

"What did you wish to tell me?" the spymaster asked.

"Magnus has left Avaldenn with Lord Lisika and a retinue of six Clawsguards. Just now."

"Where? And why?"

He had held a meeting with the king, Prince Rhistel, Lord Roar, Lady Qiren, Lady Ithamai, and selected jarls just that morning. The king had called his banners and made sure that the faithful great houses were amassing their armies. He was preparing to strike the moment Neve showed her face. Magnus was already paranoid that Neve had gathered an army.

He was wrong, but if Lord Riis's sons had done their jobs correctly, Neve and Vale would already be on their way south. They'd treat with House Balik, and after all that had transpired in the Courting Festival, Leyv believed Neve would soon begin building her army.

He intended to add his soldiers to her cause too, when the time was right, and the young hawk recognized the fullness of her power.

"He wouldn't say and did not allow me close enough to learn."

So the king had wished to keep his plans a secret from his wife, not allowing her to touch him and read his intentions.

"It must have been based on something Lord Roar said, though, as he's traveling with the king. More importantly, they're traveling on gryphons—my own father's racing stock. They're the fastest in the kingdom."

A gryphon's aerial speed was unmatched. And their stamina was second only to pegasi, which were far more rare. If the king took gryphons, he wished to get somewhere far away, and he wished to do so quickly.

"They flew southwest. Any idea?" Inga looked up at Leyv.

Anguish simmered in her blue eyes. Eyes that had entranced him when he was but a youngling being dragged to his liege lord's castle with his mother. Leyv fell in love with Inga before he'd known the true meaning of the word.

"Last I heard, Vale was in Vitvik, which is that direction. However, that was days ago. I doubt they're still there."

"What if they are?"

"Vale loves Neve. You should have seen him when he thought they were related. It destroyed him, hence why I told him the truth. He won't let her go, Inga, I'm sure of it."

She did not look surprised. "I expect not. He's much like his father in that way. Never lets go."

Lord Riis smiled softly, happy to have passed down something to his son. If it was his steadfast love for a female who returned his affections, all the better. "Not unless the object of his desire wishes."

"She doesn't," Inga said with a sigh. "They fell in love before they knew they were doing so."

"Now that the king is gone, what of the Courting Festival?"

Inga laughed. "It's already fallen apart. My husband has

gotten a few alliances from it, but whatever is in the south seems to have captured his full attention."

Silence hung between them before Lord Riis whispered, "We cannot let him harm Vale or Neve."

"No, it's time to do what we should have done many turns ago."

So she was on the same page as him. He should have known. After all, Inga was the only reason Leyv had been able to free Duran from the dungeon. She wouldn't have bothered if she did not see the threads of fate weaving through the tapestry.

"You'll speak to Rhistel?"

"Do you think it unwise?"

"Rather the opposite," he replied. "I can see Vale coming out with the truth to support Neve's legitimacy. And I have to say that if she can bring Winter's Realm out of the long night we're suffering, I am for a new ruler."

"As am I," Inga replied. "I tire of Magnus's foot on my neck. If he is gone, I'll give it all up."

She'd said as much before, but now that Magnus might fall and with it, his ability to tell the realm Inga's secrets, Leyv burned with a hope he'd never allowed himself to feel before.

Her love was all that he'd wanted his entire life. He'd searched for a replacement in countless other females, but never been satisfied. Never been able to replace her. Finally, he'd stopped his dalliances, but not before fathering a small army of bastards, all of whom he loved, even if he could not have the relationships he wished with each of them.

"Shall I come with you to tell Rhistel about us?"

Inga swallowed. "I'd like you nearby, but this is something I must do alone. I've always wanted to spare my children pain. It's the reason I've done everything I have, and with you there . . . Well, Rhistel might not like that."

Lord Riis's heart sank with the truth. He'd always gotten on better with Vale. The younger of the twins had been, and still was, more open to a relationship. In truth, had Rhistel ever wanted to spend quality time together, Lord Riis believed that they would have a lot in common.

They were both thinkers, manipulators. Of course, with Rhistel's whispering magic, he could get whatever he wished, not that Leyv would ever say as much. No one, save for Inga, was aware that Lord Riis knew about Rhistel's powers. He'd never put his son in danger by speaking of them.

Inga turned to him. "I saw some of the Falk children die. I regret that with all my heart. I regret that, when I was young, I was careless, and Magnus was able to use my weakness against me." She sniffed, the slightest sign of emotion that hid a mountain of regret. "If war comes, I will not watch my children, not our sons or Saga, suffer the same."

"Will you tell Saga about us, too, then?"

Lord Riis wasn't against it. As a seer whose powers developed by the day, Saga might have a vision pertaining to them at any moment. Thus far, she had not. Or if she had, she'd kept it to herself.

"I'm not sure. Rhistel first. He deserves that much." Inga took a step forward, touched the tree. "If you wish to watch, go to my waiting chamber. I'll be there soon."

"I'll be watching," he assured her. "Good luck, Inga."

294

She bowed her head before the Crown Drassil in prayer.

Through the lattice that would have hidden a lady-in-waiting from view but kept her close enough for the queen to call upon her, Lord Riis watched Inga wait.

While Inga often lamented loudly that she could not keep a lady-in-waiting for more than a few moons, both of them privately realized it was a boon for them. With no highborn lady waiting to attend to the queen's whims, Lord Riis had often used this entrance to sneak into her quarters undetected and see Queen Inga.

Or, on a day such as this one, he could watch Inga tell their oldest son a great secret. Perhaps if it went well, Inga would call for him to reveal himself. His heart squeezed at the idea as a knock came at the queen's door.

"Enter," Inga called out, seated on a settee by the fire. Ever clever, she'd asked for wine to be brought to her quarters.

The heir to Winter's Realm appeared, dressed in Aaberg blue and gold, dark smudges on the fingertips of the ice-spider silk gloves he wore. One black smudge of ink streaked across his cheek.

Leyv eyed the gloves that protected the heir from inadvertent use of his magic. They were one of the few things Lord Riis had been able to give his blood son over the turns. Unless you were brave enough to steal from or bargain with the giant spiders, or you had the right connections, ice spider silk was nearly impossible to come by.

Being from a wealthy merchant family that sourced only the finest materials, Lord Riis had the necessary connections.

"You called, Mother?" Before she answered, Rhistel gestured to the door as he shut it. "Where is your guard? In times such as these, you should have two with you."

"I required privacy and therefore took it." The queen arched an eyebrow. "I might say the same to you. Where are your guards?"

Rhistel crossed the room. Inga poured him a goblet of wine, which their son took with grace as he sat in an armchair closest to the fire.

"They're not allowed around me during my studies, so I also relieved them of their duties. What is so important that we need to speak now?"

"What were you studying?"

"Considering recent news, I thought it prudent to brush up on the Falk and Skau line and their histories," the prince replied. "Perhaps what I learn will help Father with his breakthrough."

"He shared what he was doing with you?" Inga leaned forward. The king had not shared the details of his travels with her. He respected his queen, but also feared her. As he should. Given too much information, Inga could destroy Magnus. It was why he only shared what he must with Inga.

"He did. I cannot say more."

"You were at the House of Wisdom, then?"

"The best place for Falk and Skau archives."

Lord Riis held back a snort. Magnus, the fool, had wanted to burn the histories of those families. To keep them out of his castle. It had been such a fight to convince him to move them to the House of Wisdom.

"Indeed." Inga let out a hum and looked out the window.

Nerves. Leyv recognized the queen's tells, no matter how slight they might be. He wished he could be beside her, holding her hand, helping her speak with Rhistel.

"So, what did you call me here for?" Rhistel asked.

"Seal the door," Inga answered.

Rhistel's eyebrows shot up, but he did as his mother requested and with a wave of his hand, a barrier of air to prevent eavesdroppers.

Leyv leaned to the side so there'd be no chance he'd be seen through the lattice. It might be foolish to be this close, but he'd waited for this day, hoped it would come for so long. He didn't want to miss a moment of the prince's reaction, be it good or bad.

"There's something I must tell you, son." Inga moved before Rhistel. She held out a hand.

He took it, but not without hesitation. "You're acting strangely, Mother."

"You'll soon understand." Her voice sounded ever so slightly strained. "I've been keeping something from you. Both you and Vale since the day you were born."

The prince stiffened. "What is it?"

"There's no way to say this that won't hurt or turn your world on its end, so I'll come right out with it." She exhaled. "You and Vale are not the sons of King Magnus."

Rhistel retracted his hand. "To say such a thing is treason."

"It is but the truth."

Leyv's breathing stopped. The queen and the prince stared at one another, still as statues. Lord Riis thought he saw Inga's gaze flicker over to him. Was she requesting his help? He'd nearly opened the partition to reveal himself, when Rhistel released a low, menacing laugh.

Inga's shoulders tensed. "Your brother already knows, and I fear he will speak the truth soon enough, for he loves his wife."

Danger glinted in the heir's brown eyes. "How would you be aware of what Vale intends to do?"

"I'm in contact."

Rhistel stood. "Is this some ploy to make sure I never sit on the throne?"

"Why would you think that?"

"There has to be a reason you never went for it yourself, Mother. I believed that you think fae with our powers should not hold such positions. You've been brainwashed into that weakness, but I assure you, Mother, I intend to take the Throne of Winter, whether through right or by might."

"My son . . . the king will not allow it when he learns the truth. Saga will be his heir."

If Magnus wins the war to come . . . Lord Riis thought from his hiding spot.

"You don't deny my reasoning?"

Inga said nothing, which seemed to be all that Rhistel needed.

"So Saga is legitimate, is she?"

"She is."

The prince took two steps closer to his mother and

leaned in so that they shared breath. "Who says the king, *my father*, will need to *allow* anything?" Rhistel raised a hand and removed the glove that kept his whisperer magic nullified. "Especially when I erase this truth from your mind. It will be like you never spoke. And as for Vale—well, I'll come up with something to explain his addled mind. He was always so dimwitted, anyway. It would not be hard to convince the masses that the whore of a Falk manipulated him."

He lunged, but Inga dodged the hand coming for her. In his hiding spot, Lord Riis gripped the wall. Should he reveal himself and use his own magic to nullify Rhistel's power? Yes, then Inga and the Lord of Tongues could come up with a new plan. He very nearly pulled aside the lattice when the door to the queen's chamber burst open.

"Stop!" Princess Saga rushed inside just as the queen grabbed Rhistel by the arm.

Leyv saw the moment Inga whispered her son. She rarely left tells, but their son—a profound whisperer himself—was no normal fae. His eyes went vacant, his body slack.

Saga stopped in her tracks. "What are you doing to him?"

"Daughter, I can explain. I—"

"You had better for I *saw* all that just happened, Mother." The princess spoke with a seer's authority. "I know what you told Rhistel about him and Vale and Lord Riis. I witnessed how my brother reacted. I thought to arrive in time to stop him from hurting you, but it seems I didn't have to worry. You protected yourself against him, somehow. The only thing I do not understand is why he looks like that." Saga pointed a finger at her brother.

Lord Riis's heart thudded. Saga still knew nothing of the whispering powers her mother and brother possessed. So she hadn't *seen* everything that had occurred.

Inga released Rhistel, and his eyes cleared to normal, though when he sat back down—unbothered, Leyv knew Inga was still in control.

"Shut the door, Saga," the queen said. "I'll explain everything. I've been wanting to for many turns." She swallowed. "Though the truth will endanger me, Rhistel, and you as well."

The princess shut the door. Before she sat, however, she turned to the lattice. "I *saw* you too, *Lord Riis*. You may as well emerge."

Inga chuckled, though there was no delight in it. "Please, Leyv."

He slid the lattice aside, and though every part of his being wanted to run and take Inga in his arms, he refrained, if only for Saga's sake. The princess, after all, did not seem too impressed with him or her mother at the moment. It would be more prudent to fight his impulses and stay away.

The princess and the spymaster gathered around the queen, all the while the prince sat there, still and without the haughtiness that was his nature.

"What did you do to him? Is this from reading his mind too forcefully?" Saga eyed her half-brother.

"No, my dear," Inga said. "I—and your brother—are whisperers."

Saga's hands flew to her mouth.

"Before you say anything," Inga said, "we did not tell you to protect you."

Silence hung through the air until Saga turned to the spymaster. "But *he* knows?"

"He," Inga looked at her first love, the love of her life, "was the first person to experience my whispering. He has kept silent for many turns and is trustworthy."

"Who else knows?"

"My family kept me a secret. So my father, my mother—stars rest her soul—my siblings too. Lord Vagle bound them to secrecy in a blood oath. Then your father knows and your brothers. That is all."

"*Half-brothers*, from what I *saw* in my vision." Saga's voice came out small, and she stared at Rhistel again. "He's one too?"

"The ice spider gloves are not because of powerful Winter magic, but because Rhistel could not control his whispering magic for a long time." Inga gave a sad smile to her son. "That is no longer the case. He looks docile but do not be deceived. Rhistel fights me even now. His thoughts, though suppressed, are not peaceful."

"What do you mean?" the spymaster asked. "Will he hurt you?"

"He'd like to, and I'm not the only one." A quick glance at Saga made the queen's meaning all too clear. "I'm afraid our plan must change, Leyv."

"How so?"

"Rhistel is already thinking about how to harm Saga. And how he'll control Magnus, take power, and hunt Vale to keep this secret. I will not allow it. I must stay here and keep control of him."

"He'd really hurt me?" Saga spoke softly, but not weakly.

"You, my love, are the only trueborn child of King Magnus and yes, Rhistel would do anything to protect his title as heir."

Saga caved inward, as though someone had punched her in the belly.

"I know it hurts to hear such a thing. It tortures me to think that my children could harm one another, but I believe you must come to terms with it, and fast." The queen turned her attention to the male who had been by her side, if only in spirit, all her life. "I've searched Rhistel's head. The king and Lord Roar went toward where the Ice Tooth Range and Red Mist Mountains meet. They're in search of the Ice Scepter. Rhistel doesn't know exactly what led them to that area, but he believes Warden Roar has something to do with it."

Lord Riis displayed no sign of shock at the mention of the Scepter. He'd known as much from Vale. The king had, at one time, suspected his own family of holding a famous Hallow of Winter's Realm.

"More than that," Inga let out a long sigh, "a coinary in a place called Eygin informed my husband that Vale was there, so I assume Magnus will go there too. He'll search for Neve."

"No," the princess cried out, but her mother did not break eye contact with the spymaster.

"Take Saga," the queen said. "Find Vale and protect them. Please Leyv."

"Remember," Lord Riis sought to assure the queen, "Vale and Neve are on the road already. Most recently in Vitvik, and while I cannot pinpoint where Eygin is, it is not Vitvik."

Inga swallowed. "A small mercy."

"Yes." He faced Inga, not wishing to say what he needed to say next. "And I will go, though, I dislike the idea of leaving you in this predicament alone."

Though the words destroyed him, he knew better than to ask her to come with them.

The queen looked out the window. "I wish so many things could have gone differently. I wish I could have apologized to Princess Neve myself, but I must stay behind. This is how I will keep Winter's Realm together for as long as possible. Rhistel has grown strong, and I cannot control him forever. When he breaks free, he will tell Magnus all that I've said. All that I've done. Perhaps I can escape before he does so."

They both recognized it was unlikely.

So this was goodbye. Unable to stop himself, the spymaster took the queen in his arms and kissed her.

Saga might have been watching, but she said nothing as they kissed, as tears ran down their faces. The merchant's son and the lord's daughter had loved one another since they were young. When the truth of Inga came out, as it always did, the realm would implode. These might be their last moments together.

"Keep Saga and Vale safe." The queen pressed her

cheek against the spymaster's chest and added. "And as for Neve, tell her I am sorry for my part in her tragedy. Tell her the *whole truth*, Leyv."

They broke apart, and after one last kiss, the princess flung herself into her mother's arms. A few moments of tearful bargaining on Saga's part proved fruitless. Queen Inga insisted she leave and told her daughter that if she did not do so willingly, she would force her.

So, Saga and Lord Riis left the queen to her plans.

The princess wiped her face and did not cry another tear. Nor did she speak, not even to ask if she might gather personal effects. She did not look at the spymaster, nor breathe in his direction. Not as they left the castle. Not as he took her to the Warmsnap to get a disguise and ready two horses.

Normally, Lord Riis would travel via a gateway. But Saga did not know of Luccan's magic, and the spymaster thought it a good idea to keep that quiet for as long as possible. The less the princess knew right now, the better. The king had closed the city gates, but Lord Riis had spiders at his service. One gate was open to him. Once they left Avaldenn, they'd simply have to ride swiftly down the King's Road to put distance between them and Avaldenn.

"The vision of you and Rhistel and my mother was not the first I saw today," Saga said suddenly. "It was the last. Before that, I saw Vale, Neve, your sons, and others."

"Did you? Were they in a town?"

Vitvik perhaps? He was not sure what would delay them, but anything that made his job of finding them earlier was welcome.

304

"No. They were traveling. Through a forest in the midlands, judging by the size of the trees."

The largest trees grew far from the raging winds along the coast and the mountains that bordered the west and south. If they'd begun in Vitvik and were traveling, Lord Riis assumed they were still going east.

"Were they well?"

She turned her reddened eyes up to the spymaster. "They'd been captured."

CHAPTER 22
NEVE

I opened my eyes to find bars. Bars in front of me. Behind. To the sides. Above and below, solid slabs of metal caged me, magic simmering on the surface.

Wards.

Sitting up, I blinked hard, trying to orient myself. The air smelled cold, as though someone opened a window or door. Each of my traveling party were also caged, all separate, all passed out. Knocked out? I felt my head, which did not pound. From a brief examination, I deduced I hadn't been hit on the head.

"By the dead gods, *it's about time.*" A voice cut through the silence.

Turning, I found stairs and to one side, cloaked in thick darkness, there was a single chair in which a female faerie sat. Locking eyes with me, she leaned forward and placed her elbows on her knees.

My blood ran cold at the sight of the black-haired archer who had tried to kill me at the Royal Theater. She was there, just mere paces away, her expression haughty, her countenance cold, her body was strong and taut. Ready to strike.

This time, however, she wore black trousers, tunic, and cloak, with no Falk insignia on her arm, declaring her loyalty. Rather, she seemed to be prepared for the elements.

A memory surfaced. Shouting, running, ice-blue eyes— *her eyes*. Then darkness.

"What am I doing here?" I asked. "And why did you abduct me?"

She laughed, though there was no joy in her face. I wondered if there ever was.

"*Abduct!* We *saved* your arses. Your guard was knocked out and the rest of you were asleep, just waiting to be devoured." She rolled her eyes, an action that drew my attention to the scar over her left eye. "Of course, we wouldn't have bothered had we known who you were, but no one stopped to have a meeting. Not with the Dream Eater so close. Why would you camp there, anyway? Don't you know anything about this area?"

I shook my head. "I don't understand. What's a Dream Eater?"

Low-hanging fruit. But that was all my muddled mind could manage. Somehow, this violent faerie found me. Which meant the rebellion had found me. And they hadn't already killed us?

"Dream Eaters are a race of fae that directs and eats dreams, *obviously*," she replied through tight lips.

I blinked. Those strange dreams, my last memories before I saw ice-blue eyes, came back to me. They'd been so fast. So odd—like the Dream Eater was pulling them from me. Creating them too, or so she claimed.

The archer snorted. "I guess what they're saying might be true."

"What are they saying?"

"That you're not from here. If you have not a clue what a Dream Eater is, I can believe it. So, are you from here, *Princess Isolde?*"

"I was once a slave in the Blood Court," I said, because why not? The fliers the king put out painted such a horrible picture of me that telling the truth could only benefit.

"And then you married into a family who has slaves. A violent past too. Not a surprise, seeing as you married the brute of the family." The female stood, a sneer on her lips. "Mates too."

A sense of violation came over us. "You searched us?"

"Searched, took any weapons on your persons, anything else of value too. And you can bet we warded those cages all the way to the afterworld."

Yes, now that I was more alert, I felt more than simmering magic. A stifling sensation had taken over inside, over *my* magic. Still there, churning deep inside, but unusable.

"If you hate me so much, why haven't you killed me already?"

A slow smile spread across her face. "I can't say I wasn't tempted. The prince and his wife? What a prize! But since seeing the posters, we're all wondering what's happening. Why a fae pretending to be Isolde Falk would be in the

309

midlands. Why she'd marry an Aaberg. You're a puzzle, and I don't like those unsolved."

"Then let me solve the puzzle for you. I *am* Isolde Falk." I stopped there. To insist too much might put me in more danger. The rebels who attacked the Royal Theater had claimed to follow the true heir. Was I a threat to that person?

"What are you doing with that human?" the female brushed aside my claim.

I winced. If only Caelo's powers had been at full strength, and he'd had the energy to glamour Anna. Everyone in the group, actually. Alas, that wasn't the case, and the only option I had was to come clean.

"She's my best friend. My sister."

The faerie's face hardened, and she approached my cage. I stood on wobbly legs. I had to assume that my general unsteadiness was an aftereffect of the Dream Eater, though I wouldn't ask this female. I needed to stop revealing my weaknesses to her.

A hand's width from the bars, the faerie stopped and flared her silver wings. Now that we were closer, and she wasn't threatening my life, I could see that the color was a shade or two darker than my silver wings. "A human friend? Have you taken Liar's Salvation?"

"No." I closed in on her, not about to show the fear that her presence birthed in me. "If you aren't sure, you could let me out of my cage and see for yourself."

Had I taken the potion, I'd be powerless. This female knew that as well as I—better even, given she'd grown up here. I would bet that she also had a intricate knowledge of black markets where the forbidden potion was sold.

"Hmmm." Her eyes, eerily like King Magnus's ice-blue, shifted to Vale. Then the Riis brothers. "I like you all where you are. The human, though, needs to be moved. Maybe I can get *real* answers from her when she wakes."

She spun on her heel and took three steps toward the cage where Anna lay, motionless.

"Don't you touch her," I commanded.

Still, no one else stirred. Not only did that mean no backup, but it brought up more questions. How long had we been out? Was this common after encountering a Dream Eater? Would they wake up soon, and would they be normal when they did?

I pushed all those questions down as the rebel laughed at my command.

"You think you have any power here? Do you think I will listen to you? A great pretender? Most likely, a liar?" She placed a hand on the door to Anna's cell, and the metal glowed blue. A faint click answered the faerie and the door to the cell flew open.

She strode in, knelt, and with an ease I admired, hefted Anna's body over her shoulder as if she weighed no more than a youngling. Then I remembered this fae had also run from a monster with me in her arms, and I weighed much more than Anna. Fates, the archer was strong, indeed.

"You should be happy to still have your heads." The rebel powered back over to the stairs.

"Please!" My voice broke as I gripped the bars of my

cage and tried to break out. The metal did not budge. "Please don't take her!"

The faerie twisted. "She's the only one I can trust. A human is no lord or lady or lackey. They see the world differently."

"I've seen it that way too!" I roared.

"If that's true, this human will know."

I slumped. This rebel was dedicated to hating me, to writing my story for me and making it one that she understood. To her, I was a commoner who married a prince for luxury. A life that most others could not afford and would never achieve. I was safe. Others froze and starved.

And worse, what she thought had largely been true. Only when I went out on my own for revenge against Roar did anything change. Not that I'd say such a thing to her.

"Don't harm her. I beg of you."

For the first time, the fae's eyes softened, though that softness did not land on me but on Anna. "I only wish to question her." She gestured to the frozen ground. "And to get her out of this dungeon. It's too cold for her kind."

Something in the faerie's face made me believe her. Or maybe it was the way she looked at and carried Anna, gently. Most fae didn't physically harm humans, but they didn't go out of their way to be kind to them either.

"We grew up together, so she's very loyal to me. She might not tell you what you want to hear, so . . ." I trailed off. How to signal to Anna that I needed her to tell this fae the truth?

I did not like the rebels, but the enemy of my enemy

might be my friend. If I played my cards right. If I got them to trust me.

"Tell her I wish for her to speak plainly to you. I swear on our twin scars I won't be mad about what she says."

I bore a crescent scar on my temple. Long ago, in another kingdom, *another life*, Anna had carved a similar one on her collarbone. Hopefully, what I said was enough for Anna to do as they wished.

And I prayed that the female was honest when she said Anna would be safe. If not, I'd never forgive myself.

"Very well." The female climbed the stairs, pausing briefly at the top, almost as if she wished to say something more, before she exited the dungeon and left me alone in a cage, waiting for the others to wake.

CHAPTER 23
VALE

I gripped the bars of my cage, as furious as the moment I awoke in a dungeon.

Without windows to let in the sunshine, it was difficult to estimate the passage of time, but I guessed we'd been here for a day with little food and water, and only a bucket each to relieve ourselves in. I'd nearly lost it when Neve had needed to use her bucket with my friends and brothers as witnesses. Cloak covering her or not, I did not want others to see her like that.

"I swear to every dead god and goddess, I'm going to *lose my bleeding mind* if they don't let us out soon." Thantrel gripped the bars and leaned back on his heels, tipping his strong chin to the stone ceiling.

The youngest Riis brother was not one to be idle. Nor was I, for that matter, though the cages had outwitted me. Whatever ward was in the metal nullified each of our magics. Rynni's dragon magic included.

"I hope Anna is safe," Clemencia whispered.

Our human companion had not returned since the rebels had taken her. That I had not been awake for my mate in her time of distress only deepened my agony.

"The fae who took her said she wouldn't hurt her," Neve assured us. "And I didn't hear anything like screaming afterwards."

"We can't hear anything at all! Nothing but the sound of our own voices!" Thantrel roared. "It's maddening! What are they doing up there? I'm dying to go see." He gazed at the stairs, as if there was some great treasure up the steps and not a horde of enemies.

"And *where* is up there?" Duran added, frustration lacing his tone from where he sat, cross-legged, in his cage.

I cast a glance at Neve. She was laying down, curled in on herself, at the bottom of her enclosure. Her violet eyes were empty as she stared into space. My heart clenched. More than anything, I wished to hold my mate. To comfort her and tell her that I'd kill anyone who harmed her and Anna, but my words would be empty.

Stars, I despise being powerless. I wish—The door at the top of the stairs banged open.

"Haven't I told you scum to be quiet!" A massive male fae with gray wings too small for his trollish frame appeared, a fresh scowl on an ugly face. Unlike when he berated us before, he didn't just shout, shut the door, and leave. This time, the fae descended the steps, glittering black eyes narrowed upon us.

In one meaty hand he clutched a shimmering silver-white cloth that contrasted with his skin, which was as dark as the night sky.

"Prince." The fae stopped before my cage. "We wish to question you."

"Where's Anna?" Neve rose from her lethargy. "That female with the scar over her eye was questioning her! Is she still alive?!"

"The human is fine. But she doesn't have all the information we require." Black eyes locked on me. "This prince might. Wrap this around your middle, under your shirt. Then tie it tight."

He tossed the item in his hands through the bars. I caught it and recognized the material. Spider silk, like the gloves my twin wore. A better look revealed the silk to be a long ribbon as wide as my hand. This amount of material was unspeakably valuable.

"You'll be going upstairs," the male said. "That'll stifle your magic."

"My magic is the least of your worries," I snarled, muscles tightening.

He chuckled. "You think you can fight me? I'm three times your size."

"I've fought orcs as large as you. I can do it again."

"There're a dozen soldiers at the top of the stairs. If you think you can free your friends before you get to the top, you're wrong. I have no power to open any cage except for yours. So try and kill me if you want, but it'll get you nothing, and if the others hear me call out before I meet my end, they'll be ready with arrows and blades."

"Vale. Go." Neve's voice was but a whisper, one that tore my chest open. "Tell them whatever you must so they'll free us."

"Bring my wife too," I commanded.

"You have the power to free her, but I'll not be the one opening her cage. It all depends on what you say to our leader," the fae tossed back lazily. "Wrap those around your middle and tie it tight. Once you're done, we'll be enchanting it into place."

Why they wished to speak to me, and not my mate, when they knew who she was—a Falk that they might be inclined to follow—was beyond me. Still, I did as my mate wished and wrapped the wide ribbon around me. I had many questions regarding the material, but one thing was clear to me. If the rebels had the silk but did not weave it into clothing like gloves or vests, which would be useful for this purpose, then they didn't have someone to work the rare material. No surprise there. Few could sew and create with the silk of ice spiders.

Once the spider silk material encased me, the rebel fae opened the door to my cage. He'd not used a key, but placed his hand on a flat part of the cage, where a lock would be located.

"Come on." He pushed me ahead of him, and throwing Neve one last look, I climbed the steps.

Just as the fae said, a dozen armed soldiers wearing the red hawk of the Falk rebels around their arms waited at the top. I found it ludicrous that Neve was a true Falk princess, not some bastard-born Falk taking a claim that was above them, and yet they did not listen to her.

Inhaling to keep my calm, I examined the swords the soldiers held, some sheathed, some out and at the ready. None of them were *Skelda*, and that at least was good news.

Upon capture, we'd been relieved of our weapons. To think of someone else carrying my sword rankled.

The soldiers escorted me down a hallway, the large part-troll, part-faerie at the front. As we went, I studied our surroundings.

The building seemed quite large. A small fortress or castle made of stone. Though clean enough, the ceiling sagged in places and stones jutted from an uneven floor. Where in all the nine kingdoms were we?

The rebels stopped before a door in the middle of a long, blank, black stone hallway. The troll-faerie opened the door and poked his head in. My name lumbered off his lips and a second later, a female voice told them to enter.

Someone shoved me in the back. My fists clenched, but I held my composure and passed through the doors to find a large room, empty save for the two people sitting around a table. One I recognized as the black-haired female who tried to kill Neve at the Royal Theater. The same faerie who had visited my mate before the rest of us awoke. The rebel who took Anna.

"Thank you, Ulfiel," the black-haired female said. "You may go."

"You're sure?" the troll asked even as he brought a fist to his chest in a gesture I'd seen before. The famous singer, Avalina Trusso, had done the same thing before rebels descended upon the Royal Theater. It was a gesture of loyalty to the rebellion. "No protection?"

The female's eyes, a sharp blue, settled on me. "I'm sure the prince knows how much is at stake. After today, we'll get to the bottom of their story. Wait outside if you must, but the prince will not harm us."

She was right. Without my mate and my friends beside me, I'd not do anything stupid.

The soldiers left, but I remained standing there, waiting.

"Sit," the female said.

"Who are you?" I asked, my tone matching her command as I crossed to the empty chair.

"For now, all you need to know is that I'm the leader here. One of them, anyway." She nodded to another female at the table, an older faerie with black hair heavily shot through with gray, light blue eyes, and navy wings pressed down her back. "This is Ratha. She'll read your mind. Give her your hand."

I balked. "If I don't?"

The younger faerie shrugged. "Then we kill you."

"Where's Anna?"

Her eyebrows arched. "You care about the human?"

"I do. She's my mate's best friend."

A long sigh left her lips. "You're a strange lot, I'll admit. One that brings up many questions for people like me. Questions you can answer—if you work with Ratha."

The old faerie's trembling hand extended to me. One might think the trembling was a sign of nerves, but there was no hint of anxiety in her proud face. Age affected this fae, not my presence. "Give it over, my prince."

There was something so familiar about the old faerie. Almost motherly. Though I did not trust them, I understood this was what had to happen.

The issue of my many secrets—that of my mother and

brother's powers and my own birth father—flitted across my mind, but I dismissed them. This female would be looking for information on Neve. On me. On others in my group. I doubted she'd search for anything about my mother and brother and well, if she learned my secret now, I'd regret that, but I had no power to change what the Fates had in store.

I extended my hand, touched it to Ratha's roughened skin. This fae had seen much of this life, and her turns had been hard.

Not as hard as yours will be if you fight, a voice rang through my head, raising alarm bells. I'd always been told that mind readers could not speak to the person whose mind they were reading. But her voice was loud and clear and powerful.

Bleeding skies, she's—

A low laugh interrupted me. *Don't fight. Just allow me to have my way.*

My body loosened as the truth crashed over me. This fae wasn't a mere mind reader—if such a power could ever be called mere. No, her magic was more distressing since she was a whisperer, able to read *and* control.

I let her inside willingly, a fool's move. Because of my many experiences with Mother and Rhistel, I recognized Ratha as her power wove through me. As she demanded answers, which I supplied mentally, unable to stop myself. And though her control was not as complete as my mother's and brother's, I was no match to stop her.

So I sat there, supplying answers as the whisperer got what she required from me. Outwardly, she remained silent, asking and searching, asking and searching. Some unknowable time later, Ratha leaned back in her chair.

She turned to the black-haired female faerie. "The human spoke true. This prince and his mate do not work with the king but against him. The princess is who she says she is."

The younger faerie leaned back and let loose a long breath. "I was *certain* the princess was lying somehow."

"What will you do now, Thy—"

"I don't know," the younger female cut Ratha off, a warning gleam in her eyes. "Most of them still have much to answer for, but if they wish to unseat the king . . ."

She trailed off as she stood. I got the sense that she had many things on her mind. "Release the prince and the others still in cages. Show him to the annex, where they can stay under guard. Wrap their middles with ice spider silk and don't give them access to weapons either."

"How do you have so much silk?" I asked. I had an idea of how much it would cost and given the state of the castle, the rebels did not seem to be swimming in gold. It was as shocking as the orcs having nets made of the material, though I was sure the orcs had stolen it, rather than paid a fair price. And the only other way to get the silk was to bargain with the spiders, an act most did not dare to commit for ice spiders took lavishly.

"We once had brave fae who risked their lives for the silk," the archer replied, her face contorting in pain. She said nothing more as she left the room.

The older faerie turned to me. She released her magic over me.

"You're a whisperer."

"We rebels use the powers that we must. I understand that you're quite familiar with my magic?" Blue eyes burned into mine.

So she had seen what I'd hoped she would not. Was this a threat to my mother and brother? The latter might hate me when I declared for my mate to take the throne instead of him, and yet, to think of someone outing his magic, something he had no control over, did not sit right with me.

"Please, say nothing," I begged.

Her wrinkles deepened as her face softened. "You're full of surprises, Warrior Bear."

"None I have from you. Not any longer."

She smirked. "I suppose not." A pause fell between us before she added. "How do I compare? To your mother and brother?"

I blinked. An odd question, though perhaps not for a whisperer. A fae with an elemental power, or even a less common one, might seek peers. They could compare skills and learn tips on how to use their magic.

Whispers could do no such thing. They remained silent, else death came for them.

"You're not as strong," I said. "Mother is the most powerful between the three of you, but Rhistel could control you too, I think."

"You were his first?"

"I was." And often, I'd been used as a practice subject for Rhistel. That was, until I demanded it all stop, which created a deeper rift between us.

She let out a soft hum. "I'm not surprised. You see, I

323

know your mother. Met her when she was around twelve turns, and I was much younger than I am now. The young Lady Inga whispered me then. My intervention startled her, maybe scared her. But, in truth, I suspect that any fear she felt was nothing to how her power had terrified me. As a youngling, she was stronger than me. Far stronger. Should she have wished to, she could have ruled all of Isila."

I swallowed. "Have you told anyone of this?"

And who? How many? Fear for my mother was building by the second and stilled only when Ratha shook her head.

"Never. In a way that only our kind can understand, we are bonded, your mother and I." She licked her lips. "And then there's the matter of our blood bond."

My spine straightened, and I took her in again. The blue eyes. They'd seemed so motherly because they were the same shade as my mother's. This female had black hair too.

Her wings lifted, spread, answering my unspoken question. Black as night. Black as my own.

Vagle wings.

"Who are you?"

"A bastard of House Vagle. One hidden for my mother's treachery and then hidden again when my magic manifested. There are many of us bastards of nobles. Fae who want a better life and a better kingdom. When your father first took the throne, I was happy. I thought he'd give us that, but he failed."

"He's not my real father," I admitted, surprised that she'd not seen the truth that burned within.

"I wondered if you'd speak it."

"I plan to speak it more. After my mate makes her claim public."

Ratha's face went blank, and she pushed her chair back. "The guards waiting in the hall will show you to your annex. They'll retrieve your mate and friends too."

"Thank you," I said, somewhat at a loss over her reaction. At so much. I looked around at the empty, vast room. "Might I ask where we are?"

Ratha chuckled. "This, Prince Vale, is what's left of Castle Valrun."

Had a band of orcs burst through the door at that moment, I wouldn't have been able to move, let alone fight. My feet froze to the floor in shock. In fear. "Val—Valrun! It's cursed!"

"That's what they say."

"But then, why are the rebels here?!"

"Where else could we be certain that we would not be found?" Ratha shuffled to the door. "If you're going to join us and survive, you'd better start thinking more like a mouse than a bear."

CHAPTER 24

NEVE

"Vale!" I gasped as I walked through the door of our new quarters. The annex, or so the rebels called it. Whatever this place was, one glance assured me it was far better than those horrible cages.

My mate took me in his arms, and the worry that had filled my chest deflated. It felt so good to touch him again. To smell him and taste him.

"Where in the bleeding skies are we, Vale?" Thantrel asked after allowing us a few precious seconds together.

My mate pulled away from me, kissed my forehead, and then turned to the group, which now included Anna. Since we'd reunited in the corridors, my friend had been crying and saying she'd done all she could to make them believe the truth.

I didn't blame Anna in the slightest. Fae had a difficult time taking humans seriously, and the rebels were predisposed to dislike us. Though now, they might not?

I studied the interior of the building. It was large but

humble, made of wood, unlike the stone castle. A newer portion, though why it wasn't stone as well was beyond my understanding. Fabrics, I knew. Castle craftsmanship, not so much.

"We're in Valrun Castle," Vale answered.

"*Valrun!*" Duran's hands went to his mouth.

"Indeed."

I was missing something. "What's wrong with Valrun Castle?"

"The place, the entire town around it too, is cursed, Neve," Clemencia, with her teacher's heart, was always quick to offer information.

"Oh." It had appeared rundown, but cursed? "How?"

Anna and Rynni appeared as lost as me. The others looked uncomfortable, but Clemencia didn't shy away from whatever unsavory thing needed to be said.

"Well, the first horrible event happened at the time of the Unification," Clemencia said. "Many generations back, Sassa Falk nearly demolished the castle. Some, or maybe most, of the destruction is from her."

"I see," I said, chewing at my lower lip. Sassa was a distant ancestor, but an ancestor all the same. It troubled me that she'd do such a thing. "But you said *the first* event? There are more?"

"Two other historical events occurred here, each worse than the last." Clemencia held up two fingers, all academic authority. "The second was a dragon flying overhead and torching the castle and the town surrounding it."

I blinked. "But why?"

"I'd like to know too," Rynni cocked her head. "Most

dragons don't come here unless they must. Too bleeding cold, this kingdom."

"It's said that the dragon's wife slept with the lord of this castle. He exacted deadly revenge."

"And the royals at the time did nothing?" Such an attack on the fae of Winter's Realm should not have gone unnoticed.

"They were preparing to fight the dragon lords when the entire family living at Valrun took ill. They died shortly after, so there was no one to fight for."

"So, that's the third event?" My stomach had twisted into knots.

"Oh, no. Something else happened. Save for the blight, I don't count illnesses as extraordinary events."

"By the stars," I breathed.

Anna leaned forward. "What else happened?"

"Valrun is at the edge of a forest, between the trees and the great lake of the midlands," Clemencia gestured to the trees out the window. I could see no lake but would take her word for it. "We're also not so far from the King's Road."

"A day or two away," Vale supplied.

"Yes," Clem continued. "And a good distance from the mountains, though not far enough, it would seem."

I swallowed.

"Frost giants came down from the mountains and they didn't stop at Myrr. The city is too fortified, the Balik host too great. But Valrun, even in its glory days, was small and susceptible. The giants appeared, killed, and ate every living soul in the town—the new nobles included. Thrice this area has seen great hardships, and many believe that it is a bad omen. That at some point, this place was cursed. Since the frost giants came down from the Ice Tooth, no one has dared settle in this area again."

While I usually found a sense of comfort in Clemencia's academic detachment, this time, it only made the news more chilling. And brought up a hundred questions, the most serious of which being: Why were *we* here?

"You're a historian?" Duran asked Clemencia, breaking the silence.

She blinked, her concentration being pulled from the histories as she turned to the dwarf. "Of a sort."

"She knows *everything*," I boasted for her, happy to change the subject. "You two would have much to talk about."

Duran's face lit up. He and Arie were often together, speaking of subjects the rest of us knew little about, but I imagined that, for a scholar, to have more people to talk and debate with, was a magic in itself.

"I'd like that," Clemencia admitted. "The House of Wisdom has always fascinated me, but my father would never have allowed me to even attempt to attend. You study there, correct?"

"I'm a lärling," Duran answered. "Arie is trying to earn his place there too."

I turned away from the trio that were now gravitating to one another and looked up at Vale. "What did they ask you about?"

He swallowed, and his voice dropped so that only I could hear his reply. "I'll tell you later. When we're alone. For now, let me show you our new home."

I nodded, somewhat surprised he was not open about the experience, though there had to be a reason.

"What do you think this is for?" I gestured to the structure built off the main castle. "It looks newish."

"I believe they kept the older parts of the castle for themselves. The walls might still retain some protective enchantment. The guard who showed me here says it's for refugees, and they rarely stay too long." Vale's lips turned down as he spoke.

"Refugees from what?"

"That, I don't know. But there are plenty of rooms, indicating that, perhaps, many families from the same town or village—or even a city—stayed here?"

Vale showed me to a space where the rebels had set baskets of bread and cheese for us to snack on before the official mealtime gathering in the dining hall. As we'd been fed while in cages and had expended little energy, I wasn't hungry, so we moved on. He showed me the first three rooms, all with two beds. The fourth was the smallest, with one single bed and a rickety wooden altar to the dead gods in the corner. Rynni had slipped into it before us and claimed that room. Solitary as ever.

The fifth and last room had only one bed, one much smaller than Vale and I were used to sleeping in, but after days of sleeping in ice shelters, it looked blissful. Though I had little reason to trust the rebels, I also did not think they'd put us in this place if they wished to harm us. For now, we were safe.

"This is ours." I spun in the bare room. "Do you think they'll bring our things?"

I was missing my sword and my mother's jewels. If they didn't offer to return both, I'd be having words with the rebels.

"I think they will. No doubt they were examining our items."

"Well, having a proper place to sleep—together, at that, is some progress. To be honest, it surprises me that they'd keep us all together, guards at the door or no."

"Don't be surprised. They used a whisperer on me."

I sucked in a breath. The reason he'd not spoken before the others emerged. "*Oh.*"

"There's no reason for them to doubt me. What the whisperer read in my mind lined up with what Anna said."

"What about your mother and brother?"

"She knows about that. She'll tell no one."

My eyebrows knitted together. "You're sure?"

"She has a valid reason not to and said she wouldn't, so I'm choosing to trust her. I have no other options."

True. When we fled Frostveil in the dead of night, neither of us had possessed the clarity of mind to snatch up flasks of the Mind Rönd potion that protected fae from most whisperers. Even if we had, we would have run out by now. If Vale was confident with this whisperer knowing his secrets, then I would trust his judgment.

"That makes us a pair," I said. "My secrets are also known to all now."

He extended his arms and wrapped them around me. His hands slithered to my arse and pulled me close, his intent as clear as the hungry gleam that sparked in his eyes.

Vale was done with catching up. He wanted to feel me after being apart for days. "Surely not *all* your secrets."

"You're right," I spoke offhandedly, as if my heart had not begun to race at our closeness. "Some are not even known to you."

"Is that a challenge, my mate?"

I tilted my chin up. "You know what? I think it might be."

"Challenge accepted." He scooped me up, and my toes curled in my boots as he strode to the bed and placed me there, lovingly, tenderly.

"Now," Vale pulled back and took his time as he examined me, his warm brown eyes lingering over my every curve and valley. "Where might I begin to find these secrets?"

My hand drifted to my breasts, grazed across them. Though I wore traveling clothes and not the gowns with plunging necklines that I'd become used to at court, one would never guess that Vale preferred one style over the other.

He looked like a male desperate to drink, to indulge, *to ravage*. And I was more than happy to oblige his every whim.

"A favored spot," he stepped closer, began untying the top of my tunic, then easing me upward, he shimmied it off. The band I wore around my breasts followed quickly, leaving only the ribbon of spider silk wrappings around my waistline. The ribbons were enchanted onto our bodies, so I did not try to remove them.

"Fates, Neve. If I go to the afterworld on this night, I'll have gone out happy." And with that, he bent and took one nipple between his lips, his deft hand teasing the other. Tugging. Twisting. Flicking.

My eyes fluttered closed as pleasure washed over me, and my hands lodged themselves in Vale's long, dark hair, sometimes gravitating toward the shaved under portion that had grown out slightly during our travels.

Vale moved his mouth to the other nipple. "So far, no secrets I have not already discovered, but I must be thorough in my assessments."

And he was thorough. So very thorough, I was squirming beneath his touch when he stopped showing my breasts attention. His head lifted, a fiendish grin on his face.

"That sweet sound you made is the secret?"

I swallowed. I'd not been aware I was making a sound.

"It was a bit like a kitten."

I laughed. "In no world would I make a sound like that!"

"Another challenge." He began tugging off my trousers, and the moment they were free, I rose to remove his shirt, leaving only the spider silk against his skin. He obliged, mock weariness in his tone when he added. "I grow tired of excelling in all these trials, love."

"That's too bad. I was about to give you another." I scooted back on the bed, and my hand drifted to my sex. Slowly, I began rubbing at the apex.

Vale's eyes widened. "Tell me."

I didn't reply right away, just continued stroking myself. My breathing deepened, and I felt a flush cross my face. Inside, my magic responded too, a cold wash fluttering through me like ice fire.

"You test me," Vale growled as he crawled over me and pressed his cock against my hand.

Test him? I tested myself! And I feared that soon, I'd fail this test of my own making, but in the best possible way.

I leaned closer, brought my lips to his ears. "Make me come so hard that I see the dead gods."

A low rumble of a laugh rolled out of Vale. "Gladly."

He pulled my hand from my sex, gripped my hips, and flipped me onto my stomach. I gasped as Vale lifted my hips, and his thick cock pressed into my entrance as he began circling my clit with two fingers.

"Hmmm, you will be the death of me, won't you, Princess?"

The question was not one he meant for me to answer, for when he thrust inside the next second, he stole all my breath. Stopped my heart. Made my mind blank.

No one had ever fit me so perfectly, nor been so deep inside me. And as Vale began to rock, and I matched his rhythm, I knew it was the same for him.

He struck that deep spot inside me, and my soulmate mark glowed, almost blinding.

"There's one secret," Vale laughed. "I've found it and so easily."

I pressed my rear into him, halting any more cocky remarks as his moan added to mine. Gripping the black fur on our bed, I rolled my hips, desperate for as much of him as possible to—

Snow fell on the bed, light fluffy flakes. I stared at it as Vale pulled me up, positioned me so that I sat on his cock with my back to him.

"That shouldn't happen," I breathed. "We're wearing spider silk."

"Another secret, possibly accessible only to the mated." His voice was filled with reverence, with awe. "Do you feel my magic upon you? It's not coming from inside me, but the magic is . . . attracted to us, I think."

I hadn't until he said something and then I noticed the swirls of air around my nipples, teasing as his hands had moments before.

"Astounding," I breathed as I rocked against him once more. Needing the friction, to release the tension building inside me in the most pleasurable way.

Vale appeared to be of the same mind, for he thrust deeper, harder, faster, one hand on my hip, the other fondling a breast. Sweat built in my cleavage, and I threw my head back. Vale's lips kissed along my jaw, taking full advantage, as we both spiraled up to the stars.

And when our release came, it was together, in a flurry of snow and air and light in my eyes, that did, in fact, make me think I might have glimpsed the dead gods.

A fist pounding on our door woke me sometime later.

"Neve!" shouted Anna, the peace-stealing culprit. "Someone is here to speak with you!"

"Who?" I curled closer to Vale, savoring the warmth of his skin against mine.

"Well, I don't know! A soldier! He has a message for you."

The three pesky Fates did not want to give my mate and me more than a moment of peace. I rose reluctantly, as did Vale.

He reached for his pants, giving me another delicious view of his malehood before his trousers covered him up.

"You spoke to no one but the guards who brought you here?"

"No one," I replied. "Odd that a message would come just for me."

"Not if they want to speak with the Falk heir. Remember who these people fight for, Neve."

I pulled my shirt over my head. In no way had I forgotten that white hawk symbol painted in a bold red across the curtain in the Royal Theater. Nor the fight.

Who did they follow? Likely a bastard, for before Harald Falk married my mother, he'd sired several children. As had other members of House Falk over the turns. Hawk Seeds, they called them.

Dressed, we left our room, and when we reached the common space, half of our friends stared. The others must be in their rooms. Resting, I hoped.

Anna watched me carefully, Clemencia, Luccan, and Arie with her. I turned to the annex door to find a faerie with only one arm waiting for me.

"Hello? What is it?"

The soldier stared at me, and in his gaze, I couldn't decide if he viewed me as an enemy, a friend, or someone he had not yet decided on.

"Our leader wishes to break bread with you. The others will eat elsewhere."

"Now?"

"Yes."

"Fine." I took Vale's hand. "Show us the way."

"Not him. Only you."

A low growl left Vale's throat, and the soldier curled in slightly, regretting his words. He found his courage, however, and straightened once more.

"She wishes only to dine with Princess Neve," the soldier said. "No harm will come to her."

"She?" I asked.

"Yes, as I said, you will dine with our leader. Her two closest advisors as well."

Could their leader be the same whisperer who had spoken to Vale? Or someone I had not met?

I should have been more cautious. With a ribbon of ice spider silk wound around my middle and stuck to my body with a magical adhesive, I couldn't access my magic, and I had no weapon. Then again, I was only a touch safer being here, with my friends and mate.

Truth be told, though, a dinner with the rebels did not faze me. That they had not already harmed us spoke volumes. And while they might take precautions around us, I had to see our release from cages as a giant step forward. It was time to take another and gain the trust of their leader.

"Vale, I'll be fine." I kissed him on the cheek. "As you were."

He locked eyes with me, a clear and heated recourse brewing inside him.

"If they wanted to hurt me, they would have already done so. We're outnumbered, and with the silks against our skin, overpowered too. Yet we haven't been harmed. Given those facts, we can assume this meal is just that. A meal. An opportunity?"

Not without noticeable effort, Vale inclined his head. "I'll be waiting for you to return."

We kissed, and I spun to face the soldier. "Show me to your leaders."

The soldier led me down the hall and until we turned the corner, I sensed eyes on my back. Vale's certainly. Probably the others too. My heart swelled with the knowledge that they cared so deeply for me.

As we walked, we passed parts of the castle that were open to the elements. A hole in the ceiling let in the falling snow and winter chill. I looked up as I went beneath and shuddered.

"Why hasn't that been fixed?"

The soldier turned, eyebrows arched. "The curse."

"That prevents repairs?"

"That and our lack of coin." His tone dipped into annoyance.

We walked the rest of the way in silence and when he stopped at a door, I blinked. "No guards on watch?"

"They don't need them." He pounded on the door.

"Yes?" a male voice answered on the other side.

"The princess is here."

"Let her in."

He opened the door for me to enter. Ready for whatever may come, I stepped through and found myself in a small dining room that was in better shape than much of the rest of the castle. The dining table in the center was meant for intimate gatherings of six people, though today only three others were present around the circle.

One I recognized: The archer, again dressed in plain, black clothing suitable for traveling or working. I studied her, and she did the same to me, until the eye contact made me uncomfortable, and I moved on. Next to the archer sat a female faerie. The white streak in her brown hair told me she was older. The last took up the archer's other side. He was a male, his dark brown skin gleaming in the candle light. Bread, cheese, and cut roasted meat decorated the middle of the table.

"Princess Neve," the male said, golden eyes flashing. "Please sit."

I did so, taking the place across from the archer.

The older female leaned closer, a small smile playing on her lips. "It's good of you to come. I'm sorry that you had to be detained, but you'll understand that we must be careful."

"I do," I said, though I'd been furious to be caged, and more so when the rebels took Anna, I did understand. "So you're the leader of the rebellion?"

The faerie laughed; the tone airy. "By the dead gods! No, Princess. As delighted as I am to be thought royal, I'm just Brynhild, an advisor."

The soldier who led me here had said the leader was a she. Which meant that it was the archer . . . But she was so young. Around my age. Shocked as I was, I did not let it show on my face.

"Nice to meet you." My attention turned to the male next, wanting to leave the younger female for last, if only because she'd been so rude when I was caged. He held himself with a powerful bearing. "And you?"

"Bac. Named for a river near my home city. A pleasure to meet you, Princess Neve."

"The pleasure is mine." No longer able to put off the inevitable, I locked eyes with the archer. A shiver darted down my spine. As ever, her ice-blue eyes reminded me of King Magnus. "And will I finally be able to put a name to the fae who tried to kill me?"

She stared back at me, the corner of her lips pulling up so slightly. Then, the leader of the rebels leaned forward to rest her elbows on the table.

"I suppose I should apologize for that day in the theater, shouldn't I, sister dearest?"

CHAPTER 25
VALE

Many eyes followed us as we trailed our armed escort through the corridors of Valrun Castle.

"Bleeding skies, we're an attractive bunch, but you'd think they'd be *a little* less obvious about it," Thantrel spoke loudly, inviting a reaction.

A few fae looked away. Some scowled. Most merely continued to stare.

Not only was an Aaberg prince in rebel territory, but the Riis brothers—with their red hair, fiery wings, and two larger-than-life personalities—never failed to draw attention. It would only be worse if Rynni had joined us in going to the dining hall, but the dragon healer had remained in the annex with Caelo, who was not completely healed yet and had wished to rest.

"I hope there's meat today," Anna said wistfully.

"You're in luck." Our escort, the same part-troll named Ulfiel, turned. He bore a smile for Anna he had never bestowed on the rest of us. Warm and sincere. "Today a hunting party returned with boar and a few birds."

"Excellent." Anna beamed at Ulfiel, and his cheeks darkened.

A moment later, Arie slid forward to walk by Anna and stole her attention by pointing to something outside a window crumbling around the edges. Luccan caught my eye and together we shared a knowing smirk.

As a youngling, I'd heard about the Curse of Valrun. Mother had told the tales to Rhistel and me. Likely because she was the mother of two males who liked to get into trouble, she considered it a cautionary tale. In truth, the story had taken seed. Being in a place such as this made my skin crawl, though I could not deny there was a hint of thrill present too.

Valrun and the town that used to sprawl around it had been empty of fae for centuries. No one dared to travel close by, which for the rebels proved both a blessing and curse. Vitvik and a smaller town were close enough for basic supplies, but they could not fix this castle. As the castle stood now, it was minimally protected. The holes in the ceilings, walls, and the eroded windows—some empty of glass— allowed the winter chill inside. The few tapestries lining the walls did not help much. They hung threadbare, perhaps from the time of the curse's final blow.

"Here we are," Ulfiel said as we turned a corner.

Sounds filtered from down the hallway, and I steeled myself for more attention, which I should have been used to growing up a prince. Though getting attention as the beloved Warrior Bear versus a prince whom the rebels despised because I'd helped imprison or kill some of their lot were two different circumstances.

"Smells good," Thantrel commented, sniffing the air, though his face turned away from the dining hall as he did so. My eyebrows pinched together. Thantrel had always been excitable, but there was something about Valrun that distracted him more than usual.

Ulfiel twisted his hand, extending in what I could only describe as a lackluster gesture of welcome when we approached the door to the dining hall. "Those inside have been told you're under protection, so expect no bloodshed. I'll wait in the hall to show you back."

"Thank the Fates we have private shitters in our annex," Thantrel muttered. "I'd hate for someone to have to show each of us there. Full-time job, that'd be."

Three steps into the dining hall was all it took before the rebels took notice our arrival. Forks and knives hit plates, conversations lowered or stopped, and heads turned.

"Ridiculous comment coming in," Luccan gestured back to his youngest brother, "Three, two, o—"

Thantrel cleared his throat. "I could teach all of you to have long flowing hair like this too." He pointed at a table closest to us. "Well, maybe not you with the raggedy brown curls, but—ow!"

Arie removed his elbow from Thantrel's side.

"Was that necessary, Arie?"

"Oh shove it, Than. I've seen Sayyida punch you harder in the side, and you didn't make a sound."

"Well, I was ready for her."

"Not sorry," Arie muttered. "I'd like to eat a full meal and not get stabbed. So you should quiet down."

At the very least, Thantrel's antics were keeping my mind off Neve. I felt certain of her safety, and proud that she was taking steps to become who she wanted to be, but that didn't mean I enjoyed being away from my mate.

I took in the spread as we approached the feast table at the front. I was more used to being served but had been to a feast or two like this before where fae served themselves. I could understand the rebels operating in this manner. From what I'd seen, anyone they could use as a soldier became one, and that likely left few people to complete tasks regarding the wellness of their home base, such as cooking and cleaning.

At the long feast table, a sole, tiny brownie offered us plates. I thanked him, which earned me two wide eyes before the brownie scurried off.

Could have been worse. I awaited when rebels would confront me.

As we'd been fed only breads and cheeses since we'd been taken captive, we were all rather hungry. We filled our plates with roasted boar, cheese, and bread. No vegetables or fruits were present, which made me wonder if they had a fae gifted with earth magic to produce such things. I selected an empty table near the front of the room, figuring it would be pointless to hide in the back or to the sides when others had been staring since we walked in.

The moment we sat down, however, something distracted me from the onlookers and my friends. Outside an intact window, standing in a courtyard, was a Drassil tree.

Of course. This once was the home of nobles. Why wouldn't one be here?

This tree, however, looked even worse than most I'd seen of late. The purple leaves, or what remained of them, drooped and were veined with a blackness that brought to mind the darkest creatures of the realm. The bark appeared dull, not shimmering, and full of life and magic. The tree was also smaller than most I'd seen. Certainly smaller than the Crown Drassil at Frostveil and the Heart Drassil at the Tower of the Living and the Dead—both trees I'd been called to tend in the past.

What did that mean for the realm? For the Faetia and the magic all around us? Drassil trees weren't only connected to the magic of Winter's Realm and the spirits of fae who once lived. It was also said that the trees were hinges, places where the veil between worlds was thin. Like gateways to the human world—though no one fae knew anything about the worlds the Drassils connected to. We believed them to be places of limerence, of pure magic, and if they died, we would live a diminished life. Or more likely, die too.

"Don't even think about it," Duran said.

I turned to my friend, shocked to find that he'd already devoured a quarter of his food. "About what?"

"Touching that Drassil. I can see that longing in your eyes, Vale. You can't."

"Why not?" Anna asked from a ways down the table,

where she sat with Clemencia, who'd been quiet since Neve left for dinner.

"The Drassils are all connected," Arie answered.

"So if Vale touched it, other trees would know?" Anna asked.

"Potentially," Duran replied. "And as we're trying to hide from powerful people who have access to the tangle of holy trees within the realm, it's best that Vale not do what he wants to do."

"It's dying," I said. "This makes our task all the more imperative."

"It does," Duran conceded.

I took a swig of ale from the rustic horns on offer and wrinkled my nose. *Sour. I suppose there's no chance of Summer Isle wine here.*

The conversation had spun to the roast, and I was about to comment when someone fluttered down to land on our table and stand before me.

"Prince Vale." A pixie glared up at me and crossed her arms over her chest. She was only slightly taller than my hand, pale as the moon, and *glowed*, a rare ability for her kind. "I require a word."

No question in the feminine tone. Nor was there a hint of reserve on her face. Both taken aback and amused at the intrusion, I leaned away, setting my horn in its holder.

"You have my attention."

"And I *deserve* your apology," the pixie's voice rose and spots of color filled her cheeks. "You killed my brother! If you're to be here, to break bread among us, I demand that you speak on your wrongs."

The skin on the back of my neck prickled. Around me, I felt my friends stiffen and was sure others were watching too.

And so it begins.

"When did this happen?" I asked.

Her face hardened. "At the most recent tourney in Avaldenn."

The tourney where I'd found Neve, left in the royal box. The one where a rebel had tried to kill the fae I'd once called my father.

But a pixie? I'd been armed with a bow and arrows. I recalled shooting three faeries, but not a pixie.

"I shot him?"

"No, but my brother got caught in your wind—thrown against the stone of Aaberg Ring. He died from a broken neck."

My heart sank. Never did I wish to harm a good-hearted fae of Winter's Realm, but at the time, I'd been defending the fae I'd called Father and the king. I'd also been defending the inhabitants of Avaldenn. In my mind, what I was doing was valiant and right. That the rebels were darkness, and we were light, and the rest of the world fell into shades of shadows.

Now, I understood that so many things were shades of darkness meeting the light. Gray, not just white or black.

"At the time, I believed that what I did was right, but believe me when I say that I don't take pleasure in harming the fae of Winter's Realm. Most of those fae are innocent and good and wish for nothing but a fulfilling life."

349

The pixie's shoulders loosened, but I wasn't done. I had much more to atone for.

I inhaled. "It would be an insult to your brother's memory for me to say that I am sorry. We both fought for things we believed in, and while my own beliefs have changed, I cannot alter the past. As much as I wish to, that is impossible for us all."

The pixie opened her mouth, but I held up a finger, halting her.

"But I will say this. I regret that the realm is divided. That it had to come to this and that you lost someone you loved. That I dealt the blow and caused you and your family great pain. Your brother might have been a good male—and I cannot bring him back. I wish I could, but I cannot, and I am truly sorry for that lacking."

Seconds passed in which she stared at me, wide eyes glowing. Though she was still, two feet solidly on the table, mentally, the pixie appeared as though she stood on a cliff's edge, and she did not know whether she wished to step off or jump back. I was not sure her mind decided as much as her heart did, but when a sniffle escaped her, she softened ever so slightly. "To be honest, he was a scoundrel, and we weren't close. Still, I loved him all the same."

A chuckle left me. "I'm related to a scoundrel, so I understand." I didn't look at Thantrel, but heard Luccan smothering a laugh and an incredulous whisper that definitely belonged to the youngest Riis brother.

"I see the world differently now," I continued. "I would not act the same as I did in the past. What I consider just and right has changed."

She stared at me, and I wasn't sure she knew what to make of my apology. I wasn't entirely sure either. But it had felt right and from the heart and it was the truth. The best I could do.

The pixie went so still and silent that had I not seen her lungs fill, I would have thought she stopped breathing.

Finally, though, she spoke. "I accept your apology and you. We were on different sides, and, from what I've heard, now we're not." She stuck out a small hand. "Don't make me regret this."

I gave her a finger, and she pressed her skin to mine as murmurs once again flooded the dining hall.

The pixie snorted and tossed her sheets of long, white hair over her shoulders. "Fates, we'll be all the gossip tonight."

"I expect we will," I said with a soft smile. "What's your name, anyway?"

"Xillia." She looked beyond me. "I think some others wish to speak with you. I'll leave them to it."

She fluttered off as fast as she arrived, and I twisted to find a line of at least twenty fae. Some were clearly ravaged by the blight. Others by battle. Some wore looks of anger, others of interest.

"Fates," Duran murmured. "I'm going to scoot down and give you and . . . all of them some privacy." He did just that, leaving a sizable gap between me and my friends.

I took another long drink of ale before locking eyes with the first in line. "Shall we speak?"

❄

An hour later, the last person requesting an apology left the table. Their frustration with me, with their king, and with the state of the realm had burrowed deep in my bones.

Of course, I'd known things in Winter's Realm were not perfect, but to learn how far from ideal the kingdom was for the commonfae rocked me to my core. My plate of food, half eaten, sat before me. The remains had long gone cold for I no longer had an appetite.

At the end of the table, my friends waited. As none had a reputation such as mine, no one expected anything of them. They'd eaten and set in on drinking ale—all the while observing me. Measuring if I was well. Occasionally, I'd give them a nod or a wave, telling them that I was fine.

The truth was, I was far from fine. But I'd needed to do this all the same. To listen to the grievances of the fae of Winter's Realm. Mostly, I could not fully apologize, and I was shocked to find that many understood my reasoning, even if they did not like it.

We are all people of duty. Of honor and oaths.

"Vale? Should we return to the annex?" Duran asked.

"Yes. I think so. I—"

"Urgent news!" a gruff voice shouted over the din of rebels. "Shut it *now!*"

The talking in the hall quieted, and all heads turned to where the voice had come from. Near the door, a male faerie with silver hair and wings stood, arms raised.

"What is it, Aleksander?" A female faerie as tall as me and with broad shoulders stood at her table.

"King Magnus and a constituent of Clawsguard have

been spotted flying about the midlands. They were not so far from here." Aleksander roared. "Lord Roar Lisika too."

I stiffened. The king and Roar? Flying together this far south?

I stood. "Were they on wing?"

Aleksander's gaze landed on me, and he scowled. "Gryphonback. Though I'm not sure I should say more with the prince about."

Silence rang through the hall and fae stared.

I left the table to walk over to the male. When we stood face to face, a jolt of recognition trilled through me.

This male had ice-blue eyes. When paired with his silver hair and wings, however, he looked much like Neve. My eyes scanned him more closely.

The same chin and nose too. I suspected I was looking at a Hawk Seed.

"Are you going to run to your father now, Prince Vale? Tell him that we've spotted him? Squeal of Valrun?"

I shook my head. "You may not know this, but my wife, Princess Neve, is indeed a Falk. And my mate." I did not tell this male that I was not an Aaberg anyway. The time would come for that revelation, but not tonight. "I stand with my mate. I'd do nothing that compromises her and that includes drawing the king here."

The male blinked.

"I only wish to ask how you saw them with such clarity if they were flying on gryphons?" The beasts were very fast. And if this fae had been on wing himself, then he'd already done the job of endangering the camp. "On wing?"

Aleksander sneered. "Do you think me a bleeding fool to

fly by a king and his guards? On a night such as this, the winds alone would damage my wings, but the White Bear? He'd hurl me from the sky!"

I did not deny it.

"Then how can you be sure?" The gryphons would bear royal markings, but they'd be too small to see from the ground.

"I'm a fylgjarn. My white hawk, Arla, saw the heraldry of the White Bear and the House of the Snow Leopard. She saw the males too, and I witnessed it all through her eyes."

My eyes widened. Skin-changing abilities with animals were very rare. It was far more common to shift, or even to be part elven and therefore able to manipulate the animal and speak with it. But to see through the animal's eyes? To have full control? And this male did so with a white hawk?

The symbol of House Falk . . . and not just any animal. A magical one.

"Putting it together, are you?" His wings spread behind him, a luminous silver.

My early guess was all but confirmed. "You're of Falk blood?"

"The son of the Hawk King himself. Born twenty turns before his firstborn, Aksel Falk, Fates rest his soul." Aleksander looked smug. To be a Hawk Seed and have survived this long reflected on his resourcefulness. "Me and your mate, we're brother and sister."

Was this the fae that the rebels rallied behind? Was he a threat to Neve?

If so, why wasn't she meeting with him? Aleksander

claimed to have come from outside and judging by the ruddiness of his cheeks and neck, he had.

"You're the leader here?" I asked.

He pulled back before releasing a booming laugh. "The leader! That's a good one, Prince!"

"At the attack in the Royal Theater, the rebels claimed to fight for the heir. That must be a Falk."

"Nothing trueborn about me, though. Well, maybe except my taste in good ale and fine wine. The stuff here is swill, but it gets the job done, I suppose." He reached to the nearest table and plucked a horn from a dryad's stand. They didn't stop him, only rolled their eyes.

"Plus, I have not a speck of Winter magic," Aleksander added after a long pull. "No Winter magic means no crown."

"I see." The next question, one I'd been wondering since Neve left to dine with the leaders, built behind my lips until it spilled out. "So, who is the leader?"

Aleksander popped an eyebrow. "Well, that's Thyra Falk —your mate's twin and my half-sister."

My knees buckled. *Neve's twin.*

Fates, I could only imagine what Neve had felt at that revelation. Neve had so wished to know her family and now she had someone close to her, so close they'd once shared a womb.

Aleksander leaned closer, and with ale-soured breath, spoke again. "Any idea where your father is heading? He flew southwest."

I drew in a breath as I considered. Southwest was the direction we'd come from. There were no great houses in the area, only the Lost Kingdom of Dergia, Vitvik, smaller towns and villages, and mountains. So many mountains.

The king might be going to the coinary from which I'd withdrawn coin and trying to follow me from there, but even that idea sat wrong in my belly. He'd send soldiers to fetch us, and yet he flew with Roar. Why would he bring Roar to hunt Neve and me down? I didn't deny that Roar would want to see Neve harmed, but the king would do that at court. He'd wish for an audience. He always did.

"I haven't a clue," I admitted. "But I'd also like to find out."

CHAPTER 26

NEVE

*S*he called me her sister.

I sat up straighter and looked the black-haired archer in the eyes. "Is this a joke?"

"I'm not the joking type," she replied. "Am I, Bac?"

"No, Lady Thyra."

Thyra. That name did something to me, opened a hole I hadn't known it was possible to open. Tears that I did not wish to show, let alone let fall, filled my eyes. My twin sister was alive. Right across the table from me!

For so long, I'd wondered if I had blood family in Winter's Realm. When I was a slave, I'd imagined a quiet family life in some small town glittering with snow outside the window of a cottage. A place alive with fae and the love of a family. Since learning who I was, I'd resigned myself to not having anyone. At least not a blood family. And I'd been happy to have those who loved me, my chosen family and my mate, take their place.

But I *did* have family, and she was staring at me with those cold ice-blue eyes. Smirking at me.

"I guess you didn't know I existed either," Thyra said. "Then, at the very least, no one can claim that you're far cleverer than me."

Her flat tone brought me back down. "Why would you say that?"

Thyra shared a pointed look with both Bac and Brynhild before answering. "You were at the Theater, Neve. You heard Avalina Trusso's song. She sang for *me*, the heir and holder of Winter's Touch. Once I learned who you were, I looked into the histories. You were born twenty minutes before me, and while I know little of your magic, you're a threat to my ambitions." She cocked her head. "You were planning on challenging that upstart White Bear, were you not?"

I leaned back, unable to believe that this moment, something that might have been beautiful, would begin like this. That my twin was worried I'd take what she thought was hers.

However, she was right on one score: As she knew little of me, I could say the same of her. I needed to take a step back and be more cautious.

Thyra had tried to kill me once, and her soldiers had wreaked havoc on the fae of Avaldenn. She was dangerous, and while a sister of blood, she may not be a sister of the heart. I had to tread as though I walked on a frozen lake with a nøkken scratching at the ice from below.

"Yes, I was planning on challenging King Magnus," I answered.

"When? How? And with what force? You arrived here with eight others, two of them cripples and one of those cripples is a human." She smirked, but Bac appeared taken aback at her tone when she mentioned cripples. "I understand that your mate is formidable. The others might be too, but your numbers are not promising."

"I wouldn't take on King Magnus with only eight—"

"Use his name. Or call him the White Bear." Thyra plucked a piece of bread from the center of the table. "Do not allow him to be king. That gives him too much power, which he does not deserve."

"There's no denying he has the power, Thyra," I retorted, my hands forming tight balls beneath the table. With every passing second, I felt more and more that she was toying with me.

"Names hold power," she insisted. "History recognizes them. Reveres them."

"*People* give those names power. And whether I call King Magnus a king or not, *others will*. At least until he meets his undoing. I will meet them where they are and, in me, they'll see a relatable fae."

Thyra snorted. "Are you aware what they are calling you right now? What they're whispering in the villages and cities alike? What they're calling your mate?"

She did not wait for my answer. "Slave Queen. Traitor Prince."

My name did not surprise or hurt me, but my belly hardened at the thought of anyone calling Vale a traitor. Vale . . . once touted as the Warrior Bear, now a Traitor Prince. That would crush him, though perhaps his fall from grace had been inevitable after he tied himself to me. I didn't think that King Magnus, who still did not know that Vale wasn't his son, meant for that label to spread. But how could it not?

Thyra shook her head. "We're both right. The people give names, *and* they hold power. But when we are dead, more fae will come after us, and I would not like to be remembered, not for a second, as a slave queen, sister."

I swallowed. "Considering my past, it's not so odd."

Thyra sipped her wine, a thoughtful expression on her face. "You mentioned ending the blight of Winter? How do you intend to do so?"

I frowned. Thus far, she'd been so mean, so unwelcoming, that I didn't want to tell her, but someone had to extend the rowan branch.

"We were traveling south, to the seat of House Balik, in hopes of gathering allies." I'd nearly said more allies, referring to the dwarves of Dergia, but they were my secret. I would not tell Thyra unless I was sure I could trust her. Fates willing, that day would come. "But we've also spoken of finding the Ice Scepter."

"So the king doesn't have it," Thyra mused. "The rumors are true."

King Magnus had never come out and said so, though I'd learned from Roar that the noble houses had surmised as much many turns ago. Apparently, the rebels had too.

"What do you want it for?" Bac asked.

"To tame Winter's hold on the land. To help with the blight—if that is, in fact, wholly related from the disappearance of the Hallow."

A small smile played on Bac's face. "The fae of Winter's Realm deserve a respite from the harsh and the cold and death."

"Do you believe the Scepter connects to the blight too?" I asked the golden-eyed male.

"I do," Bac replied. "You'll see many in our forces affected by it, either directly or indirectly."

My gaze shifted to Thyra. As if expecting this, she shrugged.

"I never said we did not have cripples in our forces. I merely wished to learn more of what you thought."

"Cunning."

"A leader needs to be."

I sighed and, already wishing for a break from the verbal sparring, gestured to the food at the center of the table. "The meat is getting cold. Shall we eat?"

"We should," Brynhild replied, her tone soft again. I got the sense that as one of Thyra's advisors, she brought a warm edge. And perhaps Bac brought reason?

I wasn't sure, but it did make me wonder what my sister would be like if she wasn't trying to investigate me. Would *we* be alike? Or was this her true nature? Harald Falk, my father, had been said to be calculating and hard. A Cold King. Was Thyra the same?

The food tasted bland compared to what I'd eaten in great halls of castles, but after days of eating on the road, and then being given only hardened bread, cheese, and water in my cage, I savored the meat, fresh bread, cheese, and wine. The others seemed hungry too, and we allowed ourselves to eat for a few moments, and it was almost easy to ignore the glances Thyra sent across the circular table. I'd nearly finished my plate when my sister pushed her plate away.

"What else do you know of the Hallows of Winter's Realm?"

I set down the piece of cheese I'd been chewing on. Only recently had I learned two others existed, one of which I had in my possession. "Not much."

"They're lesser known," Brynhild offered, at the same time Thyra tossed up her hands.

"Fates! She has no idea about anything!" Thyra hissed. "Why are we tiptoeing around this?"

"You brought it up." Bac did not look at Thyra as he spoke but glared at his plate. "We said we would not. Not yet anyhow."

"Yes, well, this entire conversation is not turning out as I expected, and I require answers." Thyra's jaw hardened. "You're ignorant about the Hallows, yet you arrived with one? How is that so?"

My jaw tensed. So she recognized Sassa's Blade when no other had. Interesting. Still, I was not ready to give her more. Not yet.

"I'll remind you that you carried me here," I said.

She rolled her eyes. "The *sword*, Isolde! Sassa's Blade! You truly don't know what it does?"

My heart skipped a beat at her using my birth name. My real name, though I had yet to use it publicly. However, hearing it from Thyra's lips—no matter who frustrated her tone—that was different. She said my name and for the first time, it rang true. It felt like me.

A well of emotion sprang up in me as the second part of her claim hit when Thyra stood from the table.

"I can't do this. She may be my twin, but she knows nothing *and less*. I need to consider how to proceed. Make the plans we discussed." She left the table and strode out the door, banging it open as she left.

I sat there, mouth hanging open at what had happened. No words could describe the mountain of emotions I'd felt during this meeting with my only surviving blood—and some of them shouldn't be said in polite company.

A feminine sigh came from the other side of the table. "I'm sorry. Thyra is worried."

"Scared," Bac said hotly.

"That too," Brynhild allowed. "She has never been good at handling surprises, and you're the biggest surprise of her life."

"We don't seem much alike, but we share that at least." I picked up my goblet of wine, noting that it was dented from use, and drank.

Brynhild watched me. "I noticed your reaction when she used your birth name. Would you like us to call you that, or Neve?"

"Neve for now," I said, surprised they would even ask. "It's no surprise who I am, but I'm still getting used to Isolde."

The older fae nodded. "Smaller changes are difficult enough to wrap ones head around. I cannot imagine altering your identity so thoroughly."

Stars, I did not want to talk about this with them, fae I

barely knew. Thankfully, I had another topic in mind. "I don't suppose you could elaborate on Sassa's Blade?"

Brynhild nodded. "It's the blade of the Unification. How much do you know about the Unification?"

"The basics, perhaps a touch more, I suppose."

"Did you know a great cavern opened in the ground? That is where Sassa banished the Shadow Army?"

"I—I did not." Nor did I see how that was possible. Or understand the implications.

"That's what they say happened. No one alive then is alive now, and many of the histories have been destroyed, but oral tradition lives on." Brynhild leaned back in her chair and rested her folded hands on the table. "It says that the blade possesses great magic. Have you experienced it?"

I jolted, shocked at the mention of the magic of the sword, but also curious for answers. Perhaps I'd found the one person who could give them. Maybe the rebels understood more than anyone gave them credit for. And maybe I should share the information I'd gleaned about the sword.

"Once. A shadow came from it," I admitted.

Brynhild's eyes flew open. "A shadow?!"

"In the shape of a man. It helped me."

The other two exchanged glances.

"Will I get my sword back?" I asked, more possessive of it than I had been since I learned they'd taken it.

"In time," Bac replied. "I must ask though, since you have one Hallow and are going after another, do you have the third?"

"I do not," I said. "I assume you speak of the Frør Crown?"

Brynhild smirked. "You have more knowledge than you let on."

"Barely." I shrugged a shoulder.

"Well, let us see if we're on the same page." Brynhild clasped her hands together on the table. "The Frør Crown is a sign of legitimacy for the ruler of Winter's Realm, and the least is known of it, but it is the third Hallow of this land. The Frør Crown has magic, like the other two, though I cannot say what that magic is."

That was what Vale said too.

"And you two learned all of this from the histories?" It was my turn to ask questions. "How did you get these histories?"

The male's lips curled up. "My mother worked in a famous library in the south. She was well respected and well loved, by one more than most." He gave an unamused chuckle. "My father, in an effort to impress my mother, allowed her access to the place where only the members of the Golden House and select keepers can go. She read of the Hallows there and told me of them."

The Golden House. I'd never heard House Balik described as such, but it fit. They were gold of eyes and deep gold of hair and certain members of the Balik clan such as Sian wore enough of the metal to weigh down an orc.

"Your father was a keeper of this knowledge?"

Bac shook his head. "Better. He was a brother to Warden of the South, Tadgh Balik."

I drew in a breath. So Bac was a highborn bastard, related to Baenna, Eireann, Sian, Filip, and the other Baliks who I'd not met. A cousin. I looked at him afresh and believed it. His brown skin and golden eyes were so very familiar.

"I've met some of your family," I said. "They're my friends and very kind."

"My mother spoke well of them, and even though my father died, and they never married, I think she loved him until she took her last breath."

Stars alive. If there was one thing I understood, it was being an orphan. I didn't think Bac had intended to draw a line connecting us, but as far as I was concerned, he had.

"I'm sorry about your parents," I said. "But I'm pleased that you entrusted me with this information."

"It's not a secret," Bac laughed. "Our rebel forces comprise of bastards, criminals, cripples, and otherwise broken fae. Sometimes just fae who want a better life for their younglings too, but all of us have seen hardship."

"That we have." Brynhild stood, revealing she was missing the lower half of her right leg.

Fates, what a life these two must have lived. And they weren't alone in this. I'd seen the disfigured fae. I'd known them. Just as I'd met broken families, and those who did not fit in with a blood family. It seemed that times were not better when my father reigned, but they weren't good now either.

"Thyra wishes to set a trial for you." Brynhild walked over, more graceful on her false leg than I would have imagined. "It's her way of seeing how reliable you are—if you're strong enough for the fight she has been planning for many turns. If you can really work together."

Thyra was plainly untrusting and equally as tough. Hardened by her past. No doubt the task would be dangerous and difficult.

But as frustrating as I found my sister and this assumption that I'd jump at the chance to complete a task for her, I *would* rise to the occasion. I had to. Not only did I wish to see Magnus thrown from the throne, but I also wanted someone worthy to sit there. And I wished for revenge. For that, I needed more allies, and the rebels already shared my cause. If I had to prove myself to Thyra to earn their help, I'd do so.

"Fine. Set the task," I said. "I'll be ready when it comes."

INTERLUDE

LORD ROAR LISIKA, WARDEN OF THE WEST, HOUSE OF THE SNOW LEOPARD

Many turns had passed since the Warden of the West had visited the site where his parents and brother died. It was rare that frost giants ventured out of their mountain peaks, but on that foul day, they had. With their appearance, a great family of Winter's Realm was broken. Nearly wiped off the face of the realm.

Roar could not recall the time after his family died well. The fever from the blight destroyed his mind for days and his body for far longer, but it was said that while their castle in Guldtown was in an uproar, a maid fled with the Princess Isolde in her arms.

When young Roar awoke, his eyes took in a changed world. His family dead. A title now upon his head. And the baby faerie he'd been commanded to wed, gone to the stars only knew where.

And though not a hint of his family's blood remained upon the snow of this cursed place, Roar felt their presence. He had each time he came here and that worried him. Had

LORD ROAR LISIKA, WARDEN OF THE WEST, HOUSE OF THE ...

their souls been denied entry into the afterworld? Had the Fates cut the threads of his father, mother, and brother, and fed it to the serpent that wound through the stars, preventing them from knowing a moment of peace, even in death?

Likely because of Roar's new leg hindering him in deep snow, the king commanded Roar to stay behind and not help search the area. A mercy, he supposed, though with the sensation of spirits all around and no distractions to occupy his mind, it did not feel like one.

To stave off the aches that came with flying, Roar shifted in his saddle only for his muscles to tighten and send a jolt of pain through his leg. Somehow that same agony extended all the way into the metal that was now a part of him. The phantom ache made Roar's jaw tightened.

Every morning when he awoke, he swore vengeance against Isolde Falk—he could no longer think of her as Neve, the stray he'd picked up and tried to love, if only because it was what his parents had once wanted. No, now he saw only a duplicitous female. *A Falk.*

Isolde, however, wasn't the only fae Roar wanted revenge on. Vale would pay too, though Roar would not bring that up around his new *ally*, the king.

Roar snorted at the notion. An ally! After all the king had put him and his family through, Roar would never stoop so low. He would marry the king's daughter, but he'd only requested to do so because that sort of request would be expected of someone who wished for an alliance with the Crown of Winter. A pardon, a place on the king's council, and the hand of his daughter—all very normal appeals when one had such valuable information. His Majesty hadn't seemed at all surprised by Roar's petition. Which was just as Roar had planned.

But a true ally, the king was not. Roar only needed to wait, to be patient. Soon enough, vengeance on those who had wronged his family would be his. Then he'd claim what he deserved.

"Nothing in the woods." The king's voice hit Roar's ear. He twisted to find the monarch and his golden-cloaked Clawsguards emerging from the trees.

"No?" Roar asked dryly.

Had the Ice Scepter been here for two decades, he, or the loyal fae he'd sent to search this area, would have found it and brought it to the warden already.

"Not a bleeding thing." Magnus swung a leg over the gryphon, and the beast, better trained than most of its kind, shifted its wings to oblige. "I wish to go to the closest town. It's the same one where Vale withdrew coin. There we can make inquiries."

Finally. Roar had suggested this course of action two days ago, but King Magnus denied him. The White Bear wished to focus on the Ice Scepter, and let others find Isolde for him, which didn't surprise Roar, but frustrated him when the warden had other goals in mind.

"An excellent idea, Majesty." Roar gripped the reins tighter. "Shall we fly?"

Roar stood in the middle of the street, assessing the village of Eygin. He'd never visited the place, though this village was, technically, under his protection. The mountains surrounding the village crawled with dangerous creatures and this particular stop on the map was simply too remote to bother with. That a place so small supported a coinary was shocking. Almost as shocking as the fact that Isolde and Vale had made it so far south with so many humans. Roar's property.

Or they had been.

His fists clenched, anger rolling through him again. He did not know what Isolde and Vale had done with the humans—most likely they were dead in the snow somewhere in the west—a feast for the wild creatures and ogres. Roar didn't care. But if they were dead, then he hoped their deaths weighed on Isolde's shoulders. He hoped that the weakness of the humans had slowed her, harmed her. He wished three times that pain for Vale.

But he wanted neither of them to die. Not yet. Not without his presence. Not without them knowing that he'd helped the king find a Hallow of the realm, one that could stifle the ever-worsening weather. Once that was done and Winter's Realm was to rights once more, he wanted them to watch Roar take the throne for himself.

Then they can die. Magnus too. Roar stared at the coinary façade where the king was now interrogating leprechauns.

He doubted the king would find anything more than he already knew about in the coinary. Rather, he'd have to speak with the locals who frequented places where one laid their head at night. Vale and Isolde would have had to stay the night in this dunghole.

Above, a white hawk shrieked. Roar had seen the bird circling the village and the surrounding mountain side for an hour, no doubt looking for mice or something else to eat. Roar took the bird's call as a sign to do something. A sign to act from one predator to another.

"Tell His Majesty I'll return soon," Roar threw the command to the Clawsguard who was waiting outside the coinary with him.

He walked toward the Frozen Toes Tavern, the best tavern in the town and with an attached inn, or so he'd been told. It wasn't much to his eye, but as Roar opened the door, he found two dozen fae staring at him. Whispers ran through the crowd as he approached the bar.

"Mi lord? What can I get you?" The dryad barkeep stood at attention, his skin bark-like and arms looked rather like stiff branches but were ready to serve all the same.

Roar leaned over the countertop, seemingly at ease in this place. Though his face was now scarred, he remained handsome and charming, and he intended to use each quality and anything else he might need to gather information.

"Your best ale, is it local?"

"We grow everything in greenhouses outside of town. The water is fed straight from the mountains."

"Perfect. Your favorite local ale then."

The barkeep poured the ale, frothing at the top, and set it before Roar.

A gold bear slid across the barter, and the tender's eyes widened.

"It's only a copper, mi lord."

"I'm looking to purchase more than ale."

The barkeep pocketed the coin. "What else do you need?"

"Information."

"'Bout?"

"Word has it that a prince and princess came through here recently. Did they stay here?"

"They did."

"Were you working?"

"I wasn't. My brother was. They stayed in three rooms."

Yes, Sir Caelo had been with Vale that night, and one human—the same one Prince Gervais had brought to court. Isolde's friend, he later learned. Roar remembered the slave's face. The dark upturned eyes, the raven-wing hair, and the small stature.

But three rooms would not fit the humans they'd liberated.

"How many were in their party?"

"Four."

So they'd put the humans somewhere while they stayed at the inn. Kept them in the woods?

"And they came from what direction?"

"West. From the deep mountains."

Roar took a drink of ale. It was rather good. He lifted his horn, which pleased the dryad.

"What's to the west of here?"

While this was his territory, Roar was not as familiar with the few villages dotting the mountain ranges.

"Nothin' much." The dryad shrugged. "Mountains all the way to the other kingdoms."

It was impossible, given the distance they needed to travel and the days that Vale and Isolde had been gone, that they'd seen the humans to another kingdom. What else could they have done with the slaves? Kept the humans in the mountains?

Or perhaps the humans had remained in the woods while the fae ventured into town and the humans were still actually traveling with them?

"Which direction did they go when they left?" Roar asked.

"They took the high road to Vitvik, or so says my son. He was huntin' goats on the mountainside and saw them leave."

Roar sat up. Vitvik was a small city, and he still found it difficult to believe that all the fae in a city would allow humans to live alongside them. He was not the only one with harsh feelings toward the weaker species.

"Are there towns or villages along the way to Vitvik?"

The barkeep appeared deep in thought as he polished a horn. "There was once, but no longer. Too many wild orc tribes in this part of the kingdom."

Once. Were Vale and Isolde taking the humans to a ghost town? Would he find both his slaves and his enemies in one place?

"Can you show me which road they took? And provide a

map showing any of the smaller ones?" Just in case, it was best to have all the information on hand.

"'Course, mi lord. I'll send the server to get one right now." The barkeep looked as though he wished to say more but did not.

Roar slid another gold across the table. "Tell me."

"The path to Vitvik is perilous. Often much colder than the surrounding area—locals think the passages trap the wind, but there are also creatures in the mountains. *Monsters.* You'll take care if you go that way?"

Roar's ears perked up. It was said that until a fae worthy of ruling Winter's Realm held the Ice Scepter, the magic of the kingdom would continue to fall into disarray. Cold came with that. Maybe the Ice Scepter had not traveled so far from the site of his parents' deaths after all?

"Mi lord? I'd be upset if I sent you that way, and you found harm."

"My party will take care," Roar assured him. "Thank you for your service." He stood, not bothering to finish the ale, and left the tavern.

He rejoined his travel party to learn that the king had found nothing of importance at the coinary. That failing frustrated Magnus and left him at a loss until Roar divulged what he'd learned. His idea about the Scepter, too, just to sweeten the deal.

The king grasped at the idea, flailing for some lead, and they took to the skies.

They followed the small road the barkeep pointed out as it unraveled through narrow mountain passages. They searched for signs of passing through, burnt wood from a fire being one sign. They hoped, with the beating of their gryphons' wings, that finally, they'd have a true lead.

"I'm going lower," the king shouted over the wind. "To ride through that tunnel through the rock."

Roar squinted and saw what the king meant. A tunnel ran through the mountain in a place where it would have been too precarious to carve a road on the mountainside. Likely of dwarven creation. In no way did Roar think that his enemies or the humans would all be in there, hiding. However, the tunnel could hold other clues.

"I'll join you," Roar said.

The king did not deny him, so the pair descended, the Clawsguards behind, following their king. Upon landing, the king directed a Clawsguard to ride first. Magnus took second position, and Roar followed with the other guards at the rear. They entered the darkness of the tunnel, and a cold set in—one even more stifling than outside.

Recalling the barkeep's words, Roar sat up straighter, a mistake as the stone ceiling dipped, and he nearly knocked himself out.

Magnus, however, continued forward, his hand running along the wall. Seconds passed before he stopped, twisted to meet Roar's eyes.

"We need to find a way inside this mountain."

"Of course, Majesty," Roar replied, heart skipping a beat. For the first time in days, the king appeared very determined. "You believe they're in there?"

"I think first of the Ice Scepter. Your own magic is frozen, is it not?"

"It is."

"Then this area needs to be investigated." The king paused. "If what I seek is not there, we continue to Vitvik, but if it is, and *we* have found it . . ." He let out a hard laugh. "Then she still cannot read her magic. A boon for me."

Isolde had been powerful in the mines, but Roar believed the king was right. The Falk princess was unable to wield them like one who knew their magic inside and out should be able to use their powers.

That lack of depth of knowledge might be her downfall.

CHAPTER 27

VALE

When I awoke, it was to find my mate already wide awake and deep in thought.

"Did you sleep well?" I nuzzled into her hair, sniffing and repressing a low moan at how her smokey vanilla scent turned me on.

"Not really. Thyra dominated my dreams," Neve murmured.

I pulled her closer, protective over the female who completed my soul as I completed hers.

A day had passed since she'd met her sister. A day of silence that was driving my mate crazy.

My mate had longed to meet her family and though she put up a brave front, Thyra's reception had hurt her.

"Also, I've been wondering about the task they're to set. Will it be something deadly? Thyra doesn't seem to like me much. What if she wishes me dead?"

"She won't harm you." I sounded sure, though doubts roamed deep in my heart. Neve didn't need to hear those, though. "And if there's so much as a whiff of danger in the task, I will join. There is no other option."

"We have other options, Vale." She turned to face me, her violet eyes searching for an answer to a question she hadn't spoken. "We could leave. Go find the Baliks like we planned. Or try to find the Ice Scepter with our friends."

"Do you now have an idea of where to start?"

"None," she admitted so halfheartedly that I suspected she hadn't really wanted to leave anyway. She wanted to learn more about Thyra and see if they could have a relationship.

"Well, I have an idea of a different sort."

"What's that?" she asked.

"Your sister wishes to see how strong you are. To test your fortitude and weigh the true faeness of you. See how much you hunger for power, like many of our kind."

"I've never been very power hungry."

"And yet you seek the Scepter."

"I do want it," Neve said. "But only to right wrongs. I want to help those I can relate to. The downtrodden. And to bring this realm back into a state in which all can *live*."

"A noble pursuit," I whispered. "You'll need power all the same for it."

"True," she exhaled. "So what do you have in mind?"

"Today we train, and you will show off all that I've taught you."

My mate smirked, and I swore the sadness in her eyes sparked and took on heat. That fire and ability to rise to meet any challenge was why she was still alive.

"I like that idea," she agreed. "Maybe they'll give us weapons? Or allow us to use magic?"

I suspected they might be satiating their own curiosity. "We can only ask."

Neve rose. "Then let's go. I want to show my twin that I'm not one to be trifled with. That I'm not weak."

We dressed and left our private room to find everyone else in the annex was already awake. At the mention of training, Luccan, Thantrel, and surprisingly, Duran claimed to wish to join. I figured that was not so many people that the rebels would worry about arming us—especially when Caelo was still abed, and Rynni had been called to the healing wing an hour back. She was to work in that area of the falling castle, helping the rebels who did not have such a skilled healer with them.

Arie, Anna, and Clemencia would stay with Caelo. Anna would work on mending our attire that had worn out in our travels, while the other two would devour books that had been brought to our annex hoping to find clues on the Hallows. I stared at the books, somewhat stunned. That the rebels had delivered the tomes Arie requested hinted that they *might* welcome us fully. Eventually.

One could hope anyway.

Once everyone was ready, we exited the annex to find the usual six guards outside our door. One arched a dirty blond eyebrow at us. He bore a diagonal scar across his face, one that brought to mind orc claws. "Do you wish to break your fast?"

"Actually," I said, "we're hoping to work stiffness from our bones. To train, if you'll allow it."

The guards exchanged glances, but none looked surprised. Perhaps their leaders had already presumed I'd asked for such freedoms. I was, after all, the Warrior Prince and had to remain fit and nimble with my weapons.

"The others will remain here?" the same guard asked.

"Yes. I suppose the others may wish to eat soon, but most of them are not the sort of fae to enjoy sparring."

He looked to Duran, a dwarf who had spent a total of three days sparring in his thirty turns of life. After a pause, though, the guard only shrugged.

"Very well, you'll follow me." He motioned for two other guards to join us. "I'm Svald, head of your escort retinue today. If you have requests while you train, ask me."

"Very well." I nodded, and the faerie led us through the castle.

Thus far, we had seen little of the cursed place. Still, I recognized many of the tapestries that we passed by. Familiar areas too. Odd, for I knew the castle to be large. I guessed that parts were so destroyed that the rebels only used a portion of it.

"Any word on King Magnus and his retinue?" Neve asked Svald, breaking my short musings.

My clever mate. Always digging for more information.

She'd been shocked to hear of the Falk bastard, another relation. Almost as surprised as she'd been to learn of the king flying overhead—on some sort of mission, I guess.

"Our fylgjarn has his hawk following," Svald replied. "So far, he and the other fae—Lord Roar Lisika being one —seem to be hunting for something. We know not what."

"Where are they now?" I asked.

"Can't say for certain. Last I heard, they entered a mountain abutting Eygin, and the hawk has since lost them. Can't go in there, can she? But she's staying nearby, waiting to see them come out. We can only hope they emerge from the same hole they entered by."

We turned a corner, and I caught the sounds of clanging metal and jeers that indicated sparring fae, when, to my right, Thantrel shuddered.

"What's wrong?" I asked.

"Don't you feel something off here?" He peered about, as if searching for something. "Like your nerves are on fire? I've felt it a bunch of times and can't help but think it must be the curse."

"Can't say I have."

Neve, Luccan, and Duran echoed me.

"Guess I'm special. Not that we didn't already know that."

Duran scoffed. "By the dead gods, your ego knows no bounds."

Thantrel scowled. "Why are you here, dwarf? You don't even fight."

"I'm curious about the castle. Wanted to see more and hear stories of it—if I can get anyone to talk."

"Oh yes, seeing a rotting castle is such a breath of fresh air," Luccan added, before Thantrel could respond, as he appeared to be about to do. The way Duran and Thantrel bickered, you'd think they were brothers too.

"We're here," Svald announced as we approached the end of the hall and stopped before an open set of doors.

Inside a large room about half the size of the training

facilities at Frostveil, a hundred rebels sparred with swords, maces, axes, and other weapons. One female fighter hurled daggers at a target. This room, unlike much of the castle, looked to be in good shape. No crumbling walls. No holes in the ceiling or blown out windows. It might be bare and cold, but it was functional.

"Where do the archers train?" Luccan asked.

There wasn't room in here, but many of us had seen Thyra shoot. She was no slouch, and I suspected there were other rebels talented in archery too.

"Outside," Svald said. "If you wish to train in archery, I'll have to request permission. You are permitted in here, though." He gestured inside. "No magic. Just weapons."

"We understand." Without our magic, we were small threats. Even if we had been inclined to fight and flee, with so many people training in the hall we'd never make it.

We entered the training area, and everyone turned to stare. Svald's presence seemed enough to dim some interest, but not all. About half of the room returned to what they'd been doing, and the others watched as we approached the weapons.

I picked a sword. Luccan took an axe and Thantrel, a mace. Neve studied the weapons before she too took a sword similar in size to Sassa's Blade. My mate was training with her sword even when she didn't have it in her grasp.

"You take the far corner," Svald instructed.

"Are you going to train with us?" Thantrel asked, his eyes darting about as if he didn't dare meet Svald's gaze.

My eyebrows furrowed. Usually the youngest Riis brother had more control. He was a master of eye contact—

either to exude how powerful he was or charisma, depending on the situation. Now, however, he seemed about ready to jump out of his boots.

"We're to stand with you. Not train." Svald motioned toward the other guards who'd come with us, all still silent.

"Too bad for you. We could show you a good time." Thantrel winked, but the gesture appeared jerky, not smooth.

"Than? Do you need water? Or food?" I asked. "You're acting strange."

"I'm fine," Thantrel shot back, all the while shuddering again. "I . . ." He trailed off, eyes widening as he turned to face the entry to the training room again. "Bleeding skies. It can't be!"

"What in the stars is wrong with him?" Duran muttered as the rest of us spun to see what had Thantrel in its grips.

"Who is *that*?" Thantrel whispered, pointing to the door. A trio of fae were entering, one of whom I recognized.

As did Neve.

Her eyes widened. "The black-haired one in front?"

"W-w-who else is there!?" Thantrel sputtered, which initiated a sidelong glance from Luccan. Had Than lost his mind?

"That's my twin, Thyra. She's the leader of the rebels."

A grin spread across Thantrel's face as he shook his head. "That's not all that she is. She's also my mate."

My heart skipped a beat. "You've got to be kidding. Thantrel, are you—"

But he was off, red and orange fiery wings spread and

389

soaring across the sparring room, above fae who were fighting a single-minded mission.

"Skies! What an idiot!" Luccan leapt into the air to soar after Thantrel.

"Come on." Neve took my hand, and we followed suit, also flying and leaving Duran in the corner with Svald.

"Thantrel!" I roared. "Stop!"

He did not heed my command. Rather, the youngest Riis brother soared all the way over Thyra, landing before her and bowing.

The leader of the rebels did not appear amused. She scowled as we closed in. "What do you want?"

"You, my love." Thantrel reached for her hand, a move I'd seen him try many times on barmaids to great success.

Thyra batted his hand away. "Don't you dare touch me. And *I'm not* your love. Are you drunk?"

I landed, Neve and Luccan right beside me. But before I could speak, Neve stepped forward.

"Thyra, he's with us. He—"

"I'm your mate," Thantrel cut her off. "Surely you feel it? I've been sensing you since we were brought here. I thought it was the curse, but it was you, my beautiful raven-haired mate!"

Thyra's face went blank, only for that shock to be replaced by a hardened jaw and narrowed eyes. "*You're* what I've been feeling?!"

Bleeding skies! She didn't deny it!

Jealousy welled inside me. I'd always heard tales of fae sensing their mate in an instant. I'd believed that was what would happen to me too. While I'd been attracted to Neve from the first moment I'd set eyes on her, the day when she'd stepped out of Roar's sleigh and quite literally stopped me in my tracks, I hadn't innately recognized her as my mate. In truth, I suspected our scenario was more common, and the fantasy, that deep instant knowing written about in tales, was rare. Exceptional. And it happened to be playing out right before my eyes.

Not smoothly, though. I winced.

If looks could kill, Thyra would have murdered Thantrel a million times over by now.

Thyra took a step toward Thantrel, her leanly muscled arms flexing, her body unyielding. Every line in her body indicated malice.

"You need to leave Valrun." Thyra punched her finger into Thantrel's chest.

He pressed a hand to where she'd made contact.

"Leave? *Together?*"

"Bleeding skies, it's bad enough that the dead gods gave me a mate with the hubris to line his eyes and plait his hair."

She waved near Thantrel's face, his green eyes lined with gold by the same nymph who colored Saga's hair. Most females were intrigued by his appearance. Thyra was plainly not one of those admirers.

"But to also send me a stupid male to bind myself with?" The rebel leader sneered. "No, we're not leaving together! I can't think straight with you here! And I have no time for a mate. Go back to Avaldenn, or wherever you came from, you prissy lordling!"

A cough came from behind the Falk heiress. The male

with brown skin and honey eyes that brought to mind Sian and Filip, stepped closer to Thyra. He must be the Balik bastard Neve told me about. One of Thyra's right-hand fae.

"Thyra," the probable Balik bastard said, "he can't leave."

She spun. "I'm in charge here, correct, Bac?"

"*Yes*, but what if his family asks questions? Or the king? He knows this is the rebel hideout. He—"

"Thantrel Riis," Than bowed low and with a flamboyant wave of his hand. "Son of the Lord of Tongues, Lord Leyv Riis."

"By the dead gods, it cannot get worse than the *spymaster's son*." Bac shook his head. "Now he *really* can't leave Valrun. Not until we're sure they all side with us."

Thyra tossed up her hands. "My bleeding luck!" Venom filled her glare as she turned on Thantrel. "I reject our bond, Thantrel Riis. Now, the rest of you, move out of my way!"

They did so, and Thyra marched past those she'd arrived with and straight out the door.

"By the dead gods," Luccan breathed. "I can't believe that happened."

"*My sister* is his mate," Neve scoffed.

I swallowed, taking in Than's expression. With his hand over his heart, and his eyes screwed shut, he seemed to be in physical pain after being rejected by his mate. "And she wants nothing to do with him."

CHAPTER 28

NEVE

I leaned back in the threadbare chair, stretching my boots toward the blazing hearth to warm my cold toes. Our mission to show Thyra our skills had failed spectacularly. After encountering Thantrel, she'd never returned to the training area. Still, I didn't count the day as a total loss.

Many *watched* us spar. Some tried to mimic Vale and Luccan. Mimicry was flattery, and I was certain the rebels would talk of what they saw.

Gossip would find Thyra's ears. Even if she was avoiding us. Avoiding *him*. I swallowed as I looked across the sitting area at Thantrel.

Others read and relaxed as we waited for dinner, but Thantrel stared at the fire burning in the hearth with forlorn olive-green eyes. After Thyra rejected their bond, he hadn't trained with the rest of us but requested to be returned to the annex. Anna told me he'd been like this since. Sullen, often with tears in his eyes.

I supposed I would be much the same. I suspected that he'd felt his mating bond thrumming in his chest since our arrival at Valrun Castle. He'd been acting so off that there was no other explanation. Their bond had not yet snapped into place, and Thyra had rejected him. Harshly so. From what little I knew of my sister; I had every reason to believe that she would not budge in that rejection.

Thantrel would be doomed to a life of agony, knowing his mate existed, knowing her and being able to see her, but never having her. Never feeling complete as I did. As Vale did.

How in the world was Thyra so bullheaded to do the same to herself? When I looked at Vale, our bond set me ablaze. Who wouldn't want that?

And why does she think Thantrel is so bad?

He was a handful, but Thantrel possessed a good heart, and no one could deny that he was gorgeous. I sighed, knowing I would not be able to help. At least not unless Thyra and I grew closer and even then maybe not. She seemed very much the kind to keep her private life extremely private.

I can only do so much. I allowed my mind to drift to other matters until a knock came at the door. I looked at Vale, who'd been stretching on the other side of the room.

"It's not late enough for dinner," he remarked.

"Rynni is back?" Clem quipped. The healer worked with injured rebels all day. Apparently, they had attacked a lord's army moving north at the request of King Magnus a day before we arrived, and many paid the price.

"Why would she knock?" The closest, Arie, opened the door. "Hello?"

"Good afternoon. Is Princess Neve available?"

I recognized that voice from last night. I rose and found Brynhild standing before the soldiers who guarded our annex.

"Hi," I said, uncertain why she'd be present.

"Might we speak in private? Down the hall?"

"Sure." I cast Vale a glance that clearly said I'd be fine. So far, there'd been no physical threats from the rebels—just verbal ones largely directed towards Vale, not me. I didn't expect any sort of threat to come from Brynhild.

He nodded, and I slipped out the door and trailed behind the faerie with the wooden leg. She paused when she was out of earshot of the guards.

"Apologies if I was interrupting a pleasant afternoon."

"We weren't doing anything," I assured her. "What do you wish to speak about?"

"Two reasons. The first being the most important." She drew a breath. "Thyra has set your challenge. You will be sent to Avaldenn to access the Falk vault there and see if the Frør Crown is inside."

My jaw dropped. "Won't that alert King Magnus?"

Our visit to a coinary in the south had given away our location, and that had been risky, but to do so in Avaldenn? A stone's throw away from Frostveil?

Utter madness.

"You will have to do so in secret."

"A heist then."

I'd often heard that no one could break into the

coinaries of the leprechauns and here my sister set me that very task. Maybe she really did want me dead!

"Correct." Brynhild gave me an understanding smile. "Only you and Thyra can access the vault, and she is desperate to possess and master a Hallow. Their powers increase one's own. Or so they say. And of course, you already have one."

"Do I now? My sword is but a memory since coming here."

"It's being kept safe. I give you my word on that."

"And what if the Frør Crown is in the Skau vault?" I asked.

A long shot as that crown had belonged to the royal house and the now extinct Skau family had only been a member of the Sacred Nobles, but it was not out of the question. Maybe my father had transferred items to my mother's family vault to keep things extra safe?

"Thyra will be breaking into that vault while you work in Avaldenn. A coordinated effort."

I laughed. She had such audacity!

"That wasn't my reaction," Brynhild shook her head. "You two are more alike than you seem."

I exhaled and brought myself under control, still full of questions. "The city that House Skau called home is far from Avaldenn, is it not? What is it called?"

I'd seen it on the map, but not been that far east. Nor had Clemencia made me memorize anything about it, as House Skau was long gone.

"Bitra is many days' ride. We're working on the schedule now."

CHAPTER 28

If any one thing went wrong in the plan, that put my potential relationship with Thyra at risk. My sister might despise me, but I didn't feel the same. Plus, I'd just found her. I didn't want to lose her to a heist gone wrong.

Then, it hit me.

Bitra was presently the seat of House Riis, not House Skau. Over time, Luccan had created gateways between all his family's properties, including the brothels and taverns his father owned. It made checking in on the lord's establishments far easier than riding for days and days.

Luccan would likely have created a gateway to their castle, as he had one tucked in the basement of his home in Avaldenn. Add that to the fact that we'd been in Vitvik, where Lord Riis owned a brothel, also boasting a hidden gateway, and this heist got far easier. Part of it, anyway. We could ride to Vitvik, which I'd heard was a day's ride away from Valrun, and from there arrive in Avaldenn and Bitra within minutes.

But that would mean outing Luccan.

My teeth dug into my bottom lip, and Brynhild let out a sigh.

"You don't have to decide now, but soon."

She'd mistaken my reaction. Not that I wasn't worried about a heist, but it was concerning to force a friend to tell their secret. To rebels, no less.

"Thank you." I needed to discuss this with those I'd arrived with. "I won't be alone if I decide to do so, will I?"

"Of course not. Groups will form. Some rebels will go with each, but you can take your friends too."

"Thank you."

She said she had more than one matter to discuss and now that she'd delivered my mission, she appeared more anxious. What else could be so harrowing? "You wished to tell me something else?"

She swallowed. "I wished to share this with you at dinner, but Thyra requested my silence in the matter."

Would what Brynhild was going to tell me be equally impactful as simply learning that Thyra existed? I didn't see how it could.

"I was the maid that ran with Thyra from Frostveil Castle the night the two of you escaped." Tears shimmered in the older faerie's eyes. "I was one of the people who used to care for you and your sister as babes. Since Thyra and I were turned away from the noble house your family believed would take her in, I've viewed her as a daughter. More than anything, I hope the two of you can reconcile. Your mother and father would have wanted it."

All the breath left me. Brynhild wasn't just an advisor. I suspected Thyra considered her a surrogate mother.

"I'm so sorry for what happened to you, Neve. I wish I could have taken you both. I wish that you and Segla did not come across such trouble. I often wondered what happened to you. Is Segla still alive?"

"Segla? She was the maid who took me?"

"Yes. We were good friends."

I hated saying the next words. "The vampire who owned me found her in the snow with a toddler in her arms. I think maybe she got lost when we fled the Lisika Castle."

"Lisika?"

"She either fled there or they captured us," I explained.

"They planned to use me as leverage. To wed me to Roar when I came of age and then use that power. Though I don't know how, I'm sure it would have been easy. I was a youngling."

Brynhild scowled. "The last Warden of the West was a vile sort of fae."

I suspected she didn't know half of it. Not that Roar's father was a gatemaker who lured humans into slavery and sold them to the vampires. That was part of how his house had remained wealthy for so very long.

"His son is no different," I replied. "Where was Segla to take me?"

Brynhild shook her head. "It matters not. That family no longer lives. Your mother didn't know, but I later learned that they were dead days before you would have reached them. An arsonist—likely one loyal to King Magnus's rebellion—set fire to their manor. All died."

My hand strayed to my chest. Sympathy for the many fae I never knew bloomed inside me. It was a strange feeling, but long overdue. Had they been alive, had Segla reached them, they might have taken me in. I might have had a loving family. Not my own, but a family of Winter's Realm.

My parents might have been wrong though. Doubt played games with my mind.

Brynhild had told me that Thyra got turned away. My heart clenched for my sister and Brynhild. Where had they lived all these turns? What had they resorted to doing to survive? We'd all been through more than a soul should have to bear in a lifetime.

"I'm sorry that you lost Segla," I murmured.

"There was so much loss during that time. Whole families exterminated." Brynhild looked at me, her expression woeful. She reached out and took my hand. She trembled, and I felt that she meant all she said. "I've wept for you and Segla often, believing you both dead. It's my greatest wish that you and Thyra bond. That you become the sisters you once were, so happy and full of sunlight."

My throat caught. "I wish for the same."

CHAPTER 29
NEVE

Vale snored beside me, peaceful in rest. I wished to join him in that lovely, soft place, but for me, slumber hovered on a far distant horizon. My mind was far too busy.

Thyra and Thantrel were mates. Brynhild was the maid who had saved my sister from death. Though I barely knew the older faerie, and my sister seemed to despise me, I found myself so grateful for Brynhild. She'd saved my last remaining family member.

Well, not the last. I corrected myself quickly.

Poor Prince Calder, my uncle on my father's side, was still rotting in the eastern dungeons of Frostveil Castle, and earlier Vale had spoken to a rebel Hawk Seed.

So I *did* have more family, just none so close as my twin. A full sibling. *A sister.* Maybe a treasure, should we get to that place.

Is that possible?

I wasn't sure and though the skin-changer would be no

replacement for my twin, I yearned to know more of my family. I resolved to ask Vale to introduce me to the skin-changer he'd met in the dining hall. Perhaps the fylgjarn and I would click right away.

Vale tugged the fur blanket, yanking it off me and ripping me out of what could have been a nice daydream of siblings reuniting. A chill washed over me as cold air nipped at the bare skin of my calves and arms. I tried to recover some of the blanket, but he was so large and somehow had already tucked the blanket beneath him.

I moaned. Not again! At Frostveil, we'd always had extra-long blankets and as many as we wanted. The abundance hid Vale's propensity to be a cover thief.

I frowned at my mate and nearly woke him out of sheer annoyance, but then decided against it. He'd worry about why I was still up and alert. I didn't wish to go over the many matters of my mind.

As Valrun Castle was falling apart, wool and fur blankets were one of the few ways the rebels fended off the persistent chill. They had provided extra blankets, and we kept them in the shared living space. I'd grab one and bring it back so I would not disrupt Vale.

Slipping from the bed, I rubbed my hands along my pebbled arms and padded out of the room. What I wouldn't give for a sauna right now.

The annex was silent, save for the volley of snores coming from the Riis brothers' room. I smirked. I'd be teasing them about that trollish racket tomorrow.

I reached the sitting area where we'd spent most of our day and stopped on the threshold. My lips flattened.

Thantrel never made it to bed, but rather he slept in the same chair he'd been in all day. No blanket covered his body, and his arms hung limp over the edges.

Careful not to wake him, I grabbed two woolen blankets from the basket by the fire and slipped one over him. The stench of sour ale wafted off Thantrel, and five empty horns littered the ground at his feet. He hadn't gone to dinner, but we'd brought him back food and a single ale. I was guessing he'd somehow convinced the guards outside the door to bring him refills to dim the pain of being rejected.

"I'm so sorry," I whispered, tucking the blanket in and hoping it was enough to keep him warm. His head lolled, and with my heart breaking for him, I turned to return to bed.

I made it three steps when a soft creak of the door opening hit my ear. Twisting, I caught a figure dressed in a black cloak slipping inside the annex.

Her wings were white and shimmering, her hair as black as a starless night sky, and her face set in cunning and hard lines—but none of that set my heart racing like the sight of her fangs or her red eyes.

Vampire. A hungry one at that.

Two more vampires, also female, slipped in behind her. They stared at me, eyes wide and as red as the first vampire's. It was as if they had not expected to find me here, though the entire rebel force was aware of where Princess Neve and her cohort rested.

I reached for my magic, but as the rebels still required us to be bound by the ice spider silk, no power came to my aid. Nor had I brought a weapon with me to get a blanket.

What of the guards at our door? One glance beyond the females brought only more questions. The guards were standing there, as if nothing at all was happening.

Compelled. That I'd forgotten that trick of the vampires spoke to how much I'd moved on from that world.

I opened my mouth, preparing to call for help, when the lead vampire blurred over, pulled my back against her chest, and slammed a hand over my mouth.

"We're not here to hurt you. Don't scream."

I stared at her, breathless. Was she serious?

"We came here to find you. To help. We promise you can trust us." She lifted her hand slightly, just enough for me to speak. "We've actually already helped you once."

"How?" I demanded.

"The Dream Eater," another said. "We chased it away. At least the first time. It circled back as the rebels approached, and we dared not show ourselves to them."

"Dream Eaters float." I gaped, putting the pieces that I'd learned since the attack together with what had happened that night. "And you have wings. That's why Vale didn't find footsteps in the snow!"

"Correct. We—"

"Bleeding skies!" Thantrel screamed.

I jerked as he leapt out of the chair, scooped an empty horn off the ground, and chucked it at the vampire holding me. "Let her go!"

The other two vampires blurred over, and one compelled Thantrel to be silent while the other held him still. The fight rolling through my friend died.

My jaw tightened at just how powerless we were. They'd compelled him so fast and with such little effort.

"Rustling in the rooms. Someone heard," the vampire who compelled Thantrel whispered.

A few thundering heartbeats later, Vale appeared, his gaze hinging from me to Thantrel, who stood limply in the room. Before Vale leapt at the vampire constraining me, she held up a hand.

"We aren't hurting her. We just wanted to speak with her. I'll let go, but please, don't make noise or attack."

And then, to my utter shock, she did as she claimed and released me.

"I'm not harmed, Vale. I—"

The others rushed into the room and suddenly all my friends were staring at me and Thantrel, aghast.

"Than?" Luccan's voice came out strained. "What's wrong with him?"

"He's compelled," I said. The fear that had filled me moments ago had dimmed. Now only curiosity simmered. "They want to talk to me. Thantrel surprised them and lashed out, so they compelled him to be silent."

The vampire holding Thantrel nodded. "I will release him, if that makes you feel better."

"*Do*," Luccan commanded.

She did, and before Thantrel sprang into another drunken attack, Luccan was at his side, calming his drunk brother.

I turned to the vampire who had grabbed hold of me. "Are you Red Assassins?"

"We are," she replied, dark eyes open and honest. "But

we're not here to kill you. We want to *join* you. To help you if you'll have us."

My eyebrows screwed together. "Why?"

Her white wings spread out behind her. "We were born in Winter's Realm, and our sire turned us against our will. We want to return home and doubt the current king will allow us to do so. However, maybe someone who has been in a situation much like ours will? Could you, if you achieved power, be different enough to change perceptions? And if you would, then we will pledge ourselves to your cause and protect you with our lives."

Yes, of course, they'd been fae and turned. The wings were one of the first things I'd noticed when they slipped into our room. Then, somehow, they became assassins.

I had to know their story.

"Sit." I invited them to take chairs. "I'll hear you out."

The small hour of the direwolf neared when the vampires finally finished telling their tale. I shivered and pulled my blanket tighter around me. We had not dared to light the fire in case the smoke from our chimney drew attention so late. As a result, the annex was frigid and not only from the cold. The vampires' story chilled me to the bone.

Sisters. Three of them. All taken from Winter's Realm. All slaves to none other than Prince Gervais and later sold to the Red Assassins to pay his staggering gambling debts.

If I thought I couldn't hate the vampire I'd killed more,

I'd have been wrong. What he'd done to these sisters was beyond horrific.

And all of that might have happened to me.

Well, maybe not the being sold to an assassin's guild part. I hadn't had the prowess these sisters had accumulated before their turning, but all the rest . . . The abuse that Gervais was famous for, *that* would have been me.

I didn't regret killing him. Not even with the consequences that action rained down on me. He deserved a hundred painful deaths.

And these faeries of Winter's Realm turned vampires deserved more than the hand the Fates had dealt them. The issue was helping them when I held so little power and influence among the rebels. Among anyone outside this small annex, really.

Vale and the Riis brothers continued to pepper them with questions, so I sat there and watched Astril, Freyia, and Livia.

Each one had wings as white as snow and skin only slightly darker. With striking hair the color of a starless night sky, they appeared around thirty turns. Their differences were slight— found only in their builds, and in Livia's charming lopsided smile. Her older sisters' smiles were straight and brilliant. It was easy to tell that they were sisters. Invisible threads of love and loyalty bound them, and one could feel those bonds.

Would I ever have that love with Thyra? My heart, though guarded around her, wished for it so.

"You hail from Virtoris Island then?" Luccan asked, and my ears perked up.

"That's why we grew up sailing," Freyia, the middle sister, answered. "Our parents were merchants before they journeyed to the afterworld."

"*Were murdered,* you mean." Astril, the oldest and the leader among the trio, scowled.

Like her sisters, Astril's eyes were still red, and they seemed to burn with hatred. Though red eyes had often terrified me in the past, now they helped me trust these sisters. Red eyes meant the vampires had not fed recently.

"I'd like to take down the entire Laurent family for what they did to ours," Freyia added.

We shared that rage, that hatred of the royal vampire family and, more specifically, the queen who wanted me dead. Some might think me crazy, past me would have, but after hearing their tale, I sensed that these vampires and I could work together.

"Did you know the Virtoris family?" I wondered where Sayyida and Vidar were now. While I hadn't known either for long, they'd burrowed their way into my heart. I hoped my choices had not put them in danger, though I doubted Sayyida would allow such a thing. None in the House of the Sea Serpent would.

"We were too lowborn to be friendly with them," Astril replied.

I doubted that very much. I'd seen Sayyida around sailors and she hadn't cared about the details of their birth at all. I doubted Vidar would either.

"But I saw the Lady of Ships many times at the docks," Astril continued. "Her mate too."

"Once, I spotted the heir of the island. Handsome, that

one was," Freyia smirked. "I wouldn't have minded getting to know him better."

"Well, he's no longer betrothed to Princess Saga," Luccan muttered. "Maybe you'll get your chance."

The middle sister's face lit up, and unable to help myself, I shot an amused look at Clem. My quiet friend loved a romance story, and one featuring a vampire assassin and an heir to a great house famed for their armada would certainly be a story worth reading.

"All of this is interesting, but I cannot help but wonder what to do with you now." Vale asked.

My mate was ever a fae of strategy, and as dawn neared, I could not deny we needed a plan. These vampires would stay, but I needed Thyra to see how valuable they could be. That they deserved to be brought in by her, as well as I.

"First, you should reverse your compulsion on the guards," I said. "The longer they stay out of it, the more likely they are to question things."

"Are they staying here tonight?" Anna asked, her voice high.

Like me, she'd spent many turns around vampires. She knew how they thought, how they lived, and how they disregarded humans, fae, and pretty much anyone who wasn't a vampire. Anna had a right to fear the sisters staying in the annex, and while I trusted the sisters, I wouldn't make my oldest friend live in fear.

"No." I turned to the vampire sisters. "I don't feel threatened by you."

A soft exhale left Astril's lips. "Thank the stars."

"But I have to discuss your arrival with the leader of the

rebels, my sister, and we're not close. Not even friends at this point."

"Do you want us present for that?" Freyia asked.

There were pros and cons to inviting vampires into the castle before I could assure others they were on our side. Fear being the biggest con. However, if the rebels witnessed how composed the sisters were, that might change things.

"I think you'll have to make a magically binding deal to stay, so yes. It will have to be quite serious too. Your protection or your death if you betray me."

"We have no intention of betraying you. Not when you could give us everything we've ever wanted," Astril replied. "When should we return? We can sneak in unseen— perhaps another selling point to keeping us around?"

With two heists in the future, and others of the Red Assassin Guild still hunting me, I had to agree.

"When the rebels are breaking their fast. They do so all together—save for a few who remain on guard. You'll smell the food, which means most of them will be otherwise occupied. I'll request an audience with Thyra at that time. Show up for that. Do you know where the great hall is?"

"We do. We spent all day scouting the castle before approaching you."

Fates, and none of the rebel lookouts spotted them. The sisters *were* good.

If I convinced Thyra and the rebels not to kill the vampire sisters, their skills could be an enormous boon.

"Then meet us in the great hall when others are breaking their fasts. Fewer eyes will be a good thing. And your quiet arrival will only prove how useful you'd be." I took in their red eyes. "Do you think you can hunt and feed enough in the meantime to dim the red? Revert them to their normal color?"

Astril stood. "There's wild game about, and we can run a great distance and still return in time. We won't appear so hungry when we see you in a few hours."

"I'll be ready to vouch for you," I echoed, and the other two vampires followed their older sister out of the annex. The door shut behind them.

All around, my friends seemed to hold their breath. I remained silent too, not knowing exactly when the sisters would release the guards' compulsion and if the rebels would notice. A minute passed, two, then three. When I heard a shuffling outside—a sound far too loud for a vampire to make—I exhaled. The guards had been released. They said nothing, though. Perhaps they also suspected nothing? I hoped so.

Shoulders loosening, I turned to Vale.

"You're sure about this?" he asked.

"My thoughts exactly," Anna cut in, "this feels crazy, Neve."

"I can see why you'd think that." I took Anna's hand. "But consider what this could mean. They had every advantage to take Thantrel and me out before you all woke. They could have done their killing and slipped away, and no one would have been the wiser. But they didn't."

My wings stretched. I'd watched the sisters doing the same often. The very fae gesture hammered home that they belonged here. That their misfortune should not be punished.

"They used to be fae, Anna. They're furious that the vampires took their lives and twisted them into something monstrous. They want some part of who they used to be back. I can relate *and* give them some consolation if I take the throne."

"But what if Thyra wants the throne? Isn't it safe to assume that she does?"

That was an issue. Well, that and the whole having to fight to dethrone King Magnus.

"I'm going to convince her that they can be useful. Surely, if someone with my past can say that, she'll listen. And if I convince her of that, she'll protect them too. No matter who wears the Crown of Winter in the end, I don't want them to have to go back to the Blood Kingdom."

Anna didn't look convinced, and I wouldn't try to force that. Once the vampire sisters made an oath, I hoped Anna would feel more relaxed.

Vale came behind me, rubbed my shoulders. "Forward thinking. That's what this kingdom needs."

I tucked up against him, savoring his warmth. "Let's hope Thyra agrees."

CHAPTER 30
VALE

T hyra accepted my mate's request to meet on the condition that Thantrel not join us. The demand shattered the youngest brother Riis, but he rolled his shoulders back and claimed he would be fine. Selfless was not usually how I'd describe my half-brother, but he knew how having three loyal vampires could benefit us.

When one did not possess an army at their disposal, any ally was welcome.

As Thyra did not yet know of the vampires, we suspected she had agreed to meet because she believed Neve wanted to speak about the heists. A reasonable assumption that we would leverage until the vampires arrived in the grand hall.

Caelo had woken up feeling nearly his old self, so my best friend, Luccan, Arie, Anna, Clemencia, my mate, and I walked to the meeting right as the scent of fried eggs filled the castle corridors. Rynni had, once again, been called to healing rebels, and Duran had decided to remain behind with Thantrel. That latter turn of events I couldn't quite fathom, as they usually squabbled, but Duran seemed to have been struck hard by Thantrel's brokenhearted state.

Crisis can bring out the worst, or the best, in us all. And there are few life events more dire than a rejected mate bond.

Our escort led us to the grand hall. We were the first to arrive. I breathed deeply and tilted my chin up, preparing for a meeting that could either sour or sweeten our relationship with the rebels.

Even in the so-called grand hall, Valrun cried out for help. The soaring ceiling was open to the elements in three areas, all of which were, thankfully, at the far end of the room. Windows that had once been stained and beautiful were boarded up and the chandelier hung by a single chain.

"Fates, they need to work on this place," Arie muttered. "A dunghole if I've ever seen one."

"Would you like to supply the coin, lordling?" Thyra breezed in with two advisors at her side.

Neve nodded as they stopped before us, both groups a dozen paces from the door. "Thyra, Brynhild, Bac, good morning."

"Is it good?" Thyra asked as the male shut the door behind them. "What did you need to call me for so early? And with so many?" Thyra gestured beyond Neve. "Can they not survive without you, sister?"

"They wished to stretch their legs." Neve spoke as if three vampires wouldn't appear at any moment, and we'd need these witnesses to vouch for them. "We're planning to get breakfast together after the meeting."

"Get on with it, then." Thyra crossed her arms.

Neve cleared her throat. "Well, there are people I wish to introduce you to. They want to join me, and as I am in your keeping and hoping to work with you, that would mean them joining the rebellion too." She carefully avoided the word alliance. Did she think it was too strong for her sister's tastes? "I realize you'll need to approve their presence."

Thyra's eyebrows arched. "How did you get a message out?"

She shot a glance at me, likely wondering if she needed to worry about the king arriving. Maybe she believed that his flying overhead on a gryphon had been down to me.

"I didn't. They found me. They've—um—been looking for me for a while. However, they're going to cause a stir around here, so we wanted a private meeting first."

"A stir? Why?"

In answer, three figures dropped from above. They landed, lithe as snow leopards, behind Thyra, blocking the door.

Astril rose first, her eyes, now a vivid green thanks to the hours they'd spent feeding, locked on the rebellion leader. "We're fae turned vampires."

I sensed the spiking of magic in the air as it radiated from Thyra. Bac was calling his powers too, though neither had struck, so I did not know what magic they possessed.

"*Vampires!*" Thyra hissed. "You said you wished to work together, Neve, and you bring these bloodsuckers here!?"

Neve darted forward, putting herself between Thyra and the vampires. "Look, Thyra, they have wings! They were once fae of Winter's Realm and turned against their will."

Thyra sliced a glare in my mate's direction. "And?"

"Their maker was Prince Gervais, so they no longer have a sire whom they must listen to. They wish to join us as protection. And they'll help with the heists."

"Last I heard, Red Assassins were following Neve. She just said you were following her, so are you Red Assassins?" Thyra directed the question to the sisters, who again were not dressed in the garb of their guild.

"We were of the guild and deserted the command to kill Princess Neve the moment we could." Freyia held up her hands and stepped closer. "We don't want to harm you or the rebels. We wish to make change in the kingdom in which we were born. To make it our home again."

Thyra scoffed. "No fae will accept that."

"They will if their leader, the fae they are fighting for to become queen, sets an example."

Thyra glared at my mate, and I felt a rush of protection rise inside me. If she so much as moved a hairsbreadth toward Neve, I'd intervene.

But my mate's twin stayed put, her stance hard as ice. "And that leader will be you, sister?"

"Me? A leader of the rebels? Please, Thyra, that could not be further from the truth."

"You know what I meant. As queen."

Neve swallowed. "We haven't discussed that, have we?"

Thyra snorted. "Why should we? As far as I can tell, I'm the only one with an army. I also have far fewer enemies—just the king. You have Magnus, the Red Assassins, *and* the Queen of Vampires hunting for your blood. Plus, I was raised in this land. I've seen its ruin, and the people suffer. You have not. As far as I can tell, I'm the obvious choice."

"That might be true," Neve said carefully, trying not to give in to her sister's obvious need to egg her on. She'd quickly gotten a read on Thyra. "However, I might be able to get many noble houses to rebel against the Crown. And if they provide armies, well, that would make us closer to equal, wouldn't it?"

Pride bloomed in my chest.

"All that is not even considering our magic," Neve added. "We have yet to see who is most powerful. Wouldn't, by the law of the kingdom, the strongest magic win the Crown of Winter?"

She was correct. My family had been an exception, for we'd hidden Rhistel's forbidden whisperer powers. To do so, we'd had to feed into the rumors that his winter magic was so strong he needed to wear ice spider silk gloves to keep those around him safe. In truth, though, Saga was not only the only real heir to the king, but she held the strongest winter magic.

Thyra growled. "I suppose we'll have to see."

"Allow me to take off these spider silk binds, and we will."

"Not yet." Thyra's gaze skittered to the vampires before returning to my mate. "You say they wish to help with the heists?"

A not so covert change of subject. Not a surprise either. Neve had known that the vampires' ability to help in the heists would be a large draw, for her sister coveted a Hallow.

423

"We will," Astril answered. "We've already committed to making an oath."

"Which is?"

"We fight for Princess Neve loyally, or we die."

Thyra's jaw set. "That won't do."

"Why not?" Neve frowned.

"They must swear to us *both*."

"You are barely tolerating them as they stand in front of you." My mate scoffed. "Are you serious?"

"Deadly."

The twins fell quiet and in that silence, one could hear the individual breaths of each fae present. Finally, Neve sighed in resignation.

"As long as they wish to do so."

"We will protect you both," Astril said. "And when King Magnus is off the throne, we will be free to live here. Not persecuted as we would be now. Whatever squabbles over the throne itself, however, will *not* be settled with our help. That is a matter between the Falk princesses."

Another silence. More glares shared between Thyra and Neve.

"Then you may stay," Thyra announced. "Your kind will be useful for sneaking about. And if we're in a bind when we flee the cities we plan to steal from, you can run ahead with the Frør Crown—should we find it. That way, it's safe. Fates be good, both me and my sister will survive, but we cannot bet on such a blessing from the Fates. Not when they seem to enjoy ignoring us."

To that, Livia, the most quiet and youngest of the

vampire sisters, cocked her head. "Why would you travel by foot when you have a gatemaker amongst you?"

I stiffened and sensed Luccan doing the same behind me.

Upon hearing about the heists, Neve had brought up the idea of using his gateways, but had assured Luccan that if he didn't wish to come out as a gatemaker—a regulated magical talent—she would understand. Luccan had told her he'd think about it.

He'd not come to a decision, but he no longer had the power to remain a secret.

To make matters worse, Livia was staring straight at him, the confusion evident on her face. "Couldn't you make gateways into the cities?"

Thyra sputtered. "Y-y-you're a gatemaker!?"

Luccan's face had gone paler than usual.

"What makes you say that, Livia?" Neve asked, clearly trying to play this off.

The vampire laughed. "I can smell magic. Gatemaker magic is rare, but I've been sent to kill one before, and I recall the smell. Even if he's bound by silks, I can tell that he's one. A powerful one."

"You had this magic before your turning?" Luccan asked.

"I did. It intensified after I became a vampire."

I supposed Luccan, as a super smeller himself, would find that interesting. I, however, was dying to know if the other sisters retained magic.

Thyra held up a hand. "Could you make gateways from here into Avaldenn and Bitra? That would save us from having to go by armies and through city gates. Save rebel lives."

"Yes," Luccan admitted, making my stomach harden.

Perhaps I shouldn't have brought my brother. In doing so, I'd placed a large target on his back.

"That settles it then," Thyra said. "If we can use your gateways, the vampires can join."

"You already agreed they could join us!" Neve said.

"I didn't have all the information. I suspect I still don't have it all, but I possess what I need."

"No you don't," Luccan said, to which Thyra's lips flattened.

"What else is there?"

"I already have gateways set up from Vitvik into both cities. I don't recommend having me make new ones, since that will take weeks, but you can use those. As long as someone with Riis blood passes through them, others can too." He paused. "I'll give you access, as long as you swear that everyone under your command keeps my secret. I'm not safe if the king learns of it."

"You're not safe now, Luccan," Neve whispered. "You've allied with me."

"Still," Luccan said. "I require secrecy."

"Then you have my word," Thyra stated stoutly. In that moment, she reminded me very much of Neve, for she looked like she cared about honoring her word.

"No one will know of your magic, save for those here today and those chosen to go on the mission with us. We will go from Vitvik in two days' time." Thyra twisted to the vampires. "I wish to see what you can do before then."

"You'll be pleased," Astril said, her tone held unbridled confidence.

Thyra hummed and switched to Neve. "I'm impressed. This was an insane plan. One that I might have killed you for, but it turned out to be something that will be of great use to us."

"That's right," Neve said, her chin lifted.

Thyra assessed her baldly for a long moment.

"Very well. Let's make our oaths, here and now." She held out her arm. "We can't use the Drassil of Valrun to perform our eiðra's. That's too risky."

"And unnecessary," I said. "An oath made between fae is quite strong enough."

Thyra snorted. "So you say. I, however, require extra assurance." She jerked her chin to the male at her side. "Third party binds are stronger than those done by oneself, so Bac, you will be the binder in my oath. Prince Vale, you will do Neve's."

I bristled at being commanded, but when Neve sent me a pleading look, I remained silent. My mate had finagled what she wanted from her prickly sister.

The price on our end was Luccan's secret.

INTERLUDE

PRINCESS SAGA AABERG, ROYAL HOUSE OF
THE WHITE BEAR

"Blast these winds." The princess yanked her wig down once again.

While she wasn't the only one in Winter's Realm with pink hair, the hue was rare among faeries like Saga. Had she been a nymph or a dryad, the princess need not give her hair color a second thought. Thankfully, ensuring she remained unrecognizable when they left Avaldenn had been easy enough. An obliging and loyal whore of the Warmsnap Tavern had given the princess the wig of obsidian dark hair to wear during her travels.

The disguise cut down on their worries, but it far from eliminated them. Walking down snowy roads on horseback left little to keep her mind occupied, so for days, Saga had worried.

Where were Vale and Neve? What was going to happen to her father and Rhistel if Neve did take the throne? Had she truly hugged her mother for the last time just days ago?

Last but not least, she worried for her friends, especially

Sayyida, Marit, and Neve. All three hung in the throes of danger.

But maybe Neve and Vale have already saved themselves? Her teeth dug into her bottom lip. *If only I'd have another vision. A better one this time.*

The princess lifted her eyes to the sky, to the dead gods resting amongst the churning stars. They never answered her pleas, but that did not stop her trying. *Perhaps give me a vision with signposts? We need them.*

The worries filled her heart, consumed most of her minutes, and there was only one way that the princess found to lessen them. Any time they were not on horseback, she wrote in her Book of Fae. Even as she thought of the journal, her fingers itched to put quill to paper.

"There are lights just ahead," Lord Riis said. "See through the trees?"

Saga sighed with relief. They'd left Avaldenn on horseback, stopped in Kethor, and then a tiny village before they were able to truly rest at Riis Tower. That night of security passed too quickly for Saga's liking and the next morning they were back on the road.

The princess had briefly wondered if she should have stayed at Staghorn Castle with her Vagle kin. The castle of House Vagle was only a short distance through the forest from Riis Tower. But her mother claimed the spymaster would keep Saga safe until they found Vale, and Lord Riis insisted on going south, only stopping in Myrr. If they did not find Vale and Neve at the Balik's castle, then they could gather a force to help locate them.

A half an hour later, they entered the village. Saga

scanned the streets. The sun fell two hours back and most fae were tucked in their homes—hiding from the winds, most like.

"This is Kalbaek, about halfway between Liekos and Odelia," Lord Riis murmured. "It's been a long time since I've passed through."

"You own no businesses here?"

"No. So this is perfect for us." He shifted in his saddle. "The tavern is right up there."

She smelled stew and spotted a small longhouse with faelights aglow and had to agree. It looked like most of the taverns in Avaldenn, if maybe a touch smaller.

They approached the establishment and stable younglings ran out, eager to make a late-night coin.

Saga beamed down at them. She'd always liked children and had dreamed of having many of them one day. The idea of future children would have been the only pleasant aspect of the couplings she'd have to endure with her future husband—a duty she could not shirk, thanks to her royal blood. When that male had been Vidar Virtoris, Saga had not relished the idea, but at least Vidar was kind and a friend.

He and Sayyida shared the same eyes. Saga had forced herself to believe that might be enough.

However, her father ended that betrothal and set another to the Warden of the West. Try as she might, Saga rarely found anything likable, or even redeemable, in Lord Roar.

"Two coppers for the horses," one stable lad said.

Lord Riis gave them four claws. "Make sure they're well

fed and taken care of. They like apples too, if you have them."

"We do, mi lord!" The younglings led the horses away, and Lord Riis ushered Saga into the tavern.

The place was rather empty, and Lord Riis approached the bar and ordered their food, while Saga took a seat by the fire. Once settled, she pulled out the Book of Fae and tore a page from the back.

Sayyida had been on her mind every day since her friend had left Avaldenn. She suspected Sayyida returned to Virtoris Island as a protest over her arranged marriage, and Saga desperately wanted to get word to her. Deeming them far enough from Avaldenn to risk it, Saga penned a quick letter to her oldest friend, asking her to join Saga in the southlands. By the time she finished, Lord Riis had returned.

She folded the paper, to which he arched his eyebrows. "What's that, Princess?"

"A letter to Sayyida. I plan to send a raven tomorrow before we head out."

Lord Riis swallowed. "You know where she is?"

"I can guess well enough."

He stared at her, his brown eyes as sad as the day they left Avaldenn. They hadn't spoken of his kiss with the queen, but there had never been intimacy between her parents. Their marriage had been political, and neither ever claimed otherwise. Because of that sharp lack of love in her family Saga could tell that Lord Riis and her mother were different. They had *truly* loved one another, and this was hard for him too.

"What does it say, Saga?"

She rolled her eyes but really, she should have expected the question. He was, after all, the spymaster. Used to knowing all that went on even more so than her.

"I asked her to come south. To meet us in Myrr."

"She can't sail all the way to the landlocked southlands."

"She'll have to hire a sleigh at some point, but Sayyida can manage. Vidar might come too, especially if he thinks Vale is there."

Vale's cabal were the most loyal of friends, and Saga had hinted in her letter that they were on the hunt for Vale and Neve.

"Tell her to avoid docking in Grindavik," Lord Riis said. "Sail into Vantalia and have her use the name Lady Glia. She should also not parade about in Virtoris colors or with their sigil, no matter how tempting the privileges. Once docked, tell Sayyida to go to the brothel flying my banner near the docks. I'll have an escort waiting for her."

"She'll be offended that you think she needs anyone to help her," Saga replied.

"Her offense is the least of my concerns. Her ship and influence over the Nava, however, might be useful."

Saga nodded slowly, unsure about all that was transpiring—that Neve was a cousin, and, if the rumors were true, might wish to dethrone her father.

A part of her hated the idea, but another part, the bit that despised her title as princess for all the restrictions that came with it, wondered if it wouldn't be so bad to no longer be royal. She could live more freely—marry whomever she wished.

Unsure about so much, Saga sighed and turned to the letter. She added the last parts stipulated by Lord Riis before closing it back up.

"You won't regret adding that, and neither will Sayyida. We'll have it sent off in the morning before we set out once more."

She looked up at the male her mother loved. Perhaps she had loved him for all of her life? Saga did not dare ask.

"What will happen if Neve takes the throne?"

His brown eyes softened. "If you fear for yourself, you need not do so. She loves you, Saga."

"I don't fear for myself."

She did, however, worry that her father and Rhistel might be harmed if Neve seized the throne. Her eldest brother did not deserve Saga's concerns, but she could not turn them off. That was a failing, a too warm spot in the heart of a daughter of Winter. A weakness.

The stew arrived before she delved deeper into her failings.

CHAPTER 31
NEVE

Three days had passed since Thyra and I made oaths with the vampires, and yet, as we rode west for Vitvik, I still felt the band of the magic simmering beneath my skin. It mixed with my own powers, now freed since we were about to undergo heists. The sensation was not unpleasant, just odd. A constant reminder of what we'd said.

"Are you well?" Vale asked, his horse coming up alongside mine.

"Fine. Preoccupied by the oath."

"Had you performed it yourself, you'd hardly sense it at all. That's why most people perform eiðra that way."

"I had no idea. When I made a pact with Roar, it was in writing."

Vale's jaw tightened. "I assume he did not want to form an eiðra to save his own hide because he knew he might have to break the pact."

Which was exactly what he'd done. Then Roar had sidestepped further ramifications of his deception by destroying the blood vials we'd been supposed to drink.

Fates, I hated thinking about that snake.

Willing him from my mind, my gaze drifted to Thyra, riding near the head of the column, her black cloak fluttering behind her in the faint wind.

In the time between forming oaths with the vampires and setting out for Vitvik, we'd spent hours training and studying old maps of the cities we'd be entering. We'd also met the rebels who would accompany us on our heists. All that time, all those opportunities to find common ground, and yet, I had not made any headway with my sister.

Nor had Thantrel, whom my twin avoided more than she avoided me. Thyra would not look at her rejected mate. Would not speak to him. If she could, I suspected she would avoid breathing the same air as Thantrel.

However, as Vale had insisted Thantrel was too good a fighter to leave behind, Thyra allowed him to join us on the heist. Presently, he rode at the back of the column with the vampires.

As for the rest of the rebels, their slight acceptance of us had backslid somewhat when Thyra introduced the vampire sisters. The only one whose opinion remained unchanged was Brynhild, and she was not joining either heists.

"I hope Clem, Anna, and Rynni will be well back at the castle," I said.

"Anna is human," Vale reasoned. "They don't seem to lump her in with us. Clemencia is sweet and has won many of the rebels over, and Rynni might be as sour as the ale they serve, but they respect her healing skills."

It was true. Rynni had been quite busy these past days. Anna too. Once it came to light that many rebels needed their clothing mended, she'd volunteered to do the work. I'd almost done the same, only to have Clemencia stop me.

"It won't do for a queen to mend the clothes of her subjects," Clem had cautioned.

Of course, she was right. Clem always was. Still, for a moment, I'd hoped it would endear the people to me. In that regard, I needed all the help I could get.

Perhaps finding the Frør Crown will do it?

"Darkness is setting. I expect that we'll be stopping for the night soon," Vale mustered. Vitvik was only a day and some few hours from the rebel camp, but we wished to time our travels so that tomorrow, we could arrive close to when the coinaries closed. That meant sleeping in the forest. "Perhaps tonight is a good time for you to speak with Thyra?"

"And you Bac?"

Vale had strong ties to House Balik and, bastard or not, Bac could be an excellent ally. If he warmed up.

"Exactly what I was thinking."

We continued to ride for another half an hour or so before Bac veered his horse off the trail, cutting through the woods.

Vale leaned closer to me, the space between our horses filling with his tempting scent. "If I were you, I'd catch your sister before she becomes too *busy*."

"Good idea." Thyra had an odd habit of being busy for someone who was traveling through the woods and really should not have much to do at all.

I rode forward, passing Luccan, Arie, and Duran on the

way. Caelo was with us too, though he rode at the back to help keep up Thantrel's spirits. Otherwise, the youngest Riis brother became despondent.

"Going somewhere?" Luccan asked.

"More like trying to corner someone."

"Good luck."

His luck, it seemed, was on my side. By the time I reached the front of the column of riders, Bac had come to a stop in front of a home with no door, and Thyra was standing there, right behind him.

Got you!

"This is where we're sleeping?" I asked, capturing her attention.

"No, Bac brought us off the trail and to a house that looks like it might fall down for no reason at all." Thyra rolled her eyes as she dismounted.

I sucked in a breath, but didn't fire back. It had been an obvious answer, but sometimes my twin made me nervous. She was so cold and unknowable.

"Right." I dismounted and reached for a topic that wouldn't earn me her ire. "Should we be worried about monsters like the Dream Eater?"

"We know where to stay to keep safe." She handed her reins off to Sigri, a dwarf rebel, who then turned to take mine.

The rebels might not like me much, but they respected that I was Thyra's sister. Unlike my friends, I had not needed to take care of my horse when we stopped for a rest.

"Thank you." I rushed off behind Thyra and caught up quickly. "Thyra, I was hoping we could talk a bit?"

"About anything in particular? Or are you hoping that I'll sit and braid your hair like your pampered noble friends at court did?"

I winced at the near truth. Clem had usually done my hair, but Saga had tweaked it when she gave me a hair pin from my mother—the queen who Thyra resembled more than I.

My heart stopped. *That's an opening.*

"Actually, one did my hair once. She gave me our mother's pin. I don't have it on me, but I have some of our mother's jewels. Would you like to see?"

Thyra stopped, turned. "You're walking around with royal jewels? How? And why did we not take them from you?"

"You did, but then one of the rebels returned them." For the sake of trying to bond, I refrained from adding *'unlike my sword'*. "Probably because I never said outright that they were from our family."

"How did you get them?"

"I took them from the castle when I thought I'd need them for payment south. I no longer need them for that, but they could be useful."

"You'd *sell them?*" she hissed.

"If necessary." I did not wish to, and Vale assured me we'd use all his coin before it came to that, but I was a realist. Where I came from, you did what you had to do to survive.

Thyra glared at me. "Do you have no pride! Those are what's left of our history."

I stared at her, shaking my head. "I don't understand you at all."

She laughed dryly. "The feeling is mutual."

"Allow me to elaborate on whatever question you have."

"Why do you go by Neve and not your true name? I can understand when you remained in the dark, but you still use the name a slaver gave you."

I swallowed. "I—I wasn't ready to change yet. But I plan to take it. And soon."

"Soon. How *encouraging*."

I pulled the pouch of jewels from the pockets of my cloak and thrust the bag between our faces. "This might be our history, but I'm *your blood*, Thyra. You've shown more interest in baubles than your twin!" I didn't mean for my voice to lift as I spoke, but it did, and by the time I finished, more people than I'd have liked had overheard.

My twin came closer, jaw tight. "You're right. As it stands, I care more about those baubles than you because I know of their past. Know that they will not hurt me or disappoint me. They're things! You're a fae with ambitions, and you may be working to undermine all that I've striven to achieve for our family."

"We want the same thing. King Magnus off the throne. Revenge for our family."

"And to sit on the throne yourself?" Thyra asked.

I wanted to sigh, to say '*not this again*', but Thyra didn't give me the chance.

"You are, after all, already wed to a prince," she plowed

onwards. "A respected one—for all his faults. But you haven't spent your life here, Neve. You know so little of the people of Winter's Realm. How can I trust you will care for them as well as I?"

"I want to help them too."

"I noted, however, that you didn't state that at first. Revenge on Magnus is a motivator for you. For me as well, but I will always think of *the people* first, for I have seen many starve. Die. I've watched Winter take them, and if I can change that, I will."

I wanted to say that I'd seen pain too. Here, and in the Vampire Kingdom, but those words lodged in my throat. She was right. I wished to save people too, but I couldn't help the fact that I had a personal vendetta against King Magnus. I'd spoken of revenge because that seemed to be what she wanted most, but Thyra was motivated by so much more.

"In time, we'll see who is worthy of the throne," Thyra said. "But until I know who you are and that you won't betray me, I'll keep my guard up. As our parents should have done with those around them."

"What do you mean?" I asked, but she was already turning away, preparing to bolt.

Unfortunately for Thyra, someone had snuck up on her: Thantrel.

His olive eyes locked on her, and the hope there made my heart break.

"I told you to stay away from me," Thyra growled.

"And I have. *For days.*" Thantrel's voice sounded

strained, as if he'd been planning this approach for some time and could barely contain himself.

"I understand your shock," Thantrel added. "I was surprised to find you as well. To recognize you as my mate. Although my appearance is clearly not to your taste, I don't understand why you wouldn't want our bond to snap into place. Doesn't it hurt you to feel it and deny it?"

Her back was turned to me, but for the briefest moment, Thyra's shoulders softened.

"I never said you weren't to my taste," she muttered. "Just that your eyeliner and hair are distracting."

Thantrel's lips curled into a flirty smile that I'd seen before, and my heart clenched. She gave him one small consolation, and he was about to run with it.

"I promise if you give me a chance, you'll come to like me," he said. "I've rarely had complaints from females—and you, well, you're not just a female I fancy. You're the one my soul longs for. Wants to protect. To love."

I pressed my lips together, shocked by his openness at what he wanted, thinking that it would have worked on many. Including me, if I was not already mated. Thyra, as always, was of another mind. She shook her head and became all tension and anger again.

"What hurts me is knowing that you have a lot of power to distract me from what I've worked for all my life." Her finger pressed into Thantrel's chest.

Though I was sure she was not being gentle, the touch made Thantrel's eyes light up.

"And if I were to accept a mating bond, it would not be with a lordling whose family was raised by the male I

despise. A new noble family who sits in my mother's ancestral home! The home her family occupied for millennia, but
now they cannot because they are all dead! What did your
father do to gain a seat at the table of the Sacred Eight,
Thantrel?"

I blinked. Thyra raised a question I'd not much considered. Lord Riis had always been kind and helped Vale and
me out quite a bit. What had the spymaster done to be
raised in society?

At her question, Thantrel licked his lips, uneasy. "I can't
say. I wasn't born until the end of the White Bear's
Rebellion."

"You never asked? Never wondered how a merchant
rose so high? How he leaped over jarls who had been
faithful bannerfae to the House of Aaberg for as long as that
ancient house existed?"

"I did not."

Thyra scoffed. "Then I'm right to reject you. No mate
of mine will be so dimwitted, and a pretty face cannot make
up for those failings." She stepped back and away, leaving
me facing Thantrel. "Leave me alone. I'm about to undertake a mission to change the fate of the rebellion. Of those
of Winter's Realm. I require no distractions."

She marched off, snow crunching under her boots.

Thantrel watched her go, longing in his eyes, and misery
written all over his lovely face.

CHAPTER 32
VALE

After an uncomfortable journey west, we reached Vitvik in the late afternoon.

The savory scent of meat pies baking for supper filled my nostrils, and my mouth watered as I pulled my hood over my head. I wished we could stay the night in Vitvik and advance in the morning, but all those involved in planning the separate heists agreed it would be best to visit the coinaries near the closing hour. Fewer leprechauns would be working meant fewer witnesses.

"People are staring," Neve whispered.

"Of course they are. We're fifteen fae riding into a small city where many fae have lived their entire lives. Keep your hood up and your hair tucked away. They won't recognize you. Or the vampires."

Aside from the fact that everyone wore unremarkable, thick, fur cloaks and kept their hoods up, we'd both already vanished our wings, making it seem like we were among the unfortunate faeries to be born with none. The color of my wings—Vagle black—and Neve's silver were too noticeable when paired together.

"Directions to the brothel? One with a tavern below for the less adventurous fae in our party?" Bac asked so many could hear.

A plump brownie arched his eyebrows at that but gave directions.

We already knew the location of the brothel owned by Lord Leyv Riis, but Bac's query was sticking to the plan. We were casual travelers, looking for a night of fun and debauchery. No one who knew that would think twice about us.

Back on our way, a soft song came from Bac's lips, one echoed by Thyra and two other rebels.

I'd spent time speaking with Bac the night prior. He didn't just resemble Sian and Filip, he acted like the Balik males too.

Along with Bac, a rebel nymph named Tanziel would join our heist party. Bac had introduced me to Tanziel the night before and though the blue-haired nymph had been distant, she'd also been polite. It was as much as I could ask from rebels when I'd been involved in hunting so many of them down.

"Here we are!" Bac sang as we approached the brothel.

Like the Warmsnap in Avaldenn, this establishment was far nicer looking than most of its kind. That was the stamp of Lord Leyv Riis, who owned no low-end establishments.

Younglings appeared to take the horses. Bac and Thyra paid a copper apiece for each horse, allowing Neve and me to hang back in the shadows.

We were waiting until the last moment to apply glamours, which we'd need in Avaldenn. That way, the magic would remain as fresh as possible in the city where so many recognized not only my face, but Neve's and Caelo's too.

With the horses stabled, we walked into the tavern on the ground floor. Here, we did not pretend to be patrons. Rather, Luccan led the way to the back and up the stairs. With every step closer to the active brothel, the scent of flowers and musk grew stronger. Faint music played, loud enough to cover up some of the less attractive noises of love-making. When Luccan reached the top, the madam smiled in recognition.

"Lord Luccan." She inclined her head. "Back so soon. Might I tempt you to stay the night?"

"Not tonight, Lady Amal," he said, though his tone sounded like 'never'. If I had to guess, Luccan was far too consumed with Clemencia to wish to visit a brothel for pleasure. "Keep the workers and clients away from my father's office. I require privacy."

"It is yours." She swept down the hallway, deeper into the brothel.

Luccan claimed the workers of the taverns and brothels did not know they had gateways in their places of employment, but I wasn't so sure. Some of them had to suspect as much, but if they held their tongues, that was good enough for me.

We entered a short, empty hallway in which only one door waited at the end. Luccan approached and placed his hand on the knob. The door lit up, and the lock clicked, allowing us entry.

Fitting so many into the office was difficult. Lord Riis was an extravagant male in many respects, but he didn't use this office often. As a result, it was on the small side. Fit we did, however, and once the door closed and locked once more, Luccan turned first to Thyra.

"I'll send your lot through first and seeing as you'll have Arie with you, returning won't be an issue."

As the only Riis in the other group, Arie not only gave them access to the gateway on the other side, but he would also get them into the coinary of Bitra by asking to access his family vault. It would likely be on the lowest level, just like House Skau's vault.

Duran was also going to Bitra. Not for connections, but for reasons involving his mind. The Skau family had a reputation for being erudite. Many of that bloodline became a Vishku of the House of Wisdom or renowned scholars in their selected field. It was a common practice for noble houses to put their own protections on their vaults. Protections particular to their strengths. House Skau might have a riddle at the door or something of that nature and for that, Duran was being brought along.

"This gateway enters into Skau Castle?" Thyra asked.

Luccan nodded, not about to correct her that *his* family now owned the palace in Bitra.

"As I'm with you, there will be no issue with the skeleton crew of servants we keep at the castle," Arie added.

Thyra let out a breath. "Then we're ready. Open the gateway."

Arie stepped forward and poked his finger with the tip of his dagger. With his blood he drew an X on the wall.

Instantaneously, a portal opened, light blinding us and hiding what was on the other side.

"You first, Riis," Thyra said.

Neve huffed at the lack of trust her sister exhibited. I felt the same.

Arie rolled his eyes, but did as Thyra said, slipping through the portal.

"I hear nothing," Thyra said.

"You won't," Luccan snapped. "I wouldn't let my brother go through first if there was a monster or something, would I?"

Thyra looked at Neve before staring at the portal again. "I don't know your relationship with your brothers, gatemaker."

Anger rose in me, but I tamped it down. Soon Thyra would be gone, and we'd be on our own mission. It was best not to take a negative attitude with me.

Sigri the dwarf followed Arie. Then Duran, Halladora, the rebellion's glamourist, and then the vampires Livia and Astril, which left only Thyra standing with our party.

My mate's twin inhaled. "Meet back here as soon as the job is done."

"We've been over this time and time again," Neve said. "We won't forget. Or fail."

Thyra did not respond, just walked through. The moment she disappeared, someone nudged me to the side.

Thantrel stepped by, and my eyes widened. "What are you—"

He sliced his finger and applied blood to the wall.

"I can't let my mate go into danger without me," he said as he passed through the portal, and it closed behind him.

Neve's mouth fell open. "He *did not* do that! Thyra is going to rip him open!"

"She might send him back." Luccan shook his head slowly. "I should have guessed Than would pull something like this."

We waited to see if what Luccan said would come to pass, but the portal didn't open again. I imagined Thantrel was earning a tongue lashing and not the kind he desired.

"Skies, I'm glad I'm not in Bitra right now," Caelo said after a full five minutes had passed. "I think Thantrel might have won that fight, but at what cost?"

"A high one," Luccan confirmed. "Should we move on to Avaldenn?"

Everyone agreed, and Luccan opened a second gateway, this one leading to his home on Lordling Lane.

I took Neve's hand. "You're ready?"

"As ever," she replied, and together, we stepped through.

CHAPTER 33
NEVE

S weat poured off Caelo's brow as he finished applying Freyia's glamour. As the sole vampire on our team, she'd required a more thorough glamour than the rest of us. Usually, that would be a minor task, but Caelo had already altered me, Vale, and himself since we could not freely travel the streets.

The Crown wanted me in chains, Vale and I were married, and Caelo was a knight, a Clawsguard, and Vale's dearest friend.

So we glamoured ourselves and had borrowed the plainest clothing possible from the rebels before leaving Valrun.

Out of everyone who had lived in Avaldenn, Luccan alone got to wear his usual clothing, and because it would be best if the leprechauns recognized him, he also bore no glamour. Bac and Tanziel, a nymph with blue hair down to her knees, would also walk the streets of Avaldenn undisguised.

I'd only met the nymph last night, and quickly realized that even though Tanziel's powers allowed her to see events and share them with others later, she was only present to watch us. A recorder, the nymph called herself. It was an intriguing talent, though we would have done better with a stronger sword in our party instead.

But my sister doesn't trust me, so we get a recorder of events rather than another competent fighter.

I hoped Bac would make up for the skills that Tanziel lacked, but that remained to be seen.

"Everyone is armed, right?" Luccan asked.

We'd decided to carry at least four daggers each, all of them hidden in our cloaks and boots. Freyia and Bac also had throwing stars.

While one *could* walk into a coinary with a sword or mace or bows and arrows, those weapons would grab notice. Potentially, the leprechauns would ask us to check them. If we said no, they would monitor us far more thoroughly, and we wished to get in and out quickly and undetected.

"I think that's enough of a disguise. Does she look fae enough to the rest of you?" Caelo stepped back from Freyia.

I examined the vampire. "It works. None of us looks like ourselves enough to alert a normal citizen." For the time being, we vanished our wings. Our hair and eye colors appeared changed and the most prominent parts of our faces altered. My new dark hair, brown eyes, and larger nose would trick even those in Avaldenn who'd known me best, like Saga and Sayyida.

Luccan led us up the stairs to the main living area of his house. I looked around for servants.

"I released them when my brothers and I left town." Luccan handed us the cloaks his servants wore outside when on errands for him. These cloaks bore the signet of the ice spider in red and black and told shop keepers that the servants could charge to Luccan's accounts or pick up items for the younger Lord Riis. "I didn't want anyone here if the king came calling with questions."

"Ah," I said. The Riis brothers and the spymaster always danced two steps ahead of others.

Outside, familiar frigid winds gusted off the Shivering Sea. I shuddered as we passed through the gates of Luccan's manor and on to the bustling street of Lordling Lane. There was much I missed about Avaldenn, but the harsh wind was not one of those things.

Vale and I flanked Luccan but took care to walk a half step behind him. The others fell in line behind us, just as a servant on an outing to help their lord would do.

"The coinary used by the noble houses is close," Luccan said. He spoke loud enough for those around us to hear, and likely for the benefit of Bac, Freyia, Tanziel, and me. As this coinary was one where all the wealthiest fae in the capital kept their money and precious items, it would be well known to those who had grown up in the city. "A few streets down."

"All the better for fancy lordlings to spend their coin," Tanziel muttered as she scanned the opulent street with a frown.

Like most rebels, Tanziel didn't trust us yet, but maybe it

was more than that. A harboring of resentment. Once I'd done the same to the wealthy, though I doubted she'd appreciate it if I said as much.

Despite my past, the rebels saw me as only one thing: A royal threat to their leader. While few of the rebels were pleasant to us, and many acted polite enough, that did not mean the majority liked us.

"Are you recording?" I asked.

"I have been since we left Lord Riis's home. He requested I not record inside, and Thyra agreed to that, so I didn't. But everything else will be documented."

"Good." I wanted Thyra to see that we worked for her cause. Working to make things better for the small folk of Winter's Realm.

If the Frør Crown does anything at all.

The unknowns about the Frør Crown remained a point of annoyance for me. In all the research Arie, Duran, Clem, and Anna had done, nothing of note had been discovered. Most people merely saw the Frør Crown as a sign of legitimacy for the ruler of the realm.

I hoped it was more than that and had to assume Thyra knew what she was doing—even if she wouldn't divulge that information. Maybe she would if we found the Frør Crown. At the very least, Thyra having a Hallow might incline her to return Sassa's Blade to me. Then, on equal footing, we could go after the Ice Scepter.

We neared the end of Lordling Lane when I heard a voice that snapped me out of my troubled musings.

"Calie, shouldn't we stop by the dressmaker? My gown might be ready early."

"And what would you wear it for? Thanks to that whore of a Falk, the Courting Festival had all but ended!"

I swallowed as Calpurnia Vagle and the tall, blonde Adila Ithamai came into view through the thick crowds. Judging by their rosy cheeks, I guessed that they'd left one of the taverns known for serving only high-end wines from far-off locales.

"Skies!" Calpurnia pointed at our group, lips parted in shock. "Luccan Riis, is that you?"

Vale glanced across Luccan at me. "Hood up."

I did as he said, and he too covered his face as much as possible. Glamour or no—Calpurnia was Vale's cousin on his mother's side. Observant and clever too. She might see someone with the same gait as Vale, someone the same size and height, and suspect something.

And if she suspected I was with him, then Calpurnia would have me thrown into a cell faster than I could blink.

"Hello, Calpurnia," Luccan said as the noble lady stopped before him. He bowed. She curtsied. I refrained from rolling my eyes at the performance of it all when so much was on the line. "Out and about today, I see?"

"I am! But I heard that you left Avaldenn?" She did not spare anyone wearing the servants' cloaks a glance.

"Interesting story. I just left my manor."

"Oh," she sounded as if she did not quite believe him. "A miscommunication, I guess. Although, I suppose there's little reason to be at Frostveil now." She gestured to the rest of us without looking at us.

"Why are so many of your servants with you?"

"I'm going to the coinary, and they are helping me carry

out items." Luccan twisted the truth and made a show of looking at the clock in the distance. "In fact, the coinary closes soon, so I'd better be on my way."

Calpurnia's lips pursed slightly. "I'll let you go then."

"Until next time," Luccan said.

As we moved around Calpurnia and Adila, I made a point of looking away, hoping not to draw attention, but fate was against me, for I'd nearly passed by Calpurnia when I tripped on a chunk of ice. I toppled to the side, right at her feet.

"By the dead gods," Calpurnia muttered.

Someone more forgiving would have assumed she was saying it out of concern, but I detected a tone of derision in her voice.

"Apologies, my lady." I spoke in a deeper tone than normal as I rose, hoping to carry on. But I could not stop her from staring at me, making my heart rate ratchet up. Her eyebrows pinched together, and I felt the air pulse. She was staring for *too* long. Did she suspect?

She shook her head. "I thought you were someone I knew." And with that, she left.

I took my place by Luccan again, face flaming. No one said anything as Luccan veered us to the mouth of a side street. We paused, and I heard Luccan let out a long breath.

"That was close," Vale whispered the words I was sure at least half of us had been thinking. Those who had experienced the vicious side of Calpurnia. "Sorry I didn't catch you. I worried about her seeing me and that distracted me."

"A valid concern." I wasn't mad at all. I'd rather eat a

face full of snow than have Calpurnia out us because she detected Vale or me. "Please tell me we'll get there soon."

"It's there." Luccan nodded down the side street, an uneasy expression on his face. "Everyone ready?"

We affirmed that we were, and once again, he took the lead for the coinary.

"We're really safe, right?" I whispered, unable to let go of that worry and needing to get it off my chest before entering the coinary. "You don't think Calpurnia suspected anything?"

"I think so," Luccan replied without so much as a glance back at me. No one was on the side street, but you never knew who might watch from the apartments and shops above. "Much has happened since the time my brothers and I left court, so Calpurnia being mistaken is not odd. As we're not the highest born males, she—and others like the king—probably cares much less of our whereabouts. Still, we should be quick."

If Luccan's face was key to getting us to the more protected parts of the coinary, Bac's powers of persuasion would be the part that got us in and out without issue.

His powers weren't exactly like a vampire's compulsion, fae mind reading powers, or whispering, but they were close. Bac could suggest something to someone, and they'd have the overwhelming urge to help him. No questions asked. Bac said there were other facets to his magic, but that this bit would be the most useful to us, so that was what we focused on. We'd have Freyia with us too and her compulsion was an option, but no one wished for her to use her magic unless it was a last resort.

Getting in. Persuading. And then leaving—walking calmly down the street and vanishing without issue. Or so I prayed.

Guards so large they had to be part troll flanked the towering double doors of the coinary. Luccan paid them no mind as he strode inside with the rest of us behind him.

Fires blazed in two long hearths that lined the hallway leading into the main chamber where leprechauns helped clients.

I craned my neck to peer around Luccan. It appeared we'd timed this right. Aside from the leprechauns on duty, of which about half the desks were occupied, only one client lingered in the chamber. The fewer people to witness this, the better.

The sounds of our boots echoing on the floor intensified as we entered the main chamber. Above, a ceiling, gilded and domed, nearly took my breath away. Emeralds cut the golden dome into sixteen equal parts and at the top gleamed a gem that looked to be a diamond. The ceiling alone made it clear that this coinary was more prestigious than the one I'd seen in Eygin.

Like the ceiling, the desks that the leprechauns sat behind appeared to be made of solid gold. The floor was white marble and chandeliers dripping with gems lined the long room.

A leprechaun with a bald, wrinkled head and extremely long ears stood from his desk, approached Luccan, and bowed.

"Lord Riis. A surprise to see you here. I'm Coinmaster Balvor. What may I do for you?"

"I wish to enter my vault and withdraw items. And I'm in a bit of a hurry."

The leprechaun clasped his hands in front of him. "Very well, no need to sit down then. Allow me to retrieve the cauldron."

The Coinmaster darted over to his desk and back. "Your hand, if you please."

Luccan obliged, placing a hand on the cauldron. Though I couldn't see it, I assumed that his name appeared on the cauldron's other side, telling the leprechaun that Luccan was exactly who he claimed to be.

"Follow me, my lord. Your servants can wait here."

"I wish for them all to come to assist," Luccan replied. We'd figured we'd come up against this roadblock, but both Luccan and Vale were sure that if Luccan insisted, they'd allow us all into The Below. Nobles brought guards and servants—perhaps this many *was* unusual, but it wasn't unheard of. "I don't care to carry it all."

We planned to stuff our pockets to make that true. After all, extra gold never hurt.

Balvor hesitated, tilting his head to the side. One of his ears flopped slightly to the side. "Can we keepers of the coin assist?"

"I prefer my own help."

Not surprisingly, Balvor's smile disappeared as he turned back to the restricted part of the bank. "As you wish, my lord. Follow me."

Luccan walked behind the leprechaun, and we followed. I didn't spot anyone watching us, and yet when we passed through a door leading into a dark tunnel that led down-ward, I sighed.

"Few people have that response to the back part of a coinary. Most find it stifling." Balvor eyed me with interest as he pulled a torch from the wall and lit it with magic. "Are you part leprechaun?"

"Uh, not that I know of," I said, unable to lie. But who knew? Maybe long, long ago, I'd had a leprechaun ancestor.

"Hmm, too bad. Watch your step. And stay away from the walls." Balvor descended the staircase.

Despite the light from the torch, inky blackness enveloped us on the way down. The staircase was wide enough for four to walk side-by-side, though after Balvor's warning, we went in single file. I took such care to focus on the steep steps that when a growl came from my right, I tripped onto Vale, who walked ahead of me. Thankfully, my mate proved more surefooted and caught me.

"What was that?" I asked.

"Theft deterrents," Balvor chirped as though he'd been waiting for someone to fear the creature I still could not see. "Monsters, caged along the staircase. All kinds, at random intervals."

"Stars," I breathed. I'd been told that we'd encounter captive creatures of tooth and claw down below, but on the steps too?

Did Luccan know what they were? Vale? As we ventured to a part of the coinary where the wealthiest and the oldest noble families in the city kept their prizes, I had to imagine that both had gone this way before. Questioningly, I looked at Vale.

"They're fairly new, and I don't know what's inside," he whispered. "But I'm sure they remain caged unless a leprechaun releases them."

And with Bac's powers of persuasion, that wouldn't happen. I swallowed but kept going.

Down, down, down we went. It felt like we'd descended at least four stories into the ground, and we weren't at the bottom.

Occasionally, another growl or snarl filled my ears, and while I did not fall again, I couldn't help but wonder what might be lurking a few paces to either side, caged and unseen down a narrow hallway that branched off the steps.

I wondered, but I prayed we wouldn't find out.

CHAPTER 34

NEVE

T he moment we reached the bottom of the steps, I exhaled, as if we'd already completed the heist when we'd only just begun.

Balvor walked the perimeter of a room, snapping his fingers every few paces. Faelights ignited, revealing hallways jutting off a circular room like spokes extending from a wheel.

My jaw set into a hard line. "Why not have faelights on the steps? It's dangerous."

"Are your servants always so outspoken, Lord Riis?"

Luccan arched an eyebrow. "Some. Answer her question."

"We prefer people to take care with the stairs rather than run up and down needlessly," Balvor replied smoothly.

I read between the lines. The steps were one of the last line of defense from thieves.

The leprechaun waved his hands and the faelights he had ignited floated over to hover in a circle around his bald head. "These faelights will follow us to your vault, Lord Riis. Come." Balvor took the far right spoke, and once he turned away, I looked at Vale.

"What if mine is down one of the other spokes?" I whispered.

"It won't be," he assured me in an equally low tone only I—and probably Freyia, with her sharp vampire senses— could hear. "The Aaberg vault is this way too. It's the best protected branch."

I reminded myself that while the protections might be intimidating, they were also a safeguard that had prevented Magnus Aaberg from entering the Falk vault, despite being half Falk himself.

The sounds of our footsteps on stone echoed through the long, cavernous corridor. When we came across the first door, I took it in, hoping for hints as to what I might come across later.

There was no name, but a tower carved into the stone. The other doors were much the same, most with insignias I did not recognize. I suspected these were the vaults belonging to lesser noble houses. Or just wealthy fae in Avaldenn.

Occasionally, a hallway would branch off the main one. From those depths, I caught the sound of growls. Were there vaults that way? Or just more monsters?

Stars, I do not want to find out.

After almost five minutes, we reached an imposing steel door. Balvor pressed his hand to the steel, and it rose like a portcullis. We passed through and the gate slammed shut, the metal teeth digging into the stone below.

We'll need the leprechaun to get back.

Deeper into the coinary we ventured. With each hurried step, the corridor grew dank smelling and darker. Worst of all, the growling returned as we came upon massive cages built into the walls, visible to us as we walked through.

On each side of us ogres towered at least five times Vale's height. Their great height shocked me, though I knew the tales. Ogres were once the same as frost giants, but long ago some left their tribes. Each generation of ogres grew more animalistic and smaller than their giant kin. Now they were something else entirely. A stream of unintelligible words came from one such loathsome being. Another barked only two words.

"Blood! Meat! Blood! Meat!"

Had they been down here, caged, for so long that they'd forgotten all else? I took in their thin forms, their patchy hairy bodies and the graying skin beneath, their teeth all sharp points. One noticed me looking and roared. His breath, reeking and rotten, washed over me.

My stomach twisted and, fearing that I'd be ill, I covered my nose, and I wasn't the only one. Tanziel's face had lost all blood.

I'd been in Winter's Realm for many moons now. In all that time, I'd never seen an ogre, and I'd been happier for it. They were as ugly and foul as I'd imagined. Starving too, from the looks of it. If those beasts got loose, they'd eat us without a second thought and once we were gone, they'd turn on each other to fill their bellies.

And yet, knowing all that, I still felt a little pity for these fae. Ogres were not bright like faeries, dryads, or other fae races that lived together in harmony. They didn't even possess an orc's intelligence, but they were also not purely mindless creatures. They spoke and thought. And they weren't supposed to live down here, caged.

I doubted those that we passed would ever see the sun again. Never feel the snow fall or smell fresh air.

"Here we are," Balvor stopped before a vault bearing a crimson ice spider in a web and a number one. "Lord Luccan, your vault."

I hadn't seen numbers on the other vaults, but those surrounding Luccan's vaults also bore ice spiders and numbers up to three. On one, only an ice spider gilded in gold glinted in the faelights. I assumed the other numbered vaults belonged to Arie and Thantrel—each having their own wealth in addition to family wealth. Lord Riis, as Head of his House, was the golden spider.

"Into the cauldron." Balvor held out the cauldron he'd carried in one hand. From inside, a dagger of gold gleamed.

Luccan took the blade and drew blood across his hand. He then held his palm over the cauldron and allowed a few drops to fall in. The leprechaun did the same, and the moment the blood mixed, the door to the vault glowed.

Luccan pressed his hand to the door. It swung open, and he stepped into the vault filled with hills of gold and other precious items. We went after him, taking gold and shoving it into our pockets as Luccan plucked five gemstones from the top of a hill of gold without a care.

Balvor's thin eyebrow knitted together when Luccan exited, and we followed. I was sure the leprechauns had thought we were intent on taking much more. Balvor opened his mouth, a question on his lips, but Bac had already moved into position, surely anticipating the questioning just as I did.

The rebel placed a hand on the leprechaun's shoulder. "Take us to the Falk vault, Balvor."

The Coinmaster jolted, and his face took on an amenable expression that surely did not stem from his heart. "The Falk vault, you say? Bad idea."

"And why's that?" Bac asked.

"You'll all die."

I stiffened. "Why do you say that?"

"Only a trueborn Falk can open it," the leprechaun replied. "Many others have tried. Some attempted to steal. They all died. Others with a drop of Falk blood in their veins tried to claim the riches inside. Those fae lived, but none succeeded in their task."

The tension left me, likely a foolish response. "We'll take our chances. Show us the way."

He smiled a lazy smile, taken over by Bac's magic, though something in his eyes gleamed, a tell that hinted he did not take kindly to us tricking him. "It's your necks."

We continued down the same hallway. Vale strode at my side, his hands tense. I had a feeling he was ready to pull one of his concealed daggers at any moment. Tanziel, the recorder, had been fairly quiet since we'd entered Avaldenn, but she was taking everything in closely. I hoped the nymph was getting a good record of the monsters and ogres we passed. Would Thyra and the others in Bitra see similar monsters?

"You shall not pass!" A voice boomed out of nowhere, making me squeal, and everyone around me startled.

"They request the Falk vault," Balvor said simply.

"Only the Coinmasters and the Blood of the White Hawk can pass!"

My heart raced, knowing this was a moment of truth. A test for me.

"I am the Blood of the White Hawk," I said, stepping forward. "Daughter of King Harald and Queen Revna."

"Oh, is she?" Balvor commented.

Bac chuckled. "Stay quiet."

"Of course."

That power of his was *quite* handy.

From a hidden door in the side of the corridor, a skeletal creature of horrors emerged. I leaned back as I took in the walking corpse dressed in old, rusted armor.

This had to be a draugr, an uncommon creature and for a good reason. They used to be living fae, but they'd long died, been resurrected, and then instructed to protect treasures of their bloodline.

Despite the terror I should feel at the creature's appearance, pity filled me. To die and then be denied a trip to the afterworld by your own family was a fate I'd not wish on anyone. What had this fae done to deserve it?

The draugr approached me, the empty sockets of his eyes seemingly burning through me as he reached for his sword spattered with rust. "Are you sure, lady? Others have claimed to be of the White Hawk line, but they were not. The odds are not in your favor, and I do not take kindly to trickery."

"How do I prove who I am?"

"Take my hand." He extended a skeletal limb. "If you are of my line, I'll recognize our bond."

I refrained from wrinkling my nose and extended my hand to meet his. The lack of flesh was disconcerting, almost as much as the strength of his boney grip, and the deep cold that radiated from the creature.

And though he had no eyes, the moment he felt the truth within me, his jaw went slack right before a horrible smile crossed his face.

"*Family*," he whispered longingly. "It has been so long."

All the bad things I'd been thinking came crashing down and guilt filled me. The draugr was pitiable, not someone I should fear. Though I'd take what his family had done to him as betrayal, all he wished was to serve our line.

"A pleasure," I said.

"What is your name?" he asked, that rotted smile still on his face.

"I've been going by Neve, but my true name is Isolde." When faced with a fae who had given up so much for his family, *our family*, the least I could do was own my name. In front of him, it felt good and right, much like when Thyra had first uttered it. "You may call me by the name my mother and father gave me. What's your name?"

The creature looked stricken, and I had to wonder if anyone had asked him that since he'd been down here. Stars, how long had that been?

"Harvadril," he spoke his name as though he were speaking through a mouth full of food, his hand coming to his chest.

"A name for a guardian," I whispered.

"In life and so beyond."

I had nothing to say to that. He seemed touched, not sad, but to me it was all terribly tragic.

"You may pass, lovely Isolde. Those with you too, if you wish for them to go. I follow your lead from here, my lady." He bowed his head. "Your faithful servant."

I exhaled, pleased but also disquieted. "Is that the only test I'll face, Harvadril?"

The draugr shook his head. "Trueborn blood protects our family's treasures. You will give some of your lifeblood to the leprechaun's cauldron and enter."

It must have maddened King Magnus to get this far, to have to touch the undead, only to fail because his father would not legitimize him.

"Thank you," I said.

"Glad we didn't have to fight him off," Luccan murmured when we were out of earshot.

"He's bones and a little flesh," I said.

"Don't be tricked. Some say that draugrs are held together by the magic of the stars and they're notoriously difficult to kill."

"Well, thank the stars, we needn't try.".

The corridor continued on, a ribbon of darkness before us, illuminated only by the faelights still following Balvor. After what felt like an age, but likely had been no more than five minutes, the leprechaun announced that we'd arrived.

The vault looked much the same as others, though with more space on either side. Larger, I guessed. On the door, a hawk made of gleaming silver spread its wings. Despite the many turns in which the vault had been closed, the silver had not tarnished.

"Let her in," Bac commanded Balvor, and the leprechaun extended the cauldron to me.

As I'd seen Luccan open his own vault, I knew what to do. I drew blood and allowed it to drip into the cauldron, then the leprechaun did the same. Inhaling, I pressed my hand to the door.

The door to the vault glowed silver. A whirring that had not sounded at Luccan's vault filled the dank hallway. Clicks followed, a lock disengaging.

The door opened on a groan, a musty scent washed out, and the first sight I got of the inside made my knees buckle. Luccan was rich with gold and gem-filled hills as tall as Vale, filling his vault.

The Falk vault was a different monster. It was at least seven times larger than Luccan's. And if Luccan had hills of gold and gems, the Falks possessed *mountains* straining to touch the stars.

"Fates," Vale laughed with disbelief. "No wonder the king wished to get in here so badly. This vault could fund a lavish court life for many decades."

"Astounding," Caelo agreed. "Now how are we to find that crown, if it's in this one?"

"Split up," Freyia suggested, tossing her curtain of black hair over her shoulder as if she meant to get down to business. "Bac and Balvor can stay out here in case someone comes down here and asks questions. The rest of us will search."

"Fine. Remember we're looking for a silver crown, heavy

with amethyst gems and a few larger diamonds. Many spikes off the top too," I said, as though they hadn't seen the drawing that Brynhild had shown us. "If it's a Hallow, we should be able to tell the difference between it and other crowns. It will have magic."

What magic, she was not sure, a smithy *had* felt the shadow magic in Sassa's Blade. Though considering I had to spill a lot of blood to activate the powers, I wasn't so sure they were useful.

I hoped the Frør Crown was a more powerful Hallow. Anything to help us in our fight against Magnus.

We entered the vault, Tanziel trailing close behind me. Aside from the mountains of riches, a line of three swords, hilts gleaming and glittering, caught my eyes.

"They no doubt have tales," Vale said, longing in his tone.

"I'd love to fight with those. They're beautiful," Caelo added, his eyes covetous.

If I had my way, I'd let them take the swords. But we needed to slip out of here without issue and leaving with three swords when we arrived with none was not exactly an inconspicuous exit. Especially if the Coinmasters recognized these swords as belonging to House Falk and not House Riis. That seemed a long shot, but I would not put it past the leprechauns and their meticulous accounting.

"Another day." I smiled at the soldiers. "For now, we search."

We split up, each taking portions of the enormous vault. Only a few minutes of searching passed when Freyia let out a string of curses.

"What happened?" I asked. We'd not gone so far into the vault that the vampire had disappeared behind all the gold. She appeared unharmed.

"Nothing. But have you noticed that everything in here has a replica?" She gestured at two identical shields, and then two twin goblets.

"Are you sure?" I looked back at Tanziel, as if she'd answer, but she was busy recording me.

"Bleeding skies, I think she's right!" Caelo shouted from across the room. "I thought I was going crazy, but no, each item has a twin."

"It's a common great house trick," Vale said. "Make identical treasures so thieves won't know which is real. When the thief leaves, if they've taken the wrong one, it becomes ash."

"You didn't think to mention that?" I scoffed.

"We planned to show you the Frør Crown before leaving anyway, and you'll be able to tell," Vale said. "There will be an imprint on the real thing, and you will recognize it."

That appeased me, but only slightly. I now had double the amount of objects to sift through. So far, we'd been lucky. But what if another Coinmaster ventured down here to check on Luccan and Balvor? Luccan *was* an elite client. What would they do if we weren't at the Riis vault?

With vigor, I walked deeper down the narrow paths between mountains of gold, searching up and down. Luccan flew above, searching for the diadem.

My hopes were plunging into valleys when I neared the back of the vault and spied a cabinet. It was familiar, much like the one my mother had in her room to display crowns, though this one was all wood.

Was this used for the same purpose?

I darted over and opened the first door of three. My heart leapt.

Many crowns stared back at me, glimmering and lovely despite being underground for at least two decades. None resembled the Frør Crown, though, so I shut the first door and opened the second. A quick glance yielded the same results. Praying to the stars that the third time would be a charm, I opened the third door.

All my breath left me in one go.

In the center sat two silver crowns, heavy with amethyst gems. Like the hawk on the door, neither piece was tarnished. I scanned the others, all beautiful but not the ones we were risking our lives to find.

"I have them!" I announced.

"Thank the Fates!" Caelo shouted. "Do you need help?"

"I don't think so. You can go to the front. I'll figure out which is the true Hallow and meet you." With trembling hands, I reached for one crown, and upon the first touch a spark ran down my arm.

Daughter of Winter. A male voice whispered. *Don the crown.*

I pulled my hand back. This crown possessed magic, and had belonged to my family, but was it wise to do as it wished? Maybe this was another spell to protect the contents of the vault?

And yet, we'd come here for the Frør Crown. I'd do all I

could to not leave without it. So slowly, I reached out and touched the headdress again.

Will you hurt me? I hoped the Frør Crown could hear me like I could hear it.

I will not. Don the crown, Daughter of Winter.

Throat tightening, I lifted the headpiece and, with a trembling hand, placed it upon my head.

The world exploded. Snow swirled, disorienting me further, and it took a moment for my eyes to adjust and see that I stood in a forest before a Drassil tree. A male fae with a sharp nose and strong square jawline was captured within the tree, just under the bark somehow.

"Are you here to make good on your bargain?" he asked.

"I—I don't know," a voice that did not belong to me replied, making me jump. I twisted, looking for another, but found no one else in the vision.

The male cocked his head, clearly shocked by the answer. Being trapped in a tree, it was the most movement he could make. Or at least I thought so until shadows began to spool around him.

A Shadow Fae! In a Drassil? Was I in Winter's Realm like the snow indicated, or was I seeing the Shadow Fae Isles?

"You used me. I allowed it because I loved you," he growled. *"And for my love, you took my power and trapped me. But you promised one day I'd be free. Are you here to deliver?"*

My fingers and toes felt like ice. Danger rippled from the fae in the tree. I didn't like being here, in front of him.

"It is not that time." The feminine voice replied.

He roared, the sound loud enough to rattle the stars, and

his darkness expanded menacingly. I ripped the Hallow off my head and stared down at the sparkling amethysts, chest heaving.

Who were those fae?

"Neve! Everything is fine?" Vale called from the front of the vault, ripping me fully into the moment.

We were still in danger, deep within the coinary and about to take something from my family vault. While it wasn't thieving, I was a wanted fae.

And I was wasting time. I glanced down at the Frør crown again, sure that I held the Frør Crown, but unsure if I should bring it with me. The vision had scared me and taking an object when we did not know its full scope of powers did not seem wise.

Someone shifted behind me, the faint noise indicating that I was being watched. I twisted to find Tanziel watching. Recording me, as was her task.

Bleeding skies.

Now I had to bring it. If I didn't, Thyra would never trust me. I needed that trust now more than ever. She, my blood, out of anyone in this world, might understand what I'd seen.

"This is it." I tucked the Frør Crown in the inner pocket of my cloak. "Let's go."

We wound back through the mountains of treasure, and all the way, I did my best to hide my shaking hands. Vale and the others waited for us just inside the mouth of the vault. At the sight of me, their shoulders loosened, relief washing over their faces. Everyone, that is, save for Vale whose eyes widened. Try as I might, I could not hide my fear from him.

"Neve, are you well?" Vale asked as the group stepped over the vault's threshold, back into the corridor to join Bac and Balvor. "You look—"

Bells rang, and the roars of ogres filled the hall.

"Thieves!" One ogre barked, and I thought I heard rock fall. Perhaps they were pounding the walls? "Let us out! We want blood!"

Metal clanged, and my stomach plummeted as footsteps fell loudly and clumsily and the ground shook beneath my feet. The ogres were free. The leprechauns knew we were here.

CHAPTER 35
VALE

"Coinmaster!" I barked. "How do they know there's trouble?"

The leprechaun looked up at me blandly, still under Bac's enchantment. "The king insisted that an alarm was to sound if anyone left the vault and one of you stepped over the threshold, triggering the alarm. He seemed to think that someone might get in another way, but if they got out, then they'd be a threat." He looked at Neve. "Seems she might be one to him, no?"

Fates. We are in trouble.

"Daggers out," Caelo said. "We know there are ogres, and they look hungry. I can't say what other monsters lie ahead but be prepared to fight all the way to the main level."

"Since we're no longer getting out of here quietly, we might need more than just daggers and throwing stars." Neve darted over to the line of three swords. They were ancient and more decorative than most swords I'd seen.

Prizes, all of them. "Take these!"

She passed me a sword, then gave the other two to Caelo and Freyia. Blades gleaming in the faelights, we took off, sprinting down the corridor. Under one arm, Bac carried Balvor. We needed the leprechaun to pass through the steel door near the entrance, but his legs were too short to keep up. Thankfully, the fae remained under Bac's magical persuasion and did not fight.

We closed in on the draugr first, and he shifted to the side, bowing at Neve jerkily.

"My lady. Until we meet again."

Neve should have kept running, should have ignored the undead creature. Instead, my mate skidded to a stop.

"Harvadril, you said you served me?"

"I serve the true Falk line, Princess Isolde. That is you and I, and no one else. Or if so, I have not met them."

Neve nodded. "I ask you to join us. Fight with us all the way up the stairs." She paused, her eyes lighting up as though she realized something. "Then, once you're done, you can either return here or come with us."

My brilliant mate!

The draugr gripped his rusted sword, thrilled by the idea of a fight. "I've been wanting to skewer those ogres for many turns."

"Have at them," Neve said and waved for the draugr to lead the way, which he did with apparent relish as we, once again, raced for the door.

I beamed at her. Draugrs were famous for their fighting skills, and they could not die. Putting this creature in the forefront was genius. Particularly as we weren't sure what we'd meet on the steps.

As we approached the first of the caged ogres. The skeletal being surged forward to meet those who wanted to drink our blood and eat our bones. With grace that most living soldiers would envy, Harvadril cut down one ogre with ease, though as he did so, another ogre leapt on his back, sinking her teeth into the draugr's bony shoulder.

Freyia caught up, sword in hand. With the speed of the vampire order, she grabbed the ogre by the head, pulled back, and cut across the neck. The second fell with a thud as four more shuffled out of their cages.

These new ogres drooled at the sight of the dead, and I got the sense they'd been waiting in the dark for death to come upon the others so that they could scavenge.

Time to put them out of their misery. I attacked one while Caelo brought his sword down on the other. The ogres were slow moving in body and mind and despite their massive size, they were weak from starvation. We flew high and targeted the veins in their necks to cut them down one by one. By the time we finished, Harvadril and Freyia had dispatched the other two.

"How many more?" Neve asked. "And why aren't they here?"

"Six," Bac said. "The other cages are empty. They might have gone in the opposite direction. Are they instructed to go somewhere, Balvor? Maybe wait by that steel door?"

"They're instructed to kill any thieves, leaving only leprechauns alive," Balvor said, still seemingly unworried.

Bac's magic was keeping him so. "We all drink a potion that is poisonous to them, so they wouldn't dare eat me. I fear that you all are in *grave* danger."

As if we didn't know that already.

"So, are there more? Near other vaults?" Neve asked.

"Yes."

"They likely ran off because they were weaker than the ones here," I said. "I expect that they're elsewhere, fighting and eating their own kind."

"How many others are there within the vault system?" Bac asked.

Balvor gave a shrug and hummed lightly. Bac's powers of persuasion were far too strong.

"It matters not how many. We have no choice but to go forward," Caelo muttered, as pissed about all this as I. "Weapons at the ready. Harvadril, at the front again."

As we raced down the corridor, I half expected the other ogres to leap out of the offshoots and into our path. They didn't though, and I caught the sounds of fighting down a few smaller tunnels. On the way here, I'd heard growls and whines. It seemed I was most likely right about ogres moving to other halls to eat their own.

Whatever the starving, pitiful fae the leprechauns had imprisoned were doing, it was not searching for us. We reached the steel door without issue.

"Your hand to the door," Bac instructed.

Balvor extended his hand, palm shaking. Was he fighting Bac's powers? If so, he failed to free himself from them, for he pressed his hand to the door as Bac instructed and the door lifted. We ran through it and down the hallway.

"Nearly there!" Luccan cried out. "Be prepared for anything."

I gripped the long sword in my hand, thankful that Neve's family had placed them in the vault. For us, they might mean the difference between life and death.

We burst into the circular room, the mouth of the never-ending stairs. I took in the space but found no adversaries. A moment of peace that was shattered by the howls and guttural roars from the steps above.

"Freyia, can you take the back?" Neve asked. "More ogres, or maybe something worse could come, and you'll hear them gaining before any of us. Plus, I trust you to catch anyone if they fall down the steps. Harvadril, you take point."

"As you wish, Princess Isolde."

"I'll be right behind you, draugr," Caelo said.

I stood by Neve. The steps were narrow, but there was no way I was letting her go ahead of me, nor behind, where I could not see her.

"Go," Freyia assured. "The longer the alarm bells sound, the more guards they'll have at the top of the steps too."

We ran, lungs burning, legs straining from the effort. With each step upward, I kept Neve in my sights. We made it only thirty steps when my heart dropped to my knees.

Emerging from the unseen cages deep in the sides of the staircase were black direwolves. I counted six. Almost one for each of us. Too bad they weren't the only foes we'd face.

A lindwyrm, technically a type of dragon native to this realm and not a worm at all, undulated down the stairs ahead of the wolves, having already spotted us. The creature was fifty paces long and made of pure muscle, but that was not the worst of it. Seemingly in control of the animals were two draugrs waiting among the wolves.

"Bleeding skies," Luccan hissed. "If we live through this, it will be a miracle!"

"The lindwyrm has venom," I shouted. "It will spit that venom, so steer clear of it."

"How will we kill it if we have to stay away?" Neve held up a dagger. "These aren't good for range fighting."

"Harvadril," I said, not wanting to risk someone with skin that the venom could burn off.

Not to mention, I had doubts that any of us could do what I was about to ask of the draugr. The lindwyrm was thick and while Luccan, Caelo, Freyia, and I were strong and experienced fighters, the draugr was more so.

"Harvadril, slice the lindwyrm in half. Then we fight our way up." I rarely prayed to the dead gods, but I did so now, singling out Tyiel, God of Battle. If no more ogres came and if the wolves and the enemy draugrs would just stay on the steps long enough for the lindwyrm to die, we *might* have a chance.

"Ogres incoming," Freyia said, dashing my faint hopes as the ground trembled with their great weight. "I'd say six or seven, judging by the cadence of their footfalls."

Of course they were. They were starving and had finished whatever mayhem they were causing in the other corridors. They'd caught on to our scent and hoped to feed more decadently.

"Harvadril, kill that wyrm!" Neve commanded, panic rising in her voice.

I grasped her forearm. She needed to keep her head. For that, I suspected Neve required a task, and I had just the one.

"Wife, shoot icicles at the wolves. Aim for their soft side."

The cold in the underbelly of the coinary deepened as Neve called upon her magic for the first time in days. Since we'd traveled to Vitvik, we'd all saved up our powers, just in case disaster struck. The time to use them had come, and no one here possessed more power than my mate.

She released four spear-like icicles as long as *Skelda*. Three hit their targets, one shattered on the steep steps behind an enemy draugr—female by the looks of her. The corpse monster let out a roar, but as the lindwyrm was closing in on us, their faraway anger was the least of my worries. My stomach danced as Harvadril climbed a dozen more steps and approached the long, thin dragon.

The lindwyrm unfurled and wasted no time in spitting venom. As Harvadril was skeletal, it went right through him and shot down the stairs. Caelo, Luccan, Neve and I ducked, but paces behind us, someone screamed.

"Tanziel!" Bac shouted.

I twisted to see that Bac had hurled Balvor from his grasp. He must have also released Balvor from his powers for when the leprechaun rose to stand, a stream of curses left his lips.

"How is she?" I called, lunging forward and stabbing a

section of the lindwyrm that had slithered too close while Harvadril battled the beast face to face.

"It's burning through her cheek!" Bac yelled back.

"Here!" Neve ran down the stairs to the nymph and froze the skin of Tanziel's cheek. "That might stop it from spreading."

Tanziel moaned, but Bac's eyes widened hopefully. "I think it's working. I—"

"They're here!" Freyia screamed as eight ogres entered the chamber.

"Skies!" I shouted. "Target the wolves, Neve. Luccan and Caelo, stab the lindwyrm."

Everyone sprang into action, and I flew back the way we'd come to take on the ogres with Freyia. They were pushing forward, attempting to overtake the vampire, but we had the high ground, the ogres were starving, and between Freyia and me, we had many turns of battle on our side. With swords skewering their eyes, we disabled four within seconds. An icicle shot from above to kill a fifth, right in the temple. I grinned, knowing it was Neve's work.

The final three seemed the smartest of the bunch. They ran back down the steps and disappeared into the spokes of the coinary. We let them go, and I twisted back to the others in time to see Harvadril cut through the lindwyrm. With a violent hiss, the beast went limp.

Neve had lanced more wolves too. I did a quick count.

Only two wolves and two draugrs left.

"Up the stairs," I shouted. "Harvadril, me, Caelo, and Luccan. Ogres might return. Freyia—"

"Yes, yes, I know. I have the back."

"Neve, help Bac and Tanziel."

Normally, she wouldn't have enjoyed being told to let others fight the hard fight for her, but Neve was heaving with the effort of taking down so many wolves so fast.

As we ran up the stairs, Luccan diverted to the lindwyrm. From its head, he pulled out a fang dripping with venom. He stuffed the fang in his cloak pocket. "Arie and Duran might want to study it."

Brilliant. If we could recreate the venom, we could use it in a weapon.

Up the stairs we ran, Harvadril and me taking them two at a time, pulling ahead of the others. The other draugrs rushed to meet us and before I could brace myself, I was steel to steel with the female undead.

The only way I knew to kill one of these was to slice off its head. Of course, the undead creature did not make that feat easy. She defended. I struck. She leapt. I scrambled back.

The others possessed the sense to remain at a safe distance, but at the rate I was failing, I'd be next to them soon. Then what? The enemy draugr would be far too close to my mate.

"For the Blood of the White Hawk!" screamed Harvadril, and a skull flew by my shoulder, down the stairs.

A shriek wrenched out of the female draugr I fought and in a pitiful moment of weakness she spun to find her peer crumbling to ash. One second was all I needed. My sword ripped through her neck, and a pile of ash formed.

Two direwolves left. That's all—

A dagger shot past me, sticking in one wolves' skull right

491

before a second blade did the same to the other. The beasts fell, and their blood ran down the steps.

Freyia laughed. "Stupid dogs."

Bringing the vampire had been a good idea, indeed.

"That's all, right?" Neve gasped as she ran up the steps to join.

"For now," I said. "More will be at the top. Soldiers."

Neve winced. "Harvadril, can you—"

"I appreciate your invitation to join you, Princess Isolde, but I cannot leave The Below," the undead corpse interrupted. "I'm sorry."

"Oh. Well, then, thank you for your help." She looked like she wanted to hug the creature. Or possibly drag him up the stairs. I would not be surprised if later, I found Neve researching how to break a draugr from its enchantment.

If we survive whomever we'll meet at the top, that is.

The alarm had ceased, but we all knew guards would be waiting in case, against all odds, we survived the monsters they'd placed in The Below to deal with thieves.

"Thank you, draugr," I said. "We owe you our lives."

Harvadril stepped aside, allowing us to pass. I didn't look back as we climbed the stairs. One by one, we reached the top. The last being Bac and Freyia, who were helping Tanziel.

"Freyia, I need you here," I said. "When we exit this door, they'll be waiting. The only reason no one has come down already is they want the monsters to defeat us and likely have the door warded against their kind."

"No." Neve held up a hand. "I have an idea. Let me go

first, and we won't have to kill anymore. I want to avoid that, if possible."

Her fingers glowed a light amethyst. She was calling her magic.

"You have enough power left?"

"I think so."

I trusted her judgment. "Be ready to strike the instant I open it."

She got into position, her chin tilted up, her spine straight and proud. I'd never seen my mate look so like the force of nature that she was.

"Three, two . . . *go!*" I flung the door open and a blast of cold rushed by me, stealing my breath before Neve crossed the threshold.

Screams came from the coinaries' main level, but they silenced quickly. Neve entered, and I shivered as I followed my mate and witnessed the destruction.

Three dozen guards stood assembled and ready to fight. Leprechauns were waiting for us to appear, not to battle, of course, but likely to give instructions. Every one of them was frozen from head to toe.

Neve wavered, and I caught her right before her knees buckled. "Thanks. I need a second. I—" Her eyes caught mine and widened. "Vale, your glamour! It's gone!"

Only then did I realize hers was too. Luccan, Caelo, and Freyia also appeared to be their usual selves.

"There was an enchantment on the threshold," Caelo said. "I bet it activates with the alarm. I felt the enchantment break my glamour when I walked through."

"There's no time for you to redo them," I said. "We have to run from here."

Everyone agreed, and we pulled up our hoods, our only means of disguise in a city that knew many of our faces far too well. Seeing in her stance that Neve had not regained her strength enough to sprint through the city, I sheathed my sword and gathered her in my arms. She didn't protest, a sign as sure as any that I'd correctly determined her energy reserves were low.

"Freyia, cover me," I commanded as we burst out of the coinary.

The guards outside drew their weapons, but I used air magic to blow them off their feet. Their heads knocked against the wall, and the guards slumped to the ground.

We cleared the first street with ease, but the sheer number of fae walking the larger roads made escape more difficult. Weaving around fae, many stared.

"Is that Prince Vale?" one person said after my hood fell down, thanks to a gust of wind. "And his wife?"

Bleeding skies!

Neve did her best to pull my hood back up, but word of our appearance in Avaldenn spread like a ripple of water. We'd made it to Lordling Lane when another alarm sounded.

"That's the city watch!" The words were no sooner out of my mouth than a shriek pierced my ears.

"I knew it! That *whore* is back!" Calpurnia screamed. "Stop them!"

"Get that female!" Adila added, her tone as imperious as ever. "The king has a bounty on her head!"

I ignored my cousin and Lady Ithamai, and barreled forth with Freyia at my side and the others steps behind. Luccan's home was in sight now. Closer. Closer still.

We reached the gate, and I shifted Neve in my arms. The wards around Luccan's home would allow me in if I gave blood.

"Here!" Luccan slammed into the gate, and at his touch, the wards fell. "Inside!"

We funneled in, Bac last as he was carrying Tanziel on his own. The moment we were safe, Luccan slammed the door shut.

"To the gateway."

I exhaled for the first time in what felt like many turns, and followed my brother inside, to safety.

INTERLUDE

KING MAGNUS AABERG, THE WHITE BEAR, PROTECTOR OF WINTER'S REALM

The King of Winter dismounted his gryphon, bones aching, magic depleted to practically nothing.

At least he was not alone in his weakness. At present, Warden Roar could not shift. His Clawsguard had no access to magic.

And yet, aching though his body may be, the king had rarely felt so invigorated in his soul.

I will strengthen in time. I will become stronger than ever before.

Stablehands took care of the gryphons, and the king and Roar strode into Frostveil Castle. Fae stared, for no matter that the two currently worked together, the Lisika warden and the Aaberg monarch were an unlikely pair.

"I require a concubine on my cock, and my belly filled with roast boar," the king said to a servant who waited at the door with two goblets of steaming mulled wine. The king took one golden goblet, the warden the other. "See that the concubine comes to my room immediately. Send the food a half hour later."

The servant walked away.

Alone again with the warden, the king's voice lowered. "Once I'm done with her, I shall call a meeting. Be prepared."

"I will, Majesty," Roar replied, no judgment in his tone, though the slight curl of his lips indicated distaste. Lord Roar did not approve of Magnus's harem. It was one reason the king flaunted it when the Warden of the West was around.

They parted, the king veering to his rooms. However, when Magnus arrived at his quarters, he found not a concubine waiting for him, but the Lady of Silks, Nalaea Qiren.

King Magnus smirked. "Here to revisit old times, Nalaea?"

Her black eyebrows pulled tight over piercing green eyes. In the corridor's torchlight, Nalaea's ebony skin gleamed like the fine silks her family sold all around Isila.

Even Magnus, a purveyor of the most beautiful fae in the kingdom, did not deny that the Lady of Silks was stunning. His physical attraction to her, as much as his need for her cunning mind, was why their affair had lasted so long. He sometimes thought that had he been a male to marry for love, he might have wed Nalaea. Although there was no doubt Inga had proved far more useful than a mare ever would have been.

"You think I'm here to bed you?" Nalaea snorted, not bothering to be embarrassed around the Clawsguards who followed the king, their golden cloaks fluttering behind them like ghosts. The knights sworn to his bloodline knew about the affair. Many did. Initially, some had dared to claim that the Lady of Silks bedded him to get ahead. They lost their tongues for the insult—and not by the king's orders.

The Qiren family was small compared to the other Sacred Eight, but they held great power. The king's High Councilor was a Qiren, and Nalaea was the Lady of Silks. She did not need to bed the king for any reason other than she wanted to.

"Magnus darling, you're filthy and smell like unwashed gryphon." Her nose wrinkled. "Your whores can have you."

Magnus let himself into his rooms. The Lady of Silks swept in after him, her face stoney. "Why are you here then, if not to ride my cock?"

"Your daughter is gone. One of my spies saw her entering the Warmsnap and then leaving—disguised—with the spymaster."

His spine straightened. "With Riis?"

"You have another spymaster?"

"I'm already tiring of this attitude."

"Then keep up." She sat in a chair by the cold hearth. "They've been gone for days now. Of course, others have noticed that the princess is not in the castle. Your wife, however, says that Princess Saga is simply not feeling herself." Nalaea's eyebrows rose. "Though that can be said for your heir, I assure you that the princess is no longer at court."

He gripped his goblet tighter. "What's wrong with Rhistel?"

"I cannot be certain. My daughter, Thalia, tried to flirt with him, but he did not respond."

"Is that so odd?"

"Thalia is a great beauty. And her skin and scent are like love potions to those she wishes to affect, so yes."

Perhaps the latter would affect Rhistel, but not the former. His heir enjoyed beauty, but he did not let it sway him. Not like Vale.

"What will you do about Princess Saga?"

"That's not your concern."

"I'm your *best* ally, Magnus."

"As you say. Now, unless you have more bad news to dispatch, leave me."

Scowling, she left, and the king took that time to drink the goblet of mulled wine and then a second. Once he washed down the wine, he scrubbed his hands and face. The concubine arrived and though Magnus's cock was rock hard at the sight of the dryad's large breasts and full lips, he knew he had to see if the Lady of Silks was right. The king told the dryad to wait in the bed for his return and went in search of his heir or his wife.

His cloak, the same one he'd worn on the journey south, fluttered around his ankles. Though it was hot, Magnus did not take off the cloak. Not until he had a safe place for the item inside his pocket.

As luck would have it, Magnus found not only his wife or his son, but both in the same place, the queen's chambers. It took him only one glance to determine that Nalaea had been correct. Rhistel's eyes were glazed.

Unlike the Lady of Silks, the king knew why. Magnus shut the door to his wife's chambers and cast a shield of air

at the door so that the Clawsguard outside—his and hers—
would not overhear.

"What are you doing to him?" he spat at his wife.

"That is how you greet your wife after disappearing to
the west?"

"It's how I greet a wife who is whispering our son. Do as
I say, Inga."

"I cannot."

"*Will not*, you mean." Frost formed at his fingertips.

Inga noticed the flex of power, but did not budge. Her
ability to alter his mind if she so wanted, the chance that she
might *make him* do as she wished, had always infuriated him.
It was why Magnus often kept a distance from his wife and
never missed his dose of Mind Rönd potion. He called off
his magic, already exhausted by that small show that did
nothing whatsoever to sway Inga.

When my new magics strengthen, she'll defer. He could not wait
for the day when he might try out the new powers unleashed
inside him. Magic lost to this world. Dark magic that his
bloodline had hidden for so very long.

"He threatened our daughter, Magnus."

The king drew back. "Rhistel said he'd hurt his sister?"

His heir was the most unpredictable of his children—or
at least that had been the case before that Falk whore arrived
at court and stole Vale's mind. Over the turns, the family
had needed to clean up many of Rhistel's messes, and as of
late, his heir had been violent towards his own twin.

Still, never in a million turns would the king have
thought Rhistel capable of hurting Saga. She was the jewel

of the family. The best of them. Pure and innocent and loved by all. Winter's delight.

Inga's chin lifted in challenge. "He did. Lord Riis was present at the threat and said he could take her away. Keep her safe."

"Until when?"

"Until *I* deem that our son is no longer a threat."

For the first time, his wife sounded uncertain. Was she lying?

Inga, like Rhistel, like *all* whisperers, possessed the power to lie. Even if his wife's magic was responsible for their positions today, which made her arguably stronger than him, Magnus did not think his queen lied to him often. But he could never be completely certain either.

"Did you succeed in your quest?" Inga asked.

"I did."

"And do you plan to use it?"

"How did you—?"

"I'm in Rhistel's head all day. Holding him, trying to reason with him. I see much."

Of course. The king was sure his heir would not have told his secret, not if given a real chance.

"You cannot keep him like this," Magnus said. "The Lady of Silks has noticed he's acting oddly."

"Why hasn't she left court?"

"I have not dismissed her."

Inga's lips pursed; the obvious disbelief written across her face. "That didn't stop the Armenils. Nor the Baliks, or those of the House of the Sea Serpent." Bright blue eyes snapped up to meet his. "Then again, I suppose when you say that you'll see Lord Roar fed to your bear and then give your daughter's hand to him when he actually reappears, the high lords and ladies don't believe they need your permission to leave court, do they?"

She was calling him weak. His word worthless.

"Watch yourself," the king seethed. "They'll see soon enough that they should have remained where I told them. I have a plan. One that will see the end to the rebellion, and any lack of loyalty in the great houses from here on out. Soon there will no longer be a Falk whore running about. Just bastards who have no greater claim than I to the throne."

"And what of Vale?" Inga asked. "Will your plan harm him?"

Magnus swallowed. He'd told his allies not to harm his son, but would they follow through?

"I've done all I can to secure his well-being. From this point forward, his fate is in his own hands." The king nodded to Rhistel. "As for that one, at the very least *loosen* your hold. We cannot have him harming Saga, but others cannot notice the state he is in, either."

She turned away, dismissing him. Annoyance and frustration warring inside him, the king left the queen's chambers, wishing that he could return to his chambers and take pleasure in his concubine. But Inga, for all her flaws, always had a way of clarifying his priorities.

The king left, and his Clawsguard followed behind, quiet and loyal, just as Magnus preferred. When the king reached his next destination, however, he turned to the soldier.

"I require a moment alone."

"Yes, Majesty."

Magnus exited into a courtyard. A break in the clouds dappled the Crown Drassil with sunlight, a rare occurrence for the tree. Magnus approached the magical tree of the realm, inherently linked to the magic of Winter's Realm, the dead gods, and the Faetia in the starry halls of the afterworld. Perhaps other worlds too.

Standing before the tree, King Magnus placed a hand on the bark. Usually he did this to infuse magic into the tree, a cycle unbroken by those with the strongest winter magic since time forgotten. Instead of pushing his power into the bark, though, he closed his eyes.

"Mighty Drassil, Faetia, and powers in the stars, I've come requesting that you fully legitimize me as the King of Winter. To be given the full power I've been denied all these turns."

Whispers filled his head, but one stood out. As ever, the whisper he heard sounded a lot like his mother.

Picturing the sad creature who had birthed him made the king squirm. He'd never had the courage to ask if the voice actually was the deceased Lady Aaberg or another fae soul or even a dead god speaking to him who was mimicking his mother's voice. He didn't think he ever would.

You finally have what we require of you? The voice separated from the whispers and spoke to only him.

I do.

Place it in the hole.

This Drassil, like many he'd seen, had a natural hole which no animals claimed. The king did as the voice

504

requested, placing the item he'd risked so much for in the hole. The effect was instantaneous.

The purple leaves above glowed, the bark warmed, and a cacophony of voices louder than before filled the king's ears. Then suddenly, the tree drew upon his magic. He stilled, wanted to pull away, but had a feeling that this was part of the ritual, one that was not written about or spoken of but just done. Those who went through this ritual came out more powerful than ever before. The only people who would have had experience with the Weighing of the Crown ritual were the rulers of the kingdom.

Son of Winter, the voices spoke in unison now. *You've found what was long lost. For that, we respect you.*

And? The pull of his magic was draining him more than he thought was possible. *Do you bless me? Do you give me magic from the beyond? Magic to change the fate of this realm?*

He pulled up his sleeve and stared at his pale forearm in anticipation. Though the Blessing Mark had not been seen in two decades, he still recalled what it looked like on Harald Falk's arm. A silver crown with a sword and scepter crossed before the crown. All three Hallows united, marking the Cruel King as the rightful ruler.

A pause in which the leaves dimmed, and the bark cooled again stole what little breath the king had. So when the tree spoke again, he sucked in air as though he'd been drowning in the icy depths of the sea.

You are not the only one who can change the fate of the realm. Nor save it. And we sense a new darkness in you. One your heart wishes to embrace. Though you have done as kings and queens long passed, we cannot give our full blessing.

The king's face screwed up in anger, but he mastered himself. Had the tree felt that spike in fury?

We did, it answered his unspoken question.

I had to accept the darkness to get what you required.

Had to? Or wished to?

A low breath left him. *I deserve this.*

Two more might deserve it as much as you. Two whose magic might bring Winter back to the glory days. We refrain from choosing until those two hearts and souls are weighed.

Two?

In the meantime, to you, we give another chance. An opportunity to do what is right for the fae of Winter's Realm. Show us, show them, mercy and righteousness. The entirety of our blessing may still be to come. We give you just enough power to make this a reality.

He wanted to say more, but a rush of magic filled him. Magnus tipped his head back, barely able to believe that the magic filling him wasn't the full blessing.

The moment the magic ceased flowing into him, the king wanted more. *Needed more.*

The only way he would get it would be to right Winter's Realm. Though he would kill the two threats the tree spoke of too, for good measure. Hopefully, his new allies could help him with that. Magnus only needed to do his part to lure Isolde Falk, and whoever the other threat was, to his allies.

He stepped back from the tree, a direction clear in his mind as he gathered the item from the hole and hid it in his cloak. Inside, the heat of the castle was welcome, though he found not just his Clawsguard waiting, but the High Councilor, brother to the Lady of Silks, was present as well.

"What is it?" Magnus asked. The High Councilor looked much like his older sister, but unlike Nalaea, Onas Qiren had tells. Whatever he had to say would not be good news.

"My king, I regret to inform you that there's been a robbery at the coinary."

"From my vault? Where is the thief?" There could be no question that he or she had been caught. The leprechauns provided many protections, and his vault possessed every single one of them.

"Not your vault," the councilor's dark eyes dipped, as if Onas wished to be anywhere but where he stood at that moment, "the Falk vault."

Magnus stiffened. "Did they see who the thief was?"

"They did. Princess Isolde Falk and your son, Prince Vale, were there. Along with Sir Caelo and Lord Luccan Riis. Others too, though they were not recognized."

She'd gotten into her family vault. Never had he imagined that she'd have the mettle to enter the Falk vault in Avaldenn, mere streets away from the castle!

And Vale helped!

Magnus's jaw tightened. His son may be further gone than he thought.

"Where are they being kept?" the king asked.

"Kept, Majesty?"

"I will see to her execution now."

As for Vale and Luccan, he wasn't sure what he'd do. It was unwise to execute a son of a Sacred Eight. Particularly as Lord Riis protected Saga at this moment. And though

507

Magnus was fuming at Vale, he was still the Blood of House Aaberg, and Magnus was no kinslayer.

"My king, they ran to the sanctuary at Lord Luccan's home on Lording Lane. We've been unable to breach the wards since."

"They escaped!"

"Yes." The High Councilor bowed, and his curtain of black hair fell to cover his face.

"And was their heist successful?"

"An inventory is being performed now. It's been difficult as the Falks had a draugr guarding their treasures. The undead creature is being troublesome."

Yes, Magnus had met the creature.

"Do we know *anything* about what they took?"

"A crown, sire. And three swords. The leprechauns are uncertain about the gold or jewels. There are so many within that vault that gold and jewels will take some time to account for."

A pit opened in his stomach. *A crown.* Could it be that hallowed crown he'd once searched for too?

"Continue breaking down Luccan Riis's wards."

"And if we cannot?"

A valid concern. The Riis family were wealthy and able to hire the best warders. They would have the strongest of wards around their properties.

Magnus considered the facts and possible scenarios before deciding on a course of action. "If our ward breakers haven't succeeded in a days' time, then call the fire fae at the Tower. They have stashes of riot fire. Use it."

"But he lives in the middle of Lordling Lane! And your son is in there!"

The king had little doubt that when faced with riot fire, those holed up inside Luccan's home would flee. Anyone who valued life would do so.

"Take precautions to protect others and the surrounding buildings, but if need be, burn Lord Riis's home to the ground."

CHAPTER 36

NEVE

The rebels had transformed the dining hall into a place of pure joy and dancing.

Getting the Frør Crown had gone a long way in helping our reputation at Valrun Castle. But it had been saving Tanziel's face from the venom eating through her skin that had made the others want to include us. Tonight they even spoke with the vampire sisters, laughed with them.

The gryphons and pegasi helped a bit too, I suppose.

I chuckled at the memory of Thyra and Thantrel returning to Vitvik on pegasi, each with smug smiles on their faces. The others in their cohort had followed them on gryphonback.

The eight beasts had quickly crowded most of my team out of Lord Riis's office. Caelo and another faerie named Halladora had stayed behind and performed a vast amount of glamouring on the creatures to make them look like horses.

They'd then ridden the glamoured mounts through the

crowded hallways of a brothel and tavern below. Surely those in Vitvik would talk of that night for many turns to come.

As those in Avaldenn would gossip about the prince and princess who robbed a coinary. Stars, we're becoming notorious.

Poor reputation or not, I had to admit Thantrel's idea of "borrowing" the pegasi and gryphons from his father's castle was brilliant. Both creatures could fly with fae aback, and their wings weren't as sensitive to the cold as ours. It made small missions and runs into villages and towns for supplies far easier.

As was obvious by the vast quantities of good ale and wine procured from a village before this celebration. One we sorely deserved after getting the Frør Crown, which I'd been all too happy to immediately hand over to Thyra.

The Frør Crown made me uneasy, and I'd been interested to see if Thyra would have a similar experience. She had not, and that gave me pause in sharing what I'd seen in the vision.

Why had it shown me a vision and not my twin? Did it speak to the Falk who touched it first? Could it be as simple as that? Though my questions resonated inside me as valid, not sharing this information troubled me. Thyra was my twin. Had we grown up together, I was certain there wouldn't be a secret between us. My heart ached, for that wasn't the case.

Is a loving relationship with her the price I must pay for saving Anna's life? I wondered, and not for the first time. Magic had brought my best friend back to life after Prince Gervais tore out her neck, and I was all too aware that I had yet to pay for that miracle.

"Your wine, my love." Vale appeared at my side. He'd gone to get wine ten minutes back but had lingered over there, distracted by Luccan and Arie, all of them watching Thantrel trail Thyra.

"Thank you." I took the dented silver goblet. The rebels had brought out the finery for the occasion. "Has Thantrel had any luck?"

"She hasn't commanded him to go away." Vale cocked an eyebrow. "Than is likely taking that as a good sign, but I'm not so sure that's the right way to think about it. Perhaps Thyra is just very grateful for the gryphons and pegasi."

I didn't know what to think about my twin's actions either. Since their comparatively uneventful mission in Bitra, of which I was incredibly envious, Thyra seemed to have warmed to the youngest Riis. As Vale said, she wasn't banishing him, or even sneering at him, but she also didn't smile or actively invite him into conversation.

"Her being mean to him might be better," I said softly. "Her current actions give him hope."

"It's difficult," Vale agreed, pulling me close and kissing me on the temple that bore my scar. "Especially when his brothers are finding their own loves."

In the crowd, fiddlers and flutes played, and a few rebels performed jigs that were nothing like the dances we'd danced at court. One satyr in particular was going wild, prompting smiles all around. These raucous, enlivened romps made my heart sing. The other two Riis brothers had taken to the dance floor, and Anna appeared to be enjoying herself with Arie. Among our friends, only Clem looked a touch nervous.

I chuckled when Clemencia caught my eye. The sheltered merchant's daughter was being exposed to a whole new world. One that she'd never bargained for. Though when she beamed at me and then turned that breathtaking smile up to Luccan, there was no doubt that she was happy to be here. With him.

"Your sister is coming," Vale whispered in my ear.

I tore my gaze from Clem and Luccan to find Thyra was indeed approaching from the right. She cast a glance over her shoulder in a way that hinted she might have just escaped Thantrel.

And she's seeking me? Interesting.

"Neve. Vale." Thyra came to a stop beside us. "Are you enjoying the celebration?"

"I am," I said. "It seems like everyone else is too."

Thyra's face softened. "They deserve it. For so long we've been out here, surviving well enough, but I'm well aware it's not a life most would choose. They only do it so that one day the kingdom can heal."

"Here's to that." Vale lifted his goblet. I toasted him, as did Thyra, though with less enthusiasm than me.

We drank, and as I lowered my goblet Thyra locked eyes with me. "Can we speak in private out by the Drassil? I don't mean to pull you from the party for too long."

"Of course." I kissed Vale on the cheek. "I'll be right back."

I left with my sister. The moment we stepped out of the

dining hall, I cocked my head to the side. Was it me, or were the Drassil's leaves a brighter purple? There were certainly fewer leaves on the snowy ground than usual. I wanted to think the tree was healing, but it was just as likely that someone had swept, and the moonlight was playing tricks on my eyes.

Above us, the night sky was painted with jewel tones of green and purple. The colors danced together, undulating like waves and sweeping over the stars. I smiled, for it seemed that nature was celebrating us as well.

"This is my first time seeing the lights in Winter's Realm," I murmured. Out of all the nine kingdoms in Isila, the lights were best viewed here, though I had seen them twice out my window in Sangrael.

"Here, when the lights appear, we say that Brae is painting the sky." Thyra stared above, her eyes, often so serious, lighting up for a moment. "They never get old."

"I'm glad that I'll be able to see them more." I dragged my gaze away from the beauty above and looked at my twin. "You wished to speak?"

Thyra cleared her throat as she met my eyes. "I never thanked you for getting the Frør Crown, and then handing it over."

My head tilted. "Did you expect me not to?"

"I . . . wasn't sure." She shrugged. "But thank you. I'm not any closer to understanding its power." I braced myself for her to ask if I had any idea what the magic of the Crown could be. However, Thyra surprised me again when she extended her arm.

I gripped her forearm, and she gripped mine in return.

It was the most touch we'd shared since finding one another again.

A lump rose in my throat. "When I was at Frostveil, I snuck into the hidden part of the castle. The part that does not abide by Aabergs or their supporters."

Thyra stared at me, probably wondering where I was going with this.

"One time, I stumbled into our mother's old rooms. It's where I got the jewels I told you about."

"The ones you were going to sell. Fates, alive."

"I won't do it. Promise." I laughed. "But did you know that our mother painted?"

"I didn't."

"I saw them. She painted portraits of her family, including one of us as younglings. Our backs were to the viewer, but we held hands, much like this."

Thyra's grip on my forearm tightened.

"The moment I realized it was me in that portrait and that I had a twin, I so wished to find you. To hold hands with you again." I stared down at the connection between us, tears pricking my eyes, halting me.

Thyra sniffled, though when I looked up to see if she was crying, she was not. There was, however, an openness to her I'd not seen before. "I would like to get to know you better, Neve. If you'll allow it. If you can see past how I've acted."

My jaw dropped. "I'd like that, but I have to ask, are you only saying that because I'm being sappy?"

"Not at all. I've been thinking about it for days." One corner of her lips tugged up. "Anyone with half a brain would understand that if you were working against me, you would have kept the Frør Crown for yourself. And you wouldn't have helped Tanziel as you did with that venom, nor acted so bravely on your mission. I've watched Tanziel's recording many times. Your heist was far more dangerous than mine." She shook her head. "All that said though, I have to admit I'm split minded about siding with your mate. Having Vale and his friends could be a boon, but is your mate *truly* settled with the idea of bringing down his father?"

Despite her doubts, warmth rushed through me. I'd been waiting for Thyra to take a step closer to me, to accept me, and it was finally happening.

"He says we're mates, and mates always choose each other." The moment the words were out of my mouth, I wished I'd thought them through more. After all, Thyra was rejecting her mate.

She didn't seem to care though. "What if imprisoning him isn't enough? What if we have to kill King Magnus? We'd be kinslayers, and while others would look down upon us for that, I can live with that label. Can you, though? Can your mate?" She paused. "And what of the queen, the prince and princess?"

That gave me pause. In no way would I condone harming Saga. The queen either, for though I did not trust her, there was also something about Inga that made me think I did not know her whole story.

Rhistel could be tossed in the Shivering Sea and eaten by kraken for all I cared, but it was more complicated for Vale. He might not like his brother, but they were twins, and

I was just beginning to understand how deep that relationship could delve into one's heart. We might be able to spare Rhistel if he went into exile. I simply never wanted to see him again.

And then there was the king.

Thyra had no idea that Vale shared Lord Riis's blood, and truly, it didn't matter. For most of his life, he'd considered Magnus Aaberg his father. I had no doubt that while he disliked his father and much of what he'd done, there was a sliver of love for the fae somewhere in Vale's big heart.

Her mention of kinslaying made my skin crawl. In the hearts of most fae, none were as cursed as the kinslayer. King Magnus was our cousin. No one could deny that.

I can live with killing him, though. I've survived far worse than gossip about what other people think of me.

"I don't want to harm Saga or the queen, and as for Rhistel, well . . ."

"They're twins," Thyra said. "I expect emotional conflict there. The rebels can easily bend on the princess and queen as they exhibit far less power. We can probably negotiate on Rhistel too, *if* he is stripped of power, but Magnus has done too much, Neve. He's responsible for so much pain. No one can defend him."

When you sat at the top, you were responsible for it all. Good or bad. And King Magnus wallowed in the bad.

"You're right. I'll make sure Vale understands the worst might come to pass."

"Good. The White Bear won't go down easily," Thyra said. "Which brings me to my second reason for pulling you aside—I want to search for the Ice Scepter now. Have your scholarly friends found any information on it?"

"Arie and Duran," I reminded her of their names. They'd gone with her to Bitra. She should remember their names by now, but then again, Thantrel might have been monopolizing all her brain power. He did have a knack for attention-stealing. "No clues have cropped up."

"Well, your scholars have been resigned to your annex but starting tomorrow, they can have free rein in the library. And your weapons will be returned to you tomorrow morning."

My jaw slackened. The rebels accepted us. For me, that meant a lot. For Vale and the Riis brothers it was more complicated—though as I spied Luccan and Arie, still dancing and happy, I thought maybe it actually wasn't. Perhaps they were pleased to be part of the movement that changed the kingdom.

Maybe they—I gasped as Luccan fell to his knees. Though I couldn't hear the scream leaving his lips, his face contorted in pain, and I saw the panic ripple across Clem's delicate features as she knelt next to him.

"Thyra, I have to go!" I rushed back into the dining hall and headed straight for Luccan.

When I arrived, Clemencia held him tightly, tears running down her face. Vale, Anna, and Arie beat me to him, and Thantrel arrived as I did. In the time it took me to run to them, Luccan stopped screaming, but he was still panting, his eyes wide.

"What happened?" I asked.

"Something broke inside me. A snap, like a bone cracking, but in my heart. Fates it *hurt*." Luccan gripped his chest. "I think someone has attacked my magic. A gateway."

"What?!" Arie shared a wild-eyed look with Thantrel. "The one in Vitvik?"

Luccan shook his head. "Not that one. This connection felt further away. I'm fairly certain that a gateway in Avaldenn is gone. The one in my house. They all have a unique sensation, and I can feel it better now that the shock is less."

Clem rubbed his back as the rest of us exchanged startled and pointed looks.

"Few things can destroy a gateway," Luccan continued. "Which is why when they're destroyed, the maker—if they're still alive—feels it."

"Many people witnessed us run to your home," Vale spoke softly. "The king might have had it investigated, and he has ample resources."

"Agreed." Luccan rose. He did so without help, so I stood back, watching him. When he stood again, he brushed himself off and said with calm fortitude, "This changes any plans we might have to move about the kingdom."

"It does far more than that," Arie murmured. "It marks our house as traitors to the Crown of Winter. The realm, as far as most fae are concerned."

My heart gave a hard thud as the danger I'd put my friends in grew ever larger.

CHAPTER 37
VALE

After what happened to Luccan, it became clear that we could do nothing to discover the truth of what happened, nor remedy the matter. Not right away anyhow. So we remained at the celebration, hoping to seize a few more hours of joy. To lose ourselves for a night.

Hours of revelry passed. Hours in which wine and ale flowed. I danced with my mate, and watched my half-brothers fall deeper in love. As the hour of the direwolf approached, a handful of rebels had requested that Caelo and I join them in a hand of nuchi. Caelo agreed, whereas I declined.

I had other ideas for how to spend the small hours. None of them involved gambling, but rather getting Neve into our bed.

Since the mate bond snapped into place, I'd wanted her more than ever before. Body. Mind. Soul. *Everything.*

As my mate, she was my beginning and my end, the very

air in my lungs and the blood in my veins, and I'd give everything I had to her. I counted myself lucky to have that pleasure.

I could have lived a thousand turns and never met my mate. Or never had one at all. For most fae, that was the reality of life.

And as that force of nature I called my wife entered our bedchamber, dressed in a thin gown that left little to the imagination, I planned to make the most of every moment we had together.

"Thought you might already be asleep," she teased. "Snoring drunkenly."

I scoffed at her cheek. "I'd never do such a thing."

"You have!" She slipped beneath the furs. "The night we fled Avaldenn. Stars alive, you snored so loudly, you sounded like a lür horn blasting through the room."

I grabbed her, flipped her beneath me. The squeal that left her lips set my heart racing. "I only recall battling a vampire that night, so I'll have to take your word for it."

"Better that way." She stroked my cheek, the heat I'd grown so used to seeing in her eyes when we made love fanning there momentarily before her face stilled, her gentle hand fell away. "Vale, I have something important to ask, and I don't want to delay."

"Delayed gratification can be fun though. Let me show you," I kissed her neck, but she pushed me away gently.

"Seriously."

I rolled over. "I'm listening."

"Thyra and I were talking—she wants to get closer."

"That's good. You've wanted that too." Who wouldn't? As a twin myself, I understood that special bond. They were a part of you that no one else could have or understand. Not even a mate.

"We're going to work on our relationship, and that does make me very happy." Neve chewed on her plump lower lip. "But she brought you up too."

"How so?"

"Your family. I told her I'd never harm Saga, and I don't want to see your mother harmed either. Rhistel, well, I despise him, but I understand if you want to spare him from death, though he'll be punished in other ways for the wrongs he's committed, and not just against me. Thyra knows all that, and she can understand those feelings as well. They don't rule the kingdom, after all. Mostly it's your relationship to the king that has Thyra worried."

Right, that. I'd imagined I might be an issue for Thyra. As the realm knew me as the son of King Magnus, she'd expect certain actions from me.

"Do you wish for me to expose myself now?" I asked. I planned to, soon. Planned to tell the realm that I was a bastard. The declaration would be freeing in a way, but it would also hurt Rhistel, which conflicted my heart even if I knew it was unavoidable.

"Not until you're ready, but Thyra wanted me to make sure you were willing to see the king's downfall."

"You know I am. He's not a good king. For a while, I convinced myself that he was trying, but now I no longer think that. And he's had ample time to prove himself. Plus, you're my mate. No one is more important than you."

525

"What if he has to *die*, Vale? What if I, or Thyra, have to do it?"

Her words made the hair on my arms stand up. We'd spoken of dethroning the king many times. I supported that change for the kingdom. Somehow though, I'd always thought of him imprisoned. Perhaps that he'd die in battle —for once we took a fight to him, the king would surely fight with his soldiers.

"Or what if you do it, Vale. What then?" Neve looked away, as if she couldn't believe she'd said such a thing.

Silence filled the room for long minutes. Outside an owl hooted, probably one of the creatures roosting inside the cursed castle. Her question ran through my mind over and over, until I couldn't deny my answer. Or her.

"I don't want to kill him. In my opinion, the best warriors don't hunger for blood but for peace. To protect, and one day even put down their weapons." I swallowed. "And to become a kinslayer is to be cursed in the eyes of the stars and all fae. I do not want that either."

Even my father sidestepped that fate when he took the throne. He'd had the Falks executed, but not by his own hands.

"I hope that if the king dies, it's by another hand. But if he goes after you or anyone I love, believe me when I say that I *will* fight him. I will defend you and our friends. And yes, I would do it to the death."

"And me?" she pressed again. "Would you blame me if his death fell to me?"

"No," I replied honestly. Neve, as much as she despised

my father and rightfully so, wouldn't kill him just to do so. She preferred imprisoning him.

An exhale parted her luscious lips. "Thank the stars."

"Were you truly worried?" My hand landed on her hip and ran lightly up and down. Whenever she was in distress, I craved two things: to solve her problem and to touch her.

"Somewhat? I don't know, but it's better to be certain. If his death, in any manner, would harm you, I'd do my best to prevent it."

I stared at my mate, loving that after all she'd been through, she still cared so much for others. Perhaps it was *because* of all she'd been through, but not everyone was that way.

Some would live a harsh life and blame the world. They'd claim that others owed them, and they did not care that others would be hurt by their actions. Neve wanted revenge on the male I'd called my father for most of my life, there was no doubt about that, and yet she cared about my feelings in the matter. I had no doubt that if my sister was here, she'd ask Saga too.

Rhistel, likely not.

Thinking, even so briefly, of my brother reminded me of the time he'd sought to kiss my wife. We hadn't known that we were mates then, but I'd nearly beaten Rhistel to death for *attempting* to taste her lips. I'd almost become a kinslayer then.

Despite the lack of any threat, a sense of possessiveness rose in me, and I slid my arms around Neve and pulled her closer so that we shared breath. Her eyes widened for a heartbeat, followed by a delicious curving of her lips.

"I'd not thought such talk would turn you on, mate."

"I've been thinking of time alone together all day."

"Stars, that is a long time to be in suspense," she purred. "You looked so very handsome at the party." Lightly, she trailed a line of kisses along my jaw, making me groan with pleasure.

"In your presence, it's difficult not to want you bare, laid out before me. Writhing and wanting more of the pleasure only I can give." I took her lips in mine and my cock went ice hard as she kissed me back, slipping her tongue into my mouth, stroking my shoulder. Her smell. Her feel. Her taste. Everything about Neve was designed to tempt me, tailored to my tastes.

Taste. Fates, I wanted to taste her now. To feast on her.

I broke our kiss and before Neve could blink, I shifted under the fur covering our bed, pushing that thin gown up as I went. Neve assisted, lifting her hips so that she was fully exposed to me.

Beneath the fur, I allowed myself to gaze at the beauty that was my mate. Her pussy glistened, wet and wanting, and the scent coming off her was enough to make me explode.

"Are you lost?" she asked, and suddenly, the fur was tossed to the ground.

"Admiring." I licked her folds.

They parted more, allowing me the deeper taste I so desired. I moaned as Neve coated my tongue.

In response, my wife pressed her core to my lips. A low laugh left me. Neve was not one to be shy about what she wanted, in life or in bed. One of the many things I loved about her.

Moving up, I sucked on her clit, savoring the way she squirmed as I did so. How her fingers gripped the sheets. I smiled into her pussy and slipped a finger inside.

"Stars," she whispered, almost as if she didn't wish for me to hear.

I thrived on her praise. It fed me, just as her body did. Slowly, knowing she could take it, I inserted two more fingers and began to fuck her with them as I nipped lightly at her clit.

My mate's back arched. "Vale, do that again."

"Hmmm?" I asked peppering kisses along her inner thigh now. "What was that?"

In answer, snow fell. Unable to help myself, I laughed. Since our mate bond formed, our powers had manifested whenever we were intimate. They were usually a sign that we were losing control.

"Already, love?" I growled.

"By the dead gods, if you don't stop teasing me, I'll freeze you down there."

"Yes, my queen." I dove in again, desperate to feel her come on my tongue, to give her pleasure that no one else could. Her channel began to quiver.

"Vale, I'm close. I—"

A moan swallowed her words, and her back arched high as sweetness coated my tongue. My mate rode out her orgasm on my face, and only when she was finished did I rise and crawl over her.

Her cheeks were flushed, her eyelids heavy with desire.

She took my face in her hands, brought it to her lips and kissed me.

"More," she whispered when we broke for breath. "All of you. I want you to fill me."

Never able to get enough of my wife, my mate, *my queen*, I obliged.

CHAPTER 38

NEVE

A new day brought new ideas. Or in this case, an old idea I'd been secretly hoping to bring to life since learning of it back at Riis Tower.

While others broke their fast, I sought Thyra and shared my dream. Her face lit up, and she accepted it readily, a sign that her wish to become closer last night wasn't only a passing emotion or desire. Creating something that we were both passionate about, something that we might *share*, was the best way to begin this new phase of our lives.

So after the midday meal, my sister and I met in the training area. Vale, our friends, and even Clemencia and Anna, were in the far corner, sparring and practicing with weapons. I'd wondered if Anna really needed to train so hard, but she'd claimed an advisor to a queen would need to be strong in body as well as mind.

I refrained from confiding to Anna that the game had changed since the day I'd accepted her as an advisor. Back then, I'd not known that my sister lived. Or that Thyra would wish to claim the throne. That decision lay before us still, though as Thyra and I were finally getting along, neither seemed keen on raising the topic. For the moment, we were just sisters, or as close to that as we could be as strangers learning of one another.

Aside from my friends, many other fae were present in the training hall. This part of the day tended to be the busiest. People had taken care of morning chores and had a few hours to hone their skills and strengthen their bodies.

Today, many female warriors sparred and practiced with their weapons of choice, just as I'd hoped. I looked at my sister after studying them each in turn.

"The vampires for certain," I said. "Do you agree?"

"As much as I hate to admit it, we have no one better. Save for me, of course." She smirked, but in a playful way. My heart leapt.

"Of course," I teased back. "Aside from *you*, who is the strongest among the rebels? I have my ideas, but you know them better."

"I'm thinking we begin with six and grow from there, if we can. With that in mind, I'd like to offer Sigri, Halladora, and Tonna." She pointed the fighters out as she spoke their names.

I grinned. We thought rather alike.

Sigri was a dwarf. I'd seen her sparring often and had deduced that her weapon of choice was a warhammer, though she appeared to be skilled with a bow and arrow too. Agile for her kind, the female was a fierce fighter. I'd witnessed her bringing males four times her size to their knees.

Halladora was faerie, like Thyra and me. She was tall for a female, almost as tall as Vale, and wielded a sword rivaling *Skelda* in length. A time or two, I'd caught Vale and Caelo eyeing the female as she sparred, nodding approvingly at her skill.

"About Tonna, is she——"

Thyra cleared her throat. "Yes, part orc."

"Right." Tonna had the greenish-gray skin typical of orcs, as well as the large and muscular orcish build. However, Tonna also bore olive green wings, hinting of faerie blood. "That's rare."

"She doesn't like to speak of it. A brute assaulted her mother, and Tonna is the result." My twin's face twisted with revulsion at the events of the past. "Tonna doesn't identify as an orc, but rather as a faerie. She appreciates being treated as such."

"Then she shall be," I said. "I only wondered where she fell among the fae races because of how she looks. Not to question your judgment."

"It's natural. Our races are so often at odds. Should I call them over? The vampires too?"

"Please," I said, and my twin beckoned the others over.

"My sister and I have been speaking," Thyra began once all six female warriors grouped before us, questions in their eyes. "How many of you are familiar with the monarchies of Winter's Realm long ago? Around the time of Sassa's reign?"

The vampires raised their hands, as did Halladora.

"In your studies, have any of you come across writings on the Valkyrja?"

Halladora's face split into a smile. "I used to *love* reading them as a youngling. My mother claims one of our ancestors served Queen Sassa herself."

"Did she?" Thyra looked impressed. "That would explain why you wield a sword as well as the Warrior Bear."

Halladora's cheeks took on a pink hue. "Thank you."

Thyra nodded in reply. "My sister and I have been speaking about how we'd like to work together. Much is still to be discussed, but we both wish to implement Queen Sassa's practice of having a Valkyrja regiment. The first of its kind in many centuries. We'd like you six to be the first members."

Tonna cleared her throat and when she opened her mouth to speak, fangs glinted inside. "How does this differ from being in the army or Nava?"

Thyra cut me a glance, and I picked up where she left off.

"It's a historic group made of all females who fight in battle for the queen or king—though many kings didn't implement the practice of anointing new Valkyrja. Under a string of male reigns, the elite group of warriors died out and, eventually, ceased to exist. Little has been written of them since the time of Sassa's reign. So while we don't know much about them, we'll honor some practices of the past, like keeping this an all-female group. Besides that, we would be writing our own rules." I smirked and looked at my twin. "Something that us Falk ladies seem all too inclined to do anyhow, wouldn't you say?"

A few more questions lobbed our way. Thyra and I did

our best to answer them. In the end, two of the vampires agreed.

Livia held back, and curious, I asked her if she had other questions or issues with such a group.

"It's not that. I rather like the idea," she said. "But I'd hoped to open a book and tea shop after the war is over, and my sisters and I have fulfilled our promises to you two."

Freyia and Astrid didn't appear surprised, so I assumed that such an occupation would suit Livia. In no way did I wish to squash a dream. Particularly when so many people stole options and dreams from Livia throughout her life.

"I understand. You're under no obligation to join."

"Thank you, Princess Neve."

The other three also agreed with the stipulation that, at least for the time being, they take orders only from Thyra.

"It's not that we dislike or distrust you after your heist in Avaldenn," Halladora said. "We just know Thyra better. For now, this is how it will be."

Trust was earned, often very slowly. Though it would make things more difficult, I couldn't rush this. "I understand."

"So where do we go from here?" Tonna asked, her eyes gleaming brighter than before. I suspected she enjoyed being asked to be a part of this exclusive group.

"You should train together," I said. "Starting today. You're all powerful, but you do not all know how the others fight. Time to learn, for who knows when Thyra and I will need you?" I thought of the Ice Scepter, and how it was our shared goal to find it. How Thyra believed it would give her understanding of the other Hallows.

I swallowed, feeling ever more guilty for keeping the secrets of the Frør Crown from her. I'd remedy that today. In private, of course.

"Does this mean I cannot train with my sisters?" Livia asked.

"Not at all," Thyra assured her. "You're not obligated to be a Valkyrja, but you should all train together. The best with the best. Just no using your fangs. Not until we meet our enemies anyway."

The female warriors agreed, and the first of the Valkyrja and Livia returned to the training area, leaving me alone with my twin.

"That was easy," I said on the back of an exhale.

"When others respect your actions, it is easy to get them to follow. That reflects well on us both." Her face was soft, loose, relaxed.

Should I take this moment to tell her?

Thyra twisted to take in the vast scope of the training room. She stiffened, all the looseness gone.

I searched for what had caught her attention, only to find Thantrel staring our way. Thyra stared right back at him, though like last night, she was not scowling or hard-faced. Instead she looked . . . thoughtful?

"He's a great person," I whispered. "The timing is horrible, but—"

"Stop, Neve. I want to focus on us. Not some male, no matter how handsome he is."

I imagined telling Thantrel that Thyra had called him handsome and seeing his face light up, but then her words sank in deeper. No, this was between them, and my sister had valid reasons for rejecting him, even if she'd done so coldly.

Then again, was that any surprise? We were Daughters of Winter. Of the coldest family to have walked this realm.

"I won't again. Not unless you wish to talk about him," I inhaled. "And actually, I have something more to tell you. Something I wanted to tell you last night before Luccan fell. I lost the thought of it after that, but now is as good a time as last night."

"What's that?" Relief that I'd dropped the matter of her mate rushed across her face.

"It's about the Frør Crown. In the vault, it told me to try it on. I did, and I saw something. Something I don't understand."

"Why didn't you say something earlier?" Her tone had hardened considerably, and she took a step back.

Annoyance lashed through me like a whip. "You've demanded much from me and given little in return. I still don't have the blade promised to me." Her face fell, and I regretted the words, even though I felt them wholly. We'd come so far in a day. I wanted us to go further. Not stall here, when we'd just started to bond. "I suppose I wasn't sure that I could trust you, but now *I am.*"

She swallowed. "I understand."

A pause swept between us before she added, "You're aware that we cannot stand together in everything, right? The throne seats one."

"Yes," I whispered. "But for now, the throne is so very far away, after all. It can wait."

Although I'd started to want the ruling seat enough to

accept a queensguard and advisors, I thought that I could give up a throne for Thyra. After all, I'd first wished to run away from that powerful seat entirely, at least until I understood how many people I could help. The fae of Winter's Realm, maybe, in time, the slaves of the Vampire Kingdom.

As long as Thyra proved that she was for the people of this realm, I could step down. I could live a fulfilled life in so many other ways.

Perhaps she thought the same thing, for she turned and gestured to the door. "Come, sister. Let me reunite you with Sassa's Blade. Then we'll visit the Frør Crown, and you can show me what you've discovered."

CHAPTER 39

VALE

My breath came out white as I helped the rebels usher the horses, gryphons, and pegasi from the stables into Valrun's great hall.

Wood chips covered the stone floor, places for the creatures to sleep. Fire fae worked at creating safe pits so the beasts might stay warm.

Putting aside all the work that came with making the great hall safe for animals and fae, our days had been fruitful on many fronts. For the most part, the rebels had accepted us. Neve and her sister had finally openly spoken of the Frør Crown and Sassa's Blade. They'd also recruited Valkyrja, the first group of their kind in centuries.

My heart swelled for my mate, for how happy she seemed to spend time with her sister. For the fact that they were finally of a similar mind and could, hopefully, continue to grow a relationship from a mere sharing of goals into something real. Something familial.

But not all had been good.

Today was the coldest day in memory. So frigid that my ears ached. And with cold came death, for even in Winter's Realm, where the fae were stouthearted and hearty, we had limits. If the cold continued, death would rake its frost-coated fingers across the land and scoop up souls by the handful.

Like Neve and Thyra and many of the rebels, I feared for the commonfae of the kingdom. And while I could not help them all, I would help the fae and animals around Valrun.

Our friends proved eager to assist too. Anna and Clemencia had spent the early hours walking the town around the castle, knocking on doors and inviting rebels into the castle. Most of the rebels who lived outside the castle were families requiring more space, but even in Valrun's rundown state, they'd be safer behind stone with every hearth burning.

The Riis brothers were gathering wood and attempting last minute patches to windows.

Caelo assisted me with the animals, particularly the gryphons, a testy bunch.

Rynni, as ever, worked in the infirmary, both with the injured and ill and with the lindwyrm venom Luccan took from the coinary. So far, she had not been able to replicate the venom.

And my mate was with her sister, looking for information on the hallowed crown and the Ice Scepter. I hoped tonight they'd find a clue leading to the Hallow.

"Prince Vale!" One rebel arrived; his hands filled with the reins of one rambunctious stallion.

"Caelo!" I shouted, knowing that while I might be able to control the horse better than the young rebel, Caelo would be an ideal choice. His elven blood gave him the power of communicating with animals, which often calmed them.

Almost effortlessly, Caelo took the lead and showed the creature to where the other horses were being kept. All the while, he murmured to the stallion, assuring him of safety and warmth and community to come.

"How many more are there?" I asked the young rebel.

"That one was the last, thank the stars. I'm done going outside for the night!"

I chuckled. "You've earned a nice meal and fire."

"And you." He smiled shyly at me before leaving.

The difference a successful heist made in the rebels' acceptance of us was day and night. I would not take it for granted. I was about to see if Caelo required help when Luccan entered the great hall.

"Wood is stocked?" I asked, noting his empty hands.

"Not quite," he replied. "I have something you should see."

He handed me the map he'd used to find Neve and me. The very map that Lord Riis had devised and used to learn where his progeny was. I took in the map of Winter's Realm, searching for what had sent Luccan to my side.

"The King's Road. Near here," he said.

Valrun wasn't on the map. Most fae in the kingdom called it a haunted ruin and thought it unwise to speak of the place. Putting the decrepit castle on a map would be worse. Alas, I'd seen where it was located in history books, and remembered the general location. With those two clues, I found what Luccan was referring to quickly.

"Your father is moving south," I said.

"Our father," Luccan corrected softy. "And yes, but that makes no sense."

"He could have many reasons. One of them being that his son was involved in a heist." I arched my eyebrows at Luccan.

"He's too far south to have left a couple of days ago. He's been traveling for longer. Plus, that he's traveling on a road *at all* makes me think something is up. I can still feel the gatcway at the Warmsnap." He tapped his heart, where apparently he felt the connections to the gateways he created. "If he needed to get somewhere, he'd usually use that."

"Why is he going the slow route then?"

"The only thing I can fathom is that he's traveling with someone. A person he does not want knowing of my power." Luccan gave a dry chuckle. "Little does he know a vampire has already outed that secret to the entire Falk rebellion."

I let out a hum. "Who would he travel with? And why?"

Lord Riis was notoriously solitary. Aside from the females he courted briefly, he was not known to socialize much. He had few friends, and his sons and daughters were his world.

And my mother, I added, sad for the male who fathered me.

He'd sought comfort in so many females because he'd been looking for someone to fill the hole in his heart that

Inga Vagle had left. None ever had. I believed that after a while, he'd stopped trying to find another great love. All his bastards were ten turns or older. Had he and my mother reignited their love affair in the last decade?

"I can't say who," Luccan said. "But if he goes to Vitvik, he won't find us there. Nor at House Balik's seat—where he wanted us to go. We need to intercept him."

I pointed to an unmarked spot on the map. "There's a country tavern here. I wouldn't call the area a village, just a grouping of homes and the tavern and one other business. If our father continues in the direction he's going now, he'll likely rest his head there at night. We can get there in time to intercept too."

"I'll send Arie," Luccan said.

"I'm sure Thyra will wish to send rebels," I added. "We're on better terms, but she'll want a show of power. Especially regarding the king's spymaster. We'll have to vouch for him."

"You're right." Luccan rolled up the map and stuck it in his cloak. "Come with me to speak with her?"

I told Caelo where we were heading. He waved us off nonchalantly, happy to be among the animals.

Together, my brother and I sought the leader of the rebels and hoped we'd done enough to ensure Thyra would not balk at bringing the kingdom's spymaster of Winter's Realm to Valrun Castle.

CHAPTER 40
NEVE

I warmed my hands in front of the fire burning in the library's hearth. The aroma of roasted meats wafted in from the hallways. Dinner approached, and I greatly craved a hot meal.

For two days now, I had spent many hours in the dusty, old library—one of the rare parts of the castle that had sustained no damage. My sister and I were desperate to know more about the Hallows.

After we formed the Valkyrja, Thyra had experienced firsthand what Sassa's Blade could do. As the blade had with me, it whispered to her and then proceeded to sap her of blood to produce a shadow. She'd only escaped a trip to the healer's wing because I'd commanded the shadow to stop pestering her for more blood. To my surprise, the shadow had bowed and vanished.

More shocking, when others tested the blade with their blood, it had not worked for them in the same way. No one called the shadows like my twin and me. No one heard their dark whispers. That confused me more.

It was said that anyone with winter magic should be able to wield the Ice Scepter, and we'd assumed Sassa's Blade and perhaps the Frør Crown too, would be similar. Vale was not an Aaberg by blood, but he was part Vagle, and that family once ruled a slice of the midlands in Winter's Realm. They possessed winter magic, and yet, Vale could not call a single shadow. As the Riis brothers were a newly raised family in high society, their failure was not a surprise, even if it was an annoyance.

Our time with the Frør Crown was not going any better.

My twin took it personally that the Frør Crown had spoken to me. Shown me something too. I'd tried to assure her that the vision was not worth envy, but she only became quiet and returned to her studies. She searched for a reason to explain the anomaly. Or a way to coax the diadem into working for her.

So while my twin focused on the Frør Crown, I focused on the Ice Scepter. I thought the lost Hallow was more important, particularly with the deep freeze.

Duran, Anna, and Clemencia had also been studying with us, searching for mentions of the Hallows throughout history. Arie would have been with us too but he'd already left to find his father. Thyra sent a trio of rebels with Arie, for the purposes of assessing Lord Leyv Riis. Though I thought it was unnecessary because Lord Riis was trustworthy, the rebels would be helpful if Arie ran into trouble.

"Toss another log on," Duran called out.

"Is that necessary?" Thyra countered.

Yesterday, she'd voiced concerns about creating more smoke than usual. The area around the castle was warded, and concealment illusions soared above and around the entire town, but smoke could float outside the wards. If we weren't careful in keeping the fires to a minimum, the fires within Valrun Castle could give away the rebellion's location.

"If you wish for me to stay, then yes, it's necessary," Duran said. "My hands are shaking so badly I can barely turn a page."

As Duran had been the only one of us to find anything of note, I was inclined to use as much wood as possible to keep him warm.

The dwarf had found a short passage stating that one Falk king had claimed the Hallows of the realm wished to be near one another. How the king had deduced that, I wasn't sure. There had been no notable interaction between the Frør Crown and Sassa's Blade, but the fact that there was some information on the Hallows gave us hope.

"I didn't know that the fae studying at the House of Wisdom were so weak," Thyra muttered, but waved her hand at the flames, indicating I should throw on another log.

I did so, and the fire caught. Heat wafted into the room, driving out a bit of the cold.

I sat again and stared down at the book I'd chosen. The subject was dry: Weather patterns of Winter's Realm over the last two centuries.

"Missing those adventure romance novels you love so much?" Clem asked. "Remember the enormous trunk we packed full of them for our trip to Avaldenn? Truly over the top."

I looked up at her. "I miss them all so much. You?"

She sighed. "Riis Tower didn't have the best collection. It seems like an age since I read something scintillating."

"You'll have to tell Luccan that their library is lacking."

"Oh, we already did," Anna laughed. "Arie was appalled that we both prefer romances to the histories." Her face straightened. "Not that I haven't been reading the histories. As I told you, Neve, I'm serious about learning more of Winter's Realm."

I cut a glance to Thyra, but she didn't seem to care about our conversation. Thank the Fates. I did not want it to come up that I'd offered Anna an advisorship when the subject of who would sit on the throne was unresolved.

"The selection at the House of Wisdom would disappoint you ladies greatly," Duran smirked. "There's much knowledge, a lot of it interesting, but nothing of the sort you're referring to."

I had no doubt. I'd been inside the House of Wisdom once and found the place of knowledge gray and drab.

"Count me out," Anna said. "But I do need to get through this passage before dinner."

Taking my friend's example, I pushed aside the yearning for a good story and continued reading about the weather. Where it got cold. How cold and for how long. How much snow had fallen. Few patterns emerged, but shockingly enough, one interesting pattern seemed to persist around Eygin.

I delved deeper into the material and had just discovered

another promising passage relating to Eygin, when Thyra groaned, pushed her chair back, and stood.

I exchanged covert glances with Anna and Clem and tried not to laugh. Sometimes, when few people were present, Thyra became *very* dramatic. Perhaps it made me a bad sister, but her mood swings amused me.

"Something wrong?" I asked.

"This is all for naught!" She paced the length of the room. "What if we find the Ice Scepter, and it doesn't work for either of us? My use of the Blade is weak, and the Crown is a trickster if ever I saw one."

"That's a possibility," I said softly, attempting to calm her, "but we have to try. The Scepter is said to be the one item that can warm the cold."

Thyra's cheek puckered. She had a habit of chewing the inside of her cheek when in thought. "Of course you're right."

Seeing as she'd already given me an opening, I asked, "I take it the Crown still hasn't responded?"

Thyra stored the Frør Crown in her quarters. I'd not seen it since yesterday, but as Thyra's mood was foul, I was sure she'd used the Hallow again. Or attempted to anyway.

"Nothing of note."

So complete silence.

"It's temperamental," I hedged, and with a soft sigh added, "I could try it on again and see what it does?"

I'd not worn the Hallow since the day I'd taken it from the Falk vault, though the vision had played over and over in my mind. I did not know what to make of what I'd learned.

Nor did I really want to wear the Hallow again. Not unless it made Thyra feel better.

Thyra shook her head. "It doesn't like me, and Sassa's Blade—well, I can't use it. Not without nearly killing myself." Her face twisted. "I need more time with them," Thyra added, as though she hated to admit such a thing. "Might I have the Blade for a bit?"

I swallowed. I felt protective of the sword, and although I admired Thyra's bravery, she pushed the limits in a way that I didn't care to.

"It's in the annex," I said, knowing that it would not do to deny my sister. "I can retrieve it after we finish here. You can use it, and I'll watch and make sure nothing goes awry."

Thyra looked like she wanted to tell me to get it now, but she sat back down.

Relieved that was over, I was about to return to the book but caught Duran's eye. Maybe he, with his scholarly mind could make better sense of my hunch?

"Duran, look at something for me?"

"Of course." He held out a hand, and I turned the book to him and shoved it across the table.

"Left page, about halfway down. Do you see the temperatures of Eygin?"

Taking no time at all to locate it, Duran's eyebrows pinched together. "Cold."

"Very. More so than anywhere else that I've found. Even places deeper in the mountains. Any idea why?"

The others were listening now, Clem leaning closer to take in the book, but no one spoke as Duran considered.

"A geological reason? The town is between large mountains and at elevation. The cold might get trapped in the valley between the peaks?"

"Possibly," I replied, not convinced.

"I can't say for certain," he admitted. "This isn't my area of expertise. I—"

A hard and fast knock came at the door. Thyra's spine straightened as she rose. Bac was traveling with Arie and my sister had given only Brynhild leave to interrupt us.

However, when Thyra opened the door, Brynhild did not stand before us. Rather, Aleksander, our half-brother who had bonded with the winged symbol of the Falk royal house, stood there.

"Aleksander," Thyra frowned. "I did not wish to be interrupted."

"Well, you'll want to hear this." He swept inside, not asking to be invited. The skin-changer's ice-blue eyes, twins to Thyra's, locked on me as he held up a scroll that gave off the scent of old leather. "I sent my Arla out last night. Had a feeling there was something she needed to see, and I was right. I came straight here after I understood the devastation I was seeing." His voice cracked.

"Devastation?" Thyra asked. "Where?"

"Move the books."

We did so, and Aleksander rolled out his scroll to reveal an age-spotted vellum map of Winter's Realm. When his hand veered to the southwest of the map, my eyes widened. And the moment he pointed to a spot tucked into the Red Mist Mountains, my heart plummeted.

"Here. The same place that the king and Lord Lisika

stopped in," Aleksander said. "Arla was flying above and things looked suspiciously quiet, so I told her to look. She did and—by the dead gods—I still cannot believe what she found. An entire town, dead."

"No," I whispered. "Are you sure?"

"I had her fly down chimneys into homes. Through the tavern's chimneys too, if she could. Most windows were shuttered, but one or two weren't and those inside were dead too." His lips tightened. "There's far more to explore, but a hawk cannot get to it all. From what I saw, though, not a soul survived."

A sob wrenched out of my throat, and Thyra turned to me. Her face had gone so pale. "Neve?"

"It's the same place I was just reading about. We traveled through there days ago. The place is called Eygin and, stars alive, the fae there were kind to us and now they're dead!"

The smile of the bard who had sung to us came rushing back, and an avalanche of emotion pummeled through me. Had I done this by traveling through there?

"Your presence didn't bring the monarchy down on them. Both the king and Lord Lisika left days ago via a nearby mountain tunnel. We saw no sign of violence in the village at all," Aleksander replied as if trying to assure me, though his face was grim as he spoke. "From what I saw, the villagers looked like they'd frozen to death."

CHAPTER 41
NEVE

Only two things kept me from succumbing to the grief that grew with each update from Aleksander. One: Vale's hand in mine, and two: The promise that soon, we'd fly west to see if we could find any survivors in Eygin.

Hours had passed since that moment in the library, and Aleksander continued to use Arla to patrol the villages. So far, my skin-changer half-brother had only supplied us with an updated body count. No good news at all.

Thyra had since called every rebel to the dining hall. Bit by bit, she put a plan in place, and the most important part had come from none other than Thantrel.

The youngest Riis's mother had been an elven noble so, like Caelo, Thantrel had great control over animals. His ability to speak with them, to reason with them, to convince them, was why so many had been able to ride the gryphons and pegasi—proud creatures, both. Thantrel had said we should take the flying creatures west, thereby cutting down the travel time considerably. Between Thantrel and Caelo, they would work to keep the temperamental creatures happy when they were flying in freezing conditions.

"I believe we should also write to House Balik." Vale added his idea to those being tossed out for review.

"For what?" Thyra's lips flattened. "Eygin is in the westernlands. If anyone should be informed, it's Lord Lisika—and that will *not* be happening."

"We're rebels, Prince Vale," Brynhild added softly. "We have done many things that the wealthiest fae in this land take offense to. Hence, we cannot simply call upon a great house for aid."

"You can't, but *I can*." Vale did not back down. "I have strong ties with House Balik, and I believe they're not pleased with the current reign, either." He swallowed. "Most importantly, they will not allow fae of Winter's Realm to suffer if they can bring aid."

"The dead need no aid," Aleksander spoke, now returned from his hawk's eyes. "I still haven't found a single living soul."

My stomach heaved. Every time he mentioned Eygin, I wanted to vomit. I only kept it in by sheer force of will.

Was anyone alive? The hawk could not get into every single building, and some establishments like the coinary had deep tunnels beneath. Perhaps fae huddled down there for warmth? We would not know unless we ventured west.

Thinking about the dead in Eygin was bad enough, but it had not taken me long to spiral into other worries. Dergia had entered my thoughts.

The dwarves in the lost kingdom were my allies. Most

surprisingly of all, I felt I'd become true friends with Princess Bavirra and Prince Thordur.

Dergia was a fair ride away from Eygin, but cold knew no bounds and something told me that this spread was not natural. Magic was behind this. Were my allies and friends at risk too?

My hands itched to seek the mirror the king had given me, but I'd come straight from the library and the mirror was in our annex.

"No great houses, Prince Vale," Thyra said with finality. "We will go there alone, and we will help those of Eygin. If there are any living left to help."

"What if it's not enough?" Vale challenged. "We have six gryphons and two pegasi, both carrying two fae a piece. That's too few rescuers, Thyra."

My sister's face whitened, and I sensed the war going on inside her. She didn't want to risk more rebels. Nor did she wish to leave any fae of Winter to a premature death.

"We can send riders out too," Thyra said.

"They won't arrive until it's far too late," Vale shot back. "According to Aleksander, it might already be so. I—"

"You need me," a voice called from the doorway.

I twisted to find Rynni standing there. Since our arrival at Valrun, I'd barely seen her at all. The rebels had been in desperate need of another healer, and she'd taken to that cause. The dragon-fae had gone as far as to sleep in the infirmary for a few nights. "I have very weak dragon magic, only one or two bursts of flame within me for any given day, but I *can* shift into a small dragon and make the flight west. I can bear around ten fae of my current size."

Rebels exchanged excited glances.

"Keep in mind, my dragon form would attract a lot of attention," Rynni said. "So I'll need an illusionist to mask my flight. Or I'll need to keep above the clouds, which I don't think any of the riders will want."

Yes, a dragon flying over the land would garner lots of attention. To be fair, two pegasi and a drift of gryphons might too, but they were not completely unseen within the realm like dragons were.

"We have light fae at Valrun who specialize in illusions. They'll make sure you're shielded from sight from below." Thyra nodded. "Your healing abilities might be of use too."

If people were alive to heal.

Thyra handpicked ten more rebels to fly on Rynni's back, including Tonna, Halladora, and Sigri, part of our Valkyrja. Once done, she returned to the crowd. "That's it then. We meet back here in ten minutes to fly through the night! Those who are coming, grab your thickest cloaks, and we'll be off."

With Vale, I left the room. We were among those heading west. Others in our group joining us were Caelo and Thantrel—both to keep the gryphons in line—and Luccan. Anna was the least likely to survive temperatures that killed off Winter fae. Clemencia and Duran were remaining with her to continue searching for clues regarding the Ice Scepter.

That is, if we weren't heading right for it.

Briefly, Thyra and I had tossed about the idea that the cold spike in the west might be due to the Hallow we sought. That could also explain why it was always colder there in general. It lined up with the events I'd read in Brogan Lisi-ka's note to Roar. The family had traveled south along the mountains and died there. Maybe the Scepter had not moved far in the two decades since. We intended to search for clues there while we helped the fae of Eygin.

When we reached the annex, everyone who was going on the mission disappeared into their rooms. The moment the door shut behind us, I sought the small bag in which I'd stashed the mirror.

Vale's eyebrows arched. "What're you doing?"

"Making sure Dergia is safe. And telling them that we'll be nearby."

His lips parted. "Good idea, they're relatively close to Eygin."

"I worry about them," I admitted as I pulled the mirror from the bag and prepared to call upon the King of Dergia.

INTERLUDE

LORD LEYV RIIS, LORD OF TONGUES, HOUSE OF THE ICE SPIDER

The spymaster gestured to the inn's door. "Go inside. Get two rooms next to each other and a table by the fire, if you can."

The princess huddled against the cold and rushed indoors. Lord Riis watched her go, a sigh on his lips.

He understood Inga entrusting her only daughter to him, but did he like the responsibility? No, and not because he disliked the princess.

In truth, he found Saga delightful, and much like her mother when they were younger. However, the spymaster knew Saga was King Magnus's favored child—his only true-born child—and that put a target on Leyv's back. His sons' backs too, and that worried him greatly.

The spymaster handed the reins to the stablefae and tipped them before grabbing both his bag and Saga's and followed the princess into the inn. Although the princess did not travel in the bright gowns she favored, and Saga had continued to wear the wig supplied by one of his employees, the princess was easy to spot in the busting tavern portion of the inn. She stood out in a crowd.

As did one other soul in the tavern that night.

Arie, the spymaster's son, sat in a distant corner, a horn in his hands and a hood raised to cover most of his face. Arie made to stand, but Lord Riis waved him back. His son caught on as Saga joined Leyv the next second, a smile on her exhausted face.

"We got the last two rooms." She jangled keys on her finger. "Ones at the end of the hall too, so they'll be quieter, thank the stars. That last inn was far too loud. I barely slept at all."

She was used to castles with thick stone walls, not noisy and bustling taverns made of wood.

"I also ordered you wine and stew to be delivered to the table," Saga added, lifting a horn of her own. He noted the cracks at the top of the horn, an indication of the quality they might have to look forward to in their bedrooms. "It's all they have. They're even out of bread. A bad sign, isn't it?"

Many of the smaller inns had seemed to be short on food. Lord Riis wasn't sure why that was. A war might be brewing, but it hadn't begun to interrupt greenhouse work-ings. Perhaps the cold had kept traders at home. Or slowed them down.

"Stew and wine will do for our supper tonight," he said. "I'll go set our bags upstairs. Why don't you find a seat." He nodded to the fire, glad to see that Arie had repositioned himself so that his back was to them—a smart lad.

The princess handed over the keys to the rooms and

went in search of a table by the fire. The Lord of Tongues made his way to the staircase leading to their chambers. He trusted Arie would follow after an appropriate length of time.

Doing as he'd said, he stowed Saga's bag in her room, the one farthest from the noise. When he exited the hall to put away his own bag, he found Arie waiting for him.

But he wasn't alone. Three fae stood behind him, their stances tight.

"Father," Arie said softly. "Why are you here with her?"

Her. The people with him did not recognize Saga, and if Arie was not naming the princess, then Lord Riis guessed they might not like her either. Leyv's stomach twisted. Who were the fae with his son?

"Her mother asked a favor of me I could not refuse."

Arie swallowed. "We saw you on the map, and I'm here to intercept you. It's not smart to speak of it here, in the corridor."

"Inside," Leyv said, opening his door. "Only you, son."

The other three glowered, but Arie held up a reassuring hand, and they allowed father and son privacy in the small, battered, but clean, single room. Once the door was closed, Arie began.

"You told us to go to the Golden House, but when we found Vale and Neve, things changed. We're staying with the rebels now."

Lord Riis's mouth fell open, a rare reaction indeed for a spymaster who often knew other's secrets before they did themselves. "Rebels? Were you caught?"

"At first, yes," Arie said. "But then they released us, and we've been staying with them. Willingly." He cleared his throat. "One is Neve's twin."

"*Thyra*," the high lord whispered.

There'd been rumors that she'd lived. None that he'd ever been able to substantiate and eventually, he'd stopped trying. He figured if the youngling had survived, then she'd earned a life safe from Magnus's reach.

Never in all his turns had he imagined that Thyra Falk would be a rallying point for rebel forces.

But then why not? His lack of belief in the previous dynasty's progeny seemed shortsighted when presented with the likes of Neve. The female had grit and grace and a quick mind.

"They're nothing alike, Father, but they are warming to one another."

"You said you're staying with the rebels," Lord Riis said. "What have you been doing while with them?"

"We went on heists with them to find the Frør Crown." Arie's chest puffed up. "I went with Thyra Falk. We didn't find the Frør Crown in the vaults, but Neve and Vale did. Luccan was with them. Than with me." At the mention of his younger brother's name, Arie looked away. The spymaster recognized that tell. Something had happened with Thantrel.

"Are your brothers well?"

"Luccan is. Than is . . . Doing his best."

What in the stars did that mean? He studied his son and could not reason out an answer, but as Thantrel was alive, and Arie did not seem too concerned, he decided it was best to move on. They mustn't be up here long. Saga would begin asking questions.

"You said vaults? As in, you robbed a coinary?" He had to work hard not to raise his voice. The rebels were outside, and the spymaster wanted as much time with his son as they'd grant him.

"We did. One in Avaldenn and the one in Bitra." For the first time, Arie's face flushed. "Foolish, I know, but it worked."

"Odan, give me strength." Lord Riis rubbed at his temples. "You're lucky to be alive, Arie. You all are. Leprechauns are vicious towards thieves."

"Forgive us for our stupidity?"

Lord Riis wasn't sure that his son was repentant. He seemed far too pleased with himself, and part of the spymaster thought Arie had a right to be. The spymaster half expected this behavior from Thantrel. Luccan and Vale too, if the right circumstances presented themselves.

Arie was the levelheaded one. But to go on a heist for a fae he believed in was not only foolish—it was also brave. The spymaster could not fault him for that.

"There is nothing to forgive. You helped a friend, and that is what I'd expect of my sons. Now, moving on to Saga . . ." The spymaster cleared his throat. "Perhaps I should continue to House Balik with her and then rejoin you?"

"I fear if you arrive with the princess in Myrr, you may be detained to get back to us."

"The Baliks have left court. I don't think they're loyal to

Magnus, though you're correct that they are rather law abiding. If the leprechauns—"

"Who are you?" a sharp feminine voice cut him off. "Why are you outside my room!?"

"Hide," Lord Riis said, but before his son could so much as try and shove himself under the bed, the door flew open.

Lord Riis sucked in a breath. The rebels were *blue*. Frozen in place. Saga had used magic on them.

"*Arie?*" Saga asked, her face morphing from furious to curious as she took in his son, poised to shimmy under the bed. "What are you doing here?"

"I—uh. You should sit down, Princess."

Saga's lips parted, as if realizing that she was supposed to be in disguise, and she'd given herself away.

"He knows you too well for a wig to fool him, Saga." Lord Riis said as she shut the door behind her.

"Well, that's true. Who's outside your door? They look shifty, but you do not seem bothered."

"They're with Arie." Lord Riis looked at his son. The truth was about to come out, and he thought it was best if Arie told it.

"I'll tell you, but unfreeze them first?" Arie asked. "I'd rather they not die."

"Everything but their feet and ankles." With a wave of her hand, Saga did as she said, and Arie began telling Saga what he'd told Lord Riis. The princess's expression grew more incredulous by the second.

"Where are Vale, Neve, and the others now?" Saga asked.

"Valrun Castle," Arie replied.

The spymaster's stomach dropped. "But it's cursed."

"What better place for rebels to hide?" Arie shrugged. "The castle is rundown, but they have all that they need. Shelter. The lake isn't far away. Towns within a day's ride for food, and some game in the area. It's ideal."

The spymaster supposed he was right. Valrun had such a poor reputation that even he did not have spiders there to tell him what was afoot. For a hidden rebellion, it was an ideal headquarters.

"I want to go there," Saga said stoutly. "Mother said I needed to find Vale."

She had, though that was when Inga, like Lord Riis, had believed Vale was making his way to House Balik's castle. Behind stone and wards that Lord Riis felt sure Valrun could not match. He was about to say as much when Arie spoke.

"We can stay the night here, and I'll take you. It's not too far." Arie cleared his throat. "You may have a bit of trouble at first, but if Vale and Neve vouch for you—Saga . . . are you well?"

The princess's eyes had clouded and widened. For a long minute she said nothing, though her body stiffened, her hands balled into fists so tight her hands turned white. Then, a scream cut through the room and Lord Riis scrambled.

He slammed a hand over Saga's mouth, muffling the sound. "Shhh, Saga, you're safe. You're safe. You're safe. It's a vision."

The princess continued to scream; her body as tight as a bowstring ready to launch. Briefly, the spymaster considered using his magic, the power to negate another's magic, to stop the vision, but would it hurt her? He did not know, so he opted for a more common course. "Arie, get water."

His son scrambled to pour water from a pitcher on the side table. With shaking hands, he returned.

"Pour it on her head." Lord Riis had no idea if this would work. Seers were rare and the ways they entered and left visions were numerous. He'd seen this happen once, and the family had jolted their seer out of it.

Arie hesitated. "She's *the princess*, Father. I—"

Saga gasped. Her body slumped over, and the spymaster released his hand over her mouth only to help hold her up.

"What did you *see*?" From the look on her face, he would guess it had not been pleasant.

"Vale. Neve. Thantrel and Luccan and others were there too." Saga let out a cry. "They were screaming and surrounded by something hard and white."

"Hard and white?" Arie shook his head. "An avalanche?"

"Fates! It could be!" The princess wrung her hands. "I'm still not in complete control over my seer powers, and this one came and left so fast that I can't be certain but that makes much sense. We have to warn them!"

"They're not in the mountains, not anywhere near them, but at Valrun Castle, Princess Saga. They're safe. See?" Arie pulled out the map his father had given Luccan, and his older brother had passed to him so that Arie could find their father with ease. "They—wait a second, Vale is moving west . . . Than and Luccan too—just as the princess said." His eyebrows drew together. "They're moving quite fast, not walking or riding."

Lord Riis shook his head. "They cannot fly for more than a few minutes in these conditions."

Arie's face turned red. He'd not told all of their story. Bleeding skies, what else had his sons and those with them gotten up to?

"When we, um, traveled to Bitra." Arie cast Saga a glance, and the spymaster nodded. She might learn about the heists, but for the time being they weren't important. "Thantrel suggested we take the gryphons from our castle. The pegasi too."

Annoyance flared in the high lord. "You mean *my* prize racing gryphons and *my* pegasi?"

Those beasts had cost him a small fortune. The Lord of Tongues valued them for they reminded him of how far he'd risen in life.

"Thantrel was trying to impress a female."

The spymaster pinched the bridge of his nose. Of course that was what Thantrel had been up to. As a youngling, just like now, Thantrel had loved attention. That desire continued as he grew and became an adult. Thantrel was as fluid as the sea in his tastes for bedmates, and he'd often done absurd things to win them over. Grand gestures abounded.

Lord Riis had often thought that maybe his son took after him in that manner. He had, after all, kept Inga's power a secret. That was far more dangerous than stealing a few gryphons and pegasi from an estate.

"If they continue at this pace, and the weather doesn't

deteriorate through the night, they may well hit the Red Mist Range by late morning," Arie added thoughtfully.

Lord Riis looked down at the map. "What's there that would draw them?"

"I don't know. Everything was quiet when I left. Fae were ready to ride out the cold at the castle."

The spymaster swallowed. "Then we must make haste and travel to Valrun tonight to find out."

CHAPTER 42
NEVE

My thighs ached as I dismounted from the pegasus and landed on the hardened snow.

We'd landed by the village gate, the same one Vale, Caelo, Anna, and I had walked through, near the out of service mine. Today no one manned the gate, which raised bumps on my arms. Before, there had been two drunken guards, and while they'd been deep in their cups, they'd still been living and breathing. Already, I feared this was a bad sign.

Above, mountains loomed, imposing craggy peaks glistening with fresh snow in the light of day. Though the sun shone brightly, the few parts of me that were exposed to the air stung. Breathing hurt too.

A shudder ran down my spine. This was no normal cold. As rebels and my friends dismounted from gryphons and Rynni's scaled back, their pained faces hinted that they felt the same.

I shifted Sassa's Blade, easing the sword into a more

comfortable position on my hip. Thyra had insisted I bring it, and she'd brought the Crown, tucked safely in a bag she wore around her hips. Her reasoning being that if the Ice Scepter was around and the cause for these people's deaths, then maybe the Hallows would react to one another. The Blade and Frør Crown hadn't done so yet, but I was willing to try anything to find the Scepter.

"Good work, Arava." I patted the pegasus's midnight snout.

To my shock, the pegasus turned to me and nuzzled my shoulder. My heart warmed at the show of affection. "We'll find you a warm place to rest. Food too."

Arava let out a winded huff as if to say that after a night of flying, she expected only the best, and pressed her body closer to mine.

"Don't take her to the stables yet," Vale said. "If the fae of Eygin are dead, then it's likely the horses are too. We don't wish to upset the gryphons or pegasi. They're proud creatures and will take offense, so I'll go check first." He gestured to a stable in view down the road and set out.

"She likes you, Neve," Caelo came up to me. "She claims a kinship with you. Thyra's pegasus, Lasvin, feels the same about her."

I blinked, and turned to take in my sister, standing with her pegasus. Halladora, Tonna, and Sigri hovered nearby, just as Valkyrja would do to protect their queen. It didn't escape my notice that the vampires had flown by me and Vale, while the rebel Valkyrja had stayed with Thyra. My sister was absentmindedly petting the pegasus, and Thyra did not seem to notice how the magical being leaned into her touch.

"Is that so?" I asked, shocked by the news.

"He's right," Thantrel, who had been not too far away, joined us.

Both he and Caelo had been instrumental in getting the gryphons to allow new riders on their backs—let alone ride them so far.

Thantrel snorted out a laugh as he patted Arava, who leaned into his touch. "My father will be upset that she took to you so easily."

"Why would that upset him?" I asked.

"When a pegasus bonds with a rider like I believe Arava is doing with you, they will accept no other after that. They will love you so much they would go to war for you. *With you*." Thantrel lifted a shoulder as if to say '*what can you do?*'. "It's a ruler's dream to have such a devoted pegasus."

"She never showed this type of affection to another?" My lips curled upward as I stroked Arava's mane.

"Don't get me wrong, she's a good mare. Obedient and brilliant, but never bonded before." He petted her mane too, and I noticed how Arava did not lean into his touch as she did for me. She tolerated Thantrel, even listened to him because of his elven powers, which so few animals could resist, but nothing more. "Father always hoped one of his pegasi would take to him, but neither did. Turns out they favored not his soul of fire, but one of ice."

I said nothing. I believed my friends and found myself thrilled that Arava felt a kinship with me too, but she did belong to Lord Riis. Perhaps I could speak with him about her? Maybe purchase Arava?

When Vale returned, it was with a grim look on his face.

"We can't use the stables. Too many dead horses. But there are empty homes." He swallowed. "I think those who owned those homes may have died elsewhere, because Aleksander's information appears correct. I haven't seen a single living soul yet."

"You haven't looked that hard," I replied through tight lips.

"Or heard a thing," he amended. "Not even the sounds of the dying. Unusual, considering it's daytime."

I could not deny that. In the few minutes we'd been in the town, the only sounds I heard came from us.

I gripped Arava's reins. "Let's shelter them in a home, then we can search for survivors more thoroughly."

We found a home empty of people and pushed aside the furniture before filling it with the gryphons and pegasi. A rebel lit the fire, and another created a barrier so the beasts would not get too close to the flames.

One glance at Arava, and I knew that she appreciated the flame. She'd nestled on the ground, right next to Lasvin, the snow-white pegasus that Thyra rode. Both tucked their hairy hooves beneath them and despite being midnight black and snow white, they looked very similar.

"I'll be back soon," I said to Arava as I crossed to the door. Her eyes had followed me, alert, perhaps wondering where I was going. "You need to rest. You earned it." At my assurance, the pegasus relaxed and looked at the fire again.

"Should someone stay with them?" asked the rebel who'd lit the fire.

"I can." Aleksander raised a hand. "I'll be using Arla to continue to patrol the area while the rest of you search the homes and businesses she couldn't get into. But I'll hear if they need anything."

If any one of us deserved a rest, he did. His white hawk had been patrolling the area for over a day. During that time, Aleksander had stayed awake to relay what Arla saw. Then he'd ridden here through the night to help. I thanked him as we left the home, and entered the street once more.

It took little effort to force our way into a home and less time to find the family who had lived there, all sharing a bed, likely for heat, embers burning in the hearth. All dead.

Though I'd known to expect this, my throat tightened as I took them in. "Do you think they died last night?"

"The fire suggests yes," Vale replied.

"If only we'd moved faster."

"We came as quickly as we could. Should we search for the Scepter?"

Thyra and I had told others about our secondary quest, and people were supposed to be keeping an eye open for the Scepter.

I shook my head. "This home is too bare; the family was probably poor. I cannot believe that it would be here when someone could easily sell it and improve their lot."

Vale held out a gloved hand. "Come to the next one. There might still be survivors."

I held out hope as we searched five more homes, none

of which housed a single breathing inhabitant. Nor any sign of the Ice Scepter.

We walked past the inn where we'd stayed, and my eyes began to water. Itham, the bard who had played us a song, was sitting in a chair outside, his instrument in hand. He almost looked at peace. Like he'd known death was coming, and he'd exited the tavern to play a tune for the town. Vale took my hand.

"He didn't deserve this. None of them did."

We said nothing more as we approached the coinary. Nearly there, Luccan joined us, also pale-faced and somber. He didn't have to speak for me to know that he had found only corpses too.

The door to the coinary hung open, a bad omen if there ever was one. Inside, there was no sound of coin being passed from hand to hand. No scratching of quills on parchment. No padding of leprechaun feet across the floor.

And as we strode deeper inside, my hope dimmed further. Two leprechauns had frozen at their desks. Were there more below?

Venturing deeper into the coinary gave us all pause. What if we triggered alarms? We had no intention of robbing vaults here, but there could be spells in place that only leprechauns could disable. Without one to guide us, we didn't know.

Rubbing my hands up and down my arms, and ever so thankful for the many warm layers I wore, we approached the door that led down into the vaults. We took the stairs slowly in case monsters had been released. When we reached the bottom we found that the vaults in this coinary were very plain—there was no goldwork on the doors or ogres on guard. Additionally, all of the vaults had been placed off of one main, circular room.

Laying between the vault doors were leprechauns who had taken refuge from the cold. When my gaze fell upon one, Coinmaster Hyknas, my throat tightened. She'd been the very leprechaun to help us here, and she looked stiff and blue. It took only a brief assessment for us to know that they were all dead.

Swallowing down my sorrow, I pulled my gaze up to the vaults, seven in total. "The Scepter might be in one of these."

Vale nodded. "If that's the case, we're out of luck. You need a leprechaun and the blood of the vault owner to open them."

"We can't know today, but if we don't find it, we can try to get our hands on coinary records for vaults later," Luccan added, his voice despondent.

"We're racking up quite the criminal records," Vale shook his head.

"Right," I said, barely listening to them, and really just wanting to get out of this room. "Let's see if the others have found anyone."

Hearts heavy, we climbed the steps. We'd no sooner stepped out into the brilliant sunshine than someone called my name.

"Princess Neve! Prince Vale!" I twisted to find Freyia waving at us.

"Have you found people who need help?" I asked,

hoping it to be true. Maybe a large group of neighbors had banded together, and against all odds, lived?

"Afraid not. No one has located a living soul. Thyra has found *something* odd, though. She wishes to have your opinion."

"Show us the way."

Freyia led us to the edge of the village, back to where the boarded-up mine sat waiting.

Thyra stood before the large mine door with Livia, Astril, Ulfiel—the part-fae, part-troll rebel who had pulled us out of the dungeons—and most shockingly, Thantrel. Luccan popped an eyebrow at his brother, but Thantrel was watching Thyra with rapt attention. She was too engaged with whatever she was doing to notice, so apparently, the youngest Riis was taking his opportunities when he got them.

"What's going on?" I asked.

Thyra turned from the mountain; her ice-blue eyes wide. "I kept hearing whispers, and I think they're coming from in there." She pointed to the mine door.

Whispers. Others seemed bemused, but I followed her line of thinking. Duran had found a passage claiming that the Hallows would interact, because they were all bonded in some way. Sassa's Blade and the Frør Crown had both whispered to me, and Thyra had heard the same from the sword when she used it. I cast a glance at the bag hanging at her side. "Did you try on the Crown again? Test your theory?"

"I did. Nothing." Her face screwed up in brief annoyance before smoothing out again. "But I did notice that the metal is warmer. Did you feel anything? Hear anything?"

"No." I'd been busy trying to find any sign of life.

"Is the sword reacting?"

I noted she didn't offer for me to try on the hallowed diadem. Thyra was as protective over it as I was the Sword.

"Let me see." I reached for the hilt of Sassa's Blade to pull it from the sheath and froze.

"What is it?" Thyra said excitedly.

"It's warm too. It's never done this." My heart rate kicked up a notch.

"This is it!" Thyra stared at the mine, determination laid bare on her face. "We need to get in there."

"It's boarded," Luccan noted the obvious.

"We'll pry the boards off."

"Right, that wasn't what I meant," Luccan arched an eyebrow, "the boards are probably there for a good reason."

"To hide the Ice Scepter," Thyra retorted.

"More like monsters," Vale supplied.

Thyra patted the leather satchel holding the Frør Crown rested inside. "That the Hallows are warm can't be a coincidence. It has to be a reaction, right? We need to get in there and explore."

"And what if that passage, or whatever is beyond the doors, really is there merely to keep monsters trapped in rock?" Freyia asked.

Thyra opened her mouth, clearly to argue, but the vampire held up a hand, halting her.

"I'm not saying that we shouldn't look around. Rather, I bring up monsters to suggest you take many with you. Not only you, your sister, and us." She gestured to her own sisters, as if it were a foregone conclusion that they'd come.

As two were members of our Valkyrja and the last was sworn to protect us, I supposed that wasn't a bad conclusion.

"I'm going," Vale, Thantrel, and Luccan said all at once.

Thyra did not argue with Thantrel, a testament to how badly she wanted to enter the tunnel. "Fine. Ulfiel will come as well. Someone get Caelo and Xillia too. We didn't bring faelights, so we'll need a pixie glow in the tunnels. No more, or it might get tight in there."

Thyra had a point. In Dergia, some tunnels had barely been large enough for Vale to walk through.

Freyia entered the village to search for help and tell the others where we were going. When she left, I turned back to the boarded-up tunnel and wondered if today was the day that the long-lost Ice Scepter would be found.

CHAPTER 43

VALE

L it up like a living faelight, Xillia the pixie led the way through the dark, wide tunnels.

Every so often the twins asked if she was fine to continue flying, or if Xillia's wings needed to warm. The pixie brushed off their every worry, claiming the light she emitted warmed her, which I thought was lucky. Despite the lack of wind, the cold inside the mountain only deepened.

Thyra's hunch might be right. The Scepter could lurk down here, a cold heart within the rock. I brushed close to my mate and shot her a glance to make sure she was well. She smiled smally back at me, her mind occupied.

Much to Thyra's annoyance, Thantrel had insisted on walking beside his mate, as I did with Neve. Thyra only allowed it with the stipulation that he remained quiet. The sisters needed to concentrate on the constant warming of their Hallows and the rare whispers that Thyra heard. Neve, too, twice now.

"Stop," Astril, the eldest vampire sister, spoke up from behind. "Something is coming."

"*Many* things," Livia corrected. "Sprinting our way."

Thantrel pulled his sword at the same time I did, and our mates' magic flared. I cocked my head. As we'd trained often during our travels and with the rebels, I recognized what my mate's magic felt like. Knew it almost as well as my own. But Neve's power felt different here. Weaker?

I felt my own powers, and noticed the same, a faint weakness. Was it the cold? The night of no rest and hard travel?

The question materialized right as the thing that had been running for us appeared from the darkness.

"Direwolf!" I hissed.

"And pups!" Neve yelped.

The mother ran in front, and at the sight of us snapped her jaws. I pulled Neve to the side, protecting her body with mine. Thantrel did the same for Thyra, and Xillia pinned her small body to the top of the tunnel.

As the mother direwolf approached, I expected her to lunge at me or Thantrel. I held *Skelda*, ready to defend. Others behind us had drawn their blades too.

The scent of wolf filled my nostrils as the wolves came closer, closer, closer . . .

The mother ran between Thantrel and me, not bothering to snap her jaws again. Not even as she wove through the others, who appeared as shocked as we were. Her pups followed, their attention never wavering from ahead.

I blinked. It was not natural for direwolves to act that way.

"What was that?" Neve asked, breathing hard. "I thought they'd attack!"

"As did I," I admitted.

"The pups looked terrified," Freyia whispered. "And the mother's heart rate was so fast. Something might be chasing them."

"We proceed with extreme caution." I twisted to catch Caelo's eye. "Watch your back."

My best friend was taking up the rear with Livia and Ulfiel.

Caelo nodded. "There can't be much food beneath this rock, and we're fresh meat."

In general, the wild mountains had that problem. The animal species of Winter's Realm were acclimated to the climate, and those that ate plants usually ate wood or stole from the greenhouses fae used. Some remote villages and towns constructed greenhouses for wildlife to supplement their food. But the mountains had fewer fae and less food than other areas, making it harder for wildlife to survive.

We continued on, dragging our fingertips along the uneven, frozen walls and more alert than before. For a long while, nothing of note happened. Still, there were no turn offs. No other creatures, save for an occasional rat. Sometimes I'd hear a skittering noise but see nothing. More rats running through the tunnels, I assumed. Vermin survived everywhere.

We'd gone another half an hour when, finally, the wall fell away from my touch. We'd walked into an opening of sorts.

"Up Xillia," Thyra instructed.

The pixie soared above, her light illuminating the high ceiling and tunnels far above our heads. At eye level, another dozen tunnels presented themselves. We weren't at a simple turnoff but a juncture of many halls of stone.

"So many options," Thyra mused. "Do you see anything in the tunnels up there, Xillia? Anything to help us choose? A sign or runes?"

"Nothing!" the pixie called, floating around a circular room. "Only lots of cobwebs and dirt!"

"Nothing obvious down here either," Livia said, having already done a quick round. "I hear no sounds of creatures, big or small."

"Me either," her sister, Astril, assured the rest.

Fae hearing was keen, but vampire hearing was the best in the nine kingdoms. If they heard nothing, then nothing lurked nearby.

"No whispers either." Thyra's lips tightened with annoyance.

"By feel it is, then." Neve patted her sword and began her own circle. With one hand wrapped around the Frør Crown, Thyra went in the opposite direction.

Thantrel fell into step behind Thyra, whereas I followed my mate closely, attention darting above often. I could not be certain that the vampires could hear deep in the tunnels above, and it would be all too easy for a monster, or many monsters, to drop on our heads.

Neve was the first to stop, to cock her head. Though when Thyra joined her not a minute later, she did the same.

"Hear it?" Neve said.

"I do," Thyra agreed. "It has to be coming from this tunnel."

"You're sure?" Thantrel's eyebrows knitted together.

"Not entirely, but it feels right." Thyra gestured to the other tunnels. "I heard nothing inside the other tunnels, and the Crown has not cooled, so I think this is it."

"As this is our first turn off since entering, let's mark it," Luccan took his dagger and sliced the bottom of his red tunic. "In case we somehow get turned around and end up here again, then we'll know not to bother."

With that bit of cloth secured, we entered the passage.

"Tighter in here," Ulfiel muttered. "Go in front of me, Sir Caelo."

He was right. This tunnel cut the space by more than half. The Falk twins had converged together, leaving Thantrel and me to follow in their footsteps.

"That means we're heading deeper into the mountain?" Luccan asked.

"Not necessarily." I couldn't fault him for not knowing, never having been in a dwarven kingdom. Until recently, I'd known little of them myself.

"Oh! The sword got hot!" Neve gasped. "Thyra?"

"The Crown too." Thyra said excitedly. "I think we're getting close."

In the end, *close* seemed to be relative. We walked another half an hour before the twins shared an excited look that raised the hairs on my arms.

"There are the whispers again, and they're stronger now. We're closing in," Thyra said.

"Actually, I think we're there." Neve pointed ahead with her sword's tip. "Do you see that light?"

I squinted and caught what she referred to. A pinprick of light shone in the darkness ahead.

We made our way forward, stopping only when we stood on a wide ledge looking into a vast cavern.

Above, like in other parts of the mountain, tunnels riddled the rock, but more eye-catching were the multitude of sunshafts and an array of mirrors that caught the incoming light. There were so many, I suspected that the mirrors caught light on all hours of the day. What they illuminated became apparent when I looked down.

"A Drassil!" Thyra gaped. "Inside a mountain! How does it survive?"

I had that question too. For many turns, our Drassils had required an influx of magic from powerful fae to survive.

Who tended this one? The fae of Eygin? Unlikely, given the boarded-up mine door and the long walk here.

And even if it got a magical boost from the network that linked the holy trees, it was so far from the others. It had to receive less power than trees in the heart of the kingdom. Although from our vantage, high above and somewhat far away, the tree looked quite healthy.

The leaves were amethyst in color, not falling or with blackened veins. The limbs did not droop, and the bark glimmered, darker than other holy trees, but nothing that set off alarm bells.

"Let's go down," Neve said.

"Wait," Astril held up a hand. "There's a smell in here though, is there not? A rot?" The vampire's nostrils flared.

Her sisters followed suit, leading me to do the same. Before I caught the scent—sweet and cloying but off-putting —Luccan nodded.

"Death," he said with surety. Of all the fae here, he was the only one I suspected could rival a vampire's sense of smell. "Maybe those wolves found something to eat and left meat on the bones?"

"Sounds reasonable to me," Neve piped up. She hadn't taken her eyes off the tree. "Or other wolves. We need to be on the lookout, right?"

"Agreed. Let's go down," Thyra added.

We could have flown down, but the air here was still cold enough to make that uncomfortable, even for the fae turned vampires, and there were stairs. Old, crumbling steps, but steps all the same.

Two by two, we descended the staircase. I watched Neve's every step and kept my hand on *Skelda's* hilt, not sure I trusted this place. The space may be deserted and peaceful in appearance, but that worrying scent lingered in the air. It set my teeth on edge, and while Neve and Thyra were quick to dismiss it in hopes of finding the Ice Scepter, I remained alert.

"Skies, if only we'd found a tunnel closer to the bottom," Thyra complained when we were halfway to the bottom. "This is—*ahhhhh!*"

She'd been walking along the edge and the step she'd landed on gave way beneath her boot. The rebel leader toppled, but Thantrel and I caught her before she could fall far. Pressed against the wall, Neve's eyes went wide.

"Are you well, sister?"

"Fine," Thyra cleared her throat, and a soft blush arose in her cheeks. I'd let my mate's twin go when it was clear Thantrel had her. His hands remained supporting her. "Thank you, Thantrel."

"I'll always catch you," he replied, his tone serious yet also, somehow, flirtatious. Something only Than could manage, I supposed.

"This is no time to succumb to Than's charms, Thyra," Luccan teased.

She rolled her shoulders back. The old Thyra returned. "Sheathe your weapons. We don't want anyone accidentally hurting themselves if the stairs give out again. From here on out, we go one at a time."

We descended the rest of the way in single file, and I swore Thantrel had a bit more bounce in his step as he trailed right behind Thyra. And for her part, the raven-haired Falk looked back once, stared right up at him before catching herself and resuming her mission.

As we reached the bottom, Neve turned, caught my eye, and winked. She'd noticed the interaction too. I took her hand in mine and pulled her close, savoring her scent of smokey vanilla.

"If you find it, be careful, Neve."

We knew about the Ice Scepter's power, or at least what the previous Falk monarchs told us. I knew from experience that might not be the entire truth. With fae, and particularly royals, you could count on many omissions.

"I will." She kissed me before turning away.

Her sister waited for her with arms crossed.

"I didn't want to investigate without you," Thyra said when Neve arched her brow. "We found this together."

Neve smiled at the inclusion, at their growing bond. "Let's take a look at this tree."

CHAPTER 44

NEVE

Thyra and I approached the Drassil. How the tree was here, bathed in sunlight while darkness ruled the rest of the cavern, baffled me.

Since arriving in Winter's Realm, I'd not seen a holy tree so alive. So vibrant. Or with as many leaves.

Like the first Drassil I'd seen in Traliska, I yearned to touch it. To see if this tree would speak to me too and, if so, what it might say. Would I hear my mother again? My father? A stronger tree had to mean a stronger connection to the Faetia and with Thyra by my side, I yearned to attempt contact.

But first, the Scepter.

Sassa's Blade remained sheathed; however, I needed to only touch the top of the hilt to know it was hot. I assumed the Frør Crown was too. Throughout the journey in the tunnels, between feeling our Hallows and hearing whispers no one else heard, my sister and I had traded assurances we were on the right track.

So *where was* the Scepter? I didn't see it down here. Nor in the branches above. The tree featured a hole that I could imagine an aura owl nesting in, but it was not deep. From paces away, I could tell no Hallow of the realm glittered inside.

Had we been wrong? It didn't feel like we were wrong. If anything, the closer we got to the Drassil, the stronger the magic that came off it. Magic that was familiar, but also somehow unidentifiable. Different from other holy trees.

"I don't see it." Thyra exhaled a long breath. "But I was so certain."

"As was I." I turned to my sister, my eyebrows pulled together. "Do you think it's beneath the tree? Buried there by purpose or chance? Maybe that's why the tree is healthier than others of its kind."

From behind, Vale cleared his throat. "It would be sacrilege to find out."

"An affront to the dead gods themselves," Ulfiel added, a tremor in his voice as three fingers went to his chest and he dragged them downward in reverence.

If people continued to die, and younglings continued to be born misshapen and weaker than generations before, would it be worth it to cut down the tree? Or, at the very least, to dig under the roots? Imagining the tree tipping if we'd dug too deep made me cringe.

Thyra gestured above. "I say we search the tunnels. An animal might have dragged the Scepter anywhere. If it's not there, we dig around the tree," Thyra cleared her throat. *"Dig with great care."*

"Don't fly for too long," Vale added. "It's utterly freezing in here. Colder than outside."

He was right. I'd managed to not be bothered by the temperature because the hunt preoccupied me. Once you stopped moving through, the cold was piercing indeed.

"Let's take it in turns," Luccan suggested.

I was about to agree, but a whisper teased my ear. I twitched. That had felt close. Closer than any had been before. I twisted toward the sound and found a dark, male face looking back at me.

"Screaming stars!" I jumped into Vale, who placed me behind him.

"What is it?" he commanded, *Skelda* in hand.

"The tree!"

A few shuffled back a handful of steps as they took in what I'd seen.

"It's rare that visitors enter my mountain." The face rasped, his voice so familiar, despite the motion of the barky face being so completely strange. "I almost thought the voices I was hearing were but a dream."

A body appeared below the face and the features sharpened and began to look more like a normal fae, though the color of him was still the same as the tree bark. The result was a male as tall and muscular as Vale with wings sprouting from his back. However, unlike our wings, they tapered to nothing at the ends, like smoke blowing away on a faint breeze.

No, not smoke. Shadows.

I stared at the male, recognition dawning at the sharp

hawkish nose, the dark eyes, and the square jaw. The same face I'd seen when I'd placed the Frør Crown atop my head.

"Who are you?" Vale asked, *Skelda* still aloft.

My mate wasn't the only one to have drawn a weapon. In fact, I was in the minority, alongside Xillia, as the only fae not prepared to attack. I righted that oversight, pulling Sassa's Blade from the sheath, and immediately regretted the action, for I swore the trapped fae's eyes lit up.

Fool. He's in a tree! His eyes are nothing but bark.

And yet, judging by the expanding pit in my stomach, logic was not convincing. Not even to myself.

"I am a visitor to this kingdom who took a wrong turn," the fae smiled and though he was undeniably attractive, it was not a thing of beauty. No, his smile set my teeth on edge.

"You're a Shadow Fae," I stated, having found my voice. "I've seen you before."

"Did you? That makes the two of us, for I've seen you before, Isolde. You as well, Thyra."

My sister's expression, as hard as a blade, revealed the slightest shock before she hid it again.

"How?" she demanded.

"I live in a Drassil tree," the Shadow Fae waved a hand up at the leaves. "Tending it takes much of my time, but like all Drassils, mine connects to others—like the ones Isolde has communed with. Like the one at Valrun Castle, the same tree you often stare at, Thyra Falk."

My sword lowered. "Have I spoken with you?"

"Alas no," he said. "I'm not of this kingdom and cannot

speak through your other holy trees, just this one. But I can listen. I can watch."

I didn't believe him. Something in the way he spoke made me think he was lying. Could Shadow Fae lie?

I knew next to nothing about the exterminated race of fae. Those that sought to take over all of Isila and bathe the land in darkness. To devour the light in more ways than one. Maybe an ability to lie was part of what made other fae despise them so? That and the Shadow Faes' tendency to violence, of course.

"When did you listen?" I needed to learn more, to see if I should trust this creature.

"The day you stopped in Traliska was the first time I heard you," the fae replied. "Then I heard whispers the day you wed the prince. A marriage blessed by the Faetia and the stars, was it not?"

"What's your name? Vale asked. "And why are you in a holy tree? Are you from another world?"

The idea hadn't occurred to me, but yes, what Vale suggested made sense. Drassils, like certain places in Isila, were said to be hinges—areas where gateways could most easily be made. Sometimes natural portals formed there ever so briefly too. Hinges were as rare as snow in the Summer Court, but they existed. Somewhere. Sometimes.

"From this world," he replied. "Once, I roamed the lands of Isila. At that time, I had many names."

"*Give one*," Vale retorted, his tone hard.

"King Érebo of House Nikao, ruler of the Shadow Isles, husband to Queen Nyxa of House Skialo."

My heart fell to my knees. He was not just any Shadow Fae, but *the Shadow King*.

"Why would a king believed to be dead be watching me through the trees?" I asked.

"You intrigue me, Isolde."

Thyra stepped closer to the tree, and Thantrel made to follow, but my sister swept a hand out, not wishing for him to protect her.

"All this is interesting enough, but we're here for the Ice Scepter. We feel it, and seeing as you're stuck in a tree, I have to ask, is it in there with you?"

Again, he laughed. "I know of the Scepter, but I believe that *I* have answered enough questions. If you wish to know more, you must give me something in return."

"What do you want?" Thyra asked.

"I wish for you and your sister to come closer," he replied. "To touch the bark of my tree, so that we may speak without others listening."

I recoiled. Nothing in me wished to comply, but Thyra cast an expectant glance back at me.

"Come on." Desire for the Ice Scepter sat heavy on her face.

"I'm not sure this is a good idea, Thyra."

"I won't hurt you," said King Érebo. "I only wish to speak privately, and no matter how low I whisper, we all know that the others will hear. Particularly the vampires."

No answer escaped my lips right away, and in the silence that permeated the cavern, a sound came from above. Skittering?

I looked up. Found nothing.

"Please, Neve," Thyra whispered. "We *need* the last Hallow. If we're to take our home back, if we're to avenge our family, we need it."

As it stood, Thyra had a band of rebels who had been fighting King Magnus on and off for many turns. I had my friends, my powerful mate, and the dwarves of Dergia. That small force could not stand up against the royal army, Roar's forces, and likely those of Houses Ithamai, Qiren, and Vagle too. Perhaps I could convince a few noble houses to side with me, but to ask them to fight their king was a very large matter indeed. They would want to be certain that we'd succeed, or the fates of their houses would be dire.

Having all three Hallows would surely help to sway the great houses I hoped to ally with.

"You won't hurt us?" I asked.

"I only wish to speak, not harm you." He pressed his palms to the bark. An invitation.

"Fine."

"I don't think this is a good idea," Vale said.

I turned to look my mate in the eyes. "The matter is mine and Thyra's to decide, my love. We need the Scepter."

For a beat, we only stared into one another's eyes. He loved me, and I loved him, and of course he wanted to make sure I was safe. But I saw the moment that Vale acquiesced and understood why he did not push. My mate was a warrior. He knew that risk was often necessary for great reward. "I'm with you."

"Until the stars fall." I smiled at my mate before moving to Thyra's side.

In step with one another, we approached the tree,

pausing only to exchange glances before placing our hands on the rough bark, right where the Shadow Fae's hands were.

It's been so long since another fae touched me. The King of Shadows sighed. *That it is you two makes it all the better.*

Why? I asked mentally.

No, first, the Scepter, Thyra countered, and I was shocked that I could hear her as well as the Shadow Fae through the tree. Somehow the magic in the Drassil was connecting us all. *We've done what you asked. Given you touch. Now you can answer us. Where is it?*

A chuckle rang out that made my skin crawl. He claimed he wouldn't harm us, but I wasn't about to mistake this creature born of shadows, a creature that someone had trapped here for what I expected might be a good reason, as anything close to a friend.

Luckily, your questions are linked. Through time and chance and blood, the Scepter cannot be spoken of without telling you why I was put here. And by whom.

I inhaled, heard my sister do the same.

It was none other than your ancestor. Long ago, the Unifier Queen Sassa Falk put me here, the Shadow King said. *Your grandmother, many times over, deceived me and stole my power.* His eyes dropped to the blade sheathed at my side. *You had to have guessed, seeing as that Blade possesses magic born of my flesh.*

My lips parted. I'd been using the Shadow King's magic that was somehow shoved into a blade?

How did she deceive you? Were you not at war for many turns? Trapping an enemy seems like anything but deceit. Thyra replied, eyes narrowed. She stood firmly on guard, as did I.

A great war raged between our peoples, yes. But something more existed between Sassa and I . . .

Behind us, the eyes of others burned holes into my back, but I remained captivated by the Shadow Fae's face.

What? I asked.

His chin lifted. *Your queen was my mate.*

You lie! I tried to pull my hand back but found the motion impossible. My hand was stuck to the bark. *I don't want to speak to you any more. Release me.*

To what do you protest?

That you were Sassa's mate, I barked back. *She wed Torre Lisika.*

And? A marriage between fae is often political. Did you not take such vows to Prince Vale? Before you loved him? Before you learned that you were mated?

We'd not been in love the day we'd wed. Both falling, but not quite there and hence, not able to take the love match vows. The Shadow King read the truth across my face.

Like it or not, your ancestor and I were mated. Both wed to another, but mates, fated in the stars. Neither would forsake our wedding vows—we owed too much to our people who were at war. In truth, we both despised one another as much as our souls yearned to be together.

Suddenly, I saw him more clearly. His clothing appeared fresh, as if he'd just put it on. A black tunic, pants, and boots. A crown, weighed down with gleaming black opals, perched atop his head. The king pulled the collar of his tunic aside and where the skin covering his collar bone would be glowed a mark. Black, not white like mine, but shimmering.

A mate mark, he said. *I expect she hatched her plan the moment* *she saw our marks emerge. Moons went by, and we met in secret. Sassa convinced me to come here for a tryst, or so I thought. Even then, even when I despised her and me **and us**, saying no proved impossible.* He scowled. *But a tryst was the last thing on her mind. She trapped me, but not before extracting some of my power for her use. To use against my people.*

Her sword. The fabled blade that was treasured in the Falk line. The one hanging at my side.

So you've been here since? Thyra asked.

I have.

My sister scoffed out loud. *Well, your kind began a war that stretched across many kingdoms. You're in there for good reason.*

His eyes glowed a vicious black, his first real sign of anger. *You would do best to release me.*

Thyra laughed. *Oh, would we? And why is that?*

Above, the veins on the leaves of the tree darkened. A few fell. Just like the tree in Valrun had been before we found the Frør Crown. Like the trees all over the land. My skin tightened. This fae was the cause of this. The cause of the blight too?

Stop! I screamed. *Please! Stop!*

For a price.

More leaves fell. Had they even been there at all? Healthy and alive? Or was this glamour? Panic flared at the realization that reality might not be real at all.

Name it! I said.

I wish to touch the magic of your line.

You want us to . . . open ourselves to you?

Only for a moment.

608

As I'd appeared conflicted when Thyra wished to touch the tree, now she seemed worried.

You swear not to hurt us? I asked again. *And to stop harming this tree?*

On the dead gods. On my people. On my blood.

With every new leaf that fell, here and elsewhere, it grew colder out. More fae were dying. More being born with mangled wings or bodies because things were out of flux. If he would not harm us, it seemed worth the risk.

Yes. I answered.

The leaves ceased to fall, and the blackness in their veins lightened. Real? Not real?

Thyra? He asked.

She swallowed. Nodded.

The Shadow King smiled, the effect full of malice and greed, and before I understood I had, in fact, made a dire mistake, shadows swirled. Climbed my legs, my torso.

I managed only another breath before darkness overtook me.

CHAPTER 45
VALE

M y heart skipped a beat as Neve and Thyra slumped to the ground, their hands still on the tree, seemingly adhered there. Shadows pulsed around the twins.

I took a step closer, ready to carve answers from this Shadow Fae if need be. Thantrel mimicked me, and the others began to close in behind us.

The fae held his palm out. "Stay where you are. I'm not hurting them."

"Then why are they like that?" Thantrel growled, his eyes ablaze.

"I'm feeling," the fae said. "And I'm already done."

Before we questioned him further, the shadows fell away, as if they'd never been. Neve's eyes fluttered open first. Then Thyra's.

"What did you *do* to me?" my mate rasped, as her hand went to her heart. "I feel—I feel, I don't know. *Wrong.*"

"Like you're meant to, granddaughter."

Granddaughter? Dread swirled inside, matched by the identical expressions of horror on the Falk twin's faces.

"That can't be true!" Thyra stood fluidly, a hint that the fae had not, in fact, hurt them, and when Neve followed, equally strong, I breathed my first sigh of relief.

"There's no way our line possesses shadow magic!" Thyra growled. "Your kind has been gone for four thousand turns!"

"Then why do you sense the shadows inside you? Churning? Begging to be released?" The fae in the tree laughed. "Sassa banished my people and trapped me, yes, but *I* survived, and I found the kernel of dormant magic inside you. I activated it."

"You changed us!" Neve gasped.

"On the contrary, I only enhanced what you *already were.* Gave you a gift—*a strength*—which you would have never been able to access without my touch. And I did not harm you by doing so, just as I promised."

The sister's eyes met, and the same anger blazing in their gazes simmered inside me. This Shadow Fae had touched my mate *inside.* He'd felt something she had not known existed. He'd changed her without consent.

A low growl built in my throat, to which the fae looked up. A slow, cunning smile formed on his face.

"You think you can harm me, Warrior Bear? That you can strike your sword against this tree, and I'll fall?" He laughed derisively. "Stab this Drassil with that sword of yours, stab it *a thousand times*, and nothing will happen to me. In fact, you'll be doing me a great favor. Should this tree die by anything but remarkable magic, I will simply be moved to another Drassil, somewhere deeper in Winter's Realm. You will have achieved nothing, other than having to live with injuring one of your holy trees."

I swallowed, believing him. Whoever put him there was clearly powerful and ingenious. No doubt they would have had a backup plan and this sounded like a good one to keep the king in place. But what exactly did he mean by a remarkable magic?

"Besides, if I am somehow harmed, who will teach the royal twins of their powers?" the Shadow Fae asked smoothly. "There's no one better to instruct them than their own blood."

The king spread his hands wide, an odd gesture for a male in a tree, but he made it appear regal. "Only I can teach these two, my heirs in this world, of their true potential. Only I can love them unconditionally. Release me from this prison, and you'll be greater than you could have ever imagined."

Rage bubbled over. "I'll love Neve, no matter her magic."

"As I will Thyra," Thantrel spat.

Thyra jerked and spared Thantrel a soft look that I'd never seen on her face before. Then she turned, her ice-blue gaze back, and on the tree. "We do not accept. We're here only to claim the Ice Scepter. If you wish to help us—if you love us unconditionally as you said—you'll give us that freely."

Another sinister smile. "I thought you might request that. Alas, you're too late. Another of my blood came first. He proved far more amenable, but he did not have the power nor the tools to release me from my prison. He might still gather strength, but I was not happy to wait and I did not need to. I knew that once he used the Scepter, once he put our plan in motion, you'd come. The trueborn blood of Sassa Falk would come."

Burning skies, that could only be one person.

"It was King Magnus, wasn't it?" Neve hissed.

The Shadow Fae smirked. "He knows what he must do with the Hallow, and he's already begun his work. Luring you to Eygin was only the beginning."

Thyra roared. "That monster used the Hallow against those fae! That's why the cold deepened so quickly. Unnaturally."

My stomach pitted at her words. At what the male who had raised me was capable of when the throne was on the line.

The Shadow King didn't deny her accusation. Rather, he looked pleased.

Neve grabbed Thyra by the wrist and shuffled back a few steps. "We *do not* align with you. We do not accept your so-called help. And we will definitely not free you. We can steal the Scepter from Magnus."

The Shadow King sighed. "I worried it might come down to this. Particularly when I looked inside your hearts. They're too stout. Too set on what the stories tell you is right. I was right to align with Magnus even if he could not free me." He raised a hand, snapped his fingers. "Alas, I have waited many millennia. I can wait a few more days for freedom. After all, given the right incentive, anything can happen."

That skittering noise I'd heard earlier rose, again from above. My heart sank as my chin lifted to the sky and understanding dawned.

Hundreds of ice spiders poured from the tunnels in the mountain's rock. Some small, a few the size of horses, and most were in between. The spiders came in colors ranging from snow white to shadow black, all with hairy legs. The stench of copper and dirt and rotting flesh rolled off them and their eight legs waved in the air, pinchers clacking, their faces alit with hunger.

My magic extinguished as strands of silk shot toward us, driving home the horror of the situation.

The mere presence of ice spiders, just like the silk wrappings we'd worn at Valrun Castle, nullified magic. But this was far, far worse. More all-encompassing.

"Together!" Caelo shouted. "Weapons out. Neve and Thyra here!"

The Shadow King laughed again, a sound I hated with all my soul. "You can run. You can fight, but unless you do as I ask, you are never getting out of here alive."

CHAPTER 46
NEVE

My magic was gone. Even the newly released shadow magic vanished in the face of the horde of ice spiders. Not that I'd know how to use it anyway.

I darted a glance at the staircase we'd come down, only to find it also overrun with eight-legged monsters. We were as trapped as the Shadow King in his tree.

I stumbled closer to the others, clumsy in my haste, and my leg hit on something hard in my interior cloak pocket.

The mirror.

Back at Valrun Castle, I used the mirror to contact the King of Dergia to make sure the dwarves were safe. I never thought I'd use it again so soon, but with a plan forming in my mind, I wrestled the mirror out of my cloak.

"King Tholin!" I spoke urgently into the mirror, trying not to draw the Shadow King's attention. "Help!"

It took longer than before, but the king's face appeared, gray rocks behind him, making him look even paler than usual. He was in a mine or something but carrying the mirror with him, just as he said he'd do. A good ally. I only hoped that he could somehow send help in time.

My stomach hardened at how far-fetched my dream was.

Dergia is a day's ride, but they have messengers. Maybe even ravens? It's possible . . .

"Princess Neve? Where are you?" His bushy eyebrows pulled together. "Are those *sunshafts* above you?"

I angled the mirror up, toward the hole in the mountain. "Yes! We're in a mountain by Eygin. An old mine, we think." Thinking he might know our exact location if given more clues, I spun the mirror toward the tree. "Look, there's a Drassil too, and we're being overrun by hundreds of ice spiders. Can you—"

A spider fell on top of me. I shrieked and batted at the creature with my hands, only to stiffen when glass shattered.

I screamed as I stomped on the spider with both boots, barely crushing it because the monster was so large. The mirror was gone. Our best chance, gone.

All we had left to do was to fight. My friends were already doing so viciously. Spider carcasses sprawled around us, but there always seemed to be more. More. *More.*

"Stop them!" I screamed at the Shadow King.

The king laughed, and the skin on the back of my neck tightened. "I cannot call my children off now, Isolde. Not when flesh has walked into their home. It already took much of their willpower not to attack you on your way here, and I believe they deserve *a taste* for their good behavior. A half-elf to start sounds good, no? I do not think they've ever tasted elf."

Thantrel. Caelo. Both already covered in blood. Red *and* black blood. Fae and spider. My stomach tightened at the reek and tang of spider blood, and my air came in shallow breaths.

It was because of me and Thyra, our needs, our hopes, that these people were here. Thyra might pretend to hate Thantrel, but I had a feeling he was growing on her. At least enough so that she'd mourn him. And I could not bear to lose either male. Vale's brothers, one by blood, one by soul.

"Maybe a pixie too?" the Shadow King crooned as one spider shot a string of silk at Xillia. "Not much meat there, but some of my smaller children might enjoy her."

The pixie soared out of the way in time to avoid being caught, though I did not miss the fear in her eyes as she dove for safety in our circle.

"Here!" I waved an arm, ready to protect with my sword in the other hand. She was almost to me when she changed course, flying backwards. Another spider soared past my face, and she veered to avoid the monster. But Xillia did not see the horror coming up behind her until it was too late. The spider, five times the size of the pixie, grabbed her and tore her head clean off.

Thyra's scream joined mine, and Livia drew her bow, shooting an arrow at the spider, ending its life for killing our friend.

I tried for my magic again, to spread ice and trap these foul creatures, but to no avail.

"Neve." Vale grunted as more enemies fell from above.

He cut one swinging from above in half with *Skelda*, and blood as black as the shadows I'd been wreathed in rained down on us. Another approached, and my mate killed it too, always protecting me, shielding me. "We need to fly out of here."

I cast a frantic glance at the hole that allowed sunshine to enter the cavern and shine upon the Drassil. That hole was our best means of escape. We were simply too deep within the mountain to run.

"We go now. Ready your blade." Vale grabbed my non-dominant arm. Perhaps only for a brief moment, no spiders rained down.

I slipped my wings through the slits in my cloak, and we rose. The others followed, and I'd never been so glad that the vampire sisters still had their wings. If we had to carry them out of there, it would have been so much harder. As it was, the feat was already near impossible. Swords waved as we flew and spiders tried to catch us, spinning half hazard webs, jumping at us, and climbing the rock walls.

One strand caught not on a rocky outcropping but on Ulfiel, still lower than the rest of us. I screamed as a spider the size of Vale's destrier pulled the rebel to the ground.

"We have to go back, Vale!"

"We can't, Neve. We—"

His words died, and when I followed his gaze upward, everything inside me died too. Another wave of spiders were coming, falling upon us.

I batted them with my sword, panicking and forgoing the moons of training Vale and his friends had poured into me.

It turned out, the training wouldn't have saved me anyway, because as the spiders fell, silk wrapped around our arms, our legs, our torsos. Fighting for our lives, we pushed higher until the moment a shower of silken strands captured our wings, binding them together. We fell, and heart-pounding seconds later, I hit the rock but somehow remained coherent enough to shimmy over to Vale. I could tear the silks binding him with my teeth. We could still fight . . .

Four arms hauled me up and suddenly, I was staring into the milky eyes of the largest spider yet. Behind its bulk, my friends and sister scrambled on the ground.

"Not her, Falagog," the Shadow King said. "Nor the black-haired female faerie. They are mine. Eventually, they will see that. Eventually, they will do as I wish."

"Which can we have, Master? My children are so hungry. Always so hungry," the spider spoke in a voice so dark it must have been born in the depths of night.

"That one." He must have pointed, and I could not see who he singled out. "Be a good girl and save the red-haired elf-blood and the prince for last."

"Very well, Master," Falagog said. "Shall I keep their eyes open?"

"Do. However, before you feed, patrol the mountain. More may have entered after the princesses." The Shadow King paused before adding. "Magnus froze the village so there are corpses to be found. You may gorge on those to your liking." A dark gleam filled his eye, making my throat spasm, though no words came out. Nearly everyone, if not truly everyone in Eygin was dead, but there were many rebels who weren't. If the ice spiders went into the village, they'd find them.

The spider picked me up, and the next thing I knew, I was spun up in silk all the way to my shoulders and being carried by Falagog through a tunnel.

My eyes adjusted to the darkness as Falagog entered a small cave. Corpses and skeletons of rats and some larger animals littered the ground, but otherwise, the cave was empty. The mother spider propped me up against the wall. Bound by her silks, which may as well have been steel, I could not move my limbs.

My friends struggled within their binds, but they made no headway. We were all the same. Trapped. I stopped trying to escape and noticed that some of my friends had fared far worse in the fight with the spiders. Slashes and bites marred many faces. Was the silk hiding worse? Would someone bleed out or lose vital organs before we attempted to escape again?

Screaming stars, how will we do that?!

The spiders carried Thyra in last and placed her next to me. Directly across the small cave, I stared at Vale and Thantrel. Spiders crawled excitedly in the middle, pinchers clicking, legs moving in the most revolting way.

I feared they'd start eating someone right away, but the Shadow King seemed to have complete control over them because the spiders began finishing their job, encasing the others' heads in silks. I wanted to scream as silk climbed up Vale's face, his eyes drinking me in until the moment his head was completely covered.

Falagog herself wove her silks around Thyra's head,

although for my twin, she left eye slits. Finally, the mother spider turned to me and applied her silk to my face, once again leaving those slits to torment me. To make us watch as they killed and ate the others.

"We'll return soon," Falagog said and disappeared from my range of vision.

I heard the sounds of spiders scuttling from the cavern, leaving my friends and I in a dark cavern, entombed in white silk.

INTERLUDE

PRINCE THORDUR, HEIR TO BENEATH THE ROCK, THE ANCIENT KINGDOM OF DERGIA

The Prince of Dergia's heart pounded as he and the dwarven forces pushed their horses down the snow-covered road.

Their small but fierce army, one hundred soldiers and twelve healers strong, had started their ride north an hour after Neve called to warn them that the deadly cold might come for Dergia. That the same cold had already taken over Eygin and killed many. It was a blow to the Kingdom Beneath the Rock. Those in Eygin were friends and confidants of the dwarves, just like the Falk princess.

The dwarven forces had been nearly about to exit the mountain passages when Neve used the enchanted mirror again—this time to call for help. Now they were not just rushing to Eygin to help the villagers who had kept their existence a secret for so long, but for *her*. Their ally.

Would they be too late?

Riding leisurely, the gates of Eygin were a half an hour from the hidden mountain tunnels. They'd attempted to cut that time in half by urging the horses to go ever faster, but Neve had already been fighting ice spiders when she spoke to the king. And though his father claimed to know exactly where the Drassil in the mountain by Eygin grew, it was deep within the rock, a part of the mine set aside for prayer and solitude thousands of turns ago. How much longer would it take to delve so deep?

The gates surrounding Eygin came into view, and Thordur stiffened. Ten people stood just beyond the village gates. He knew from previous trips to Eygin that the old mine's entrance was right by the gate. From how one person pointed in that direction, he could guess that they were considering entering.

"Those are not our allies!" Thordur yelled over the pounding sounds of hooves.

"I can see that," the king replied, his voice muffled beneath his helmet, the largest and most grand of them all.

"Are we ready for our secret to be widely known?"

"The day has been coming since the Falk heir entered Beneath the Rock, son." The king looked askew at his heir. "It's time for Dergia to stop hiding. To take a stand against those who wished to bend our knees and backs. If we help her, if she takes her kingdom back, she will allow us into the open air."

The open. He looked up at the wide blue sky and though he wore a warm and protective helmet, a thick cloak, his leather coated armor, and woolen layers, a chill ran through the prince. Soon they would no longer be forced to live and work and remain Beneath the Rock for all of their lives. His sister, Bavirra, could finally go on adventures.

Thordur loved his people and his kingdom just as they were, but the thought was enticing indeed.

No one stood guard atop the village gate, and those who had been examining the mine did not stop the dwarves from riding through, though they did draw their weapons.

Flinty eyes stared at the dwarven king, and Prince Thordur could not help but feel immense pride in his father when the king dismounted.

One figure, a male faerie with silver hair and glacial blue eyes approached. The male did not hold a weapon. Instead, he carried a white hawk on his arm. The beast did not so much as blink as it took them in.

"Who are you?" the male asked.

Thordur bristled at the brusque tone directed toward his king, though his father just removed his helmet and inclined his head, not taking offense.

"King Tholin of Dergia."

The male's lips parted, and many of the faces behind him displayed the same shock, indicating that Neve had kept their secret. One of the faces in the grouping caught Thordur's eye. A female with long red hair and—scales behind her ears? The prince blinked a few times, trying to discern if his vision was playing tricks on him.

"That's impossible," the male faerie found his voice. "Dergia is lost to the ages."

The king smirked. "My kingdom is alive and well and formal allies to Princess Neve, or perhaps she is now going by Isolde?"

Prince Thordur marveled at how steadily his father told

their secret. He truly was ready to bring Dergia out of the darkness.

The male cleared his throat, shook his head slowly.

"Whatever the name you know her by, I believe the Falk princess is in great danger." The king pointed to the mine. "She called for aid just over a half hour back. Ice spiders were upon them. We have answered that call, and I don't want to waste time on debates regarding the existence of my kingdom."

The male sucked in a breath. "Some ice spiders were just in the village too. Smaller ones and we killed them pretty easily, but that's actually why we're here. Prints in the snow told us they came from there." He jerked his head to the door of the mine, now broken down, before catching the king's eye again. "I'm Aleksander, half-brother to Neve and Thyra."

Thyra. Thordur sucked in a breath. After Neve came to Dergia, the prince had thoroughly researched her family. Thyra was Neve's twin.

"A pleasure," the king said. If he was surprised to hear that another Falk twin lived, he did not show it. "Your sisters are indeed in danger. We need to infiltrate the mountain. There's a chamber with sunshafts where an ancient Drassil grows. They were attacked there."

"Sunshafts," Aleksander breathed. "I've only read of the ancient dwarven mines, but those are openings to allow light through right?"

"They are."

"So they'd be visible from above?"

The king nodded. "Unless they're covered in snow, but I

saw that these ones allowed light through, so that is not the case."

"Are they large enough for people to slip through?"

Where is this line of thinking going? Thordur thought, though the king just nodded again.

"Arla, my hawk here, can fly above and find them," Aleksander turned to the keen-eyed bird. "I'm a skin-changer. I can see through her eyes, then we'll know what's happening."

"My father *knows where* they are," Prince Thordur cut in. "We need to move. To run the tunnels and get there, for unlike some of you, we dwarves don't have wings. And I doubt there are enough of you to take on the number of ice spiders we believe are in the mountain."

"You may not have wings to fly, but we have animals that can." The female who had caught his eye stepped forward, her red hair tossing in a gust of wind that swept through the mountain passes, "and if they're not enough, I'm part dragon. I'll carry the rest of you."

CHAPTER 47
NEVE

Whimpers filled the cave.

Only Thyra and I had been given eye slits, which was not a mercy, but a way to make us watch when the spiders began eating those in our party. Our friends, my mate, the rebels, and vampire sisters that I'd been slowly forming a relationship with were all to be eaten, just as soon as the spiders cleared the mountain tunnels. For maximum effect, the others had been propped on the opposite wall. As their faces were shrouded in silk, I couldn't see exactly who was crying, but thought it was Ulfiel. My heart bled for him. For all of us.

I saw only one possible way out, and that was giving the Shadow King exactly what he wanted. Freedom.

How he was so certain Thyra or I could do such a thing, I did not know. Nor did I want to unleash him upon the kingdom. But if it came down to it, I couldn't watch the others die. Especially not Vale.

Did it make me weak that I was thinking of putting an entire kingdom in danger for just a few?

"Master," Falagog's midnight voice drifted out of the central cavern and down the short passage into the cave, "those of my children we sent out have nearly gone through all the tunnels and found no one. Some of them have already returned and are waiting. Might they begin to feast?"

By the dead gods. How had they traversed all the tunnels so quickly? It had taken us hours! I shifted in the silks as much as I could and felt the claustrophobic press of my cage.

"What of those in the village?" the Shadow King asked lazily.

"I've not heard back."

"Wait then."

"Neve!" Thyra hissed at my side. "What are we going to do?"

It was the first time she'd spoken to me since we'd found ourselves in this predicament. I couldn't see her face, but it was easy to imagine her expression, a storm of fury.

"Free him," I said softly. "It's the only way I can think of."

"Do you have an idea as to how?" Her quick acquiescence shocked me, but perhaps it shouldn't. I wasn't sure how deeply she felt toward me, but Thyra loved the rebels and did not want to see them dead.

"None."

"Me either. I—"

The wall rumbled, and the sound of rocks falling echoed

through the larger cavern—where the Shadow King and Falagog were talking.

Another whimper came from Ulfiel, and muffled shouts emerged from the other cocoons of silk.

"Neve! What's going on?" Vale shouted louder than the rest, or maybe I was just more inclined to hear his voice.

"We don't know!" I wished that, at the very least, I could twist and see the entrance of the cave we'd been placed in, but the silks prevented even that slight movement. "Rocks falling, for sure! Quiet so we can listen! I—"

A screech rang through the large cavern, raising the hairs on my arms. Was that . . . a bird?

The answer came a moment later when a white hawk zoomed into my field of vision.

"Arla!" Thyra screamed. "We're here! Help!"

The winged predator pivoted in midair only to soar out of the cave again.

"Do you think the other rebels are here?" I whispered.

Before Thyra could venture to guess, a roar sounded.

"Fire!" The Shadow King screamed, and I almost envisioned him running before remembering he was trapped within the Drassil.

A blast of heat pummeled down the hall, washing over all of us. My friends shouted in fear, still blinded by silks, still having no idea what was happening. On the back of their screams, a roar rang through the rock. I sucked in a breath.

"That had to have been Rynni!" I shouted. "They're here!"

How the dragon had gotten through the tunnels and found us so quickly was a mystery. One of many that formed in my mind as what had to be a hundred or so war cries filled the air.

"We're in here!" I screamed.

Thyra joined my shouting, but the others stayed quiet, perhaps knowing that their muffled cries would be unhelpful. My heart raced as the war cries continued, a symphony to the sound of metal hitting rock and spider shrieks.

Then, footsteps approached.

"Help! We're here! It's Neve!"

A moment later, a gasping Aleksander stopped in front of me. He was joined by an armored dwarf.

"Thordur!" I sucked in a breath as the prince took off his helmet. "How—"

"No time for talking. Aleksander, watch the opening."

My half-brother did so, as the Prince of Dergia turned to me. "There have got to be around seventy spiders out there. Thanks to your dragon friend, the big one is on fire, but she's still killing dwarves. Now, press your body back as far as you can."

I did so, and the prince's axe hooked onto the silk right at my nose. He pulled down, slicing through the spider silk so close to my skin that I barely dared to breathe. Despite the frigid temperature in the mountain caves, sweat formed between my breasts and along my forehead.

"*Zuprian* steel. Dwarven made, at that." When he cleared my face, neck, and belly, I allowed an exhale. "A good match for spider silks."

"Thank you." As he reached my legs, I had enough room to step out of the confinement. "I need to get my sword. We all do. Did you see weapons in the cavern?"

"I didn't. But I was only looking for you." He moved on to Thyra, freeing her too.

I nodded to the opposite wall. "Everyone there is with us."

"Fates," Thordur swore, but went to work, freeing each person we'd come with, taking great care as he did so. One by one, they emerged from the silks unharmed, but when Thordur cut through Ulfiel's prison, the rebel collapsed out of the cocoon of silk.

"No!" Thyra yelled and ran over to him.

"His heart stopped about three minutes ago," Freyia said softly. "I believe he was suffocating in there."

Tears pricked my eyes. Today, my sister had lost both Xillia and Ulfiel, both rebels who had joined her in this search. People loyal to her. She must feel so responsible for their deaths, but as Thordur came to my side, I knew there was no time for grief. We had to move.

"An army of dwarves is fighting for you. I will not risk them for longer than I need to." Thordur's hands gripped his axe. "We entered by the sunshaft, and we will leave the same way. Air workers are waiting with the dragon up top. They'll begin lifting those without wings to the shaft the moment they see you enter the cavern."

"I understand," I said and gestured to Ulfiel. "Can we take his body?"

Thyra sniffed and stood. "No. He's too large, and we won't be able to fight. He wouldn't want anyone to die just to bring his corpse back to Valrun. He hates it there."

I wasn't sure she believed that, but no one else put up a fight and with Aleksander and Thordur in the front, we rushed out of the small cave. When we reached the opening of the larger cavern, I gasped.

The dwarves had sent a small army, and in the middle of the melee, fighting right beside the imposing Valkyrjas, Halladora and Tonna, was a dwarf with such an extravagant helmet he could only be King Tholin. I watched in awe as the king sliced one ice spider in half with his battle-axe.

Falagog fought many dwarves and rebels, but she had also been hit by dragon flame *and* two gryphons had soared through the enlarged sunshaft to attack the mother spider too.

And still Falagog is nearly winning. My stomach plummeted as one dwarven soldier barely escaped being hurled into the cavern wall by her massive hairy leg.

"I see our weapons!" Vale pointed to the right.

They were all piled together, tossed carelessly at the base of the Drassil. Even though the Shadow Fae seemed to have retreated to wherever it was that he went deep within the tree, I didn't want to go anywhere near the Drassil. But we had to arm ourselves, so I shoved down my discomfort and sprinted for the weapons.

We reached the Drassil, and Vale immediately grabbed *Skelda* and Sassa's Blade. He handed the latter to me, while everyone else picked up whatever weapon they touched first.

"You have the Frør Crown?" I asked Thyra.

"Still in my pouch." She patted the bag hanging off her hip. When they'd captured us, the spiders took our weapons, but hadn't stripped anyone of their bags or clothing.

"Thank the Fates," I said. "I—"

"You have another chance!" The Shadow King appeared in the bark of the tree. Although the cavern was a cacophony of battle cries and the shrieking of spiders, somehow the Shadow Fae's voice carried all the way to my core. "Free me, and I won't hunt you. Free me, and I'll forgive those who came to find you."

I snorted and was about to retort, but Thyra had other ideas. She drew her sword back and slashed the blade against the tree, right at the Shadow Fae's throat.

Of course, just as the king had said when he taunted Vale, Thyra's sword did nothing to the creature inside the tree. In fact, he almost looked disappointed, his gaze flicking to me and, more pointedly, to Sassa's Blade. My heart stuttered.

He'd looked at my sword like that before. At first, I'd thought it was just because his mate had carried this very same sword, but now . . .

He's looking at it like he wishes I'd been the one to stab the tree with my sword. Can Sassa's Blade free him?

Immediately, I suspected that was the case, and I was glad I hadn't acted on my impulses of violence against the tree. But were there other ways to free him?

There have to be other ways if the Shadow King thought King Magnus might free him. Magnus didn't have Sassa's Blade, and he would have known it too.

"No one touches the tree again," I said quickly. "We don't know what will free him, and we need to run anyway."

The king glared at me and beneath the bark, though it seemed impossible, I swore that shadows churned. "Only the most remarkable magic can free me. Only the most powerful creatures."

Able to call shadows, Sassa's Blade was truly remarkable. Having gotten my answer, and wanting desperately to leave the cavern, I turned my back on him.

"I *will* find you," the Shadow Fae continued, his tone lower, more deadly in his promise of violence. "Mark my words, granddaughters. And when I do, you will rue the side you chose."

"Like you said, you have to get out first and that doesn't seem like your strong suit!" I shouted as a dozen spiders the size of direwolves scurried our way.

The Shadow King roared in fury, but we pivoted and with Vale, Prince Thordur, and Caelo in the lead, we rushed the spiders. Blades cutting and arching through the air, the best warriors took out the first wave of monsters. Two more died by arrows flying from above, archers positioned at the sunshaft. The rest of the eight-legged horrors leapt over Vale, Caelo, and Prince Thordur and extended their legs straight at our back line.

A web shot for my face. I ducked and thrust my sword up and forward. The spider coming for me skewered itself on my blade and dark, black blood ran down and onto my face.

"I'm going to be ill," I muttered, spitting spider blood from my mouth.

"We need to fly," Vale said, and I was relieved to find that while I'd been dealing with one attack, the others had already taken care of the rest of the spiders. "But why are so many dwarves still down here?"

"The air workers can only handle one or two at a time," Thordur said, as he pointed to the sunshaft. In addition to what seemed to be four air workers, gryphons were diving down, gathering dwarves and soaring upward. Only the king and a force of twenty or so remained, most of them still battling Falagog. "The moment they saw you enter this cavern, they were to begin the process, and it looks like they did, but we brought so many down here."

"Wings out," Vale said, scrutinizing the escape that was underway with the eyes of a male who'd led many battles. "The air workers are going too slow. We'll grab dwarves and carry as many of them as we can on our way out."

I slipped my wings out from the protection of the cloak.

"Neve, you take Thordur," Vale said.

I wanted to argue, because by giving me the dwarf farthest from Falagog, he was protecting me at the cost of everyone else.

"He's your ally's heir," Vale added, as if knowing what I was about to say.

I could not argue with that. Prince Thordur was an ally and a friend and as such, incredibly important to save.

If anyone else felt bitter about the favoritism, they did not show it, for as I rose into the air to do as Vale said, the others flew off to secure the dwarves fighting Falagog. "Grab my ankles and hold on, Thordur."

Thordur did so with one hand and continued to brandish his battle-axe with another.

"Just don't hit me with that thing. Here we go!" I beat my wings and rose slowly. But I was as strong as I'd ever been so while it took great effort to lift us both, I managed.

639

Sweat dripped down my face as I aimed for the sunshaft and rose higher and higher. Smaller spiders leapt out of the tunnels riddling the rock, four of which Thordur deflected with his axe. Three were felled by the archers above before they got close enough to harm us. We were in a moment of quiet when a rebel faerie healer dove from the hole above. She offered her leg to the prince.

The prince wasted no time situating his axe behind his back and grasping the healer's ankle. Together we flew for the hole, faster and stronger.

With the healer's help, we reached the hole quickly, soaring out together and then out of the way of those who were, hopefully exiting after us.

"Where are the others now? Close?" I asked, breathless not because I had been flying for my life, but due to the flaring of my magic. Outside the cavern, the ice spider's influence was nonexistent. My power was rushing back at full strength, stealing the air from my lungs.

"They're coming. Most are more than halfway here," said Sigri, another one of our Valkyrja, the dwarven member, who stared down into the hole and took careful aim with her bow. She loosed an arrow, and by the savage smile that lined her face, I was willing to bet that she hit her target. "Vale is nearly here. He's carrying two. The others are behind him, including four that the air workers are lifting. No more on the ground, but spiders keep leaping from those holes. That's what's slowing them."

"Everyone get ready to leave!" I yelled.

The rebels were mostly helping injured dwarves. Rynni waited, still in her dragon form, just a few paces from the sunshaft—poised to fly people to safety. Above, Arava and Lasvin flew in circles. Shocked as I was that the others had gotten the pegasi to come, I swore Arava's eyes brightened when I caught sight of her.

I joined Sigri at the hole and when I peered down, a relieved exhale parted my lips. Vale was so close, and holding onto his legs were the king and another dwarf.

Falagog was alive, but between Rynni's pointed attack and the dwarves axes, she'd sustained great damage. The mother spider lay on the cavern floor, her legs twitching and shuddering and two dozen of her children swarming her, presumably trying to help. I only wished they'd managed to end the bloodthirsty beast for good.

One after the other, Vale, Thyra, Luccan, and Caelo emerged from the hole, carrying dwarves in various states of injury. The King of Dergia released Vale's ankle and stood stoically, not a scratch to be seen on him.

Tonna and Halladora followed, neither of them had carried dwarves, though they'd been fighting off spiders leaping from tunnels the whole way up. As a result each Valkyrja was covered in dark spider blood.

Livia came next, emerging unharmed.

Thantrel rose right behind the vampire, and was nearly to the top when a spider the size of a boar leapt from one of the tunnels high in the rock. I screamed as the spider landed on Thantrel's back and tore into his wing.

Somehow Thantrel ripped the spider off his back, only for the creature to fall on the dwarf he carried. It knocked off the soldier's helmet, revealing none other than Princess Bavirra.

"Bleeding monster!" she shrieked and wriggled which did not help Thantrel, now injured, as he continued to fly for freedom.

"I have him!" Thyra leapt into the hole, wings spread and soared their way. When she reached them, she offered her own ankle not to Bavirra, but Thantrel. "Grab on!"

Thantrel did so, and I couldn't decide what shocked me more: that Princess Bavirra had been allowed to leave Dergia and fight or that Thyra was letting Thantrel touch her.

"Sister! What are you doing here?!" Thordur bellowed.

I winced, realizing how wrong I'd been. Bavirra was not here by permission. She'd snuck out. Disguised as a soldier no less. Both the Prince and King of Dergia glared down at their family member, a mixture of worry and anger in their eyes.

But there was no time for me to fixate on their family issues, for the next second, Thyra, Thantrel, and Bavirra appeared, followed closely by Astral and Freyia and their dwarves. Lastly the four soldiers being lifted by the air workers soared out of the sunshaft.

I double checked below. Everyone was out.

"Time to fly!" Sigri yelled when it became clear that King Tholin and the prince were in no shape to give commands. They were too focused on Bavirra.

Everyone dashed to a creature, just as Arava appeared at my side. She snorted, her eyes wide and wild as she cut a glance to the sunshaft.

"Ice spiders are one of the only creatures pegasi are terrified of," Aleksander said, mounting a nearby gryphon.

"But we needed more fliers for the dwarven army and told the creatures. Your pegasi seemed to understand you and your sister were in trouble. They recruited the gryphons."

My throat tightened. Arava and Lasvin hadn't fought the spiders, but they'd done what they could for my sister and me.

"Good girl," I mounted the pegasus.

"Everyone's up!" Vale yelled, from where he sat right up against Rynni's neck. "Ready to fly!"

"Fire, Rynni!" Thordur's voice boomed from above, where she circled the sunshaft on gryphonback.

Fire? What does that—

The answer came when the dragon lumbered toward the sunshaft hole and bent her neck so that her maw entered the hole. Heat built in the air, and I stiffened as what the Shadow Fae King told me came rushing back.

"Only the most remarkable magic can free me. Only the most powerful creatures."

Rynni had already targeted Falagog. This time, I had a hunch that she was going for utter destruction.

"No!" I yelled just as the dragon loosed her flame—one of two good ones that she had per day, or so she'd once told me.

The blast of heat made me recoil, and Arava launched into the sky.

"Wait. I need to see inside the mountain!" I yelled into the wind, and though I could tell she didn't want to Arava circled toward the shaft.

I peered down at the flame filling the cavern, and dread welled inside me.

Never could Rynni have known what her fire had the power to do. Dragon flame was *easily* one of the most destructive forces in our realm. A remarkable magic. From a powerful creature.

The Drassil was wildly aflame, just like everything else—living and dead—in the cavern. The purple leaves shriveling, the bark darkening, and as darkness coiled from the trunk of the tree, I felt my blood pound harder through me. Slowly, the inky tendrils extended out of the tree, as if stretching for the first time in many, many turns. The shadows expanded to fill the cavern, twisting and devouring the light in their path.

The Shadow King's low, menacing laugh filled my ears.

"I'll be seeing you soon, Princesses!" he boomed and a moment later, the tree split down the middle, the fire having done its damage.

The dragon beat her wings and rose. Arava did too, and once we were a safe distance from the mountain, I urged Arava toward the dragon. Vale caught my eyes, his face moon pale.

"We just did exactly what he wanted, didn't we?" He shouted into the wind "He's truly freed?"

I swallowed the lump rising in my throat and nodded. "I'm afraid so."

EPILOGUE

PRINCE RHISTEL AABERG, HEIR TO WINTER'S REALM, HOUSE OF THE WHITE BEAR

For days he waited. Lurked, listened, and prepared. Trapped in his mother's powers, Prince Rhistel bided his time, waiting for the moment she would least suspect his escape. His turn of fate.

His leashing of *her*.

The queen was confident in her whisperer magic, as she should be. However, her firstborn son had also grown in his magic. For over a turn, he'd been practicing without the queen's knowledge. Rhistel was now as good as his mother. As powerful.

And far more ruthless.

He needed only to wait until the right time to test this belief, to slip out from under her thumb.

What would he do when he regained his freedom?

Turn on the female who birthed him, certainly, for while she'd suppressed his mind, he'd also learned of her past. All of it. Every traitorous inclination. Queen Inga could not be trusted, not for what the heir wished to put into motion.

Once his mother was indisposed, Lord Riis and Saga would be next. Saga—darling of the realm—would not be allowed to take what Rhistel had worked for all his life. Then, with those threats neutralized, he'd speak with his father.

Surely, the king would not harm the male he thought to be his son. After all, King Magnus was a bastard brought up by a male who was not his father. The king, though lacking in honor in many regards, would act honorably in this instance.

If not, Rhistel had the power to deal with Magnus Aaberg. To make the king a puppet on a string until such a time when Rhistel arranged the king's death and claimed the crown for himself.

The only person he did not know precisely what to do with was Vale.

As often as the twin princes did not see eye to eye, they once had. They'd once been true brothers. Rhistel saw in his mother's mind that Vale had learned they were bastards. Could this unfortunate truth bring them back together?

As long as he forsakes his whore. Which I can get him to do.

Yes, if it came down to it, when he met his twin again, Rhistel would whisper the Warrior Bear. Getting rid of Neve would be easy enough when Vale believed he no longer wanted her at all.

He'd have his twin back and a strong protector. A good plan, if he did say so himself.

Rhistel tested the shackles around his mind again, finding his mother's power there, but not as strong as before. There were chinks in her armor.

She was tiring. He was waiting.

He'd strengthen for a few more days before breaking free and seizing his fate the stars seemed determined to strip from his grasp.

BONUS STORY

I hope you enjoyed A Hallow of Storm and Ruin!

There are many stories going on at one time in this kingdom. Thantrel's and Thyra's heist in Bitra did not fit structurally into A Hallow of Storm and Ruin, but I wanted to write it anyway. So here it is, as a bonus story, for your enjoyment.

All the magic,

Ashley McLeo

CHAPTER ONE

LORD THANTREL RIIS, HOUSE OF THE ICE SPIDER

"I reject our bond, Thantrel Riis."

Those six words, coming from her beautiful lips, cut me far deeper than any blade ever could.

I took a half-step back, staring at the black-haired beauty with piercing ice-blue eyes, hoping I'd heard her wrong. Placing a hand over my heart, I closed my eyes and prayed to the dead gods I'd so often mocked with my actions that this wasn't true. That it wasn't really happening.

When I opened my eyes again, Thyra Falk had left, and a fresh wash of pain flooded me, entering every crook and crevice of my body and soul so thoroughly, I would not be surprised if I never felt another emotion.

Many fae surrounded me, their eyes wide, and lips parted, unsure what to say. One male with honey-brown eyes and golden-brown skin had entered with Thyra and now watched me with blatant pity.

Since we arrived at Valrun Castle, I'd been feeling . . . off. Strange in a way I couldn't quite describe. Energized, desperate to move, to act, and with the distinct feeling that something I wanted—no something *I needed*—was right around the corner. Until Thyra appeared, I didn't know what that something was. A person, the other half of my soul.

The moment I saw her, the strange searching sensation stopped. I'd found her. Thyra, Neve's sister, was my mate.

And she'd rejected me.

CHAPTER TWO
THYRA, LEADER OF THE REBELLION

The cold, cracked wood of my door creaked loudly as I pressed my back against it. My chest felt tight as I tried to catch my breath. Tried not to explode.

Anger and anguish warred within me in equal parts, and no matter which one won, I couldn't let anyone watch me falling apart. Leaders did not fall apart.

"You're only fae. We all bend and break at some point. If you don't, I'm not sure that you're living." Brynhild's often-uttered words of wisdom filtered through my mind, her voice calm and familiar.

Brynhild was the faerie who saved me from certain death by the hands of the White Bear and raised me as her own youngling. Often, she'd said those very words to me when things got to be too much. When I felt the weight of the kingdom on my shoulders and rushing against me like a wicked winter wind—both feelings I'd experienced since I was only nine turns old.

But no matter how much I loved Brynhild, nor how

much I took her other advice to heart, I would not allow myself to believe that line. My family had been murdered and taken from me. I'd been forced to flee and live in hiding. And now, I was the leader of a rebellion. So many had sustained injuries, or even gave their lives because they believed in me as a leader.

Falling apart? They didn't deserve a leader who fell to pieces, and since my sister's arrival, I'd been close to doing so too many times.

Build the wall.

I stood in my small and drafty, but private, crumbling tower room. However, in my mind, block by block, a wall of ice formed around me. This frigid room was one of my safe places where I privately handled things. Or tried to.

Frustratingly enough, my usual method of calming my nerves didn't work. My hands clenched and my chest grew tighter and tighter. Since Neve and her friends had arrived, I'd failed in that often. Today, a red-haired male peeked over the wall before I finished building it, shattering the illusion of my control over myself.

My throat constricted and hot tears threatened to fall. I wiped them away, went to my bed—a rickety old thing— and face-planted, furious that this was happening.

Once or twice as a youngling, I'd played pretend with others my age. In the game, we all found our mate while undertaking some epic adventure or at an elaborate ball, but that was the only time I'd considered such a thing happening. To have and find a mate was simply uncommon. That my mother and father had been mates and found each other seemed so exceptional, like they might have taken all the luck of my bloodline. Of course, that was proven wrong when Neve arrived, and I saw she and the prince bore identical mate marks.

That *I* had a mate too was unbelievable, but the moment that long-haired, too-pretty-for-his-own-good male had landed in front of me, I'd recognized him just as easily as he'd recognized me. My heart had *sung* for Frea's sake!

I'd shut down that reaction, though, knowing I had no time for a mate. He would only be a distraction. Perhaps he might even lead to the demise of all I'd worked for.

Certainly, Thantrel Riis would hinder my ability to wed for an alliance—a far-fetched idea considering the current state of the kingdom, but one I held on to all the same.

I had a kingdom to take back. People to save. A mate would only get in the way.

Worse, he's the spymaster's son. So tied to the White Bear! This could put the rebels in danger.

Another thought struck. Thantrel's father was now the lord of the castle that once belonged to House Skau. My mother's ancestral house. My blood boiled at the idea of a new family, one that had undoubtedly backstabbed my own to earn such a high place in society, living lavishly at the castle in Bitra.

I growled and rolled over, half wishing to blame this turn of events on Neve. But I couldn't. Anyone could identify the shock on her face when Thantrel spoke. If he'd had any idea that we were mates, he hadn't told a soul before announcing it to so many in the training hall.

I'd heard from others that the tall, lithe, Riis brother never kept his mouth shut. That he was too loud. Too much.

Having just met him, I was inclined to agree.

A knock came at my door, soft and in a cadence I recognized in my bones.

"What?" I yelled, sounding far too much like the whiny teenager from a decade past.

"Might I come in?" Brynhild asked.

I didn't answer right away, but she seemed to take my silence as an invitation. The door creaked open, and Brynhild walked inside. Her wooden leg echoed when it hit the floorboards as she came to sit on the bed with me.

"Bac told me what happened. Do you wish to talk about it?"

I glared. "Talk about the fact that my mate is here, and his father works with my enemy? That his father has, on *many occasions*, been the reason so many of our friends died? No, I do not wish to talk about that."

"But what of the male himself? Thantrel, I believe his name is?"

A scowl took over my face. Even his name sent my heart fluttering. "That's what he said."

"The son didn't do those things, Thyra. You're not one to be distracted from what you want, but this might be a boon in more than one way."

"Please, just don't," I whispered. "I cannot accept a mating bond. Not now."

"That doesn't mean you can't ever."

"I already rejected him."

A beat of silence passed between us, and Brynhild took one of my hands in hers. She was one of the few fae I'd allow to touch me in this way.

"Your mother didn't send you fleeing from Frostveil so you'd live as we have all these turns, Thyra. She wished to save you so you'd live a life full of love. He may be inconvenient, but a mate is the truest love one can hope for."

"My mother should have fled the castle with me," I whispered. "With *Isolde and me.*"

Using my sister's birth name was unintentional, but it felt far more true to me. Would Neve ever be able to feel the same?

Brynhild swallowed, nodded. "I told her as much, but Queen Revna knew she'd not make it far. Too many knew who she was, and she loved you too much to trap you and your sister."

"She made a mistake," I murmured. "The truth is, love blinds us, and I can't afford to have blinders on." I caught Brynhild's eyes. "I rejected him, and I stand by my choice. Now, I know you came to help me, but please, leave. I want to be alone."

Brynhild loosed a sigh, but did as I requested, leaving my room, leaving me to pull myself together and pretend like my heart wasn't breaking into a million pieces.

CHAPTER THREE

LORD THANTREL RIIS, HOUSE OF THE ICE SPIDER

DAYS LATER

My mate rode at the head of the column, her back straight and proud as the fae of Vitvik stared and whispered at our passing. Thyra was regal without even meaning to be and though she'd repeatedly made it clear that she wanted nothing to do with me, I loved her for it. Loved her for all that she was without even meaning to.

The truth made my wings tighten beneath the thick fur cloak protecting them from the cold. Long days had passed since my mate rejected me, many of which I'd spent in a drunken stupor. In fact, I'd still be drunk if not for the coinary heists we were about to undertake.

In no way would I allow my mate to put herself in such danger while I just sat at Valrun castle, drunk and wallowing in my heartbreak. I might not be what Thyra wanted, she might even hate me, but I'd never be able to live with myself if I did that.

And though I tried not to admit it to myself, I kept

thinking that maybe, *just maybe*, if I showed Thyra I was someone worth knowing, someone worth loving, she'd change her mind and accept our bond.

A few horses ahead, one horse that was smaller than the others stopped and allowed the others in our group to pass. The outline of the form riding the horse made it obvious who it was.

"Duran." I neared the dwarf, who began to ride alongside me.

"Thantrel." The dwarf, a close friend of Luccan's, nodded at me. "Feeling alright after yesterday?"

When I'd tried to approach Thyra yet again and she'd reiterated her disinterest. The memory made my heart ache.

"I'm upright. Hoping I might change her mind today."

Duran arched his eyebrows. "Finding the Frør Crown in Avaldenn will do that?"

I don't plan on going to Avaldenn at all.

Of course I didn't say that. I only laughed. "That will probably be Neve who does the finding. I'm only hoping to do something brilliant that will catch Thyra's attention."

The dwarf's lips twitched. "She's intelligent. It will take more than you're used to giving."

"Hey!"

"Not that you're unintelligent," Duran amended. "Quite the opposite, actually. But those you choose as bed partners are . . . how do I say this politely . . . ?

"Don't." I frowned, though what he said was true. I didn't have a record of choosing my romantic entanglement based on the power of their brains.

Duran smiled, an unusual reaction. The dwarf only

smiled so unguardedly at members of the cabal, which I was not a part of. Perhaps he smiled at those in the House of Wisdom too, though I couldn't be sure. I'd only set foot in the drab, cold place once and vowed never to return.

"More than feeling the heartbreak, it's odd," I admitted, before I even knew I was doing so.

"What's that?"

"I've never had to work for affection before. And I'm not even sure what I'm doing will affect her, but it's all I can think of doing. Be a hero. Help her. Be devoted. Let her know I will love her forever."

I looked away. Stars, I felt like such an idiot admitting such things. Even if they were truths I felt all the way down in my bones. No one could compare to my mate. I understood that much just by being in her presence.

Duran cleared his throat. "I can't relate to that, but I've been heartbroken before too. She wasn't my mate—just another scholar I fell for. I have to admit, I admire you being out of bed right now."

I twisted to face him again. "A romance in the House of Wisdom?"

"Learning isn't the only thing that happens in those vast libraries."

A smirk crossed my lips and for the first time in days, I laughed. The feeling was light and so good. A slight relief.

Ahead, others turned. I didn't miss the expressions of astonishment on my brother's faces.

Nor, if my plan worked, would it be the last time they'd wear such expressions today.

CHAPTER FOUR
THYRA, LEADER OF THE REBELLION

P assing through the gateway felt strange, unlike anything I'd experienced before. However, when I stepped into the castle on the other side, that oddness fell away.

Blue and copper decor gave the room I'd stepped into, a sitting room, a calming ambience. Bookshelves lined each wall, and the panels in-between were lined with tapestries, paintings, and a singular statue of a female faerie with an aura owl perched on her raised hand.

My eyebrows pinched together. *Midnight blue. Copper. Aura owls . . . Not an ice spider in sight. Has the Riis family not changed everything?*

The colors and the animal belonged to House Skau, remnants of my murdered family line. My mother's blood. While I always made it a point to call this place Castle Skau in front of the Riis males, that name was no longer accurate anywhere but in my heart. Most of the kingdom called it by the official name of Eruhall.

"Would that we had time to visit the library," Duran the dwarf whispered, looking around. "I've heard wondrous things about it. The offerings from this library impress even the Vishkus."

Of course they were, for House Skau had been known as the noble House of Scholars. Brynhild taught me that in the past, each generation of House Skau had sent a member to the House of Wisdom, and they always journeyed to Avaldenn with a book from the Skau's personal library. My mother had been one such offering to the House of Wisdom. She'd intended on becoming a Master Healer, but then she'd met Harald Falk, and everything changed. Revna Skau had gone from a noble fae studying healing to a Queen of Winter's Realm.

And now she's dead.

The anger I felt every time I thought of my family, dead at the hands of a kinslayer, was a wild and raging thing. I'd become practiced at not showing the simmering fury inside me, but it was always there.

"What are *you* doing here?" shouted Halladora, our party's glamourist, and one of the best warriors in the rebellion. "You're supposed to go to Avaldenn!"

I spun, and when I saw who she was talking to, I forgot how to breathe. Thantrel stood there, watching me, a closed gateway at his back.

"Change of plans," he said.

"Open the gateway and go back," I said through gritted teeth. "You're putting us at risk."

"On the contrary." He strode closer, as if he had a death wish. "I'd be putting those in Avaldenn at risk if I went with them because I'd be thinking of you the entire time. Wondering if my mate was safe." Thantrel came to a stop in front of me, his back straight and proud, and his delicious scent filling my nostrils.

I narrowed my eyes. "*We're not together.* Why can't you get that through your skull?!"

"I know that, but I'm a fae male. I can't ignore the urge to protect you, and I will not turn away. Not this time. I'm coming with you."

We stared each other down, and I tried not to notice his stupid gold eyeliner. It looked the same every day, which led me to believe it was magically applied, and annoyingly it wasn't horrible. Rather, the liner brightened his pretty olive eyes.

I hated this male for the predicament he put me in, but even more so for how beautiful he was. It made denying him over and over and over more difficult.

Halladora, the glamourist in my party, cleared her throat. "I'm already done glamouring the vampires to make them appear more fae, as well as small bits for Duran and Sigri. As the Riis male—sorry, maybe it's males?—don't need glamours, and you don't want one, we're ready, Thyra."

"And already wasting too much time," Duran added as a bell chimed the hour outside. "The coinary will only be open for another two bells, and we might have to wait to get into the vault level, right?"

"Right," Arie said. "The thing is, Thyra, you could send Thantrel back, but I know my brother and his antics. He won't go quickly, and we need to move."

"Bleeding skies! Fine," I shouted, throwing my hands to the ceiling. "You're on point because if you're going to force yourself down my throat, you might as well be useful."

"I plan on more than proving myself, princess," Thantrel replied.

"Don't call me that," I said childishly. As long as I was with trusted people, I didn't care if others called me princess. It was more the way he said it . . . like it was a pet name.

"Arie, show us out of the castle." I turned my back on Thantrel and waved at the door. "We have a vault to break into."

CHAPTER FIVE

LORD THANTREL RIIS, HOUSE OF THE ICE SPIDER

"You owe Arie and me," Duran whispered as we left the sitting room behind the others in our group.

"Don't I know it." I exhaled. "I don't expect anyone to be happy about my choice to shoot an arrow in the plan, but I needed to be here."

"I would be surprised if you felt otherwise." Duran shrugged.

Eruhall was fairly empty, which was normal for the castle. Though it was my father's noble seat, he rarely visited the city of Bitra. He preferred to stay in Avaldenn, as did my brothers and I. So Eruhall ran with a skeleton staff, all of whom my father ensured were very loyal.

Tarlu, the first member of staff and also one of the oldest and most steadfast, having come from serving my father at Riis Tower, was so shocked when he came upon us he jumped. Then he fell into a deep bow.

"My lords, we didn't know you were visiting today," the butler said.

No questions. No mention of how we had arrived unseen. Just as father liked it. If the servants suspected we had a gateway in Eruhall, they never said such a thing. At least not to my family's face.

"We have an errand to run, but will leave right after," Arie said.

"Of course, my lord. Will you need a sleigh?"

"No, thank you."

Tarlu left, and we continued on our way. We approached the main door to the castle when Thyra pointed above.

"Why are those all still up?" She asked as if she didn't want to but was also unable to hold back her words.

I glanced above. Stone effigies of the aura owls watched us. In fact, they still lined many of the larger corridors.

"Do you dislike them?" Arie asked.

Thyra snorted. "It's not that. I don't understand why your house kept them. They belong to my mother's bloodline."

Arie shrugged. "We're almost never here, and Father did very little to the castle when he came into possession."

Our father had instructed that the color scheme be changed in the most trafficked rooms. He'd added stone ice spiders here and there to show that our family claimed the castle, but mostly, he'd left the decor alone.

"That's strange," Thyra said.

Arie shrugged, and I could not help but add, "We spend the vast majority of our time in Avaldenn."

Thyra didn't turn, didn't even acknowledge that I'd been the one to speak when she asked, "You didn't even grow up here?"

I laughed, even though the disregard cut me up inside. The laughter must have shocked her because it got her to turn around. "Arie, Luccan, and I basically grew up in a brothel."

Thyra's eyes widened slightly, and I swore I could see a question on the tip of her tongue, but she turned away from me, and we continued walking to the door of the castle in silence.

Outside, the cold wrapped around us, though I noted it was warmer than the area around Valrun. And definitely warmer than Avaldenn with the never-ending winds coming in off the Shivering Sea.

Bitra was in the east of the kingdom, right off the River Skatuá, which provided freshwater for the city. It was one of the nicer cities in the realm, though it lacked the excitement of Avaldenn. I thought it might be my fourth choice for a place to live after the capital, Grindavik, and Myrr.

The streets were relatively empty, as most fae were preparing for, or already, eating their evening meal. Just as we'd hoped. Fewer witnesses if things went wrong. The coinary loomed only a couple of streets away from the castle, so the building, white and expensive looking, came into view in no time.

"The river is over there, right behind the building," Arie said for Halladora's, Sigri's, and Livia's benefit. "The mechanism the coinary uses is marked by their signature cauldron. Should be easy enough to spot."

"On it," Halladora said, and the trio split off from us to wait by the river.

Like all coinaries, this one had strong magical protections. Unlike other coinaries run by the leprechauns, the Bitra location used the river to maximum effect. Had our family not possessed a vault here, as well as in Avaldenn, we wouldn't know such a thing, but the leprechauns were required to tell vault holders certain secrets.

One such secret was that the vault area had motion sensing spells, so the leprechauns always knew if someone was down there—whether or not they should be. The much larger secret, however, was that should there be a break-in at the coinary, the hallways the vaults were off of would be flooded, using the water from the River Skatuá. What was more, the leprechauns kept water monsters below and those monsters' cages would shatter, allowing the beasts to swim within the river water and attack thieves.

Halladora, Sigri, and Livia would wait by the river in case an alarm sounded. They would be able to stop the leprechauns in charge of diverting water into the vaults. Or that was the plan.

"Than, you may as well join me," Arie said. In the original plan, he was to be the one to request access to the family vault. It would look odd to hang back, so I joined my brother.

Astril, Duran, and Thyra, all in nondescript clothing and black cloaks, would act as a merchant group interested in buying something from my family. A vampire, unlike fae, could outright lie, so Astril would be playing the lead part. She'd also later compel the leprechaun who showed us down to the vaults so he or she would not sound the alarm.

"Let the show begin," I muttered as my brother and I pushed open the coinaries' large double doors.

CHAPTER SIX
THYRA, LEADER OF THE REBELLION

T hantrel and Arie took the lead down the long, grand hallway that led into the heart of the coinary.

As much as I disliked that Thantrel had forced himself upon us, with a few more minutes to reflect upon the intrusion, I thought it might be a boon. Arie was a lord, the same as Thantrel, but the latter had a presence Arie lacked. A charm and a way with people. We might need that today.

"Masters Riis," a leprechaun rose from his desk, one of the first in the main room where his kind saw clients, and approached. "What brings you in?"

The Coinmaster was tall for his kind, more rounded too, and with long white hair down to his knees. He walked slowly but confidently on bowed legs. I'd put a few golden bears down that he'd been in the profession for many, many turns.

"Coinmaster Gorun." Thantrel stopped before the leprechaun and inclined his head. "A pleasure. We're here to access the family vault." He gestured to the rest of us. "As you can see, we've brought others. They're interested in the contents of the vault."

Carefully chosen words that were Astril's cue to slide forward.

"The Masters Riis have items that my company is interested in purchasing."

Coinmaster Gorun nodded. "Your business?"

"Traveling merchants," Astril replied smoothly.

I'd been anxious and angry when Neve presented me with the vampire sisters, but already, I was seeing the benefit of having bloodsuckers working with the rebels. Had our party been composed of only fae, we'd have to consider our words far more carefully.

"I've spoken with the Lord of Tongues about certain items we're interested in purchasing for a family in the elven court," Astril continued. "The high lord himself is, of course, too busy to come to Bitra, but sent his sons to open the vault so we might examine the items in person." She waved back towards me and Duran, and I offered a confident smile to the leprechaun as he took us in.

"Very well," Coinmaster Gorun replied. "You're in luck. No one else is below right now. I shall get my cauldron, and we can descend."

He left, and I allowed a slight exhale. Once we were below, as the leprechauns called the vault area, Astril could compel Gorun without the other leprechauns noticing. The rest should be easy—as long as no alarm went off.

The coinmaster returned, and we followed him to a door at the far end of the rectangular room. I had never held a vault at a coinary, but I'd heard from others what to expect, so I wasn't surprised when Coinmaster Gorun opened the door to a staircase and utter darkness.

"Watch your step." With a wave of Gorun's hand, faelights illuminated all the way down.

Even with the added light, the steps were narrow and steep, and I did indeed have to watch myself. When we reached the bottom, the Coinmaster placed his hand on a door. Runes glowed, and the door opened. From what Arie had told us, the vaults were located over this threshold.

I cast a glance at Astril. The moment had come for her to do her work.

As smooth as water rushing over ice, the vampire slipped through the Riis brothers to walk behind Gorun as we entered The Below.

"Coinmaster Gorun?" Astril spoke as though she were about to request something of him, and dutifully, the leprechaun turned.

The moment the vampire's compulsion took over was obvious to all. Gorun stiffened, his eyes glazed over slightly, and his jaw went slack before Astril remedied those tells and gave the leprechaun some composure.

"Take us to the Riis vault first," Astril said because that was the plan, if only to make everything Thantrel had said the truth. "Then that of House Skau."

If Gorun found the request odd, it didn't show on his face. He nodded and continued on, marching through a tunnel in his bandy-legged way.

A shudder ripped through me. Vampires held far too much power for my liking. How had my sister dealt with them for so many turns? And how had she allowed the three sworn to us into her heart so quickly? In so many ways, my sister was vastly different from me.

The hallway we'd entered opened up once again, and we found ourselves in a circular room with corridors branching off in every direction. Well, every direction except for one.

As the Riis brothers had said there would be, to my left, next to the hall we'd entered through, was a large glass cage built into the underground wall. Inside the cage swam a muddy brown sea serpent with gleaming yellow eyes locked on us.

Imaginary claws raked down my spine. The serpent had to be at least fifty paces long, his head the size of an eight-person sleigh, and the many jagged teeth that filled that large skull were as tall as me.

As if the creature knew I was examining its teeth, the serpent opened its mouth into what I could only describe as a macabre smile, and slammed its muscular tail against the glass. The barrier shook violently, but held.

"Stars alive," Duran whispered. "That is hideous."

"The cage must be enchanted to the afterworld. And go very deep into the ground," Astril added. She had halted Gorun while we took in the area because he stood there, like a puppet.

"It does," Thantrel replied. "I asked during my first visit and got a very thorough explanation of how they made it happen. There are more creatures in that cage too. He's the dominant one. And those," he pointed up and for the first time, I noticed small glass circles above, "are where the river water would come through if the alarm sounded. See how the influx of water would be positioned to strike the serpent's cage? Once the water from the river hits at the speed it would tunnel through, the glass breaks."

I swallowed, knowing what happened after that. The room we stood in and the corridors leading to the vaults would be flooded, the door leading into this area locked down, the sea serpent and other monsters were released, and whoever lurked down here at the time drowned. Or they became monster food. Though we'd been told all this before, it was different being here and seeing it for myself. I wanted to get out of here as quickly as possible.

"Let's go," I said, and we moved on, following Gorun down the center corridor, which I noticed was wide and tall enough for the giant serpent to swim through. The leprechauns missed nothing when they developed their theft deterrents.

The Riis vault was quite a ways down the hall, but when we reached it, my heart soared. The ice spider on the door indicated Arie and Thantrel's noble house, just as the face of the aura owl on the door across from their vault had to indicate House Skau's holdings.

"Did you know they were so close?" I asked, gesturing to the vault that belonged to my mother's house.

"I haven't been here for many turns, so no." Arie shook his head.

"Me either," Thantrel replied. "But it makes sense, as now our house holds the same standing that House Skau once did."

My jaw tightened. Admittedly, the Riis brothers seemed

like good-natured fae. Even Thantrel, though he had many annoying quirks to be sure. What I did not like was the reminder that their house had replaced my mother's birth house, which I knew they were not responsible for, but it still angered me. Why had House Riis risen so high and so quickly? What had they done to earn that honor?

I put the questions out of my mind, for they did no good for me now, and stood aside as Arie performed the ritual to enter his family vault. A little blood dripped into Gorun's cauldron, and the leprechaun's hand pressed on the door, and the vault opened to reveal gold, jewels, and items of great value. The brothers entered and filled the pouches they wore with gold and jewels.

"Want to buy this?" Thantrel asked Astril as he held up a small figurine.

Out of all the items in the vault, it looked to have the least worth, but fae could not lie without hindering their magic so this was all part of the plan.

"A silver stag for it?" Astril asked with a grin as the brothers exited their vault and the door closed behind them.

"Done." Thantrel tossed her the figurine, and she reciprocated with the coin.

Astril turned to the leprechaun. "I have made a purchase, and now we'd like to enter that vault." She nodded to the Skau vault.

"Do you have an heir to House Skau?" The leprechaun held out his cauldron.

"We do." I stepped forward, and took his proffered blade, poked my pinky finger, and allowed a few drops to enter the cauldron. The inside of the magical container glowed blue, and Gorun placed his hand on the second vault.

The door, however, did not open. Rather, the eyes of the aura owl blinked and the creature that once symbolized my mother's house before its demise spoke.

"Blood of the House Skau, you've come to collect what is yours?"

I swallowed. "I've come to access this vault, yes."

The metallic owl blinked, as though shocked by the answer. "I thought I'd never speak to one of my house again."

"I'm one of only two survivors."

Anguish rippled across the owl's face. "The cauldron tells me you're Revna's girl?"

"I am. My twin also lives."

The owl nodded as much as he could, being a piece of metal inside a door. "I'm happy to hear that. Now, to access this vault, you must first answer a riddle."

No one had been sure what to expect, but it wasn't unheard of for the highest noble families to add extra protections to their vaults. As House Skau had been known to be scholarly, we'd guessed that any additional protections they would have added might have been in that vein. We were right.

"Can anyone help me?" I asked. We'd brought Duran and Arie because they were well read and even if we hadn't known what to expect, it seemed prudent. I hoped the owl would let them help me if I needed it.

"With help from others, you must answer two riddles."

"Fine. No one helps unless I ask," I said, wanting to leave as quickly as possible. "What's the riddle?"

"I am born in fear, raised in truth, and I come to serve the cause of need."

My heart raced, but I could not allow such a thing. I had only one shot here.

A slow breath left my nose, forcing my heart to slow, pulling me back from the brink of panic. *Work it out, bit by bit.*

Born in fear. When I was scared, I either wanted to run or fight. Those were the options I'd start with. I moved on to *raised in truth.*

My head tilted as I considered. When I was right about something, and *I knew* I was right, I was unmovable. Even in the face of large obstacles. Or. . . I linked the second line to the first—fear. When I knew I was right, or in the owl's words was *raised in truth*, I was also unmovable in fear.

Or maybe more like I was a fighter? *Fearless?*

I gasped as the answer became clear. Obvious and designed as though for me, a fae who would need much of this very thing in the future.

Just in case, I ran through the last part in my head. Yes, I was right. I was sure of it.

"I have the answer," I whispered, a smile blooming on my face.

"Then speak it," the owl replied.

"Courage."

The vault door swung open.

CHAPTER SEVEN

LORD THANTREL RIIS, HOUSE OF THE ICE SPIDER

The contents of the Skau family vault glittered and gleamed. So many jewels and coins, piled as tall as me, and those hills separated by random objects—some mundane in appearance, some extravagant. No matter what they looked like, I was certain each object in here was of high value.

I wonder if anything in here was purchased from Father?

Before he became a high lord, Leyv Riis was a merchant of fine goods. He'd sold jewels to Queen Revna when she was alive. And once her identity came out, he told us Neve had even worn a phoenix opal he'd sold the Falk queen to the Courting Festival Ball. According to my father, that night, Neve had looked so like her mother that our father had begun to question things. Perhaps Queen Revna's birth family had bought other things from him?

"If the Frør Crown is in here, I'm guessing it will be prominently placed, or hidden within something that would protect it," Thyra said. "So I don't think we need to dig through piles of gold."

I agreed with her and such reasoning would cut down the search time.

"Gorun, stay on the threshold of the vault," Astril said as we entered the vault and split up to search.

I stayed close to Thyra, but not too close, for I did not wish to push my luck. So while she took one path, I took a parallel one through the piles of gold.

Still, I could not help but steal glances at my mate as we searched. The way her black hair caught on the faelights still following us around, and how her ice-blue eyes searched with intent—it was all so sexy. Everything about her was designed to captivate me, and she did so easily. It was inevitable that she'd catch me during one of my longing glances, and catch me she did.

"You're going to miss the Crown if you keep staring at me." Thyra twisted toward a cabinet; its dusty doors closed for so many turns. "And that's not something I can forgive."

"Apologies," J said, because what else could I say? She'd made her position clear, and I simply did not want to believe this was my reality.

Thyra tried the doors to the cabinet. It didn't budge, and she swore. "Keep searching. I want to get out of here. The sea serpent creeped me out."

I was about to walk a few paces and linger in a more unobtrusive manner when she tried the doors again, and I stopped, a glimmer of recognition sparking in my mind.

Carved into the doors was the figure of a banshee, one bony hand outstretched. Ruby eyes and onyx stones created an elaborate cloak. A memorable one too. Finally, I recalled why this piece struck me as familiar. My father had sold that very cabinet to House Skau. It was one of his more memorable sales, not because the cabinet was so beautiful.

But because a banshee was trapped inside. One whose song not only foretold death but brought the never-ending night to those who heard it.

I opened my mouth to warn Thyra, but she'd already used her magic to freeze the handles—and was preparing to strike the metal again with magic. A strike that would, undoubtedly, break the door open.

"No!" My wings snapped out, and I soared over the pile of gold as she blasted the cabinet with her winter magic.

The next seconds passed in slow motion. The cabinet shattered at the lock, and a low laugh rang through the air.

Thinking fast, I blasted Thyra to the side, and then pushed a wave of air at the lock, creating a shield. When I landed, Thyra had regained her footing. She stormed over to me and slammed her palm against my chest. I fell backwards into the cabinet, and not wishing to test the limits of my shield, I grabbed her hand, pulled her closer.

Her breath hitched, but a scowl covered it up. "What in the afterlife was that about?"

Her skin on mine, my hand touching her arm, it sent a fire rushing through me. With great effort, I doused the flames, not wishing to anger her further.

I nodded back to the cabinet. "There's a banshee inside that thing. One with a song that doesn't only foretell death but kills anyone who hears it."

"How do you know?"

"Because my father sold it to House Skau many turns ago, before the rebellion. Look at the carving." I moved away from the cabinet, drawing her with me, still very aware I was touching her and soon her anger would subside, and she'd realize it too and pull away. "A banshee, see?"

Thyra stared at the cabinet, swallowed. "You're sure?"

"Positive."

"Well, I—" she looked up at me, and no anger remained in those ice-blue eyes. "Thank you, Thantrel."

She retracted her hand. I drew breath, regretting that we were no longer touching.

"You saved me, and now I'm in your debt."

I wanted to say that it was my duty as her mate. That I would always do so. That to see her die would kill me, and she didn't owe me a thing.

Instead, I nodded. "Of course."

Thyra exhaled, took a step back. "Will your shield hold?"

"It will, for a while. I'll have Astril tell Gorun to fix the cabinet before we leave—for the safety of anyone who comes here in the future."

"Right." Thyra spun and stared out over the gold. "What if there are more dangerous objects? I didn't think about that."

"It's not unheard of for noble houses to have dangerous objects," I replied. "My father has told us about many."

She let out a soft hum. "Maybe there is a better way to do this?"

"The leprechauns have registers of what objects are in each vault, but that means going back up and asking."

Thyra's eyes brightened at the mention of the scrolls documenting the contents of each vault and its value. "But they may not be the only ones who know what's in this vault." Her wings snapped out, and she flew over the gold, back to the door.

Unable to help myself, I followed, and when she landed in front of the owl, right next to a placid Gorun, I understood.

"Can I ask you a question?" Thyra spoke to the owl.

"You may."

"Do you know the contents of this vault?"

"I have seen every item brought in and taken out of this vault."

"Do you remember them? "

The owl looked offended. "Of course I do."

"Is the Frør Crown inside? Do you know what that is?"

The owl paused for an instant that seemed like an eternity. "A Hallow has never entered House Skau's vault."

Tension I hadn't known I'd been holding left my body. We had certainty now.

Footsteps sounded, and at their echo, Thyra shot me a frantic look and scurried inside the door. Together, we peeked around the door right as another leprechaun appeared down the hall.

"Gorun! Is all well? We got a notice that the Skau vault is open, and seeing as you're in the doorway, it seems true! What's going on?"

I cast a wild glance around for Astril, and found her flying towards us, jaw set in a hard line.

"Gorun?" the other leprechaun cried out again. "Should I sound the alar—oh!"

Astril burst from the vault and soared for the leprechaun before he could turn around. She caught him, and his body went slack with compulsion.

"Fill your pockets with gold!" Thyra yelled. "We have to go!"

She began scooping up gold from the nearest pile. I wanted to tell her it wasn't necessary, but then again, after all this, I wouldn't be entering a coinary any time soon.

I, too, began grabbing up handfuls of gold, and once we were weighed down with the stuff, Astril commanded the second leprechaun to wait below while Gorun showed us the way to the top level of the coinary.

Heart racing, I jogged alongside the others. Our time in Bitra was up.

CHAPTER EIGHT
THYRA, LEADER OF THE REBELLION

The moment we exited the coinary, my shoulders loosened. The cold winter air had never felt so good.

Astril had commanded Gorun to wait for an hour, then tell the others about the cabinet with the banshee inside. The other leprechaun was still deep in the vaults until the effects of the compulsion wore off. Still, we weren't sure if Gorun's colleagues would ask questions about the Skau vault and send another person to check it out, so we remained in a hurry, speed walking down the street and around the coinary to collect the rest of our party. With each step, I did my best to wipe the memory of the moment I'd nearly killed us all by opening a cabinet from my mind.

Thantrel saved my arse back there, no doubt about it. His own, and everyone's inside the vault too. And somehow, the life saving was not the thing that had affected me the most.

No, his touch, his silken skin on mine and the way electricity had filled me made me lean closer. Made me want more of him.

By the dead gods, I hated that he had an effect on me. A strong one at that. Thantrel was not in my plans, and I had to remember that, had to stay strong.

"What in all the nine kingdoms?" Astril hissed.

I blinked. Our other friends had come into view, but by the way the vampire spoke, I'd have expected to see something odd.

"What?" I asked, unable to figure out what would be distressing.

"Livia compelled the workers."

I groaned.

"You can tell from this far?" Duran asked, squinting.

I did the same. Three fae stood on a platform jutting out over the river. The mechanism to flood the river water below the coinary was somewhere on that platform.

"I can. Let them come to us."

We stopped walking and did as the vampire said. The moment our friends joined us, Astril spoke to her sister.

"What happened?"

"They were asking questions, and we knew we couldn't leave the area." Livia shrugged. "Why are you so upset?"

"I had to compel two leprechauns. The more we influence, the wider the trail we leave. What if someone comes up to them, a co-worker, and notices how off they are?"

My stomach tightened. Astril was right. We were leaving too many breadcrumbs. We needed to exit Bitra.

"At least we're all safe," I said. "We may attract a little

extra attention, but let's run to the castle. I want to get out of this city as soon as possible."

We pivoted and ran through the streets, aiming for Eruhall. The moment the bronze gates came into view, I breathed a little more freely. It was unlikely an alarm would sound now, but even if it did, we were moments from stepping through a gateway into Vitvik. Safe.

The guards saw Arie and Thantrel and opened the gates for us. We ran through, and only then did we slow to catch our breath.

"I can't believe that we didn't even sound an alarm," Arie murmured. "Truly, I thought we'd be swimming for our lives."

I was about to agree when a creature rose into view on the other side of the castle. Pure white and gleaming in the waning sunlight, the pegasus flipped in the air. My breath left me in one go, which, of course, Thantrel noticed.

"You like her?" he asked.

"Obviously." Who wouldn't like a pegasus? They were rare and majestic magical creatures.

"Father has two," he said, and shot a covert glance at Arie before adding. "Actually, he has gryphons too. And he's not using them. What do you say we put them to better use?"

I blinked, pivoting to face him. "I'm not sure what you're saying."

"It takes forever to get supplies to Valrun Castle. We can change that with a couple of pegasi and gryphons."

"Won't your father be furious?" I asked, though I didn't truly care. The idea of having those creatures for the rebellion was exhilarating, and as far as I was concerned, the spymaster could deal with the loss of a few animals.

"He will be," Arie said. I glanced at the middle Riis brother. Though he'd spoken, he also didn't push, which gave me the sense he wouldn't stop Thantrel.

Thantrel shrugged, eyes still on me. "I'm willing to risk it."

His unspoken words rang loud and clear in my ears.

For me. He's willing to risk it for me. His mate. My chest tightened. *I should not allow such a thing. Shouldn't make Thantrel think that there's a chance between us.*

But as I stared at the pegasus, only to watch a second one join it, I knew it would be stupid to deny this help. The rebellion needed assistance.

"Then, on behalf of the rebellion, we accept your offer," I said.

Thantrel grinned, and despite myself, despite every wall I'd built, my heart warmed when he winked at me. "Let's saddle up."

THE NINE KINGDOMS OF ISILA

The Blood Kingdom - vampire
The Elven Kingdom - elves
The Winter Kingdom - fae of various races
The Autumn Kingdom - fae of various races
The Spring Kingdom - fae of various races
The Summer Kingdom - fae of various races
The Wolvea Kingdom - wolvea shifters
The Dragon Kingdom - dragon shifters

*** Each kingdom is colloquially described as a court, though technically, the court is a specific place or places in the larger kingdom.

Some kingdoms have additional names, such as the Winter Kingdom being called Winter's Realm or the Dragon Kingdom being called the Kingdom of Flame.

THE HIGH NOBILITY OF THE KINGDOM OF WINTER

HOUSE AABERG - ROYAL HOUSE
King Magnus Aaberg
Queen Inga Aaberg née Vagle

Children
Prince Rhistel Aaberg
Prince Vale Aaberg
Princess Saga Aaberg

The royal house is not a part of the Sacred Eight.[1] They do rely heavily on the families of the Sacred Eight but the royal house is distinct from all others.

Before the White Bear's Rebellion, House Aaberg was a member of the Sacred Eight. Since the rebellion House Riis took their place as a reward for loyalty to House Aaberg.

The Sacred Eight Families of Winter's Realm

* Lord Sten Armenil - Warden of the North - Head of House
* Lady Orla Armenil née Balik
Children
* Marit Armenil - female
* Connan Armenil - male
* Rune Armenil - male
* Tiril Armenil - female
* Jorunn Armenil - female
* Raemar Armenil - male

* Lady Vaeri Ithamai - Warden of the East - Head of House
* Lord Tiarsus Itamai née Skau - deceased
Children
* Hadia Ithamai - female
* Adila Ithamai - female

* Lord Tadgh Balik - Warden of the South - Head of House
* Lady Kilyn Balik née Armenil
Children
* Sian Balik - male
* Baenna Balik - female
* Eireann Balik - female
* Saoirse Balik - female
* Fionn Balik - male
* Garbhan Balik - male - deceased

* Carai Balik - female

* Filip Balik - squire to Prince Vale of House Aaberg - male

* Colm Balik - male

* Lord Roar Lisika - Warden of the West - Head of House

Unmarried

No children

* Lord Leyv Riis - Head of House

Unmarried

Children (only the children at court are included)

* Luccan Riis - male

* Arie Riis - male

* Thantrel Riis - non-binary

* Lord Airen Vagle - Lord of Coin - Head of House
* Lady Eliana Vagle - deceased
Children

* Queen Inga - married to King Magnus Aaberg

* Captain of the Royal Guard Eirwen Vagle - Father to Lady Calpurnia Vagle - his wife has passed to the afterworld

* Fival Vagle - acting lord in their family seat in the midlands - male

* Selah Vagle - married to a wealthy Jarl in the midlands - female

* Lady Nalaea Qiren - Lady of Silks - Head of House
* Lord Virion Qiren née Ithamai - deceased

Children
* Aenesa Qiren - female
* Thalia Qiren - female
* Iro Qiren - female

* Lady Fayeth Virtoris - Lady of Ships - Head of House
* Lord Kailu Virtoris née Oridan, from the Summer Court
Children
* Vidar Virtoris - betrothed to Princess Saga of House Aaberg - male
* Sayyida Virtoris - female
* Njal Virtoris - male
* Amine Virtoris - female

House Falk
King Harald's royal house
House Skau
Queen Revna's birth house. She married into House Falk and had six children with King Harald.

Beneath the Sacred Eight there are hundreds of lesser houses. These are led by jarls of various territories.

---

1. Prior to the White Bear's Rebellion, the Sacred Eight were actually the Sacred Nine, with House Skau being the ninth member, and House Falk being the royal house.

ACKNOWLEDGMENTS

This book, like the first and second in this series, was such a joy to write. I can't wait to continue the story of Neve and Vale and Winter's Realm. Big things are coming with the Winter family and I hope readers enjoy it.

First and foremost, thank you to my husband, my biggest cheerleader and best friend. I still can't believe I get to do this life with you. I know I say that nearly every book, but I mean it!

A huge thank you to my ARC team and especially the following members for typo-hunting for me: Lauren Searcy, Chantelle Tebaldi, Lacey Mullins, Fran Fox, Tia Brumbaugh, Colleen Hepler, Saundra Wright, April Stacey, Kaylie Willis, Brandy Freeman, Mortisha Johnson, Debbie Turk, Bobbie Jo Schultze, Shalee Bolton, Liz Ford, Donna Diagle, Sadie Nickles, Francesca Knowles, and Taylor Snow.

And thank you to my beta reader, Elyse. Your opinions and suggestions helped me make the book even better for other readers.

All the magic,
Ashley McLeo

ALSO BY ASHLEY MCLEO

The Winter Court (Crowns of Magic Universe)

A Kingdom of Frost and Malice

A Lord of Snow and Greed

A Hallow of Storm and Ruin

A Crown of Ice and Fury

Coven of Shadows and Secrets (Crowns of Magic Universe)

Seeker of Secrets

Hunted by Darkness

History of Witches

Marked by Fate

Kingdoms of Sin

Bound by Destiny

Standalone Novels

Curse of the Fae Prince (The Spring Court: Crowns of Magic Universe)

Spellcasters Spy Academy Series (Magic of Arcana Universe)

A Legacy Witch: Year One

A Marked Witch: Internship

A Rebel Witch: Year Two

A Crucible Witch: Year Three

The Spellcasters Spy Academy Boxset

The Wonderland Court Series (Magic of Arcana Universe)

Alice the Dagger

Alice the Torch

The Bonegate Series - A Fanged Fae sister series

Hawk Witch

Assassin Witch

Traitor Witch

Illuminator Witch

The Bonegates Series Boxset

The Royal Quest Series

Dragon Prince

Dragon Magic

Dragon Mate

Dragon Betrayal

Dragon Crown

Dragon War

ABOUT THE AUTHOR

Ashley lives in the lush and green Pacific Northwest with her husband, their dog, and the house ghost that sometimes makes appearances in her charming, old home.

When she's not writing fantasy novels she enjoys traveling the world, reading, kicking butt at board games, and frequenting taquerias.

For all the latest releases and updates, subscribe to Ashley's newsletter, The Coven. You can also find her Facebook group, Ashley's Reader Coven.